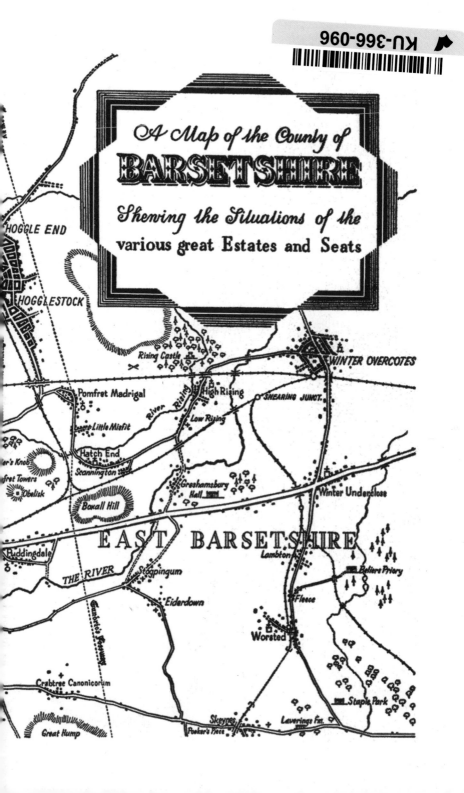

Other books by Angela Thirkell

Three Houses (1931)

Ankle Deep (1933)

High Rising (1933)

Demon in the House, The (1934)

Wild Strawberries (1934)

O, These Men, These Men (1935)

August Folly (1936)

Coronation Summer (1937)

Summer Half (1937)

Pomfret Towers (1938)

Before Lunch (1939)

The Brandons (1939))

Cheerfulness Breaks In (1940)

Northbridge Rectory (1941)

Marling Hall (1942)

Growing Up (1943)

Headmistress, The (1944)

Miss Bunting (1945)

Peace Breaks Out (1946)

Private Enterprise (1947)

Love Among the Ruins (1948)

Old Bank House, The (1949)

County Chronicle (1950)

Duke's Daughter, The (1951)

Happy Returns (1952)

Jutland Cottage (1953)

What Did It Mean? (1954)

Enter Sir Robert (1955)

Never Too Late (1956)

Double Affair, A (1957)

Close Quarters (1958)

Love at All Ages (1959)

JUTLAND COTTAGE

A Novel by

Angela Thirkell

MOYER BELL
Wakefield, Rhode Island & London

Solihull
LIBRARIES & ARTS

Published by Moyer Bell
This Edition 1999

Copyright © 1953 by Angela Thirkell
Published by arrangement with Hamish Hamilton, Ltd.

All rights reserved. No part of this publication may be repro-
duced or transmitted in any form or by any means, electronic,
or mechanical, including photocopying, recording or any information retrieval system, without permission in writing from
Moyer Bell, Kymbolde Way, Wakefield, Rhode Island 02879
or 112 Sydney Road, Muswell Hill, London N10 2RN.

**LIBRARY OF CONGRESS
CATALOGING-IN-PUBLICATION DATA**

Thirkell, Angela Mackail, 1890–1961.
    Jutland cottage : a novel by
Angela Thirkell.
      p. cm.
    ISBN 1-55921-273-X (pbk.)
    I. Title.
    PR6039.H43J88   1999
    823'.912—dc21   98-37617
                      CIP

SOLIHULL
PUBLIC LIBRARIES

IC0001539509 9

L4470 CE M

Cover illustration:
A Cottage Garden
William Stephen Coleman

Printed in the United States of America
Distributed in North America by Publishers Group West, 1700 Fourth
Street, Berkeley, CA 94710, 800-788-3123 (in California 510-658-3453).

CHAPTER I

We have at times been accused of putting so many people into our books that no one can remember who they are, in which stricture we entirely concur, as we often cannot remember who they are ourself (or selves). We have often been urged to provide some sort of genealogical chart of Barsetshire families, and several kind and gifted young admirers have even gone so far as to make a rough table of affinities; but, to tell the truth and shame him that shall be nameless, we have allowed matters to get so far out of hand that it is now almost impossible to reconcile the various discrepancies of dates and ages. For this we have no excuse and shall therefore offer two: the first that we find we get just as muddled about generations and relationships in real life as we do in Barsetshire; the second—in the words of *The Water Babies*—that it is all a fairy story and you must not believe a word of it even if it is true. Those who are at the grandmother stage will understand how completely addled one is apt to be by the generations. A generation is usually considered as thirty years, and if everyone had married and had children at thirty ever since Genesis things would be simple, though even then they would have to have had all their children simultaneously to keep the ranks abreast and seen to it that they all married simultaneously for ever and ever. But children are born with all kinds of intervals between them, and there have been well-authenticated cases in good families where, owing to a fruitful first marriage followed by a fruitful second marriage, children in their early teens have been seen pushing their uncles and aunts about in perambulators.

This brief apologia is only meant to discourage any reader who is kind or rash enough to begin tabulating families and dates, and to beg that kind and rash reader to accept a cloud-cuckooland that has grown in a way by itself. Anyone who has lived in this world knows how confusing it is, and sometimes all we can do is to snatch at some person or some event before the passing moment flies—just indeed as one does in real life. All of which is a prefabricated excuse for the difficulty we ourselves have been having of late with the Leslie family.

To go back to the days before the Second World War to end War, when Mr. Leslie and Lady Emily Leslie lived at Rushwater, is like a dream. There they had lived for the whole of their married life when we first knew them. Their eldest son had been killed in the 1914 war, and Martin, his young son, was living mostly in the house he would inherit. Their second, John, was a young childless widower. Their lovely daughter, Agnes, was happily married to Colonel Graham (as he was then), with her growing brood of handsome gifted children, while their youngest son David, rightly stigmatised by his father as bone-selfish, was pursuing his easy-going career of taking jobs and dropping them with facile charm. And in that summer a niece of Colonel Graham's, one Mary Preston, had spent several months at Rushwater, and in her the young widower had found exactly the wife he wanted.

Curtains have fallen and risen upon changed scenes. Martin Leslie and his golden wife Sylvia now reigned at Rushwater and were filling their nurseries. David and his well-dressed well-bred wife and their young family were much in America or abroad. Agnes Graham, now Lady Graham, had married two daughters young and still had a third in hand, while her three sons were doing and promising well. Of John and Mary Leslie not very much has been seen, for they lived their quiet, comfortable, slightly dull and very happy life over Greshamsbury way where John had bought the Old Rectory, a good late Georgian house standing in its own grounds. A former incumbent, the Reverend Caleb Oriel, whose grandfather, an Anglo-Indian general, had left him a considerable fortune (popularly supposed to have been made by torturing Rajahs and Begums), had put the kitchen quarters and the stabling in excellent repair, and successive tenants had so cared for them that, apart from the fact that the first were too large for these over-taxed days and the second more or less useless owing to a total vacancy of hoofs, John Leslie was able to make the whole place very livable without much expense. Neither he nor his wife had much of what is called taste; but as their taste consisted in having handsome and comfortable furniture, whether old or new, we think they will do just as well as the people who have experimented in wallpapers with feathers or shells, tables made of not quite stainless tubular steel, chairs with no hind legs so that one cannot feel safe even if one is certain that one is, and so-called kitchen units with drawers too heavy to pull out with one hand when the other is covered with flour or sticky with cutting up the dogs' meat, and with a gift for getting damp inside from condensation that amounts to genius.

In these very pleasant surroundings three sons had been growing up. As we have known them since they were at Southbridge School, we shall continue to call them Major, Minor and Minimus, though as a matter of fact they were called Henry (after John's father), John (after their own father) and Clive (after a Preston uncle who was killed in the 1914 war). All three boys had been at Southbridge School, rather to the surprise of the county who said "Why not Eton?" though not aloud in John Leslie's presence. Not that he would have minded in the least, but he was not a talker except with his wife and sons and his near relations and saw no reason to discuss his choice of school in public. We think it was partly a strong county feeling (for

Southbridge School was, as a former grammar school, as old a foundation as Eton) and partly a kind of tribute to his father, who had for many years been a governor. Henry, or Major, had now gone to Oxford with an exhibition. Minor and Minimus were still at Southbridge; and Minor, who had climbed everything in the county, including the great tulip tree in the Palace grounds and the very nasty spire of the School Chapel, was now also considering Oxford with a view to the spire of St. Mary's; while Minimus, who had no head at all for heights, was considering the Royal Air Force on the grounds that if that didn't cure him of feeling giddy then nothing would, and also, we think, because his uncle, David Leslie, had been a temporary flier during the Second World War to end War. To the young Leslies Uncle David, in spite of being a not at all so young married man with an increasing and delightful family, and two paths of baldness from the temples which made an appreciable yearly progress towards the back of his head, remained a figure of romance—largely because he always arrived unexpectedly, usually by air, and never stayed more than a night at that.

At the moment when our chronicle begins to continue its well-meaning but eccentric (in the scientific sense) way, it was a nasty cold day in early February. But in the Old Rectory all was pretty comfortable owing to the excellent central heating which would heat pretty well anything and the supply of wood from the Gresham estate. Mr. and Mrs. John Leslie were having breakfast with the heat at full blast and a good fire and not feeling in the least too warm. Indeed a great many of us, owing to the years of fuel and food shortage, will be like Harry Gill and our teeth (though we have not earned our fate as he did) will chatter still; and not to be warm enough is a state which leads us to hope for hell unless we can be authoritatively assured that heaven has a good reserve of whatever fuel it uses, with the rider that if people like Aunt Cecily—who comes into the room in mid-winter merely to say "What a fug! I don't know how you can bear it!" and open the windows wide—is in heaven too, we shall strike.

As with all England and indeed with a large part of the world (except those whose breakfast-time is much earlier or later owing to geography), the chief, the governing, obsessing thought of every day was: "How is the King?" A monarch, selfless, dedicated to his people's service, taking the heavy burden of kingship which had come to him by default, had been desperately ill. If the prayers of an Empire, spoken or unspoken, formulated or only emotionally felt, could save a life, that life was saved a million million times; but the answer to prayer as we would have it is not always given by one whose mysterious ways are not to be foreseen by us. At least the bulletins of His Majesty's health had been more reassuring of late and he was now in his country home, the Norfolk squire, shooting and walking among his own people.

"I think it is so nice for His Majesty that he lives in Norfolk," said Mrs. Leslie to her husband. "It feels so safe."

Her husband said, "Why safe, or any rate why safer than anywhere else?"

"Because," said his wife, "of Liverpool Street."

John Leslie put down his cup with almost a bang.

"And what on earth has Liverpool Street to do with it?" he asked.

His wife, whom many years of happy married life had not entirely accustomed to the general denseness of husbands, smiled in a gently superior way.

"If," she said accusingly, "you *think*, John, you will see that Liverpool Street was simply built to keep people out of East Anglia."

Her husband said that might be, but it was the only way of getting there.

"Exactly," said Mrs. Leslie, "so one *has* to use it. But just think of it, John. To begin with, it's all in the wrong place. I mean it isn't where you think it is."

Her husband said it rather depended where you did think it was, to which his wife replied that it was always farther round the corner than you thought. John Leslie said it depended where you thought the corner was.

"I don't," said Mrs. Leslie. "But it always is. And it is so dark and banging and so many platforms and so many trains going to places one doesn't know that used to be country. And London goes on for ever and ever. Besides, they have stopped that nice little real country line that goes from Bishop Stortford to Braintree and turned it into a motor bus. And the DIRT! I've got to go to Barchester this morning. Are you coming?"

Mr. Leslie said he had to go and see Francis Brandon on business and would like to accompany his wife, and they might have lunch at the County Club, and he thought they ought to ask the Brandons to dinner as Francis had been really very useful to him about some investments and his wife was so charming. Mary Leslie, to whom her husband's will (and a very kind and just one, we must say) had been law almost from the day she had first seen him, agreed to this and went away to see the cook for, thanks to good county roots, they always had a staff of sorts, and so long as good-will reigned in the kitchen its employers were willing to meet it more than halfway, so that what with tradesmen and an old gardener and the odd man (who was also in the proud position of being the village idiot and could take an egg from under a hen without ruffling her feathers or her susceptibilities and could charm warts) and the postman and the old keeper from Greshamsbury Park and anyone else who happened to be about, the yard outside the back was, as John Leslie's brother David had so truly remarked, not unlike "Bolton Abbey in the Olden Time." And if there are readers who do not know this picture, or rather the engraving of it, usually framed in a peculiarly hideous light-brown wood of concave shape lengthways (if we make ourselves clear, as we almost despair of doing), we can, like Miss Fanny Squeers, only pity their ignorance and despise them.

So the Leslies went about their various businesses and then drove into Barchester and left their car in the Close. This was strictly illegal, but the Chancellor of the Diocese, Sir Robert Fielding, had a good many visitors on ecclesiastical business; and as John Leslie was a churchwarden and had known the Fieldings all his life, he was considered as privileged and acted accordingly. The Close was almost empty of people. The Leslies walked round to the stone archway and out into the town. As they had to pass the White Hart, John said he wanted to have a word with Burden, the old head waiter. The hall was empty. John looked through the glass door of the dining-room and, seeing Burden there, went in. The old waiter was arranging glass and silver (so-called) on a table. John knew he was rather deaf and did not wish to startle him, so he went round to the other side of the table. The old man looked up with a face so altered, so stricken, that John was alarmed.

"What's wrong, Burden?" he said very gently.

"Haven't you heard, sir?" said Burden.

"What?" said John Leslie. "Nothing wrong, I hope, Burden?"

"His Majesty, sir," said Burden. "It was on the wireless, just a moment ago. I didn't know what to do, sir, so I came in the dining-room. These forks want cleaning. He's gone, sir, God bless him," and the old waiter applied himself again to rearranging the silver and cutlery, but his hands trembled and it was obvious that he didn't know what he was doing.

"Do you mean the King is *dead*?" said John Leslie, quickly assuming, as we all do, a kind of mask or shield of incredulity against news of disaster.

"In his sleep, sir, like a baby," said Burden, and even in the shock and grief of that moment John could not help reflecting how inapposite the comparison was, for babies—we are thankful to say—are far more apt to wake and yell than to slip from a night's sleep to a lasting sleep.

"Are you sure?" said John, uneasily hoping that it was all a bad dream, willing to snatch unreasonably at any respite from what was ineluctably before him—and before the whole Empire.

The old man nodded his head, blew his nose on a large

red-spotted handkerchief and went on with his work, but he did not see very well and dropped a fork.

"Here you are," said John, picking it up and giving it to him. "Bear up, Burden. It's a blow for us all," which words he felt, as indeed they were, to be singularly unhelpful. But the old waiter, with the wide philosophy of the uneducated, said Mr. Leslie was right, and if a man—he meant a King—died in his duty, that was all a man could do.

"Well, you have done your duty for a great many years, Burden," said John, obeying the instinctive reaction of the governing classes (for so they remain by faith, charity and tradition) to come to the help of a dependant. "Cheer up. We must think of the Queen, not of ourselves."

"Which Queen, sir?" said Burden. "There's three Queens now, sir."

"Lord! So there are!" said John Leslie. "I was thinking of His Majesty's own Queen, Burden—Queen Elizabeth." And then he realised that already there was a new Queen Elizabeth, her father's successor, and everything was too difficult. He gave the old man a friendly but carefully gentle slap on the shoulder as a mark of good-will and left him to his knives and forks.

In the hall he found his wife pretending to read an illustrated paper upside down.

"John!" she said. "Have you heard?"

"Burden told me," said John Leslie. "God bless him—and us all, for that matter. Let's get what we have to do done and have lunch and go home." So they went first to the bank, where already everyone was hushed and the noise of coins being shovelled into brass scoops felt like sacrilege. John's business with the manager took some little time. When he had finished his talk he collected his wife.

"I'll go to Brandon's office now," he said. "Will you come?" But Mary said there was some household shopping that she ought to do and she would wait for him at the club when she had finished, so he went away and Mary went up towards the High Street.

By this time the cruel news had spread. It was only a very short time since she had been at the White Hart, watching from the window the ebb and flow of shoppers on the pavement. The pavements were still crowded, the shoppers ebbed and flowed, but with a difference. Under a common, a national impulse, there was hardly a woman but was already in some kind of black. Some had almost widow's weeds. Some who probably had not a black suit had put a black coat over what they wore. Some strange black hats had been exhumed or rescued from the jumble-sale box. Some women had tied a bit of black chiffon or black veiling over their hair, for it is not everyone who has a black scarf to hand. Some had neither coat nor dress of black and had pinned a knot of black ribbon or material to their dress, as dark or light-blue favours are pinned on the day of the Boat Race. For the men a black band for the sleeve had in many cases been found at home, or bought, or possibly made in haste from an old sock.

Mary Leslie, unprepared for this morning's woe, had a horrid feeling of guilt that she was not in deep mourning and was just going into Bostock and Plummer to buy at least a black scarf or a ribbon for token, when she ran into Mrs. Crawley, the wife of the Dean, who was already in a black coat and hat.

"Josiah is in the Cathedral," said Mrs. Crawley without any preface. "Not exactly a service. A kind of anybody who likes coming in and praying for His Majesty. Will you come?"

"I should love to," said Mary, "but I don't feel properly dressed."

"Come back to the Deanery," said Mrs. Crawley, "and I'll lend you something. Not that it really matters, but one feels safer somehow. Oh dear! There are so many people to be sorry for that one doesn't know where to begin. Do you suppose royalty always have some black things just in *case*? My father always said every woman should have one black dress in her wardrobe because you never know," to which Mary Leslie replied that it was all very well, but you weren't always at home when people died and then you couldn't get at your blacks; but luckily the Deanery was close at hand, so this problem could be neglected. Here a black scarf was found and Mary with Mrs. Crawley went across to the Cathedral.

In London when there is any national crisis the people crowd to Buckingham Palace. So in the crises of His Majesty's illness had thousands of people waited night and day, in rain or shine, as if the fervent good wishes of his subjects could help him—as indeed they may have done. So now hundreds of people who never came to church except on Sunday, and often not that, had thronged to the great space enclosed by the white walls of the Cathedral, with cold winter light filling the clear windows. Silent black multitudes thronged the nave and the transepts. In the choir county dignitaries could be seen among the clergy. Lord Pomfret, tired and hard-working as ever; Sir Edmund Pridham looking twenty years older than his already consider-able age; landowners and titles belonging to the county—all with the feeling that a father had left them, summoned by a power greater than thrones and dominions. The Dean said—not without difficulty—a few words about the late King. The oldest Canon, who was popularly and incorrectly supposed to have been present at Queen Victoria's accession, also spoke, and was quite inaudible, though less from emotion than from lack of teeth and a rooted distrust of dentists which had made him refuse to have false ones. The brief service was over and the worshippers went about their ways, rather unwilling to speak.

Halfway across the Close Mrs. Crawley and Mrs. Leslie were overtaken by the Dean, who had brought Mrs. Morland, the well-known novelist, away from the Cathedral with him. That worthy creature had been crying, her face was most unbecom-ingly blotched, and so incapable was she of coherent speech that Mrs. Crawley took both her ladies to the Dean's study and sent for tea.

"You will have tea too, Josiah?" she said to her husband. "And don't be pompous about it," she added in what was for her an unusually sharp voice. "We are all unhappy, but at least we can be simple."

"*I* can't," said Mrs. Morland, pulling her hat a little more crooked as she spoke. "What is so *awful* is that all the time I'm putting what's happening into words. I know I oughtn't to, because one ought to be thinking of *nothing* but His Majesty, but I can't help it. I suppose it's because of having earned my living for so long by writing that I have to think aloud—only not *really* aloud, only aloud to myself inside myself. Oh dear, I can't explain."

But though no one of her hearers was a writer, unless we count the Dean's sermons and his articles in the *Spectator* about his trip to Finland and other even duller ones in the *Church Times*, they all understood in part. For most of us, we think, tell ourselves stories about what we are doing and the way we are behaving, almost unconsciously, though not all of us—luckily—get the thoughts patted and banged and pushed and humoured into words. The Dean, feeling we think that he perhaps ought to say something but didn't know what to say, oozed out of the room. The three ladies all had another cup of tea and tried to talk normally.

"You know," said Mrs. Crawley, "Rose Fairweather is down here with her children. Her husband is to be at the Admiralty for a few years. They are staying with her people at Winter Overcotes and want to find a house. You don't know of one, do you, Mary? Somewhere over this side of Barchester? I forget how many children they have."

A better antidote to true grief for a departed king could not have been imagined. Rose Fairweather, the incredibly beautiful and even more incredibly silly daughter of Mr. Birkett, the former Headmaster of Southbridge School, was always what is called news-value. Her husband, now Captain Fairweather, R.N., with every kind of medal and order and distinction, had risen steadily in his profession, not unaided by his wife whose devotion to him, whose lavish and undiscriminating affection for everyone combined with an exquisite ruthlessness in getting her own way, had been of considerable advantage to him. A woman whom every male from retired full Admiral to smallest midshipman worships at sight, who calls everyone darling and is known to adore her husband above everything and to renounce cheerfully a night-club or a world première (as they say) of Glamora Tudor and her male star of the moment on her husband's account, whose broadcast affection for practically everything in trousers no gossip has been able to touch, may be an unusual wife for a naval captain; but a better wife in her own artless way than Rose Fairweather did not exist, and her husband was fully aware of it.

"I don't know all of a sudden like that," said Mary Leslie. "Yes, I do, though. It might do. I wonder."

"Do tell me," said Mrs. Crawley, adding a little unkindly, "then we could wonder, too."

"I am so sorry," said Mary Leslie. "I was just thinking. That house where the Umblebys used to live—just outside Greshamsbury Park. The people who live there are going abroad for two or three years—I really don't know why—and I believe they want to let it. Shall I ask? It has quite a nice garden, and the bus stop is just down the village street. Where is Rose now?"

Mrs. Crawley said she was at Winter Overcotes with her parents, so Mary said she would telephone and now she really must go as John would be waiting for her at the club, and the party dispersed.

While she was in the Cathedral His Majesty had seemed less far away. While she was at the Deanery she had forgotten England's loss, as we all so easily (and thankfully) forget even our own heavy troubles while we are with friends and talking. But no sooner had the hospitable Deanery doors closed behind her than the feeling of loss and an empty house came over her again, so heavily that she went across to the Cathedral and knelt—not alone—trying to find words for her feeling, though beyond "Please, *please*, God, make His Majesty happy" she could not think of anything to say, till she remembered His Majesty's Queen-mother and his Queen-widow and his elder daughter suddenly called to her high responsibility. But even then she could not manage anything better than "Please, *please*," without any definite prayer. So she gave it up and went on her way to the club—but not altogether uncomforted.

At the club Mary found her husband waiting downstairs, so they went straight to the dining-room where John had booked a table; most luckily, for the morning's news had driven many people to seek among a crowd of friends or acquaintances, or even strangers, forgetfulness of the journey which the King had taken alone, though not, they felt, even if they could not put the feeling into words, unfriended or unguided—rather supported and accompanied by the Master who does not leave His good and faithful servants strangers in a strange land.

During the morning the tide of black had been rising, and there was a hush in the dining-room and a general feeling that somehow gin or whisky weren't the thing, but a half bottle of red wine would not offend. For this we have no explanation. One came, like a shadow, into a back corner of our mind and was gone before it could materialise. But we think we should have felt the same, though why, we have not the faintest idea.

The Leslies exchanged news. Mary told John how she had been to the Cathedral and gone in to the Deanery. John said he had had a very satisfactory talk with Francis Brandon and gathered that there were quite definite hopes of a new baby, and Lady Cora Waring was going to be godmother.

"Four is a very nice number," said Mary, not wistfully, for her three boys had filled her heart and life very comfortably, but as a mathematical fact, to which John replied that he quite agreed, but three was somehow a nicer number than four; adding rather sententiously a Latin tag about the gods liking odd numbers.

"Anyway," said Mary rather conceitedly, "three is a prime

number. I remember that from school. Why prime, I wonder?"

But John said it wasn't worth wondering about and they might as well go home. Mary did say something about mourning, but John said—and very properly, we think—that mourning in the country simply looked silly, and so long as she didn't put on a red dress with spangles and dance the Cachuca down Greshamsbury High Street she would be quite in order, with all of which she agreed—as indeed she always had agreed with what John Leslie said for nearly twenty years.

Those who know Barsetshire will remember that the old Greshamsbury consisted of one long straggling street about a mile in length, with a sharp turn in the middle, so that the two halves of the street were at right angles. Inside this angle was Greshamsbury House, where Greshams still lived, with its gardens and grounds. Within the last hundred years or so many changes had come of course. The village had grown considerably and not always for the better, pushing out towards the railway, where there was a quite large working-class suburb. Of the great wealth that had come into the family through the heiress Mary Thorne, who married young Frank Gresham, much had been lost or confiscated through deaths and taxation and a good deal of the large estate sold. The property had, since the end of the war, been made over to the National Trust. Trippers came in roaring motor coaches and cars through the great gates and up the lime avenues; they walked in the terraced gardens and were shown the principal rooms. But Greshams still lived there. The house had been divided of late years. The present owners, a quiet elderly couple whose family were mostly in London or abroad, lived in one part of the house. The big rooms were kept aired and dusted for the National Trust visitors, but not used. The smaller wing was let to cousins: Captain Francis Gresham, R.N., and his wife Jane, daughter of old Admiral Palliser, a connection of the Omniums, over Hallbury way. Several years as a prisoner of war in Japan had not done Captain Gresham any particular good, and to his great grief he had not been allowed much active service, but he was at the Admiralty during the week and came down for weekends. Their only son Frank, born some years before the war, was now at Southbridge School; and there were two little girls, born after their father's release, but of them we do not know very much at present except that they were eminently kissable and quite fairly good.

With Captain and Mrs. Gresham the Leslies had become very friendly. There was a good deal of coming and going between Greshamsbury Park and the Old Rectory, and Frank Gresham was a devoted admirer of the Leslie boys, especially of Minor, whose Alpine feats on roofs and towers he tried to copy. Not always successfully and least so on the night when he had scaled the Headmaster's House by what was known as the Everest route, including a nasty col between the built-out bit at the back and the main building, where he suddenly found himself looking in at the window of the nursery bathroom where Mrs. Carter's nurse was giving her uppers and unders their special Saturday-night purification. Nurse had with great courage opened the window and asked which boy that was, but having only put in her uppers her articulation was not very clear, which made Frank have the giggles so much that he slid down the sloping roof, fell into the box hedge and so escaped to his House and to bed—but not unseen, for next morning Matron had reported him to his Housemaster, who said he had tried that way several times himself but couldn't make it and Gresham could take a hundred lines and think himself lucky. After which Frank had boasted quite unbearably and Leslie Minor had taken the same route two nights later and seen Nurse putting her front hair into curlers, and Nurse had seen him and screamed, and the Headmaster had told his Housemaster that officially he ought to make a row, but if he would put the fear of God into Gresham and Leslie Minor he himself would overlook their behaviour. All of which was duly done, for though Everard Carter was universally liked he was also feared by evildoers, not one of whom had been known to get away with his evil doing.

At the moment, being February, all their young gentlemen were away at school, and the Leslies went back to a quiet home and about their various businesses and after tea walked down to the village.

Had the Frank Gresham who married the heiress Mary Thorne nearly a hundred years ago—and yet their story feels as new as though it were happening today—been walking down the village street in the February dusk he would not have noticed any very great change. Some of the smaller houses, hardly more than cottages, had been in the phrase of the Vicar's wife at Mrs. Keith's Working Party in the first year of the war "arted up." Doors had become alarmingly flat and were bright blue, pink or yellow. Sash windows had pushed themselves out into badly shaped bows. Several thatched roofs had, through time and the decay of thatching as a profession, decayed and fallen to pieces and been replaced in some cases by wavy red tiles, in others by a flat roof with a parapet—not, as in Mrs. Gamp's time, in case of fire but rather to conceal from a still fairly uncorrupted villagery that the highbrows were lying in exiguous bathing suits on Li-los (if that is how they are spelt) with a lot of tan cream on their faces, necks, arms, legs and practically everything that was theirs. The little inn had put a dancing-room in its little garden and a rather dashing counter in its little bar. But on the whole the village was not much spoilt and, being off the main road, did not get the great motor-coach traffic. There were two good houses which had on the whole kept a dignified appearance. One, already mentioned by Mary Leslie, had been lived in by the Umbleby's, agents and lawyers to the estate, and the present tenants wanted to let it for a term of years which might suit the Fairweathers. The other and smaller house had, since the Old Rectory had been as it were secularised, mostly been lived in by the clergyman of the moment, about whom we hope to hear more.

As the present occupiers of the larger house, nice uninteresting people called Green, were pleased at the idea of tenants who were known to the Leslies, it appeared that if the Fairweathers were equally willing there need be no difficulty, so Mary promised to put both parties into communications as soon as possible.

"By the way," said John Leslie to his hostess as they were leaving, "have you heard that our new Rector is appointed? I don't suppose you have. I only heard it at the club today. I'm glad it is settled. One got a little tired of having unknown locums to lunch on Sunday. Goodbye."

"But you didn't say who it was," said Mrs. Green.

"No more I did," said John, who was apt to confound people by never apologising unless he felt an apology was necessary. "It is Fewling, from Northbridge."

"Oh, but isn't he frightfully High?" said Mrs. Green, looking alarmed.

"High but moderate," said John Leslie. "And an ex-naval man with a fine record in the 'fourteen war."

"If you say so," said Mrs. Green, looking at him with trusting eyes. "But not *incense,* I hope."

"I'm not going to answer for anything," said John Leslie. "I must say that the only time I went to St. Sycorax—Fewling was only priest in charge there, you know—it was a bit too incensed for my taste, but a lot of people liked it; and Villars—he is the Rector and a very sound churchman—said Fewling was an admirable coadjutor and got a lot of people to church that usually didn't go. I shall keep an eye on him and have him in good training by the time you come back. The church has been pretty empty lately, hasn't it?" And the Greens had to admit that they didn't go very often themselves, rather weakening their case by saying the service was so dull.

John did not make any comment, but as he and Mary walked back to the Old Rectory he said he wondered what exactly— if anything—Mrs. Green meant. That the service—whether morning or evening—could in itself be dull to anyone was almost beyond his conception. And if, he said, Mrs. Green called it dull in one breath and grumbled about incense in the next he didn't know what she wanted.

"I wonder," he said, talking half aloud to himself and half to his wife, "if the church is still open. I should feel more loyal—and more comfortable—if we could go in. When I was with Francis Brandon this morning it didn't come into my head to go to the Cathedral. I am really ashamed of myself." But his wife would not hear of any such state of mind in the husband of her young love and her continuing deep affection and they took their way by the side gate and the steep path to the church, which stood a little higher than the village.

Greshamsbury Church was of quite respectable age and had not suffered too much from zealous hands—partly because it was not old enough to have people uncovering considerably damaged wall paintings as they had at Pomfret Madrigal; partly because it had been lucky in its Rectors, who mostly kept the noiseless tenor of their way. The nice square pews to which the Reverend Caleb Oriel had taken such exception were, alas, gone, but otherwise, apart from the unfortunate Memorial Window for the 1914–1918 war, it was much as it had been within the memory of the oldest inhabitant—only we doubt whether his memory would have been much good, as he went to a very small Ebenezer chapel away by the allotments and took a senile pride in never having set foot in the parish church. There was not, we are glad to say, a Children's Corner, and the banner of the Greshamsbury Mothers' Union was in a nice dark place.

The side door at the top of the steep path was open. In the church a few lights were on. In the choir seats was a kneeling figure which got up at the sound of their voices, revealing itself as the stout form of the Rector designate.

"Good evening, Fewling," said John Leslie. "I can't be the first to welcome you, as you have already been welcomed. But Mary and I—you do know my wife, I think—are very glad you are coming and hope you will be very happy. I am your senior churchwarden, John Leslie."

"Thank you so much," said the new Rector, shaking hands almost painfully with the Leslies. "I know I shall be. It always takes a little time, you know, to settle down in a new ship, but under a good Captain all will be well," and he looked towards the altar, beyond which the east window glimmered as the moon came through a cloud.

"If it isn't a bother, will you come back to supper with us?" said Mary Leslie, and then wondered if she ought to have waited till they were outside the church. But the new Rector appeared to take it all as a matter of course and accepted at once, saying that he would be at their disposal as soon as he had taken his leave.

"I always say a prayer when I come in or go out of a church," he said. "It seems more polite in someone else's house. You will forgive the delay," which indeed the Leslies had no difficulty in doing and knelt while he bade his silent farewell, and then they all walked through the frosty moonlit evening to the Old Rectory, where there were welcoming light and warmth.

Those who had known Father Fewling as priest-in-charge at St. Sycorax in Northbridge might have been surprised for a moment at their old pastor's appearance. His rather monkish black dress had changed to an eminently respectable black suit. His rather ugly shoes (for those who said he wore sandals were not speaking the truth) were from a better maker and very clean. His collar, above the neat black vest, was shiningly white, and—if the expression can be applied to a figure which almost approximated to that of the unfortunate West India sugar-broker in the Bab Ballads—he had a general air of being a fine upstanding gentleman.

In the drawing-room, besides a good roaring wood fire, John Leslie mixed a generous amount of gin with an adequate amount of vermouth and handed a glass to his wife and a glass to the Rector designate. Then silence fell on the party, for when a

King has literally died in the service of his people such words as
"Well, here's fun" or "All the best" do not appear appropriate.
The new Rector was, however, in full charge of the situation.

"God bless our departed King," he said, as if it were a prayer,
and then added in a lighter voice, but still—or so the Leslies
agreed afterwards—as if it were a prayer, "and may He bless our
new Queen," at which heartfelt words both the Leslies felt the
pricking behind the eyes, which means that tears are not far
away. The glasses were raised and the toast honoured in silence.

"Look here, Fewling," said John Leslie, "there's one thing I'd
like to know. Do you still call yourself—I mean do you like us to
call you—Father Fewling?"

"I wish you would call me Tubby," said the Rector. "They all
called me Tubby in the Navy and I'm used to it—and really it
does suit me," he added, looking not without complacence at his
figure. "As for the Father—I have thought about that. I am
always Father for people who like to use the name. I was Father
to everyone at St. Sycorax. But if people here prefer to call me
anything else I hope they will. There's something else——" and
then he paused.

"Well, Fewling, it's for you to say," said John Leslie, amused
by his Rector's perplexity.

The new incumbent looked uncomfortable, yet at the same
time rather proudly pleased. John Leslie refilled his glass.

"Put it down, Padre," he said, "and take your time."

Thus adjured, and in language familiar to him from his old
naval service, the Rector did put it down in the naval or festive
sense.

"I hope you won't think I'm boasting," he said, with a kind of
subdued pride, "but I have been made an Honorary Canon of
Barchester. So if you like to say Canon Fewling? Not but what I
like the name Father, and I think my people at St. Sycorax liked
it. But now I have a church of my own I feel perhaps Canon
would be more suitable. Why I think it, I don't know," he added
in a burst of confidence.

"My congratulations, Fewling," said John Leslie, shaking his Rector's hand warmly and emerging bruised from its clasp. "And I hope they'll make you a Doctor of Divinity, too. It's the first time I have felt happy since the news this morning."

"I know," said the Rector. "Faithful below he did his duty, And now he's gone aloft. God bless him and his," and their glasses met and the toast was again silently honoured.

"I saw HIM once," said the Rector, when their glasses were again refilled and they had sat down by the leaping wood fire.

Mary Leslie asked if it was in the Navy.

"Oh no, in one of the big blitzes," said the Rector. "I asked Villars if he would object to my going up for a night or two, though I daresay I'd have gone all the same."

"I don't think you would," said Mary Leslie.

"Well, perhaps you are right," said the Rector. "Captain's orders come first. Anyway, I went up to see if I could help and, by Jove, I could. I rang up an old pal who had a church away down by the docks and went down for the night and, by Jove, we got it! The Hun bombers were having the time of their lives. Our fellows couldn't do much but, by Jove, what they could do they did. Do you know what it made me think of?" he asked, turning to Mary.

Mary weakly said she couldn't think.

"Tennyson," said the Rector triumphantly.

John Leslie said, "Why?"

Ship after ship, the whole night long, their high-built galleons came,
Ship after ship, the whole night long, with her battle-thunder and
*   flame;*
Ship after ship, the whole night long, drew back with her dead and
*   her shame;"*

said, or rather thundered and chanted, the new Rector, suddenly showing a side of himself unsuspected by his hosts. "Not," he added, returning to his normal voice, "that we could do much, though the A.A. chaps were doing their level best and so were our fighters—the one and the fifty-three. But that's neither here nor there, and what I'm coming to is that next morning there was His Majesty—and her Majesty too—walking through the ruins. A lot of them were still burning, and all the little houses were gone, as far as the eye could see, and the roads were gone, and there was nothing but smoking ruins and heaps of brick and rubble and people holding a teapot or a pail—all they had left—and the women crying—quite quietly, and a lot of poor chaps on the ground with their toes turned up and a bit of cloth or something over their faces. And then along came Their Majesties and talked to us. And a middle-aged man who had been working like a demon with us all night—black from head to foot he was, and a nasty cut on his head—came up to His Majesty and said, 'You're a *good* King, sir.' And His Majesty looked him in the eyes and he looked round at us all and said, 'And you are a *good* people.' God of battles, what a KING! Sorry, Mrs. Leslie, I forgot where I was. I almost thought I was back in London—on that night."

Emotion had by now reached a point at which anything must be an anticlimax, when most luckily dinner announced itself. The meal passed very pleasantly. The advantages of an honorary canonry were discussed and the Rector's face beamed as he described the beauty of his stall in the Cathedral with its oak canopy and the stall-back and cushion beautifully embroidered in gros point by the ladies of the Society of the Friends of Barchester Cathedral, each with its own blazonings.

"And, do you know," said the Rector, "I have the right—I mean any Honorary Canon has the right—to preach in the Cathedral once a year."

Mary Leslie asked when he would best like to preach.

"I have often wondered the same thing myself," said the Rector. "October the twenty-first would be a good day, especially if it would come on a Sunday, but it will be Tuesday this year. I looked it up. And one would have to wait five years for a Sunday."

John Leslie said, "What about Leap Year?" which led to such countings on fingers and statements unsupported by any knowledge of the facts that everyone would have gone gently mad had not John Leslie suggested the Glorious First of June as an alternative.

"I did look that up too," said the Rector mournfully. "Unfortunately, though I know I ought not to feel it so, the Bishop has chosen that day of all days to preach. Well, in God's good time Trafalgar Day will come on a Sunday and then——" and he fell into a kind of muse, thinking of the Great Admiral and the Royal Navy and his new church and his stall in the Cathedral.

"You know, I sometimes feel like the Queen of Sheba," he said. "The half was not told me. I mean I had often been in your church and admired it, but I did not know—no, I will ask you to guess what I found. And no one else knew it."

There was a silence while his hosts wondered whether he had found the key (reported to weigh forty ounces) of the muniment chest, which key had been lost for fifteen years, but as nothing was in the chest nobody had bothered about it. Or perhaps a squinch, a word which John Leslie said made him feel dull at once and he always wondered if he really meant a squint.

"What was it?" said Mary Leslie, with a good hostess's feeling that a silence must not last too long.

"You will never guess," said the Rector, his large kind face beaming with pleasure. "I went up the tower and while I was looking over the edge, what do you think I saw?"

Mary, in despair at her husband's cowardly silence, said she hoped the gutter had not gone anywhere again. Her husband, in mock despair at the folly of women, said gutters didn't go—they stayed where they were.

"No, but seriously," said the Rector. "A golden-crested mippet's nest. Just where, if you lean over far enough, you can see that gargoyle with a devil sitting on a man's head and pulling his ears. I thought I knew all about mippets. I have often been out with Wickham—the Noel Mertons' agent, you know; he knows more about birds than anyone in the county except Mrs. Crofts at Southbridge—and he told me it was quite unknown for mippets to nest in lead gutters. And there it was, nest and mippet and all. A bit early in the year, but it's the south side and well sheltered."

The Leslies knew birds in a country way. They were not experts, but could tell a hawk from a hernshaw and they congratulated the new Rector warmly.

"There's only one thing," he said. "I would like to know if she has laid an egg yet, but I can't very well climb over and see. I've got a pretty good head, but I'm too heavy now."

He looked so dejected that Mary's kind heart at once thought of some way to comfort him. Then, like a Spartan mother sending her son forth to battle, she suggested that John, better known to us as Minor, should on the occasion of the next school exeat go up and look.

"He would *love* it," she said. "He always wanted to do the outside of the tower, but I was afraid. If you could perhaps lean over and give him your hand, Mr. Fewling——"

"Canon, not Mr.," said her husband. "I don't know much about clerical etiquette, but I think I am right, Fewling?"

"Quite right," said the Rector. "I mean, I like it. But it *would* be very agreeable if someone called me Tubby."

"If you will swear not to let Minor do anything dangerous, Tubby, I'll call you anything you like," said his hostess, to the new Rector's great pleasure. "And when do you come and live here?"

The Rector said he had already looked at the Rectory and liked it. A respectable widow who had looked after him at Northbridge was willing to come as housekeeper and he wondered if she could get some help in the village. Mary Leslie said she would speak to her cook about it; and then talk gradually came back to the nation's loss and there was a silence. But not a difficult silence. A communion of loyal and respectfully loving thoughts for a mother, a wife, and a daughter whose loss was the loss of England and English peoples in every quarter of the globe.

"It occurs to me," said John Leslie, "that we may have seen the Last of the Kings."

His wife asked him what he meant.

"Exactly what I say," said John Leslie. "Where are the Kings of yesteryear? The Kings of France, Spain, Italy, Prussia, Hanover, Bavaria, Servia, Bulgaria, and, to be quite boring, Israel and Judah? I suppose Abyssinia thinks it has a King, but I wouldn't stand for a King called Negus."

"A very respectable English name though," said Canon Fewling. "A Colonel who gave his name to a very respectable drink. But what about the Scandinavian bloc, Leslie?"

"Good well-meaning people," said John, "but not much security of tenure and far too apt to be seen bicycling to Woolworth's or whatever it is called up there. Holland has Queens, one must admit that, but Queens are not Kings be the other who he may. And as for Belgium——" and he paused.

"But, John," said his wife, "they are all foreigners and have revolutions."

"Which," said Canon Fewling, "are child's play compared with our revolution. I don't want to be depressing, and I hope that God will see fit to guide our steps at home into the way of peace. We have a Queen now. But who can say whether we shall have a King?"

Mary said indignantly that there was Prince Charles, and if it came to that Princess Anne and probably more to follow.

"Yes, indeed," said Canon Fewling. "But at the rate we are going who can be sure of a continued monarchy? God send such a thing may never happen to us as to become a republic——"

"If I may interrupt you," said John Leslie, "it is more likely to be a Commonwealth with a King or Queen disguised as a Protector."

"And if it is," said Canon Fewling, "we come back to what you were saying, Leslie. A King of a Constitution. And they tried that in France and look at them now. No. Constitutions won't work. A great many people don't believe in the Divine Right of Kings now—then what happens?"

"Look here, Fewling, I'll have to do the preaching myself. If they don't believe in the Divine Right of Kings, why was everyone wearing in Barchester black and a lot of the women crying?" said John, rather basely changing his position.

"I think God had touched their hearts," said Canon Fewling, but so simply that neither of his hearers felt uncomfortable. "Perhaps His Majesty's death was a kind of sacrifice for us—for our manifold sins and wickedness. Kings have a duty, but they haven't all done it. In the Royal Navy duty is duty. Nelson knew it. His Late Majesty was a naval man and he knew it too. And he did his duty and more than his duty. If," said the Rector, "it is not asking too much of heaven, I should like to think of His Majesty being received by all our great Admirals. *What* a night it would be."

"Rather like the Kipling poem about all the great men who welcome Jane Austen," said Mary. "I cry every time I read it. I think I am crying now," and indeed her eyes were misted and she had to bang them with her handkerchief.

"*He* knew," said Canon Fewling, referring this time not to His Late Majesty but to a poet. "He knew almost too much. I have sometimes thought that after a hundred years or so he will be recognised as a prophet. If I were literary I should like to write something about his prophetic works. Now, there's one called *The City of Brass* and it says word for word everything that has happened and is happening in England. But no one ever mentions it," and the Leslies had to confess, to their eternal shame, that they had never come across it.

"Then there is something I really *can* do for you," said the Rector, beaming at the thought of being useful. "I have got his collected poems, a great fat red book it is, and when I am settled and have unpacked my books may I bring it over and read it to you if it wouldn't bore you? It really *needs* reading aloud—I don't mean by me particularly—because half of it depends on the stresses and the cross-rhythms and the internal rhymes and assonances. No one has ever done anything like it."

Mary Leslie said they had got a complete Kipling but she had never read the poem.

"If I got the book, would you read it to us, Tubby?" she said. "I'll go and get it."

So away she went, and the two men talked a little of parish affairs about which John Leslie as a landowning church-warden knew a good deal, till his wife came back with a fat red volume which she gave to Canon Fewling, open at a certain page.

He looked at it with great satisfaction and began to read in his pleasant, sonorous voice, beating out the rhythm and emphasising, just enough, what he had rightly called the stresses and the cross-rhythms and the internal rhymes and assonances, but before he had got very far a noise which had been growing in the hall burst into the room manifesting itself as Captain Fairweather, R.N., and his wife Rose.

"I say, Mrs. Leslie, we're not too late to come in, are we?" said Rose Fairweather. "We were having dinner with the Carters at Southbridge and we thought we might just come and see you."

Mary Leslie, too polite to show her disappointment at being interrupted, welcomed the Fairweathers and began to introduce Canon Fewling, who was to be their new Rector. But the words were still coming out of her mouth when Captain Fairweather, saying "Tubby!", hit the reverend gentleman violently on the back. The rest of the company were then completely cold-shouldered while Canon Fewling and Captain Fairweather compared naval notes ranging over some twenty years. Captain Fairweather, it appeared, had been a midshipman in a ship where Canon Fewling was an officer before his retirement into the Church, and they made so much noise about the night the Old Man had kicked the cook's cat out of his cabin where it had been clawing his best-loved leather-seated chair that the rest of the party were silent. His wife meanwhile made up her face, gazing the while at the company with the curious but fearless look of the savage who sees white men for the first time.

John Leslie, seeing no end to his naval occasion, fetched his whisky, kept for occasions of special merit, and put a glass into the hand of each disputant.

"Well, here's to you, Tubby, and all the best," said Captain Fairweather. "I'm sorry, Mrs. Leslie, but it was like old days to see this fellow again."

Mary said, quite truly, that she was delighted to see old friends meeting and asked Rose if she would like some whisky, but Rose, for some reason known only to Providence, hardly ever touched alcohol, and partook of orange juice and soda water while Mary Leslie told her about the house that might be to let in the village and Rose said it sounded too shatteringly marvellous and she would go and see it next day.

"Mummy and Daddy sent their love to you," said Rose to her hostess. "And I saw two of your boys at Southbridge. They had come to Sunday supper with the Carters. They were lambs. One of them can climb up outside houses like a cat burglar. I wanted him to show me, but it was all so shatteringly sad about the King that he didn't. I mean, one does feel so *awful*, Mrs. Leslie, and I keep on hoping it isn't true. And the other was *quite* shatteringly amusing and he told me about how he climbed up an edifice or a muniment or something and couldn't get down till someone came and helped him. They are dears. What are their names?"

Mary Leslie, too wise in the ways of the young to be at all surprised by a beautiful young woman who didn't know the name of two young men with whom she had spent an evening, said it was John, the second, who was a great climber, and the other was Clive and wanted to go into the Air Force. Rose said, "How frightfully shattering," and, catching Canon Fewling's eye, so distracted the naval part of it that he quite lost track of what Rose's husband was saying to him.

"Sorry, Tubby," said Captain Fairweather. "My wife has no manners. Never had. But a good heart and very nice children," which of course made Mary Leslie enquire about the Fairweathers' family and wonder again at their mother's air of perpetual youth and come privately to the conclusion that to be very silly made life much easier—as it doubtless does.

"Oh, Father Fewling," said Rose, "you're coming to be the rector here, aren't you? I simply adored your church at Northbridge with all those candles and the divine clothes and the choirboys singing, quite shattering. It will be too marvellous to have it here. You know John and I are looking for a house for two or three years and we may have that nice house just outside the gates of Greshamsbury Park. I shall come to church every Sunday, because I always do, and even the shatteringly early service."

"Does anyone want the late news?" said Mary, feeling that Rose's artless prattle had better be checked, and turned on the wireless. The same heart-breaking news was repeated and the world was told that the young Queen, flying back from Africa, would shortly be in her own land.

"What a burden for such a young Queen," said John Leslie, and no one disagreed when Rose, whose lovely eyes were most becomingly full of tears, clutched her husband's hand and said, "But the Queen has got her husband to help her, so she will be all right, won't she, darling?"

Captain Fairweather, to whom His Royal Highness was not unknown in the Senior Service, said Her Majesty would be absolutely all right and told his wife to stop sniffing and dry her eyes, which she obediently did.

"By the way," said Captain Fairweather, "the Francis Greshams live round here, don't they? I saw a good deal of him in the bad days out east, before the Japs got him. Good fellow."

Mary, delighted at the prospect of helping old friends to meet, said, Yes, indeed, the Greshams were living in part of Greshamsbury Park, the big house of the neighbourhood, and as soon as the Fairweathers were settled in The Laurels, which was the dull name of the house which the nice dull Greens were letting to them she would ask them all to meet, and if it weren't so late she would ring them up and ask them to come over. Then Captain Fairweather said he must take his wife home and they would look forward to seeing the Leslies again very soon and so went away. As the last news had been at eleven-fifteen on that night it was close on midnight and Cannon Fewling also took his leave, thanking his hosts warmly for their hospitality.

"I'll run you over to Northbridge, Fewling," said John Leslie. "The last bus went at nine-fifteen."

Canon Fewling looked confused.

"I don't want to seem proud," he said, rather in John Gilpin's spirit, "but I have a car. I left it in that little lane by the church unless anyone has stolen it. You never know."

So horrified was John Leslie at this thought that he insisted on walking up to the lane with his guest to assure himself that the honour of Greshamsbury was intact. All was well. A car was standing in the little lane and though it was not a particularly large one John could see that it was of the best and newest make.

"That's a very nice car you've got, Fewling," he said.

"It is," said Canon Fewling. "I think I did well."

"'All my own invention','" said John Leslie, at which Canon Fewling laughed and John thought even more highly of the new Rector.

"You see, though it's not my own fault," Canon Fewling continued, "I'm pretty well off now. An old uncle and aunt died last year and left me quite a nice sum of money, even when the death duties were paid. I did think perhaps I oughtn't to take it, but I had a talk with Villars—the Rector at Northbridge, you know—and he said I would be a fool if I didn't. He was really very kind and I felt quite humble."

John Leslie, amused and interested by these midnight confidences, asked, "Why humble?"

"Well, you see," said Canon Fewling, "I can help such a lot of people. Sometimes at St. Sycorax I used to wish I could sell myself as a slave to get money for my old and poor friends, but now I am, as it were, the steward in charge of this money and can really help people who need it. It is rather self-indulgent, I fear, but it gives me such pleasure that I hope it is all right. And one real piece of self-indulgence is the car. I had never had one, and bicycling does take a long time when people are ill and want you in the night to comfort them. So I took very good advice with an old friend, Wickham, the Mertons' agent over near North-bridge, who knows all about birds, and he said I would be a fool if I didn't buy the best as it paid in the end and I could give so many people lifts in it, or get to them quickly if they needed me in the night. She's not bad, is she? Do you think I did rightly?"

John Leslie was able to say with all his heart that the new Rector had done a most sensible thing and although it was late and very cold, he allowed his new friend to point out the many beauties and qualities of the car. Then, after a farewell grip which left his host gasping, Canon Fewling got into the car and, handling her with great skill, backed her, turned her and drove away through the village. John Leslie walked back, thinking of the Rector as the master of a man-of-war, taking his craft with all her sails spread and a favouring gale through grey seas, an eye open for enemy ships, for rocks, for reefs, for signs of storm; confident in strength and knowledge and not unmindful of the Giver of those gifts.

"*What* a nice evening," said his wife, already halfway upstairs.

John said indeed it was and he thought they were very lucky in their new Rector and how lovely Rose Fairweather was, to which she agreed. And we think that this was partly because, in a quite different way, she was herself a woman of quietly handsome and distinguished looks. For, whatever people may say, most good-looking women whole-heartedly admire beauty in their own sex.

CHAPTER 2

The stately measured ritual of a great King's last journey took its appointed course. His mortal remains lay in state in his parish church, among his people, watched and guarded by his people, while his royal daughter was proclaimed as Queen. His mortal remains were guarded and escorted by his soldiers from King's Cross Station to Westminster Hall where he lay in royal state while his Lords, his Commons, and his people moved endlessly past him. On a February day, the day after St. Valentine's Day, his mortal remains were drawn by his Royal Navy, guarded by his Army, raised shoulder high to the train by men of the King's Company of the Grenadier Guards, and so taken to be laid in the Chapel of the Knights of the Garter in his royal home of Windsor Castle, followed by four Royal Dukes and by three Queens and a Princess Royal, veiled in black. Then the young Queen took up the burden of royalty among the prayers of her people and life went on.

In Greshamsbury the departure of the nice dull Greens was followed by the excitement of the new Rector's arrival, heralded by his housekeeper Mrs. Hicks, the mother of the head housemaid at Northbridge Rectory. Greshamsbury was not quite sure whether it was going to approve a foreigner like Mrs. Hicks, but when it transpired that her late husband's aunt was a cousin of an old man whose grandfather had been employed about the stables at Greshamsbury Park all barriers fell. Luckily Canon Fewling was not much of a tea-drinker, so Mrs. Hicks was able to entertain her new-found connections on a generous scale and was considered to have paid her footing and be one of themselves. This liberty was then extended to the new Rector who found, not altogether in his displeasure, that his parishioners meant to use him as a kind of William Whiteley or Universal Provider and to bring every trouble to him, from the loss of ration books to complaints about false teeth that didn't seem not to bite proper somehow, and enquiries as to how to address a letter to Uncle Tom who went to Australia or one of them places in 1898 and had never been heard of since. But to all this the Rector was well accustomed, and such was his kindly disposition that he really enjoyed it.

"You know, Leslie," he said to his churchwarden some weeks after his arrival when his house had got into shape and his church services were at any rate not less well attended than his predecessor's, "it is really a great advantage not to be married," to which John Leslie replied he wasn't a good judge himself, as he had married quite young and had always found it a good thing.

"You don't look much like an old married man," said the Rector generously. "And certainly your wife doesn't. It is ridiculous to think of her with three almost grown-up boys. She might almost be their sister."

"You know I was married before," said John Leslie, feeling, as so many people did, that Canon Fewling was interested by everything that touched human life. "Gay was her name. She died very young and we had no child. Perhaps as well. One doesn't know. And then Mary came to Rushwater—my people's place—and brought peace into my life again. Look here, Fewling, I have answered a question about myself. Will you listen to a question from me? Do you ever consider marrying? No business of mine really."

The Rector laid his strong capable hands on his skirted knees—for he had just come away from the church where he always wore his cassock, though for ordinary life he wore ordinary clothes—and was silent.

"Look here, I'm sorry," said John Leslie. "Take it as not said."

"Not at all," said the Rector cheerfully. "I'm not a professional celibate if that's what you mean. But I've never felt that anyone thought enough of me to want to marry me. I have always been fairly poor till lately, which was against me. And really, Leslie, if you knew how female church workers can persecute a priest, you would be surprised. I remember sometimes, during the war, with the black-out, I used to beg Mrs. Villars, the Vicar's wife at Northbridge and a delightful woman, to walk home with me from tea-parties as a kind of chaperon—to take me into protective custody as it were. If one had wished to fall in love with a happily married woman with grown-up sons, one might have done worse," said the Rector, who appeared to be enjoying emotion recollected in tranquillity. "But she never thought of me. And I must say," he added with a frankness that his churchwarden found touching and amusing, "I don't see why anyone should. Just look at me."

"Not romantic perhaps, Tubby," said John Leslie, "but an extremely good fellow and, what's more, a very good churchman," which appeared to please the Rector, though we are pretty sure that he and his churchwarden put rather different interpretations upon the last words.

"What exactly do you mean, or rather think you mean, by your last words, Leslie?" said the Rector.

John Leslie, after a pause for reflection, said he didn't quite know himself, but he thought the Rector had done most wisely in giving the village—or almost town now, alas—the kind of morning service it wanted.

"I am delighted that you think they want it," said the Rector. "I sometimes miss St. Sycorax, you know. It was rather a dark church and the candles looked so well in it and I did like incense. Villars gave them the other service, and he was most kind in giving me a pretty free hand. But I do feel that a priest ought to think of what his parishioners would like. I took a good deal of pains, you know, before I came here, to find what your Greshamsbury people wanted, and I felt it was my duty to give it to them. And there is always the early celebration," he added, half to himself. "And I am really grateful, Leslie, truly grateful, that I have been given room to deny myself. One isn't in my place for oneself, you know. It doesn't do to strive to wind ourselves too high for sinful man beneath the sky."

"What's that?" said John.

"Only a bit of another verse out of 'New every morning is the love,'" said the Rector. "It never got into Hymns Ancient and Modern, I don't know why. One does think of lots of queer things, and when you are a priest you really must try to please your people."

"Even to a Children's Corner?" said John Leslie with some malice.

"No!" said his Rector. "Come rack, come rope, NO. I say, Leslie, are you going to the Carters' on Sunday? Crofts is coming over to take the evening service here, you know, and I'm taking his at Southbridge."

"That seems very suitable," said John Leslie. "He was a full Colonel and you were——"

"Only as far as Commander," said the Rector a little wistfully. "Perhaps if I'd stayed in the Navy till I was an Admiral I might have made a better parson," at which words John Leslie told his Rector not to be a fool, and it was arranged that on the following Sunday the Rector would, after the morning service, drive the Leslies over to Southbridge that they might the better appreciate and glorify his expensive car.

We hope that some of our readers were at Southbridge School, or have had sons or grandsons or nephews there, for it has, through a friendship of many years' standing, become so familiar to us that we take it for granted. Perhaps it will be enough to say, as we have said before, that it was an old foundation which after a poorish time in the middle of last century under the Rev. J. J. Damper (better known by his little volume of *Perambulations in Palestine*, long since deservedly out of print, and author of the *Carmen Southbridgiense* with its refrain of

> *Alma Mater, Alma Mater,*
> *None than thou wilt ere be greater*)

had been pulled up by a succession of good Headmasters, and recently by Mr. Birkett, father of the beautiful Rose Fairweather. Mr. Birkett had retired some years previously to the Dower House near Worsted on the branch line from Winter Overcotes. His place had been taken by Everard Carter, who had married Kate Keith, a sister of Mrs. Noel Merton, and had three delightful children. He had gone quietly at first, but gradually the old order had changed, giving place to the new so gently that few people observed or resented it, and on every Speech Day the School was able to show a fine array of distinguished Old Boys.

The lunch on this Sunday was to be of a friendly nature, with not more than ten guests, though the dining-room table with the leaf in it could accommodate as many as fourteen, and after lunch the Leslies proposed to take their sons out for a long walk on the downs. When the morning service at Greshamsbury was over Canon Fewling proudly introduced the Leslies to his car, which Mary had not yet seen.

"Now if you will sit in front, Mrs. Leslie," he said, "you can tell me, if you will, when I am driving too quickly for you. I am afraid I have once or twice gone rather fast, but I can assure you that I am very careful," and he helped her into the front seat, a kind of help for which one is never really grateful, for whether your host drags you up from inside or pushes you up from outside you are apt to arrive all askew on your seat, with your legs twisted, or one arm behind your back, or even to plunge on all fours against the steering-wheel.

"What I would really like," said Canon Fewling, taking the turn of Greshamsbury High Street practically on one wheel, "would be to drive a racing car at Goodwood. It would be almost as good as a destroyer."

Mary Leslie said, "What fun, but wouldn't the Bishop object?" and as neither speaker knew exactly what a Bishop's powers were in the case of one of his clergy taking part in motor races the conversation came to an end. It was a fine day and the country in its winter bareness had an austere beauty which summer visitors do not know. Skirting the grounds of Boxall Hill, once an appanage of Greshamsbury Hall, now an appanage of the Barsetshire County Council, they crossed the main road above Stogpingum and began to mount the downs by the line of Gundric's Fossway, and when Canon Fewling suggested that they should take the rough track over Great Hump no one gainsaid him. At the top of the hill the car was allowed to stop and take breath in the thin keen higher air. The county lay spread round them. Barchester, even on a Sunday, now lay under a thin veil of smoke which a north-west wind was bringing from the city and from Mr. Adams's works at Hogglestock, but a ray of sun had caught the spire of the Cathedral, gleaming white over the city. To the east the rich country of the Woolram valley was in cold sunshine. To the south the downland stretched away to its last barrier, beyond which lay the sea. To the west it sloped with grazing land and arable land to the water-meadows of the river, where lay Southbridge, the end of their journey. Looking before them and to east and west, that lovely land of down and water-meadow had hardly changed in the last hundred years, and many of the villages were still images of what they had been.

"You know," said John Leslie, who was on the County Council, where he made himself extremely useful by never speaking unless he knew more about the subject in hand than the other speakers, "they are talking about an aerodrome down Allington way," which depressed his hearers and led to a short and highly uninformed discussion as to whether, in the event of such interference, the rates would go up or down.

"But there's one thing," said Canon Fewling hopefully. "The illegitimate birthrate can't be much higher than it is," to which there did not seem to be any reply. From the north came the long sound of a bell, almost dying as it reached them.

"One o'clock by the Cathedral," said Canon Fewling. "We mustn't be late," and he drove as fast as was reasonable on a Sunday morning in almost empty side-roads down into the river valley and so to Southbridge School, and drew up with a flourish at the door of the Headmaster's House.

Here they were welcomed by Everard Carter and his wife, she who was Kate Keith. No one who met Kate Carter for the first time would have guessed that she had been married for some fifteen years. Time is perhaps one of the most confusing things ever invented, and if anyone had asked Kate how long she had been Everard's wife she would probably have had to count on her fingers and been just as surprised at the result as we are, until she looked at Miss Angela Carter and Masters Bobbie and Philip Carter and realised that Bobbie, her eldest, had gone to his public school and her other children were rapidly ageing. But to us, who have seen Kate at intervals ever since we first met her, she is still the Kate we first knew.

"It is only a small party, Mrs. Leslie," said Kate Carter. "Just Mr. and Mrs. Birkett and Mrs. Feeder, who is the mother of one of our masters and lives in Editha. You will like her," which remark is apt to make one take a determined hatred of the person mentioned, but, coming from Kate Carter, had to be believed because she was not only very kind but also very truthful.

"I ought to explain," said Everard Carter, seeing Canon Fewling's eye glazing with want of comprehension, "that Editha is the end cottage in Wiple Terrace down in the village. Not a female guest," by which explanation the Canon was considerably relieved. Then in came Mr. and Mrs. Birkett, whom Canon

Fewling already knew, and everyone had another glass of sherry, till Mrs. Feeder arrived, a spare elderly woman in black, with a black ribbon round her bony throat, who must have looked at thirty exactly the same as she did at sixty-odd and would doubtless at eighty-odd if spared.

"I've heard of you," said Mrs. Feeder, fixing Canon Fewling with an Ancient Mariner eye by which even his naval courage was daunted. "You were in the Mediterranean."

Canon Fewling said that was so, secretly terrified of having made an admission which seemed somehow to bring him under Mrs. Feeder's displeasure.

"That's all right," said Mrs. Feeder. "So was the School Matron's nephew. He raced jerboas with Mr. Shergold, the Senior Housemaster here."

"Not Shergold in the old *Gridiron*?" said Canon Fewling.

Mrs. Feeder said, "The same. And," she added, holding out her sherry glass, "we'll have one on that. Fill up, Padre," all of which would have frightened most clergymen, even Honorary Canons, out of their wits. But Canon Fewling, with the greatest good-nature, refilled Mrs. Feeder's glass and assisted her to drink the toast with the dregs of his own, and they all went in to lunch, where Kate Carter very prettily asked Canon Fewling to say grace, which he did in two words of the Roman tongue.

Talk, as is but reasonable with two sets of Headmasters past and present, their wives, and the mother of an assistant master, was largely technical, but so is sea-talk. Canon Fewling got on very well with Mrs. Birkett, especially when he expressed his admiration for her beautiful daughter Rose Fairweather.

"She rang me up to tell me all about it," said Mrs. Birkett. "She liked you so much and is looking forward to Sundays at Greshamsbury," which interested Canon Fewling, who said he was delighted to hear it, as somehow he had not imagined Mrs. Fairweather as much of a churchgoer.

"I know she doesn't look like one," said her mother sympathetically, "but she has always been very good in that way, in spite of which she was never engaged to a clergyman."

That, said Canon Fewling, was a striking non sequitur, and then wondered if he was being pedantic, but Mrs. Birkett, well used to the conversation of her husband's friends, who were mostly educated in the higher sense, said that though Rose had been very troublesome as a girl, getting engaged to anyone and everyone beginning with the Art Master at Barchester High School when she was sixteen, she had never tried her hand on a clergyman, and then wondered whether she had gone too far. But Canon Fewling, well up to date by now in the history of the diocese, said it made him think of the notorious Signora Vesey Neroni, daughter of Dr. Stanhope, a practically non-resident divine in the middle of the nineteenth century, about whom there were such extraordinary stories. Mrs. Birkett, delighted to find someone who knew the history of Barchester, said he must get the Dean to tell him more about it, as his, the Dean's, grandfather had known most of the people concerned. Canon Fewling asked who the Dean's grandfather was.

"Oh, a clergyman called Crawley," said Mrs. Birkett. "There was some kind of trouble with the Palace people, as there always has been in Barchester, but he came out of it all right, and Mr. Grantly at Edgewood is his grandson—or is it great-grandson? Time and generations are so confusing, and the older you get the more confusing they are. I sometimes feel so like my own mother that it is quite difficult to remember who I am. You will find it so presently," she added, looking very kindly at the Canon, and then they were claimed by their neighbours.

As soon as lunch was over the party adjourned to the drawing-room where the men, freed from the shackles of tradition and etiquette, were able to talk to one another, reinforced by the arrival of the School Chaplain, better known as Holy Joe, burning to discuss with Canon Fewling the Bishop of Barchester's letter to *The Times* about extending to our Russian friends an understand-ing which should transcend all national politics. Canon Fewling, quite rightly, said he felt that as a parish priest he ought not to question his superior officer's point of view in public, which statement made his views so plain that a most delightful and unloving conversation took place about the present incumbent. From this talk John Leslie presently withdrew himself as he and his wife were taking their two younger sons for a walk on the downs, and the party began to break up.

"Oh, Canon Fewling," said Kate Carter, who had been out of the room for a few moments, "that was Mrs. Crofts, our Vicar's wife, ringing up to say would you come to tea at the Vicarage, and the Leslies too, but I know their boys are giving them tea in their House. What shall I say?"

Canon Fewling said he would be delighted.

"And after the service I hope you will come and have a glass of sherry with me," said Mrs. Feeder, to which Canon Fewling replied that as he was driving the Leslies home he must be bound by what they wished to do but would like to come if it suited them.

"They will probably go to our service in the School Chapel," said the Headmaster; so it was agreed that the Leslies should be asked to come on to Mrs. Feeder's afterwards, and the party dispersed.

If Canon Fewling, or his host and hostess, had at all wondered how to fill the afternoon, which indeed was almost past by now, everything was decided by an S O S from Mr. Shergold, the Senior Housemaster, asking if Canon Fewling would come over to his House before he went to tea at the Vicarage and talk naval shop, which invitation was gladly accepted.

Kate Carter, who always thought of others and for others, said really Canon Fewling had better go over to Mr. Shergold's House fairly soon because naval men always had so many things to talk about, which suggestion, softly and kindly made, was tantamount to a semi-royal command. So Canon Fewling took leave of the Carters, repeated to the Birketts his admiration of their lovely daughter and went away to Mr. Shergold's House accompanied, not altogether to his pleasure, by the School Chaplain, who insisted on showing him the way; and as the Canon did not know Southbridge School this was truly an act of kindness, though slightly marred by the Chaplain insisting upon showing his guest the really revolting interior of the hideous School Chapel which, as our readers know, was designed by the same architect who had designed Pomfret Towers and combined darkness and inconvenience to an unparalleled degree, not to speak of the hideous east window (Munich 1850 style) and the Gothic pitch-pine stalls and panelling. But a consecrated building none the less, Canon Fewling reminded himself, and then gratefully was absorbed into Mr. Shergold's House for a happy talk about naval occasions, but did not forget to go over to the Vicarage, where tea was early so that the Vicar might have plenty of time to go over to Greshamsbury and take the evening service.

Here he was received by Bateman, formerly batman to Colonel the Reverend Edward Crofts, and taken into the large, ill-proportioned drawing-room, which had been made warm and comfortable though not beautiful by its present owners. Apart from some handsome Indian curtains and some good family portraits in the schools of Raeburn and Lawrence which looked very well on the walls and had the additional merit of distracting the eye from the far too high cornice, there was nothing of note about the room, the fact being that neither the Vicar nor his wife minded in the least what their surroundings were like. An attitude for which, in these days, there is something to be said.

"This is very good of you, Fewling," said the Vicar. "I don't think you know my wife," and Canon Fewling said he was delighted to meet her and had long known and admired her bird-drawings. For Mrs. Crofts, through the medium of Mr. Wickham, the Noel Mertons' agent, himself a bigoted bird-lover, had met his uncle Mr. Johns, the well-known publisher, who had subsequently made a comfortable and steady income for her and for himself by reproductions of her exquisite bird-studies, rather stylised, but with a deep sympathy for the glitter of a bird's eye, the rounded hardness of its shoulders, the grip of its feet on the twig and the delicate shading of its feathers.

Mrs. Croft's rather harsh features softened with pleasure at what was obviously genuine homage to her work, and then she thanked Canon Fewling for his exchange of pulpits.

"The thanks should be mine," said Canon Fewling. "Your husband will give Greshamsbury something valuable. I shall do my best here."

"They are all right," said Mrs. Crofts, alluding to her husband's parishioners. "I have asked Admiral Phelps, the Vicar's warden, to tea and his very nice wife and daughter. What are yours like?"

Canon Fewling said nothing could be more agreeable than his warden John Leslie and his delightful wife. The other warden, Mr. Umbleby, also seemed a very good sort. Then the Vicar claimed his guest and the two reverend gentlemen fell into delightful small-church gossip till tea was brought in simultaneously with the arrival of Admiral Phelps, Mrs. Phelps and Miss Phelps. Admiral Phelps was a small, spare, dry-faced man. His two ladies looked so capable that Canon Fewling, having had more than enough of capable women at Northbridge, nearly got under the table in his fright. But this piece of escapism was not necessary, for the Admiral, pouncing upon a junior officer of the Royal Navy, at once dragged him into naval shop and retailed for Canon Fewling's benefit a very long story about his losing struggle with their Lordships of the Admirality to get posted to an active job in the late war.

"A.R.P. was the end of it," said the Admiral, sadly and without rancour. "But I kept my fellows here on their toes. Our black-out was the best in the country. How did you do in Northbridge?"

"I was only an air-raid warden, sir," said Canon Fewling, metaphorically saluting the quarter-deck. "But we managed a nice little wardens' post. Underground it was and I fitted it up like a cabin. Unfortunately we never got a bomb at Northbridge, but I believe our little dug-out would have stood anything short of a direct hit. We had bunks for sleeping, and portholes—not real, of course, but they looked well—and I got the wheel of the old *Scrapiron* when she was broken up and hung a Union Jack over it, and a splendid ventilating system."

"By jove, I wish I'd seen it," said Admiral Phelps. "But, my dear fellow, I must tell you about our black-out here. It was really my wife's idea and Margot's—that's my girl," he added, looking proudly at his large spinster daughter of uncertain age. "It was a thick curtain across the inside of the door and you went through it; and then there was another curtain, only the way you went through it wasn't opposite the way you went through the first curtain, if I make myself clear, so that the light from the hall, which was really our sitting-room, only we usually had naval men on leave sleeping there, could not possibly get through."

Canon Fewling, though not quite grasping the Admiral's safety device, said it sounded excellent; and then, of course, the two men fell into naval talk again, in which they were joined by Miss Phelps, who had no nonsense about her and would have been good-looking if she had ever taken the faintest trouble about her looks. But a habit of considering all junior ranks as younger brothers had discouraged what possible suitors she may have had, and Southbridge had mentally written her off as a permanent spinster.

"You know, Canon Fewling," said Miss Phelps, "we really did miss the war. There was so much to do. Mummy and I often slept on the floor because we had so many boys here on leave, and it made one feel one was really doing something," with which rather addled statement Canon Fewling wholly agreed, saying that the nights he had spent in his little A.R.P. shelter were—apart from the Royal Navy—among the happiest hours of his life. Miss Phelps then described in detail the hens, ducks, rabbits and goats that she and her mother had kept, thus appreciably reducing the tonnage required for food from over-seas.

"I can't tell you," said Canon Fewling earnestly, "how much I admire you for knowing all about animals. My housekeeper, who is a very nice woman from Northbridge, says I ought to keep hens, but I don't know how to begin. She could buy them for me, she says, from a cousin of hers, but then there is the question of hen-houses and food. They need a pail of some kind of mixture that smells rather unpleasant, don't they? I seem to remember the smell when I was a boy."

"Oh, you get used to it," said Miss Phelps, looking at Canon Fewling with a tolerant eye, as a rather grown-up kind of sub-Lieutenant who needed assistance. "Where do you live in Greshamsbury? In the Vicarage?" which question was not so unreasonable as it sounds, since all over England the houses where the clergy used to live have been disestablished for lay use because the incumbent cannot afford to live there.

Canon Fewling said he did, only it was a Rectory, and there was a bit of land at the end of the garden that would do nicely for fowls, or so his housekeeper said.

"Well now," said Miss Phelps, putting her hands in her jacket pockets, a habit formed by putting her hands in the pockets of the trousers which she had worn pretty well day and night during the war, "I'd better come over and have a look. What you want is a few layers to start with and some broodies and the right kind of eggs. I could sell you some. They're really good."

"That is most kind of you," said Canon Fewling, grateful, though slightly alarmed by Miss Phelps's size and self-confidence.

"I say, Irons!" said Miss Phelps in a loud voice. "Sorry, Padre," she added, noticing that her guest was perplexed. "It's only father. He was with the destroyers in the Iron class. He was a Lieutenant in the *Flatiron* and Commander of the *Scrapiron* and Captain of the *Andiron* and was with the *Gridiron* on her trials."

"What is it, Margot?" said her father, answering her hail.

"Look here, Irons," said his daughter. "The Padre wants to

start hens. I could take some over on my bicycle, and there are some bits of wood and wire I could tie on behind. I'll see that you get the right sort of birds, Padre. Who is your housekeeper?"

"Her name is Hicks, from Northbridge," said Canon Fewling. "She looked after me in lodgings there."

"Oh, the Hickses are all right," said Miss Phelps. "I'll let you know as soon as I have a free day and bring everything over and have a talk with Mrs. Hicks."

Canon Fewling thanked her with real gratitude tempered by a doubt as to whether his housekeeper would approve, and asked if she would like to go over the church, which offer Miss Phelps accepted with pleasure, saying that she would come over early as she had never seen Greshamsbury Church and loved poking about in those old places. Then, her thoughts taking a sudden turn, she asked which came first, Canon Fewling or Colonel Crofts.

"I'm afraid I don't quite understand," said Canon Fewling. "If you mean is a Rector more important than a Vicar, or the other way round, there's not much difference. Where there is a Vicar it usually means that the church was originally dependent on some larger community who put in a priest to do the work. The name Rector is a bit more independent than Vicar," to which Miss Phelps replied that she got him; and in Scotland, where she had a lot of cousins, the Universities had Rectors, which showed. And if this was a rather muddled kind of understanding, that is all that most of us can manage. Then Colonel Crofts said he must be getting over to Greshamsbury and begging his temporary locum tenens to remain at the Vicarage till it was time for the evening service, he went away.

"It is very nice to have you here, Canon Fewling," said Mrs. Crofts, when her husband had gone. "I hope you will find our church all right. There is one step going up to the pulpit that is rather higher than the others, so be careful. My husband is used to it, of course, but I always warn people."

Canon Fewling asked if it could be altered.

"Well, I suppose it could," said Mrs. Crofts, "but it comes in an awkward place, where the steps go round the corner. We did have Guy Barton over to look at it—do you know him? he is rather an authority on church work and married the Archdeacon's daughter over Plumstead way—and he said it would be a pity to alter it, as it would cost a good deal and there was no need for anyone to fall down unless they wanted to. Our man Bateman—he was Edward's batman in the war, which makes it rather confusing—will show you where you can dress in plenty of time if you want to make any change," but though she was as a rule rather self-confident in her role of parson's wife, there was a hesitation in her voice as she looked at Canon Fewling's new and resplendent clerical suit.

"How thoughtful of you," said Canon Fewling. "I came over as you see me, in my ordinary clothes. I hope you won't think me foolish, but though I wear a cassock in church, I gathered that Southbridge prefers an ordinary suit outside, so I came as I am. It is rather a good suit, I think," he added with a kind of shy pride that amused and touched his hostess. "You know, Mrs. Crofts, the Old Adam dies hard in one. When I go from the Rectory to the church at Greshamsbury on rainy days, with a priest's cloak over my cassock, I sometimes like to pretend that I am in the Navy again and wearing my officer's cloak on a wet rough night after spending a few hours ashore."

Mrs. Crofts said it was a delightful and romantic thought.

"Do you really find it romantic?" said Canon Fewling. "I am so glad, because I do too, only being a little on the stout side—my friends always call me Tubby—I wonder if I am like the people that say they have no sins," and he paused, realising that almost speaking aloud to himself he was perhaps not making himself quite clear to others.

"Do you mean you are deceiving yourself?" said Mrs. Crofts. "Of course not, Canon Fewling. I rather wish sometimes that Edward had a cloak. But he was a Full Colonel in the Indian

Army and I don't think he would quite like it. If he could wear his belt and his sword——" and her voice trailed away.

Canon Fewling said he didn't know if there was any law against wearing a belt and a sword, and after all lots of the people in the *Pilgrim's Progress* had swords.

"And sometimes, you know," he went on, finding, as most people did, that Mrs. Crofts was an unusually good listener, "I like to feel I am still in a ship. Not during the service, of course, but when I go into the church sometimes at night, alone, I pretend I am the officer on duty. Do you think it foolish?"

Mrs. Crofts had an almost uncomfortable choke in her throat as she assured him that she didn't, adding that when her husband, as he often did, went to his church alone late in the evening she felt that he was still a soldier looking for where his duty lay.

"I should like to tell you something," said Canon Fewling, who had taken a quick and trustful liking to the Vicar's wife.

Mrs. Crofts waited intently but did not speak.

"It is the last chapter of the Book of Revelation," said Canon Fewling, "when we read that there shall be no more sea. I don't want to be selfish about my own feelings and I expect your husband has night fears too, if he thinks of swords being beaten into ploughshares. But whoever wrote such things about the sea had missed a great deal in his life."

Mrs. Crofts, casting about as to how she might comfort her guest, said probably St. John sometimes got tired of living on an island and wished he could get back to the mainland and his words about no more sea were what people now would call wishful thinking. Much to her pleasure, this quite silly remark had a very cheering effect on her guest, who thanked her earnestly and said it was a lesson to him not to lose faith.

"And it has just occurred to me, Mrs. Crofts," said Canon Fewling, his kind round face again itself, "that Kipling has a very good poem about that very thing and how the mariners will be allowed to keep their sea for ever. And he *was* a prophet, you know, though most people haven't noticed it."

And now it was time for Canon Fewling to prepare for Evensong, so Bateman, Colonel Croft's old servant who so confusingly had been his batman, took him away, the rest of the company following a little later. The church was quite well filled by villagers, various people from the School who preferred the church to the School Chapel and a sprinkling of outsiders. Admiral Phelps was doing his duty about the church. His wife and daughter were singing valiantly in the choir, for Barsetshire is not a naturally musical county and one or two people who are not afraid to open their mouths and sing out are a great help.

Mrs. Crofts whose thoughts, although she was a clergyman's wife, were just as truant and rebellious as anyone else's, found herself wondering how a stout and not very tall middle-aged parson who had once held a commission in His Majesty's Navy could suddenly become so commanding and important. But it was all too difficult and the only thing to do was to submit oneself, in everything, to a Will greater than one's own small imaginings. The mere act of kneeling, the very sound of the noble English as the service came to its close, calmed her spirit and she prayed rather incoherently and very sincerely for Canon Fewling to be very happy, though she did not feel equal to pointing out to her Maker any specific way of bringing this about. So absorbed was she in her wrestlings that the little congregation had left the church when she lifted her head from her bowed hands and went out into the churchyard.

Here she found a small crowd surrounding Canon Fewling, among them two old friends, Miss Hampton, the well-known writer of powerful and best-selling novels, and her friend Miss Bent, which two ladies had lived for many years in Adelina Cottage at the end of Wiple Terrace in the village. Them she asked to come back to the Vicarage for a few moments and then they could all go down to Mrs. Feeder's party together. So they walked across, followed by Canon Fewling who was deep in talk with Admiral Phelps, and were soon in the Vicarage drawing-room, where Bateman had kept a roaring fire going for them.

"Well, Mrs. Crofts, we missed your husband this evening," said Miss Hampton, whose mannish tweed suit, felt hat, thick stockings and heavy brogues were highly suitable for a chill spring evening. "But we had a very good service. Introduce me, Mrs. Crofts."

"Oh, Canon Fewling," said Mrs. Crofts, tearing him away in virtue of her position as Vicar's wife from Admiral Phelps, "I do so want you to know Miss Hampton, an old inhabitant of Southbridge and a great friend of ours. Canon Fewling, Miss Hampton—and her friend Miss Bent."

"Good of you to come," said Miss Hampton, grasping Canon Fewling's hand with the grip that every boy in the School envied. "Don't like to see the church empty. And you gave us a good sermon. Like a good sermon with meat in it. This is My Friend," and she brought Miss Bent forward.

"Hardly as many people in church as one would like to see," said Miss Bent, holding Canon Fewling's hand and making no move to release it. "Still, it's better than those hikers who giggled last Sunday."

"Hikers!" said Miss Hampton with profound scorn, and before anyone could get a word in she continued, "If my dear father had seen *me* in trousers, or shorts, and uplift brassières in church, he would have sent me to bed."

"And would you have gone?" said Mrs. Crofts.

"Certainly," said Miss Hampton. "Discipline. Duty. Those were father's watchwords. Canon Fewling knows what I mean. England Expects."

"Your father must have been a gentleman of strong character," said Canon Fewling.

"How right you are, Canon Fewling," said Miss Hampton. "He liked a woman to *be* a woman. He would have beaten me with a strap if he had seen me in trousers like those girls wore. I have always honoured my father, and I've never worn anything but coats and skirts all my life. No need to prove all things if you know what is good when you start. That's what St. Paul didn't know. Would know it now if he were alive."

"Hampton has to pay fifty guineas for her suits now," said Miss Bent with mournful pride. "But I always say money is worth as much as it will buy. And what is money worth now?"

"Nothing," said Miss Hampton. "So I spend it," she added, gradually drawing the whole company into her orbit. "I've been saving all my life for my nephews whom I educated. What's the good of saving now? None. So Bent and I went to Mixo-Lydia for the skiing in February, and I am buying a lot of drink. Bound to go up again, you know. Bent got her suit in Mixo-Lydia, Canon Fewling. Like it?"

Canon Fewling as a sailor was equipped with a ready-made character for gallantry, but for once found himself quite at a loss. His defection was ably covered by Mrs. Crofts, who nearly fell over herself in her admiration of Miss Bent's Mixo-Lydian attire, though as a matter of fact its embroidered baggy blouse, its full skirt of gay peasant weave, the brightly coloured hand-kerchief that was tied over Miss Bent's unkempt grizzling locks, her necklaces and bracelets of coloured wooden beads, were so exactly like what she always wore that only the eye of faith, or the tact of a good clergy-wife, could have noticed any difference.

"I suppose we are going to Mrs. Feeder's party," said Miss Hampton. "Bent and I will walk down with you. Is that your car, Canon Fewling, down by the Vicarage gate? When did you get it?"

Canon Fewling said he got her just after Christmas and was still running her in quietly, but she could do seventy on her head.

"Stout fellow," said Miss Hampton approvingly, at which Mrs. Crofts, though not possessing a very keen sense of humour, nearly had the giggles. "Times are hard. That's why Bent and I have decided to buy a new car too. Spend, dear man, spend. That's the way to show any Government what you think. Here am I, working and slaving all my life for my four nephews, all to find it's no good. So I decided to buy a new car and tell my accountant to charge it as literary expenses."

"I really feel quite a thrill when I think of it," said Miss Bent, raising eyes of worship to Miss Hampton. "Hampton can't drive, and I haven't driven for some time, but I'll soon get the hang of it again," which interested such of her hearers as had always thought (in all honour) of Miss Hampton as the competent male and Miss Bent the clinging vine. "It is a Parkinson-Greely 1949 model. They are better than the later model and have the inferential distributor above the magneto, not below."

Though the world was reeling round her, Mrs. Crofts kept her balance and asked what they were going to call it.

"If you could tell us that, dear woman," said Miss Hampton, "we should be delighted. We have thought in vain for a suitable name."

"Hampton thought Wiple, as we live in Wiple Terrace," said Miss Bent, "but we felt it might annoy Mr. Traill and Mr. Feeder who, after all, live in The Terrace too. My idea was, I think, a better one, but Hampton won't hear of it."

Canon Fewling politely enquired what name Miss Bent had chosen.

"Hampton Court," said Miss Bent proudly.

A complete silence followed while her audience collected their wits.

"Can't be done," said Miss Hampton in a firm voice, but with a wistful look in her eyes. "Not fair to Bent. She has been typing my new book all this summer and I owe her too much. I cannot take advantage of her generosity."

"Hampton is Weak about me," said Miss Bent. "It is Give and Take between us. If I Give, can she not Take? And have I not had the privilege of being the first to see her new book? It has left me quite literally Stunned by its power," and Miss Bent flung her arms wide so that her Mixo-Lydian necklaces and bracelets clashed, the better to express her feelings.

Canon Fewling, with a horrid feeling that he might be

intruding upon the rites of the Bona Dea and be torn to pieces in the Vicarage garden, asked what the new book was to be called.

"Tell them, Bent," said Miss Hampton.

"It is, quite simply, *Crooked Insect*," said Miss Bent reverently, to which her audience could find no better reply than "How nice."

"There will be some who will *not* find it nice," said Miss Bent grimly. "Let them. It will do them good. A poniard will go to many a heart when that book is published. Hampton, we must be going. Churchill is in the garden," and she tapped at the french window. A short-legged dog with shaggy black hair, a head far too large for his body and mournful eyes, came trotting across the lawn and was let in.

"Dear me, is he Churchill now? I thought——" said Mrs. Crofts and then paused, for as the dog had had a new name every year since the war began and often more than one name in a year that all heroes might be suitably commemorated, his friends were sometimes a little behind the times.

"Who else could he be?" said Miss Hampton. "The wheel has come full circle. Our great Prime Minister is under the shadow of the Little Man, but we, fearlessly, pay our homage; as of old, so today. Come along, Churchill."

"Oh, Miss Hampton," said Mrs. Crofts. "About your car. I was only wondering, as you don't like Hampton Court for a name——"

Miss Hampton was heard to murmur, "Domine, non sum digna," or, as Canon Fewling afterwards affirmed, "Domina, non sum dignus."

"—I just thought," continued Mrs. Crofts, "that there is Littlehampton and Northampton and——"

"Minchinhampton," said Canon Fewling, who though he had rather lost the track of the conversation was very ready to support his hostess.

"—and Minchinhampton, of course," said Mrs. Crofts. "So I just thought, I mean only an idea, what about Benthampton?"

"Eureka!" exclaimed Miss Hampton.

"And," said Canon Fewling, who was afraid he was going to laugh, "you could always contract it to Bampton. There are some very good lectures at Oxford called the Bampton lectures."

"My thanks, dear man," said Miss Hampton, extending her hand and grasping Canon Fewling's in a way that made him, though an ex-officer of the Royal Navy, almost utter an exclamation of anguish. "How I wish my father had known you. Come, let us be going," and she strode down the hill towards the village, Miss Bent and the dog in her train.

"Never say that village life is dull," said Canon Fewling, enchanted by the scene we have just described.

"I didn't," said Mrs. Crofts.

"There is going to be plenty of it at Greshamsbury, I think," said Canon Fewling; "but though I am already bursting with local pride, I don't think we are as good as you."

"I am sure you aren't," said Mrs. Crofts. "Admiral, are you and your wife going to Mrs. Feeder's party? We can all walk down together."

The Admiral and Mrs. Phelps were already engaged to go to the School, but Miss Phelps said she was invited to Editha and would love to come with them, so they walked down the little hill and along the village street as far as a row of four two-storied cottages in mellow red brick, with a wide strip of grass lying between them and the road. They had been erected by a Mr. Wiple, a small master builder of the neighbourhood, as a monument to his four daughters, Adelina, Maria, Louisa and Editha, calling each cottage after one of them. They were surmounted in the middle by a kind of long low gable (if we make ourselves clear) in stucco, on which the words "Wiple Terrace 1820" are still faintly visible. The property now belongs to Paul's College, who also own the Vicarage and the living, and has always been run in a very friendly way, the tenant of longest standing having a shadowy claim to pre-eminence, which position has now for many years been held by Miss Hampton and Miss Bent, the tenants of Adelina. At Maria lives Mr. Traill and at Louisa Mr. Feeder, both assistant masters at the School, while Editha at the far end has been tenanted for some years by Mrs. Feeder, the widowed mother of Mr. Feeder. In Mrs. Feeder the ladies of Adelina had at once recognised a kindred spirit in the matter of drink and there was altogether a strong spirit of cameraderie in the terrace.

Mrs. Feeder's cottage, Editha, was the nearest to the Vicarage. The front door was open.

"I do hope," said Mrs. Crofts, as they walked up the path of the little front garden, "the door hasn't been open for long. We shall be frozen," but when they reached the house they found another door a yard or so down the passage.

"Shall I ring?" said Canon Fewling; but before Mrs. Crofts could answer, Mrs. Feeder herself, holding a glass in one hand and a cigarette in the other, appeared from inside.

"Come in," said Mrs. Feeder. "I had this extra door put in to keep the house warmer. Good idea, what?"

As the passage was very narrow it was impossible to make introductions and the party followed Mrs. Feeder into the drawing-room, or living-room as one pleases to call it, in which through smoke and above the chink of bottles could be seen and heard seven or eight people.

"You know them all," said Mrs. Feeder, waving her cigarette towards the company. "Here's my boy. He does the drinks. Look after them, darling," and she flattened herself to make way for Mr. Feeder, who advanced with a large tray.

"I'm so sorry I can't shake hands, but there isn't anywhere to put the tray," said Mr. Feeder. "What can I offer you? I'm afraid we're a bit low because Miss Hampton threw a party on Friday and the Red Lion was pretty well cleared out. French, It, gin, bitters, whisky, rum, orange, a spot of brandy, lime, and the fixings. Give it a name."

Thus adjured, the new visitors were unable—as one always is

when faced with a generous choice of drinks now—to make any decision.

"Come on, Mrs. Crofts, give it a name," said Mr. Feeder, which, of course, compelled the Vicar's wife in an access of selfconsciousness to ask for gin and It, though disliking both the drink and the expression.

"If I could just have a small whisky and soda," said Canon Fewling.

"I say, you *are* sensible," said Miss Phelps admiringly. "Father always says you can't go wrong with whisky. Same for me, please. Here, don't drown it. Mr. Traill, come and talk to Canon Fewling."

Thus adjured, the tenant of Maria shoved his way through the crowd, or rather through the crowded room which could not have held more than twelve people at the most in comfort and was rapidly approximating to the Black Hole of Calcutta.

"This is Mr. Traill who lives in Maria and has a frightfully good gramophone," said Miss Phelps, pleased to be able to present something nice to the guest. "He and Mr. Feeder, who has a wireless, have awful rows about it; don't you, Mr. Traill?"

"Feeder has the rows, not me," said Mr. Traill, as heedless of grammar as the Monks and Friars of Rheims.

"Well, you have the gramophone, not him," said Miss Phelps with considerable spirit and equal lack of grammar, "and anyway this is Canon Fewling who took the service this evening."

"How do you do, sir," said Mr. Traill. "I say, I don't know if it's etiquette or not, but I did enjoy your service. I had to scoot off the minute it was over to help Feeder with the drinks. The Vicar's awfully good too of course, but it makes a change to see something fresh."

Canon Fewling, well accustomed to people who were inca- pable of expressing in words what they might be feeling, took these remarks as they were meant, but not so Miss Phelps, who turned upon Mr. Traill and told him not to be an ass and get

Canon Fewling another drink. Mr. Traill, slightly abashed, asked if Canon Fewling would like the same again.

"No more, thank you," said Canon Fewling. "But if I might have the pleasure of greeting my hostess? I met her at lunch and I don't want to seem discourteous, but I simply can't get at her," and indeed the room was by now so tightly packed that movement was almost impossible. Mr. Traill, eager to give pleasure, began a slow process of worming himself through the crowd.

"He didn't mean not to be polite," said Miss Phelps suddenly, or so Canon Fewling thought, looking like a little girl who is lost at a children's party and would like to go home. "Please excuse him."

"But, my dear Miss Phelps, there was nothing to excuse," said Canon Fewling. "If we could just get out into the passage for a moment perhaps we could hear what we were saying. I like Mr. Traill so much. By the way—you will forgive my interest and not treat it as curiosity, I beg—I notice that there is much less use of Christian names here than one usually meets."

"Oh, you mean me saying Mr. Feeder and Mr. Traill," said Miss Phelps. "Well, you see, there are millions more surnames than Christian names. You've only got to look at the telephone book to see that, so really it's easier to know who people are that way. I mean there are quite a lot of masters at Southbridge who have the same Christian name—I don't mean they all have the same name, but quite a lot have the same name as another one, so I call them Mr. Whatever the name is. They don't mind."

"And what about you?" said Canon Fewling, who had by now managed to back himself and Miss Phelps to the end of the little passage where at least they did not have to strain their voices.

"Me?" said Miss Phelps. "Oh, I see. You mean them not calling me Margot. Oh well, I'm older than quite a lot of them and anyway I've always lived here ever since father retired and I expect they think I'm a bit of an old stick-in-the-mud. A kind of universal aunt. That's all. Let's go back and I'll see if I can get at

Mrs. Feeder for you," and she began to shove herself into the room, followed by her guest.

By this time Mr. Traill had with some difficulty cut out the hostess from the ruck and punted her into position near the door, so that Canon Fewling was able to say how much he had enjoyed the party and was afraid he must be going, as he was giving the Leslies a lift home from the School, and hoped to see her and her son at Greshamsbury when his house was fit for visitors.

"I'll come with you a bit of the way," said Miss Phelps, taking him in tow again. "I've got to go back, anyway, to get the parents' supper. Irons doesn't much like drink parties. There's too much noise and he gets tired. We live at Jutland Cottage. It used to be The Hollies, but father was in the Battle of Jutland so he called it that."

The walk was not long and was enlivened by Miss Phelps with descriptions of local celebrities, such as old Propett, who was sexton when Colonel Crofts first came to the Vicarage and had lived in very squalid sin with an old woman for over sixty years and died a few years previously, largely of too much drink consumed during that period; and how the old woman had died on the same day owing to drinking all the port which good Samaritans had sent him; and how on his disgraceful and dirty death-bed he had extracted from Colonel Crofts a promise that Bateman, Colonel Croft's old soldier servant now acting as gardener and sexton, should not ring the passing bell for him because he had rung it man and boy for sixty year and didn't want no one else to ring it; and how Colonel Crofts, having given his word, rang the bell himself, ninety-two strokes. By which time they had got to Jutland Cottage.

"You couldn't stay to supper, could you?" said Miss Phelps. "Irons does so love to talk to naval men."

Torn between two duties, Canon Fewling thought for a moment and then said he would like it of all things, but he had promised to take the Leslies back by a certain hour and it was getting late.

"But if your mother would allow me," he said, "may I come over on a special visit soon? I should love to hear your father talk about his experiences. And you are, very kindly, going to let me know about some hens, aren't you?"

"Rather," said Miss Phelps, who had inherited from both her parents a strong impulse to assist and from her mother a distinct pleasure in managing other people's affairs. "I'll let you know as soon as I can get over. It rather depends on the parents. If Irons gets one of his bad days, or mother is very tired, I'm done. The village nurse is awfully good, but she's busy and I must stick to the ship," and with a hearty handshake she went into Jutland Cottage and Canon Fewling went on to the School. Here he collected the Leslies and drove them back with all due care. Of course they asked him to come in for a drink and of course he accepted, for he liked people and never needed much sleep; though to do him justice he was quick in feeling when his hosts were tired and rarely outstayed his welcome.

"And I hope you had a pleasant time with your boys," he said, when they were settled with beer (John Leslie and the Rector) and an orange drink (Mary Leslie).

Mary said, "Very nice indeed," only Minor now walked too fast for her and she was afraid that Minimus soon would do the same.

"I used to get rather impatient with them when they were small, because they couldn't walk as fast as I did," said their mother, "and now they get rather bored with me because I can't walk as fast as they do. I suppose it happens to everyone."

"You will have to grow old along with me, my love," said her husband.

"One of the silliest things Browning ever said," his wife answered with some spirit. "I don't think the best is yet to be in the least. If the last for which the first was made is just getting feebler and sillier, I really don't think much of it. What about you, Tubby?"

"Do you know," said Canon Fewling, with the engaging candour that sat so well upon him, "I hardly ever think about it. I suppose I ought to, but I'm an ordinary kind of chap and really I find so much to do all the time that I don't worry much about what will happen later. I do trust that at the end I shan't at any rate be worse than I was at the beginning, but meanwhile there doesn't seem to be much time for philosophy. Cheerfulness *will* break in, as that old friend of Dr. Johnson's said."

"I expect you are right, Tubby," said Mary Leslie, who was tidying some papers and sewing and other odds and ends which lay on a large round table. Canon Fewling, looking towards her, noticed a number of capital letters strewn on the table, such as used to be in vogue for the game called Word Making and Word Taking.

"I used to have some letters like that when I was a little boy," said Canon Fewling. "We played games with them and made anagrams. May I play with them before you put them away? What a charming set. We had one just like it when I was a boy—ivory squares with the capital letter on one side and the little letter on the other. My mother started my education with them."

As he spoke he collected the letters and began to make words, idly.

"It's a pity one can't make an anagram out of Fewling," he said. "I tried every way. Is Leslie any good? I can nearly get LISLES, but I'm not sure if that's fair. Ladies do, I believe, have lisle stockings, but I doubt whether they talk about Lisles," and Mary said she was sorry but she didn't think they did.

"I'll try something else," said Canon Fewling. "Surnames are nearly always awkward. I might try books. That very remarkable woman Miss Hampton was talking about her new book."

"What is it to be called?" said Mary Leslie.

"*Crooked Insect*," said Canon Fewling, collecting the letters as he spoke and arranging them in their correct order, the better to get his bearings. Mary and John looked on ready, as lookers-on always are, to make unnecessary and irritating suggestions.

"CROOKED INSECT," said the Rector, aloud to himself, hoping, as we all do, thereby to promote thought, while he looked carefully at the letters. "C-R-O-O-K-E-D and then I-N-S-E-C-T. Oh my—— I mean, Oh my hat! *What* a woman!"

"What on earth is the matter, Tubby?" said Mary Leslie.

"I've only just seen it," said the Rector, gazing with a kind of respectful horror at the letters in front of him.

"Come on, Tubby," said John Leslie. "It can't be as bad as all that. Out with it. Think of Nelson."

Thus adjured, Canon Fewling pointed to the second word.

"You see that," he said.

"Well, what about it?" said his host.

"If," said the Rector, fixing his hosts with a firm and resolute countenance, "if you make INSECT crooked, what do you get?"

"Dear Tubby, do talk sense," said Mary Leslie.

"I am," said the Rector. "Look at INSECT. Make it crooked. Change the letters. You only have to change the place of two of them."

"My God, Tubby, you are right!" said John Leslie, beginning to laugh, while his wife indignantly asked what there was to laugh at. "*What* a woman! If the Free Church press tumble to it, there'll be trouble with the circulating libraries," at which point his wife suddenly saw light and fell away into unmatronly giggles.

"They won't. It takes the Church of England to see a thing like that," said Canon Fewling proudly, at which his host and hostess laughed more than ever.

"Well, after that I'd better go home," said the Rector. "I liked Miss Hampton immensely when I met her and now I really respect her. Good night. It has been a delightful day."

The Leslies thanked him for taking and returning them in his car and he drove away to his house. The Leslies tidied the room and put the letters away.

"John," said his wife as they were going upstairs, "do you think Tubby is likely to get married? I don't like to think of him alone. He is such a good fellow."

"He won't get married to Miss Hampton, nor to Miss Bent neither too," said her husband, quoting from the now forgotten but once by us and our contemporaries fondly loved Follies.

His wife said with dignity that she wasn't thinking of that in the least.

"He is far more likely to fall in love with Rose Fairweather," said John. "I've yet to meet the man who hasn't."

"You didn't, darling," said his wife.

"Well, I didn't when I was young, because I never met her, and anyway I'm years older than she is," said John . "But now they have come to live here, beware," to which his wife replied that he was a goose and to hurry up and go to bed because tomorrow was Monday.

CHAPTER 3

The friendship begun between the Croftses at Southbridge and Canon Fewling at Greshamsbury had ripened with leaps and bounds. Both clergymen were ex-service men. Mrs. Crofts and Canon Fewling were united by a love of birds, and when his duties permitted he would drive over to Southbridge in his new car and go bird-watching with her. Both were deeply interested in the possibility of the golden-crested mippet nesting on the Greshamsbury church tower and called into consultation Mr. Wickham, the Noel Mertons' agent over at Northbridge, with whom she had before and after her marriage to Colonel the Reverend Edward Crofts pursued and almost persecuted birds all over the county in his shocking little rattletrap of a car.

"Take it from me," said Mr. Wickham, who had dropped in on Mrs. Crofts with a bottle of real audit ale from Paul's College, acquired by him no one knew how, unless it was true, as Lady Cora Waring had said, that he was magnetic where drink was concerned, "that if she is a mippet, she won't budge till she has hatched those eggs," which comforted Mrs. Crofts, who had visions of the mippet leaving her brood to get cold and addled if approached by man. "Talk of dumb beasts," said Mr. Wickham, skilfully opening the audit ale without spilling a drop. "There's more sense in a mippet—though, mind you, she's a bird, not a beast—than in most people. I've taken long time exposures of mippets and they've never batted an eyelid. I'd like to see this one."

"Are you going up the tower, Wicks?" said Mrs. Crofts, but Mr. Wickham said he might have been in the Navy during the war but not in Nelson's time and had no head for heights, and then in came Miss Phelps.

"Come and have some of Wicks's audit ale, Margot," said Mrs. Crofts, who had a good deal of affection and respect for the Admiral's daughter. "How's your father?"

"Oh, Irons isn't too bad," said Miss Phelps, "but I feel so sorry for him at night, coughing and trying to get his breath. I read the Riot Act to mother and said I'd leave home unless she let me do the night nursing. She was killing herself," and both hearers noticed that she did not speak of her own night watchings at all. "I say, this is good, Mr. Wickham," to which Mr. Wickham gallantly replied that if she would call him Wicks, as all his friends did, he would be much obliged.

"I'll do my best," said Miss Phelps, looking with a kind of dispassionate interest at Mr. Wickham, "but if you've called a person Mister for absolutely ages it seems a bit sudden. I say, Mrs. Crofts, can I use your telephone? I wouldn't bother you, but it's rather important," and having been told to use the one in the study, as the Vicar was out, she went away.

"Out of order as usual?" said Mr. Wickham. "I've just had a fine strafe, not to say blitz, about the telephone at Northbridge. They are trying on some damn nonsense about party lines. And, what's more, I'd have to be responsible for the other bloke's bills if he didn't pay them. If Jutland Cottage is on a party line, God help them. I'm sorry for that girl. She's a bit long in the tooth, but she has guts. Well, here's to her," and Mr. Wickham finished his ale.

"They haven't got a telephone at all," said Mrs. Crofts.

"Stinkers!" said Mr. Wickham, alluding not so much to Admiral and Mrs. Phelps as to whatever powers dispense or refuse telephones.

"They can't afford it," said Mrs. Crofts, not raising her eyes from the table where she was working on one of her exquisite bird-illustrations.

Mr. Wickham was silent, and Mrs. Crofts continued her delicate brushwork.

"Now, that's the kind of thing that brings it home," said Mr. Wickham. "I read a book once, by some woman it was, about a woman whose people were silly asses and left her pretty badly off. Not a cheerful book, but it rather got me. It just showed you how you ought to be careful with your money. It was bad investments and so on, and she tried to find jobs and couldn't because there was nothing she could do."

Mrs. Crofts, intent on the delicate feather of the splay-footed bumblegobbler, said, "How sad."

"And," continued Mr. Wickham, looking into space, or possibly having the strange visual memory, not to be understood except by those who possess it, which literally sees the printed words on the page, "what made me think was when she needs a new bit of soap and has to wait till next week's little bit of money comes in before she can wash her hands properly. Enough to stop one marrying."

Mrs. Crofts asked why.

"Well, if you were mug enough to get married and let your family down like that you'd feel no end of a rotter," said Mr. Wickham. "Only the father was dead in this book, so you can't say what he felt. I say, Effie, you don't suppose Margot Phelps is really as poor as that, do you?"

"Don't exaggerate, Wicks," said Mrs. Crofts calmly. "The Phelpses do have enough to eat. I'd see about it if they hadn't. If you have a telephone you get into the way of using it and then it mounts up. Edward and I are keeping an eye on them. I'm sorry for that girl, though. I really don't know what she'll do when her father dies. You can't take a pension with you, but equally you can't leave it with your family. I suppose Mrs. Phelps would get something. I really don't know. Edward and I have often discussed it, but it's not much use discussing."

"It's enough to make one think," said Mr. Wickham. "I'm not much of a fellow, but I've a snug house and some good pals and a drink to offer them. And if——"

"No, Wicks," said Mrs. Crofts, putting her brush down. "No good. You're only sorry for her. Do you remember when you felt sorry for me once and proposed to me?"

"Rather!" said Mr. Wickham. "Not that I really wanted to marry you, Effie, but there didn't seem to be anything else to suggest."

"You behaved like a gentleman," said Mrs. Crofts. "I was pretty down and out then and you wanted to help me. I remember you said you had a head like teak. I nearly accepted you on that."

"Good thing you didn't," said Mr. Wickham. "You wouldn't have married Crofts if you'd married me, and he's twice the man I am."

"Ten times," said Mrs. Crofts placidly. "But never mind, Wicks, you are one of the best. Did you get your call, Margot?" she said as Miss Phelps came back.

"Oh yes, thanks awfully," said Miss Phelps. "I rang up the exchange and they said it was threepence," and she took an old purse out of her jacket pocket and laid a threepenny piece on the table.

"Damn silly things, those threepenny bits, with straight sides," said Mr. Wickham, trying to disguise his compassionate admiration for Miss Phelps under a grumble about the currency. "Like what those filthy Japs have."

"Thank you, Margot," said Mrs. Crofts calmly. "Come in if you want to telephone again any time. Only next time don't try to pay. I'm keeping this one for luck."

Her head was, perhaps deliberately, bent over her work so that she did not see Miss Phelps's face. But she felt it, if the expression may be allowed.

"Thanks awfully," said Miss Phelps. "It was only to tell Canon Fewling that I could bring the chickens over, if it isn't too late. I simply couldn't leave father before. He said it was all right and I'm going over tomorrow. I can take the chickens on my bicycle."

"Look here, Margot," said Mr. Wickham. "Here's a proposition. Tubby is doing a spot of bird-work tomorrow on his church tower. If it was the lesser gallowsbird I'd say call it what you like and good luck to him. But a golden-crested mippet in the gutter of a church tower! It's against nature. Now, I'm going over to see fair play. It's only a matter of a few miles from Northbridge to get here, and I want to look in at the Red Lion on the strict Q.T. Brown *may* have a spot of Navy rum, though never ask me how. Say I pick you up and tootle you over with your hens."

Miss Phelps looked helplessly at Mrs. Crofts.

"It's not the chickens. I can manage them on my bicycle," she said, "but I'd promised Canon Fewling some wood and wire and things we've got knocking about. I daresay I could tie them on somehow."

"And why the hell can't old Tubby come over and fetch them?" said Mr. Wickham, finishing the audit ale in one angry draught. "What's the Royal Navy about?"

"Not with that *wonderful* car," said Miss Phelps. "He *couldn't*, Mr. Wickham. It might scratch the paint."

"Wicks to you, my girl," said that gentleman. "Tomorrow at ten-thirty ack emma, sauf contre-ordre, I turn up at Jutland Cottage, hitch your old trailer and the doings on behind my car, put the chickens in the boot and anything else you want and deliver you as per invoice at the Rectory. I can see about the rum on my way back."

"Well, thanks awfully, Wicks," said Miss Phelps, not so much blushing as unbecomingly suffused with red. "I didn't want to let Canon Fewling down. And I do rather want to sell those chickens and the broodies. They do eat such a lot. Canon

Fewling says his housekeeper can get some nice eggs for setting because her uncle has a job at the Vicarage at Northbridge."

"Which," said Mr. Wickham, "makes my dream come true."

"And thank you, really, very much," said Miss Phelps. "Goodbye, Mrs. Crofts," and she went away.

"I suppose she'd have cried if she'd stayed," said Mr. Wickham reflectively. "Great mistake to be grateful. Or to be kind. I've never yet seen a man help a blind beggar across a road but he found his house burnt down when he got home. Goodbye, Effie. I'll look in tomorrow for a moment on my way to Jutland Cottage. My wicked uncle sent me some books for you, so I kept them and read them first."

Mrs. Crofts enquired what they were, for Mr. Johns, Mr. Wickham's uncle, was a publisher of enterprise and considerable taste, who had for some years published bird-books with her loving and exquisite illustrations.

"There's a new Lisa Bedale; she's still writing," said Mr. Wickham, alluding to the present Countess of Silverbridge who had written some excellent thrillers under that pseudonym, "and Mrs. Rivers's new book, *Lad's Love*," which name, taken from a flower, made Mrs. Crofts and Mr. Wickham have irreverent giggles. "Middle-aged woman has comeback with young man. Wonderful how she keeps it up. And a lovely bird-book from South America with illustrations, all called *Hoxacatapopokettl* or words to that effect. Well, time's up," and putting the empty audit ale bottle on a side table, he got into his noisy, useful little car and drove away.

When the Vicar came in his wife told him about her visitors.

"I wonder," said he, "what the Phelpses really live on. I suppose one could find out what his pension is. I could ask Admiral Palliser; we meet pretty often on a Diocesan Committee. Not much for three people and one of them an invalid, anyway. I know Phelps hasn't much besides his pay. He told me so. He got me to witness some transfers for him once and I remember him saying, rather proudly I thought, that he married a wife without a penny of her own. What *does* happen to unmarried daughters then?"

"I was thinking about it, too, and worrying," said Mrs. Crofts. "She did everything in the war and she knows all about goats and pigs and poultry, but there's not much of a living there unless you have some capital. There isn't even an old aunt at Bournemouth who can give her board and lodging and bully her and then leave her money to the Mission to Ice-Bound Esquimaux. I don't suppose her parents *meant* to be selfish——"

The Vicar said parents hardly ever did and he didn't think he had been particularly selfish himself, but one always might have done more.

"And then you did it for me, my dear," he said; for he had long been a widower when he married the almost penniless Miss Arbuthnot, and she had been a true friend as well as affectionate stepmother to his grown-up children.

"Any children of yours, dearest," said Mrs. Crofts, looking at her husband with pure love while he in his turn looked at her with what might almost have been called a besotted look, for with both these dull, sensible middle-aged—or, in the Vicar's case, elderly—people, deep affection was always present in their looks, their thoughts, their ways.

According to his promise, Mr. Wickham turned up at Jutland Cottage by half-past ten on the following morning and quite illegally took in tow the Phelps's rickety old trailer loaded with bits of wood and wire. Miss Phelps, in her well-worn tweeds which sagged where she sat behind and had darns across the knees in front, put two baskets of shrieking fowls into the back seat and got into the front seat. Mr. Wickham, who had been lashing the trailer to the back of his car in a nautical and shipshape way, then got in beside her and made a quite dreadful noise with the gears.

"Never stripped them yet," said Mr. Wickham to his guest, making his voice heard above the engine as if he were an old sea-captain with a speaking trumpet. "The nearest I got was the day peace was declared, after we'd all had one or two in Barchester and another one or two all the way back. Man called Tommy Prescott—you wouldn't know him; one of the best, even if he did lift his elbow a bit—wanted to drive her, and when we got to the bottom of Fish Hill he nearly tore the guts out of her," which valuable information Miss Phelps received quite calmly, being used to letting men talk. Apart from the trailer bumping into the car when Mr. Wickham slowed down and nearly getting loose as they topped the steep road over the downs, the journey was uneventful. The hens in the car shrieked rape and murder, but Mr. Wickham and his passenger, entirely unmoved, conducted a conversation at the top of their voices about foot-and-mouth disease till they got to Greshamsbury.

"I don't suppose Tubby wants them in the garden," said Mr. Wickham, pulling his little car up on its haunches so that the trailer gave a final bang against the back bumpers and the fowls again shrieked to heaven. "Where's his paddock?"

Miss Phelps didn't know, but luckily the Rector had heard the noise, which had indeed attracted the attention of anyone about in the street, and came quickly down the garden path.

"Good morning, Miss Phelps," he said. "How good of you to come. Could you take them round the corner, Wicks, and through the second gate into my field. I will meet you there," and he hurried back through his house while Mr. Wickham drove up the lane by the Rectory. It was narrow and rutty, and Mr. Wickham drove with care lest the trailer should at last get loose, till they came to the gate which the Rector had just opened for them. Mr. Wickham drove through it onto the grass and stopped the car. Several boys of various ages gathered round it.

"Good morning, sir," said Leslie Minor, always the first to speak. "I brought these brothers of mine along in case you needed help. Major isn't frightened of hens. I am. And this is Minimus."

"Always plenty of trouble when you chaps are about," said Mr. Wickham cheerfully as he got out of the car. "Who are the others?"

"Frank Gresham, sir," said Major, "and those kids are Mrs. Fairweather's, but we don't count them, they're too young. Hullo, Miss Phelps," he added as Miss Phelps began to lug a crate of shrieking hens out of the car.

"That's enough from you," said Mr. Wickham, without heat. "Margot, allow me to present to you, in order of age and probably of depravity, Leslie Major, Minor and Minimus, and Frank Gresham. Also some young Fairweathers." Miss Phelps, who had at once recognised the Leslie boys as Southbridgians, shook hands with them all, while the Fairweather children skirmished in the background. "Miss Phelps," added Mr. Wickham, "knows all about cows, pigs, hens, turkeys, geese and ducks."

"Don't forget goats, Wicks," said Miss Phelps, straightening herself and dusting her skirt. "We kept goats all through the war," she added to the boys, addressing them as equals.

"Their milk is supposed to be awfully good, isn't it?" said Frank Gresham.

"Stinking, if you ask me," said Miss Phelps with great frankness. "But some of the refugee babies liked it. Or if they didn't like it, anyway, they thrived on it."

"Or throved?" said Frank Gresham sotto voce, thus causing Minimum to have the giggles.

"Put on weight, if you can understand that," said Miss Phelps to whom the young of the male sex were a very well-known quantity. "Where do we go from here, Canon Fewling?"

A chorus of instructions rose from the boys.

"That's enough," said the Rector, suddenly quelling a mutiny. "I have been putting up some wire, Miss Phelps, so we can let the fowls in at once," and he led them to a carefully wired-off enclosure neatly arranged in compartments.

"Well, that's a jolly good piece of work, whoever did it," said

Miss Phelps, who had done that kind of job herself for the last twenty years or so.

"I can't tell you, Miss Phelps, how pleased I am to hear you say so," said the Rector. "I made it myself. I've always been a bit of a handy man. I did wonder if I was taking the bread out of any worthier person's mouth by doing it, but my friend John Leslie—I expect you know him, Miss Phelps—said I wouldn't. And as he has lived here for a long time and is a churchwarden, I expect he knows. I hope he does, for it would be dreadful if the Rector took bread out of the mouth of people who need it. And I do so like doing odd jobs."

"You couldn't possibly take bread out of anyone's mouth here, sir," said Leslie Major. "Full employment except for the ones that just don't like work. At least that's what my father says. Oh, Miss Phelps, my mother asked me to say how glad she would be if you would lunch with us. We live in the Old Rectory."

"That's awfully kind of your mother," said Miss Phelps. "I'm afraid I'm not exactly got up for lunch, though," and she looked apologetically, though quite without false shame, at her shabby and not very clean tweeds, her cotton stockings of the type that does not have a back seam and falls into crumples over the instep, her shabby strong brown shoes, which, however, were well polished, and her gloveless work-worn hands.

"The lunch isn't exactly got up either," said Leslie Minor, smiling in a most engaging way at Miss Phelps. "It's only fish, because our cook, who lives in the village and comes in by the day, has a cousin in Barchester who is a fishmonger, and she doesn't like the money to go out of the family, so she takes the butcher's money out of the housekeeping money and buys fish with it. I say, do come, Miss Phelps."

Miss Phelps did not particularly want to go to lunch with strange people, but as usual Leslie Minor's charm, of which he was, or so his elder brother and a good many other people considered, unnecessarily lavish, worked as it almost always did.

"Right. I'd love to come then," she said. "Please thank your mother. What's your name?"

Leslie Minor said his name was John, but as his father was John he was always called Minor. Nothing to do with cigarettes, he added.

"I didn't suppose it was," said Miss Phelps, well used to dealing with cheek in the agreeable male young of the human species. "And what are your names?" she said to the other boys, but before they could answer the irrepressible Leslie Minor had answered for them, "Major—that's him—is really Henry, and Minimus there is Clive. It's not his fault. And this one is Frank Gresham."

"Mine's Margot," said Miss Phelps. "Margot Phelps. And now," she went on, turning to the Rector, "What next?"

"Well, I suppose to get the hens into the pens, if that's the right thing," said the Rector. "I've got some nice hen-houses for them, with proper perches and egg-boxes to lay in and drinking troughs with water laid on. There's a spring in this field and no one knows how old it is. The sexton says it has been here since the Saxon days."

"Might have been," said Mr. Wickham, whose love and knowledge of the county's past history was extensive and peculiar. "Used to be called Gunter's Spring, but I think myself it's a corruption of Gundric. You know there's Gundric's Fossway that runs right through the county south and north. Not that anyone knows who Gundric was," he added. "Rum what a lot of Johnnies there were and no one knows a thing about them. Lord Stoke came over here once when the Barsetshire Archaeological met at Greshamsbury and he said it ought to be Gerda's Spring. Some kind of a Norse goddess she was, and he has Vikings on the brain. I believe he thinks he has found a gargoyle with Scandinavian influence here. Anyway, if you must drink water this isn't bad. Not like those stinking spas abroad. I'd as soon drink cabbage-water. Well, talking of drinks, let's get this job done and we'll see if I've got anything in my car."

"And meanwhile, Miss Phelps, you must rest for a bit," said the Rector, coming up with what looked like a soft easy-chair without any arms or legs. "I got this in a sale over at Northbridge the other day. It's made of rubber. It's quite light to carry, and you put it on the ground with the back against something. Dear me, there ought to be a tree. Supposing I put it against the side of the car. Will you try it?"

With great good-nature Miss Phelps sat herself heavily and rather ungracefully down and pronounced the seat to be very comfortable, and the Rector looked so happy that she determined to sit there for as long as she could bear it, though to be idle amid activity, or indeed on any occasion, was by long habit alien to her nature. Luckily she was not too severely tried. The various fowls were decanted into their pens, the broodies were incarcerated and the workers came back to her. From the back of his car Mr. Wickham produced six bottles of beer, remarking that he thought they would all have burst when the engine got so hot going over the downs. The whole party camped in various attitudes of discomfort on the grass. From the garden gate Mrs. Hicks was seen approaching, a large Thermos flask in one hand and a bottle of milk in the other.

"I did take the liberty, not knowing your tastes, Miss Phelps," said the Rector, "of telling my housekeeper to bring some tea. I often drink it myself, and ladies sometimes like it. But, of course, if you prefer beer——"

"Well, I used to like it," said Miss Phelps, "but it got so expensive and it seemed a shame for father not to have his and he really needs it, so I took to tea."

"Reward of virtue, my girl," said Mr. Wickham. "Also reward of vice—that's me—because I shall drink your beer—I mean the beer you would have drunk if you'd drunk it. Well, here's to the hens, Tubby."

The boys, having taken with extreme politeness a glass of beer each, then unobtrusively melted away to their own amusements, leaving the elders by the car.

"I *do* like them," said Miss Phelps, looking after their retreating forms. "We used to have naval boys in and out of the house all through the war. There were two such nice ones in the first winter, but I can't remember their names. We just called them Tubby and Bill."

"That you?" said Mr. Wickham, looking at the Rector.

"I wish it had been," said the Rector, "but no such luck. It wasn't Tubby Smith-Hetherington, was it?"

"I believe it was," said Miss Phelps. "His ship had been torpedoed and his parents were dead and he spent his leave with us."

Mr. Smith-Hetherington then turned out to have spent two days leave in Northbridge during the war, which at once destroyed any slight shyness that might have been between Canon Fewling and Miss Phelps. One common friend or acquaintance after another was discovered. Mr. Wickham, as a dispassionate onlooker, wondered why he hadn't noticed how pleasant Miss Phelps's expression was and her air of eager attention to her host's words—an attention which might not be real, but was, in any case, convincing and rather taking. Then the conversation gently died down. In the lee of the car the sun shone quite warmly and Miss Phelps, who rarely had an undisturbed night, felt herself sliding into temporary oblivion while the men argued as to whether old Dogger Banks was the one who got tangled up with the barmaid at Southsea good and proper, when the clock from the church tower played three quarters.

"Sitting here won't get our hands washed for lunch, my hearties," said Mr. Wickham, getting up. "Lord, how stiff my old bones do be. You're like a two-year-old, Tubby. How the devil do you do it?" he added as the Rector rose.

"I really don't know," said the Rector. "I suppose, having always been a pretty thickset sort of chap, I just had to. Can you cross your arms and squat down and get up all in one, Wickham?" and with perhaps pardonable pride he folded his arms and, bending his legs, sank and rose three times without apparent effort.

"Simply a trick," said Mr. Wickham. "I gave up those schoolboy showings-off when you were in knickerbockers, Tubby. Well, I must be getting along," but at this his host protested violently, saying he had counted on him for lunch and the expedition on the church roof.

"And what about me, Wicks?" said Miss Phelps, also getting up, though not so elegantly as her host. "You can't leave me here to get back on my own."

"If it was only that," said the Rector, "I would drive you home with the greatest pleasure, Miss Phelps."

"Splendid!" said Mr. Wickham unchivalrously. "His car's much better than mine. I'll run you down to the village, Margot, for your lunch. Back in two shakes, Tubby," and he hustled Miss Phelps across the field to his car. The drive was short, barely more than crossing the road, turning to the right and straight on up the little hill, so that they were at the Old Rectory within three minutes. Miss Phelps thanked Mr. Wickham, went into the porch and rang the bell. Almost at once a boy appeared.

"Hullo, Miss Phelps; come in," he said.

"I know you apart when you are together," said Miss Phelps, looking at him, "but not when you are alone. Are you Minor?"

"That's sixpence," said the boy. "I betted Major you'd know it was me and he betted me you wouldn't. Thanks awfully. Here she is, Mummy," he added, opening the drawing-room door and Miss Phelps was greeted by her hostess. We will not say that Miss Phelps was shy, but there were not many people who knew her really well. Perhaps her older friends and acquaintances took for granted too easily the Margot Phelps they had known all their lives, the cheerful, hard-working, not so young daughter of naval people who were generally known to have little beside the Admiral's pension. We do not by this for a moment mean to say that Southbridge's attitude to him and his family was influenced by his income, but it had become evident to most people that

Miss Phelps's parents were living on a very narrow margin, a state of things not improved of late by their poor health. The clothes in which, during the war, Miss Phelps had tramped and bicycled and dealt with hens, ducks, pigs, goats and other recalcitrant animals, were still in use and could never look like anything but what they were. Miss Hampton and Miss Bent, in the real kindness of their hearts, had now and then been able to persuade her to accept a skirt, or a suit, or a jumper, but it was clear to Miss Hampton who had keen eyes and understanding, that unless Miss Phelps could repay in kind with eggs or a fowl—though at goats' milk Miss Hampton drew the line—she would not feel at ease, so Miss Hampton, being a woman of good instincts, accepted these repayments without protest.

"Proud myself, you know," she had said to Miss Bent after Miss Phelps, almost in tears, had firmly declined a black jersey with a polo collar and a tailored shirt of emerald-green silk. "Father was like that. But he could afford to be proud. Independent income. I can afford to be proud as long as I sell my books. When I can't I shall probably still be proud. Stiffen the sinews," at which fine words Miss Bent, moved to tears, had said she had a hundred and fifty pounds in the Post Office and Hampton could draw on it whenever she liked, and Miss Hampton, also much moved, had hit Miss Bent on the back and said, "Gentlemen's agreement, Bent," and they had gone over to the Red Lion together.

But on this occasion it was quite impossible for Miss Phelps not to feel at ease. Mary Leslie was so quietly kind, her boys were of an age that Miss Phelps liked and understood, and when John Leslie mentioned that he had done some temporary naval service at the very end of the first war she felt safe.

"I rather wish I had stayed in the Navy sometimes," he said.

"Do you, darling?" said his wife.

"No, not really perhaps," said her husband, looking at her with an affection that a settled life and three growing boys had, if possible, strengthened. "Was your father by any chance in a

destroyer of the Iron class at Portsmouth just after the first war,
Miss Phelps? I remember a very pleasant officer of that name.
Shortish, very efficient, didn't talk much unless he had something to say," which was so obviously her father that Miss Phelps
forgot to be shy and told the Leslies about her parents' war work
and how her father had bronchitis every winter since the war and
this year he couldn't shake it off and her mother had a heart.

"It's partly the money, of course," said Miss Phelps, feeling
safe in a semi-naval atmosphere. "If you have a pension and
everything gets more expensive all the time it's a bit difficult.
Mother's a splendid manager and we sell our eggs and chickens.
In the war I kept goats, but there aren't enough cranks now to
make it worth while. We had loads of cranks at Southbridge and
lots of Mixo-Lydians."

The boys then burst into the talk with stories of how Admiral
Phelps had spoken to the Upper School on naval history.

"That's father's hobby," said Miss Phelps, delighted by the
boys' enthusiasm. "And his other hobby is astronomy. He's got
an awfully good telescope."

"You must ask the Rector to show you his," said John Leslie.
"He's rather good on stars. He used to do star-watching with
Miss Hopgood's aunt when he was at Northbridge. Miss Hopgood's aunt's husband was head of the Matthews Porter Obser-
vatory in Texas for some years, and she gave his telescope to
Canon Fewling. If I said that Miss Hopgood's aunt's husband
discovered Porter Sidus, would that mean anything to you? I
know it wouldn't to me," he added hastily.

"Nor to me," said Miss Phelps, "but I expect father would be
awfully pleased to hear about it. I must remember to ask Canon
Fewling. He's a good sort, isn't he?" at which words the whole
Leslie family burst out in praise of their Rector.

"And, what's more," said John Leslie, "he is quite comfortably
off as things go now. Not," he added hastily, "that one's well-
offness or otherwise affects one's being a good clergyman, but I
do think it is easier to be good if one isn't *too* poor, whatever the

camel and the needle's eye may say. I am sure that high hopes can faint on a cold hearthstone just as easily as on a warm one, or even more so."

"Well, ours isn't exactly cold," said Miss Phelps. "But I do sometimes feel a bit depressed when I think of the things we *can't* get for father and mother. Things like a winter abroad. But there are hundreds of people worse off than we are."

"I don't think that's any comfort at all," said Mary Leslie firmly. "I'd much rather think of *millions* of people being happier than I am. Not that they could be," she added, looking at her husband and her sons.

"Well, even if there isn't much happiness one does manage to be happy without it," said Miss Phelps, which philosophy touched her hosts more than they might have cared to admit.

"No more pudding, Minor?" said his mother, rather surprised at her second son's abstemiousness.

"No thank you, mother," said Minor. "If I'm going on the church roof after that bird I don't want to feel too full. It might make me a bit giddy," and then he wished he had not said it, for his mother quite obviously saw him lying mangled at the foot of the church tower while a golden-crested mippet exulted in his downfall.

"Anyway," he added, "the Rector's got a splendid rope. And if I'm at one end and the Rector's at the other I can't possibly fall," at which words his elder and younger brother burst into irreverent laughter, which their parents made a slight and obviously insincere pretence of checking.

All the Leslies and their guest, accompanied by young Frank Gresham who was usually to be found in the wake of the boys, then walked up to the church, which by now presented a lively resemblance to the gates of Clumsium upon the trysting-day, though Canon Fewling, unlike Lars Porsena, was not unduly elated. Not only had bird-persecutors (or, if preferred, bird-lovers, though there seems to us but little difference between them) rallied, but Lord Stoke, representing the Barsetshire

Archaeological, had just driven up in his dog-cart with something very like a real groom sitting behind, who jumped down and ran to the horse's head, thus afflicting all older persons there assembled with heart-rending nostalgia. We must add that his lordship, who on the whole divided birds into Game Birds and All Other Birds, had not come over because of the mippet, but to verify if possible his private theory that the gargoyle near which the mippet was nesting showed traces of Scandinavian influence. A contingent from Northbridge was already waiting in the churchyard, headed by the Rector, Mr. Villars, with his wife, who kept up the most friendly relations with their former priest-in-charge of St. Sycorax. And rather apart from the rest might be seen the squat massive form of Miss Pemberton, the Provençal scholar, with her lodger and co-worker, Mr. Downing.

"I can't tell you how glad I am to see you," said Canon Fewling to Mr. and Mrs. Villars. "It reminds me of the delightful times we spent watching on your church tower in the war. Do you remember what the wind was like on the roof? It reminded me of the Horn. You know I did go round it in a sailing ship once," at which the Villarses very kindly expressed their delight and surprise, for it was the one subject on which Canon Fewling was a little snobbish, and it was so innocent a snobbism that they liked him the better for it.

"You know, Tubby," said Mrs. Villars, "I thought ships were *always* wrecked when they went round the Horn, at least if they went one way, only I forget which. I expect you went the other way. Do we all have to go up the tower? You know how it frightens me."

"Well, really the fewer the better," said Canon Fewling, "because, to be quite truthful, I think the battlements are a bit weak on the north side and if too many people came crowding up one of them might fall off. I mean one of the battlements, not the people. If you will be kind enough *not* to come up, Mrs.

Villars, it will really be a help, because lots of people will take courage when they see you don't go."

Mrs. Villars said nothing would give her greater pleasure than not to go, and if being a coward would be a help there was nothing she would like better, and everyone else could go as much as they liked.

"Oh, I didn't mean *quite* that," said Canon Fewling. "I meant if you were kind enough to say in a careless way, rather loudly, that you were afraid to go up it would encourage people wonderfully. Encourage them not to go, I mean. I know Mrs. Leslie won't go because her second boy is going over the wall and she would rather not see him. But he will be perfectly safe," he added, seeing in Mrs. Villars's face that she sympathised with Mrs. Leslie, "because I shall be holding the rope. I fastened the rope onto a beam in the church yesterday and went up myself to test it, and short of someone coming with a sword and cutting it the boy can't possibly come to any harm."

"Can you still climb a rope, Fewling?" said the Rector of Northbridge, though more with envy than disbelief. "Do be careful," which the Rector of Greshamsbury took in very good part.

"I think," said Canon Fewling, suddenly speaking in his best naval voice, guaranteed to carry through the most howling of gales, "that we had better begin. But there isn't room for more than six or seven people at most because of the way the lead roof goes up to a point behind the parapet. And I shall want plenty of room to handle the rope. Minor is going to be roped, of course. That makes five with his brothers and Frank Gresham and Mr. Wickham, who knows all about birds. We can take one more, but that is all."

As most of those present looked upon the dark winding stairs of the tower with distaste and fear, there was no immediate response.

"All right, we'll go as we are," said Canon Fewling.

"I should like to join you, if I may," said Mr. Downing, a spare, grey-haired man in the sixties.

"Certainly not, Harold," said Miss Pemberton, his hostess and—in the most respectable sense of the word—protectress. "You know you have no head."

"But, Ianthe," said Mr. Downing, "you know we agreed when we were reading that poem of Camargou's about the breeze that brings her lover's voice to the Dame de Mistigris imprisoned on the roof of her husband's tower how valuable it would be to know what the words "cuers m'eun paréiou miradéiéou" meant exactly, and you said one would have to be on the top of a tower to understand the exact feeling."

"In that case, Harold," said his Egeria and hostess, "go onto the tower. I have nothing to say," so that Mr. Downing, knowing from long experience that saying nothing would mean saying a great deal and saying it probably at intervals for the whole evening, retired into miserable silence.

Captain Gresham then asked to be allowed to join them on the specious plea that his son Frank was quite capable of being sick when excited. The party were just going into the tower, which had an outer door to the churchyard, when Captain Fairweather and his wife appeared.

"Oh, Canon Fewling," said Rose Fairweather, who was wearing tweeds that every woman envied—though it was not a grudging envy so much as a wistful envy, nor had any of them Rose's lovely figure, "I simply *must* come too. It must be simply *shattering* to be up there."

The Rector who, like every male—and for the honour of our sex we must say every female too—could not keep his eyes off Rose's lovely deliberately wind-swept fair hair, her exquisite and restrainedly artful complexion and her unexceptionable legs, said very courageously that he could not allow any more people to go up.

"In that case," said Miss Pemberton, her strong ugly face

looking quite pleasant, "I am sure Mr. Downing will give up his right."

"Oh, how *divine* of you, Mr. Downing," said Rose, at which the unhappy Mr. Downing, torn between his natural courtesy to women, his intense wish to go up the tower and his ever underlying fear—not to put too fine a point upon it—of his hostess, went red in the face, stammered something and cut a very poor figure.

"Look here, Fairweather," said Canon Fewling, "I'm sorry, but I really can't——"

"Of course you can't," said Captain Fairweather. "Up that tower you do not go, my girl."

His wife was heard to say that it was all too foully shattering and anyway the stone stairs were bound to ladder her nylons.

"But Tubby," said Mary Leslie who had been watching and listening. "What about Miss Phelps? After all, she did bring your hens today. And she's an Admiral's daughter."

"My dear Miss Phelps, how could I be so forgetful," said Canon Fewling. "I do apologise. Of course, you are the very person we want. You were so kind about those hens. Will you come up the tower?"

Miss Phelps, not accustomed to being praised or noticed, went deep red in the face.

"If you really want me——" she said doubtingly.

"Take it from me, my girl, if Tubby says a thing he means it," said Mr. Wickham. "Come on. Bundle up."

Thus adjured, Miss Phelps followed Canon Fewling up the steep winding stair, lit at irregular intervals by narrow windows calculated to let in the maximum of dirt and cold and wet and the minimum of light, which last was further thwarted by the stout form of the Rector as he paused at each slit to admire the various views. At last the whole party emerged safely from a low door and stood looking over the parapet and arguing as to whether that was Bolder's Knob or the Great Hump and getting the points of the compass remarkably wrong, considering, as

Captain Gresham very intelligently put it, that there was the weathercock just above their heads. It was then observed by all present that the cock was turning his tail to the wind in a very craven way.

"Oh dear, it needs oiling," said Canon Fewling. "The Sexton told me it was oiled last year. It must have stuck again," which comment was so reasonable that no one could make suitable answer. "There is, I believe, a little can of oil just inside the door," he continued, "but I fear I am too heavy to go up. Oh dear!"

"Please, sir," said Leslie Minimus, "can I do it?" upon which both his brothers, using the words Chump and Great Fool, said it was like Minimus's cheek and he'd only get stuck and have to be lifted down, as witness the time when he stuck on the peaked top of the Temple at Rushwater and had to be rescued ignominiously by Captain Belton, R.N.

"Now, you boys," said Miss Phelps, with all the easy authority of an Admiral's daughter who has lived among those pleasing anxious beings all her life, "stop teasing. Now, Minimus—your name's Clive, isn't it?—up you go. I'll catch you if you fall."

Inspired by these words and feeling confident that this new-met friend would stand between him and death, Minimus took the oil-can, hoisted himself up, liberally anointed the part on which the cock turned, spilling a good deal of oil on his own clothes, swung the cock a few times and came down triumphantly.

"I knew you could do it," said Miss Phelps, as she took the oil-can from him and made no further comment. But when she looked at the elder boys' kind if patronising approval of their young brother and saw his embarrassed pleasure she was satisfied.

Mr. Wickham, who had been leaning over the parapet, now straightened himself and said that as far as he could see, with the nest in such a plaguily awkward place, she was a golden-crested mippet all right, but she had got her head down and a bit of gargoyle got in the way. It was just possible, he said, that she was

Mippetta Calva Horrida, and not unless he could see her head would he like to pronounce on it.

"So over with you, my lad," he said to Minor who, asking nothing better, had already put the rope round him in the most approved and seamanlike way and handed the slack to Mr. Wickham. He then climbed over the parapet and began his walk, quite unconcernedly, along a narrow ledge towards the unsuspicious mippet. Young Frank Gresham, looking over the better to mark his progress, turned a nasty green, which being observed by his father that provident officer took him to the other side of the tower and so safely to the stairs. Halfway down the light was blocked by something that resolved itself into Lord Stoke, heaving himself up the winding stairs pretty well for a man of his age.

"All over, eh?" said his lordship good-humouredly.

Captain Gresham said, Not at all, but his boy felt giddy and he thought he would be better down below.

"That's right," said Lord Stoke in the loud voice of the very deaf and patting Frank Gresham on the head, much to that young gentleman's annoyance. "Mustn't be sick in front of ladies. You'd better take him up again, though, Gresham. Get his nerve back. First time I fell off a pony when I was a little boy my old father, though he was a good bit younger than you are then—I mean he was younger then than you are now, but that's all a long time ago and doesn't much matter. What was I saying?—oh yes, the first time I fell off my pony he said, 'Up you go again, my boy.'"

"And did you fall off again, sir?" said Frank Gresham, now that the horrid gap between sky and earth was bridged, quite himself again.

"Yes, my boy. And I fell off three or four times every day for a week, and after that I never fell off again. I won't say that I didn't take a few tosses hunting, but that's all in the day's work. Well, well," and, raising a finger to his well-known brown hat, a

mixture between a tallish bowler and a shortish top hat, he went
slowly on up the stairs.

When he got onto the tower the company were all at the far
side, and by the time Lord Stoke had reached them he saw
Minor being pulled over the parapet with something in his
hands.

"Well, boy, what have *you* got?" said his lordship, for whom
everyone made way.

"We aren't sure, sir," said Minor politely. "Canon Fewling
says she's a golden-crested mippet, but Mr. Wickham says she's
Calva Horrida. What would you say, sir?"

"Betty Baldpate in these parts, my boy," said his lordship.
"Known her all my life. Any eggs?"

"Three, sir," said Minor. "Pale green with brown spots. I took
one and left two in the nest. Here's the one, sir," and he held out
his hand with an egg in it.

"Quite right," said Lord Stoke approvingly. "And where did
you find her?"

"Over here, sir," said Minor, pointing over the wall and
downwards. "She'd made her nest just beside the gargoyle.
That's what made it a bit difficult to catch her, but the Rector
and Mr. Wickham held the rope."

"Now. This gargoyle, boy," said Lord Stoke. "Did you notice
anything about it? Anything special, I mean?"

"No, sir," said Minor. "Just a kind of head like a dragon for the
rain-water to come out of."

"No carving?" said Lord Stoke. "No runes?"

"I don't think so, sir," said Minor. "At least I've never seen a
rune. What are they like, sir?"

"You'd know soon enough if you saw them," said Lord Stoke.
"When first you see them they look like letters and then you find
they aren't. Not our sort of letters."

"There's a very good book in the School library, sir," said
Major, who had been holding as it were a watching brief for his

younger brother, "called *Italy and Her Invaders* by a man called Hodgkin with a picture of runic writing."

"Now, is there?" said Lord Stoke. "I must read that book. What did you say the name was?"

"*Italy and Her Invaders*, sir," said Major. "Eight great whacking volumes. And there's a kind of alphabet of runes, with the letters all gone wrong. I mean you think it's going to be a real letter, but it isn't. All a bit spiky they are."

"But there wasn't anything like that on the gargoyle," said Minor. "Its head's supposed to be the Bishop of Barchester—I mean the one then, whenever it was—but it looks jolly like this one," at which Mr. Wickham said that was enough, and everyone went down again, leaving the mippet to sit upon her eggs, as indeed she had done all the time and had no intention of doing anything else, observing the world below her with a glassy eye and thinking of absolutely nothing till her husband came home and said she had better go and get a cup of tea and he would look after the children for a bit. And whether either of them noticed that one of the children had been ravished from them we cannot say. Probably not.

Meanwhile the bird-lovers and their families had walked across to the Rectory where Mrs. Hicks, the Rector's housekeeper, had provided a superb tea.

"Well, Mrs. Hicks," said Mrs. Villars, who had an almost royal memory for the faces of all her husband's former pupils (for he had been a Schoolmaster for some years) and parishioners, "how are you? And what a nice tea you have got for us. John came to see us last week and he sent you his love. You know he has two little girls now."

"Well, fancy him thinking of me," said Mrs. Hicks, while Mrs. Villars prayed inwardly to be forgiven for having told such a whopping untruth, simply in an insane desire to give pleasure. "I remember as plain as anything the day he came back on leave, madam—in the war it was."

Mrs. Villars, suppressing an insane desire to say it wasn't,

congratulated Mrs. Hicks on her memory and said she was sure
John would be so glad to hear what a splendid tea Mrs. Hicks
had given them and so escaped. The air was thick with the noise
of a few well-bred country people talking to friends they met
every other day, and Mrs. Villars felt she was in the macaw
house and blamed herself for being so pernickety.

"I have brought you some tea, Mrs. Villars," said Canon
Fewling, materialising beside her. "You look rather tired," at
which Mrs. Villars began to laugh, though very pleasantly.

"I'm so sorry, Tubby," she said, "but it reminded me of the
war. Do you remember a Captain Holden who was billeted on us
at the Rectory in the second winter?"

"A good sort of fellow," said Canon Fewling. "Something in
the literary line, wasn't he?"

"He was," said Mrs. Villars. "And is. He is Adrian Coates's
partner now, the one that publishes Mrs. Morland's thrillers.
He had a respectful regard for me and expressed it by always
saying in a fierce kind of way that I looked tired. As indeed I was
when he was about, because *you* know, Tubby, how awful it is
when people are devoted to you. I often wondered how you
managed to live through it in Northbridge with all those ladies
adoring you at St. Sycorax. Do they adore you here?"

"Thank goodness, NO," said Canon Fewling. "If anything
makes one feel a fool it's being adored, and yet you can't be rude
to them."

"I wonder if Sir Andrew Aguecheek was ever rude to his
adorers," said Mrs. Villars.

"Never," said Canon Fewling with conviction. "He was one of
Shakespeare's gentlemen. Rum, how many of the Bard's gentle-
men are cads. I suppose Shakespeare saw a good many cads in
London and couldn't help using them."

Enchanted by this new light on the Bard, Mrs. Villars begged
Canon Fewling to explain. By this time several Shakespeare
lovers had gathered about them, each eager to put forward a new
and earth-shaking theory. Canon Fewling said it was hardly fair

to ask anyone to give chapter and verse for a random observation, but in his opinion any person who at a party in Rome made a bet with an Italian, in the presence of another Italian, a Frenchman, a Dutchman and a Spaniard, about his wife's fidelity, apparently in the hope of winning ten thousand ducats by her frailty, could hardly be called a gentleman in any sense of the word. Several other guests were drawn into the fray, instancing the egregious Bertram, the unworthy nitwit Claudio, and others.

"Well, well, what are you all talking about?" said Lord Stoke, who dearly loved a discussion, by which he meant not letting anyone else get a word in edgeways and making the very most of his deafness.

"Bad manners in Shakespeare," said Rose Fairweather, who was celebrated among her friends for having seen a play called *Shakespeare* three times, which had turned out to be *Hamlet*, and about which she appeared to remember nothing but the name of the principal actor.

"Bad manners in Shakespeare, eh?" said Lord Stoke, amused by this new game. "What about the man that gives a dinner-party with nothing to eat but some warm water? Shocking bad manners."

"And then throws the dishes at the guests," said Mrs. Villars, warming to the game.

"The fact is," said John Leslie quietly, "that Shakespeare can't ever have dined in good society."

While this quite idle chatter was going on Miss Phelps had stood a little apart, enjoying the good tea, enjoying the party, but just not of it. Rose Fairweather, who had been a hostess in many ports and done it very well, looking round to see if everything was satisfactory, saw Miss Phelps rather alone and at once went up to her, asking Miss Phelps if she remembered her as Rose Birkett, when her father was Headmaster of Southbridge School.

"Of course I do," said Miss Phelps. "I always rather envied you."

"But why?" said Rose.

"You were such a lovely girl," said Miss Phelps, with the real admiration that women—and more of them than one might think—feel for beauty in their own sex. "And you had such lovely clothes. It got me down a bit sometimes, when I was doing the goats and the hens in slacks and you looked like something in a story. But it was such a pleasure to look at you that I quite got over feeling how plain and dull I was."

"But that is *very* nice of you," said Rose who, though used to admiration, was always pleased to meet it. "I used to wish I could wear trousers and go on the land, but Mummie wouldn't let me and then I got married. Are you staying with the Leslies?"

Miss Phelps said she had only come over for the day and Mr. Wickham was going to take her back.

"I hope he'll be ready soon," she said, looking anxiously at the clock, "because of getting supper on. Father does like me to read to him a bit before supper. He is reading all Mr. Churchill's books. We get them a bit late, because the County Library can't have enough copies for everyone. We are still waiting for the last one."

"I've got them all," said Rose. "Look here, I'll lend you mine. Where's Mr. Wickham? Oh, Mr. Wickham, Miss Phelps ought to go home, because of getting supper."

"I say, I'm sorry," said Mr. Wickham. "Look here, Margot, just ten minutes. Downing is telling me about a man he knows in Cyprus who is selling local wine in casks. Might be worth trying. I shan't be more than five minutes."

Miss Phelps said it didn't matter, but it was clear that she was anxious.

"Selfish old man," said Rose. "Quite too shatteringly selfish. Tubby!"

Canon Fewling turned from Lord Stoke—not unwillingly, we may say.

"Look here, Tubby," said Rose, her lovely face flushed with the excitement of doing a good deed. "Mr. Wickham said he'd drive Miss Phelps home and now he says not just yet. He is too shatteringly selfish. She has to get back to her father. Will you take her?"

It was clear that Canon Fewling did not want to leave his party, but at the same time was very anxious for his guest's comfort.

"It's all right," said Rose Fairweather. "No one will notice. There won't be much traffic on that road. You can go as fast as you like. Or look here. Lend me your car, Tubby, and I'll be back before the party's over. Come on, Miss Phelps."

Canon Fewling made a protest to which Rose paid no attention at all and went away, taking Miss Phelps with her, leaving Canon Fewling a prey to the laws of hospitality, rather anxious about his new car, concerned for Miss Phelps, and full of combined admiration for and slight terror of Rose Fairweather. With complete want of fine feelings Rose hustled Miss Phelps into the large car and without a word turned it and drove at a quite excessive speed, or so it seemed to Miss Phelps, right over the downs and so into Southbridge, mostly on one wheel. But so well did she drive that after five minutes Miss Phelps forgot to be frightened and enjoyed it very much. Rose reined the car up on its haunches before Jutland Cottage and let her guest out.

"Oh!" said Miss Phelps. "I forgot the trailer," and Rose had an impression that she might be going to cry. "Wicks took it over behind his car, and we shall need it tomorrow. I *am* so sorry," she added, with the foolish way we so often have of apologising for what isn't our fault.

"If Wicks took it over to Greshamsbury, he can bring it back," said Rose, adding some powder to a perfect face. "And if he doesn't, Tubby shall. Don't worry," and she kissed Miss Phelps with a kind of careless kindness and was gone. Miss Phelps went into the house and, much to her relief, found that all was well. Her parents were pleased to see her and enjoyed hearing about the excursion to the top of the tower. Then Miss Phelps read aloud to her father while her mother finished getting supper.

While they were having their evening meal a loud roaring noise burst into the quiet evening and stopped outside their house.

"It sounds like an aeroplane," said Mrs. Phelps, "but it could hardly be one at this time."

Her husband said, kindly but precisely, that it wasn't so much the question of time as that an aeroplane could not possibly land in the lane. A strange voice was heard outside, and Miss Phelps came back with the Rector of Greshamsbury.

"It's Canon Fewling, mother," said Miss Phelps, "and Mr. Wickham," which gentleman followed them.

"You will excuse me, I hope," said Canon Fewling to Mrs. Phelps, "but Mrs. Fairweather told me you had not yet got the last volume of Mr. Churchill's book and I know how dreadful it is not to have a book one wants, so I drove Mrs. Fairweather back to her house and she asked me to bring you her copy. She says she bought it, so please keep it as long as you like. I did it in seventeen minutes," he added proudly.

"And there was I, bringing your trailer, Margot," said Mr. Wickham rather sulkily, "and if Tubby doesn't come along a-bulging and a-biling, so I went all out on the top of the downs, but he had the legs of me. Well, good night all," and he went away and so back to Northbridge.

Canon Fewling, pressed thereto by Mrs. Phelps, stayed and had some supper with them, and both ladies noticed with pleasure how Admiral Phelps responded to a younger naval man and at once looked less grey and tired, and when it was discovered that Canon Fewling had been in the *Scrapiron*, what time Admiral Phelps was commander, the two men were not at a loss for conversation. Miss Phelps washed up the supper things, saw that all her animals were safe for the night and came back just as Canon Fewling was getting into his car.

"Good night," he said. "If I can be of any use to your father, will you let me know? Not," he added hastily, "but what he has a very good friend in your Vicar. Crofts is as good a man as I know. But if there were anything that is perhaps a little difficult for you to get, will you let me know? I could run into Barchester and be out here with anything you needed quite quickly. I am very proud to know your Admiral-father, Miss Phelps. And thank you for all your help with the hens and on the tower. I cannot be grateful enough to Mrs. Fairweather for having made it possible to help your father and mother, even a little," and so he drove swiftly away towards the downs, thinking as he went of the courage and simplicity with which the Phelps family faced life. And then the thought of Rose Fairweather and her kindness in letting him know that the Admiral was wanting the last volume of Mr. Churchill rose in his mind. Beauty lived with kindness, he felt, and sang the words aloud to himself as he drove.

"Shall I shut up now, sir?" said Mrs. Hicks when he came in. "It all went very well, sir, didn't it? And Mrs. Fairweather quite a portrait, sir."

So she shut up and retired to her own quarters. Left alone, Canon Fewling opened the piano, one of the chief joys that his comparative wealth had brought to him, and played a song by Schubert, singing it softly to himself. Beauty lives with kindness. Yes indeed.

CHAPTER 4

There was no doubt that Greshamsbury had become more alive during the spring of that year. Canon Fewling, taking the duty of a good parish priest very seriously, had modified his natural inclinations to the taste of his parishioners. If he sometimes thought wistfully of St. Sycorax and the mild smell of incense, he very sensibly set against his loss all he had gained by his translation. No longer did his congregation consist almost entirely of single ladies who adored him and were each (on no grounds at all) slightly jealous of the others. No longer did he have to ask some married lady of his acquaintance (as he used to ask Mrs. Villars) to walk home with him from tea parties as a moral protection. Here, in his own rectory, with Mrs. Hicks to cook for him and try not very successfully to bully him, he felt that a clergyman's home was his own castle. From this fortress he could sally forth, dressed by an excellent clerical tailor, and dine with the John Leslies, or the dull but pleasant Greshams, or with Captain and Mrs. Fairweather. Or he could speed in his expensive car to the County Club in Barchester, where there was a very good cellar, or to Gatherum Castle, or Pomfret Towers, and to a choice of the most pleasant houses in Barsetshire. And in this spring he also reached his highest ambition and had an article in the *Church Times* on St. Paul's qualifications for the Royal Navy if he had lived today, of which article he had asked for a good many offprints and took great pleasure in giving these to his friends.

Meanwhile the cottages accepted him, which is always a good sign, and the attendance at Sunday School went up by seven and a half, the half being Mrs. Hick's niece's little boy, who wanted to go to school on Sunday because his elder sister did; and though Canon Fewling was at first doubtful about so young a scholar, Master Hicks sat in a corner and went to sleep as good as gold. Alms were dispensed in the shape of Mrs. Hicks keeping open house at her employer's expense for any tradesman or friendly passer-by who wanted a nice cup of tea, and in this way Mrs. Hicks was able to be of considerable service to the Rector, for through her it became known that he had put off his holiday to marry Mrs. Hicks's other niece, just in time, and his popularity increased. Of course, his parishioners married him twenty times over to ladies of different degrees of ineligibility, but as far as his friends could discover he preferred the less young married women like Rose Fairweather and Mrs. John Leslie, as indeed he had to do, for there was a marked absence of unmarried women in Greshamsbury. However, Canon Fewling seemed quite happy in his single condition and dined out a great deal.

It was on one of those delightful spring evenings when a dry east wind has wrecked every flower garden and blighted the early vegetables that Captain and Mrs. Fairweather had a small dinner party and invited their Rector. Rose Fairweather had entertained for the Royal Navy in more than one foreign country, and when there was an unmarried senior officer he would count himself lucky to get Mrs. Fairweather an acting hostess. Under her apparently careless touch servants who knew their work rose from the ground, and not even when the Mixo-Lydian Admiral (of one out-of-date gunboat on a lake) arrived late and rather drunk with two ladies of colour did Rose's exquisite complexion show any trace of pallor or her manner any sign of annoyance, but somehow the ladies were wafted away and the Admiral so tamed that he went home vowing eternal fidelity to his hostess. But on this evening no such trouble was likely to occur.

The party was Rose's parents, Mr. Birkett, the late Headmaster of Southbridge School with his wife, the John Leslies and Mrs. Morland, the well-know writer of thrillers from High Rising. All the guests knew and liked each other, and those who had not yet met the new Rector were more than ready to be friendly, especially Mrs. Morland, who had rashly introduced a clergyman into the book she was writing and wanted to get local colour, as it were.

At dinner a good deal of the conversation was about School matters, for during the early part of the war Mrs. Morland had lived in Southbridge School and helped Mr. Birkett as friend and secretary. Rose had been in South America with her husband then and had seen but little of Southbridge since, so she turned to Canon Fewling as a fellow outsider and they had a very pleasant time exchanging naval scandal. What struck Canon Fewling particularly about Rose was her unforced admiration for other women and in particular for those who were good-looking, and he ventured to mention this.

"But of *course*," said Rose. "I mean if someone is good-looking you simply *must* look at them. I mean it's like a sunset, or a frightfully good dress show at one of the big houses. I went to one once when John was naval attaché in Paris," and she mentioned a name which makes any female hearer feel like a Peri permanently outside the doors of Paradise.

To Canon Fewling the name meant nothing. Mrs. Morland basely deserted her host, so upsetting the whole dinner-table, to ask Rose for more details and the promise of a good long talk after dinner. For Mrs. Morland, whose permanent heroine, Madame Koska, had a highly fashionable dress establishment with mannequins of surpassing beauty, rank and even virtue, did it all by that peculiar sixth sense that sometimes tells writers how to describe things about which they know practically nothing. Rose, who had the admiration of the savage for anyone who could write (her own correspondence being a natural and highly illiterate production which endeared her to those who knew her best and drove everyone else mad), would cheerfully have talked across the table for the rest of the meal had not Mrs. Morland turned back to her neighbour, John Leslie, and enquired after his three boys with an apparent interest which quite took him in.

"I say, Canon Fewling," said Rose. "You know Mr. and Mrs. Crofts are going away for a fortnight."

Canon Fewling didn't know this, nor was there any particular reason why he should. It did come into his mind that Rose might be as it were an ambassadress to ask if he could provide a suitable locum tenens for the Vicar of Southbridge, but his mind at once rejected such a foolish idea.

"Well, who do you think is coming while they are away?" said Rose. "That quite shatteringly awful man who was there with his awful aunt."

Canon Fewling said it sounded dreadful, and could she tell him the name of the locum, in case he knew him.

"His name was Dunstan and his aunt was called Monica," said Rose. "He was older than his aunt because of his grandfather being married twice."

Canon Fewling, much interested in this family history, said what he really meant was, what was the surname?

"Oh, their *name*, you mean," said Rose. "It was something like Porter, only it wasn't that. Mummy might know. I say, Mummy." she called across the table to Mrs. Birkett, "do you remember the name of that man that was the clergyman at Southbridge with his aunt? The ones that they were always quarrelling."

"Now wait a minute," said Mrs. Birkett, shutting her eyes the better to think. "It wasn't Barton."

John Leslie said if he had been a clergyman called Barton his Christian name ought to have been Amos, but this Victorian literary allusion fell to the ground unheeded.

"It was Horton," said Mrs. Birkett. "I am so sorry, Mr. Leslie. Rose never had any manners," and she resumed her talk with him.

"That's the name, Horton," said Rose, becomingly flushed by her exertions. "It's pretty ghastly, isn't it?"

Canon Fewling, though ready in principle to agree with everything his charming hostess said, had to confess that he could not see anything particularly repellent about the name Horton. It was, he said, the name that Charles Ravenshoe assumed when he took service as a groom with Lieutenant Hornby; but as Rose had never read any book by Henry Kingsley nor probably ever heard of him, this particular conversation did not get any further, especially as Rose had an important idea in her mind and was all anxiety to let it loose.

"Well, look here, Tubby," she said. "It's this. You know old Admiral Phelps and Mrs. Phelps aren't well, and I asked Dr. Ford about it and of course he said he couldn't discuss his patients, so shatteringly official."

"So then I suppose he told you all you wanted to know," said Canon Fewling, for Dr. Ford, a much loved and respected physician of many years' standing in that part of the world, was a splendid gossip; though it must in justice be said that no unkind word from him had been known, nor any that could do harm.

"Of course," said Rose, mildly surprised at the question. "Now look here, Tubby, it's this. Mr. Crofts goes to see the Admiral quite a lot and the Admiral loves it. They both served out in the East, and they have quite shatteringly dull talks about things like old Bill in the gunroom. But this man Horton isn't a bit like that. He's what I call a professional clergyman, if you see what I mean. And, what's more, he's the Principal of St. Aella's Home for Stiffnecked Clergy, which sounds quite shatteringly disagreeable," and Canon Fewling had to admit that he knew exactly what she meant.

"But I don't quite see what I can do about it," he said.

"*Really*, Tubby," said Rose Fairweather, "you're as bad as the people in the Bible who have ears and hear not. What you've got to do is to go over to Southbridge as often as you can while the Croftses are away. You can do it in fifteen minutes easily."

"I've only done it in seventeen so far," said Canon Fewling, obviously attracted by this suggestion.

"You'll do it in fifteen all right, Tubby," said Rose and turned to her other neighbour, who was her father, to have a really interesting talk about her children and her sister Geraldine Fairweather's children (for the two sisters had married two brothers), but not particularly interesting to us.

By this time the question of Admiral Phelps had become of general interest. Except for Canon Fewling all the guests had at some time either lived in Southbridge or had strong ties with it through the School, and they fell into a very comfortable all-talking-at-once kind of conversation about old days and the years of the war and the changes that had taken place, changes some of which even Mr. Birkett, the former Headmaster, had to admit to be good. Canon Fewling might easily have felt a little out of it, but so long as everyone was happy he was content and sat looking benignly upon them, till Mrs. Morland claimed his attention.

"We are being dreadfully rude, Canon Fewling," she said, "but you know the war was such fun in some ways that one can't help talking about it. I lived at the School for the first year and simply loved it. I suppose you were at sea," and then it was discovered that Commander Fewling, R.N., during World War One had been on the China Station, where during World War Two one of Mrs. Morland's sons had also been, which, of course, made the Rector and the distinguished novelist friends at once.

"I cannot tell you how lucky I feel," said Canon Fewling, "not only in having such a nice Rectory but in finding so many naval people about. Mr. Leslie did some service in the first war, you know, and there are the Fairweathers and the Greshams, and Mr. Wickham often comes over. And, of course, the Phelpses at Southbridge. Do you know them?"

Mrs. Morland said of course she did and gave Canon Fewling a vivid description of the great Christmas party in the first winter of the war for all the evacuated schoolchildren and how Mr. Hedgebottom of the Hiram Road School, a professed atheist, had been publicly brought to shame by one of his most promising scholars, who, on seeing the crèche, contributed by Mme Brownscu, one of the more unpleasant Mixo-Lydian refugees, had pointed a very dirty sticky finger at it and said in a loud voice, "What's that?"

"It was Mrs. Phelps who did our Christmas tree," said Mrs. Morland. "She had done Christmas trees all over the world because of her husband being an Admiral. She wore blue serge trousers and a zip lumber jacket with a flowered overall over it and looked very majestic. Do you know her well?"

Canon Fewling said he had met the Phelps family and liked them very much and would like to know them better.

"Well, really that would not be difficult," said Mrs. Morland, looking at him dispassionately. "With your car you could get anywhere in no time. You could take Miss Phelps for a drive."

Canon Fewling was secretly a little frightened of Mrs. Morland because she wrote books, an attitude which is not uncommon though one cannot account for it, and said rather nervously that he didn't know Miss Phelps was an invalid.

"But she isn't. It's her mother," said Mrs. Morland with the patient voice of one who is talking to a stupid child. "Everyone does things for the Admiral because he isn't well and anyway men always get things done for them in this world. And doubtless in the next world too," the gifted author added, thus impressing Canon Fewling with a deep sense of his own unworthiness. "But no one does things for Miss Phelps. Do you know, Canon Fewling, I took her to lunch at Barchester and a film—it was Glamora Tudor with Hake Codman in *Moslem Love*—and when I took her home she nearly cried, because she said it was so wonderful to have a treat. And that," said Mrs. Morland rather severely, "just shows you."

If Mrs. Morland had been looking at Canon Fewling's face instead of—as we all do—turning her attention inward as it were, the better to enjoy the sound of her own voice producing winged words, she would have seen a look of such kind compassion, mingled with some shame at never having noticed what Mrs. Morland had now made so patent to him, as would have moved that kind creature's heart, for she had not meant in the least to imply that the Canon had failed in duty or kindness, but merely to make it clear that of Admiral and Mrs. Phelps and their daughter, it was in some ways Miss Phelps who needed the most help.

A general discussion then took place about how cold it always was now, especially when summer-time began, and whether it wouldn't on the whole be better to be frank about it and have winter all the year round, because then at least you could draw the curtains at tea-time.

"But rather fun when people dined early and could walk on the lawn afterwards on warm evenings," said Mary Leslie. "The old Greshams, who live in the wing of Greshamsbury Park, have some photographs—at least they are on glass and rather dark—of a party at the Park on the lawn after dinner in the summer. I think it was when the young Gresham of the time was engaged to the heiress who brought Boxall Hill back into the family and lots of money, though, of course, it's pretty well all gone now. Such pretty creatures in their crinolines, but somehow the men look much more caddish. I can't think why, but having one's coat buttoned up very high has a particularly caddish look. Most of the young men are like stable helpers, but the women are terrific ladies."

"But how good those photographs were," said Mrs. Birkett. "The other day I was over at Edgewood and Mrs. Grantly showed me some old photographs of the Close with the Dean and some clergy with luxuriant whiskers," which remark led to a discussion as to whether the present Bishop would be improved by whiskers. Rose Fairweather, who was not much in contact with the Close, said he would look too shattering for words, with which everyone agreed, with mental reservations as to the kind of shattering, and then Rose withdrew her ladies to what is in some ways the most satisfactory part of dining out, for much as we love and admire the gentlemen, there is something very restful in pleasant female society; and doubtless the men feel the same when the ladies are removed. Now could Mrs. Morland have a really comfortable talk with Mrs. Birkett whom she did not often see; now could Rose, who saw Mrs. Leslie nearly every day, have a really comfortable talk with her about Canon Fewling, in whom both ladies took a very friendly interest, which interest, as so often happens with our sex, took the form of feeling he ought to be married, though neither lady seemed to have any very distinct reason for it or any particular spouse in view.

"I suppose," said Mrs. Leslie, "it would be all *right* for him to be married."

"Well, he hasn't got a wife," said Rose, "or, if he has, he has been quite shatteringly secret about it, so that's all right."

Mrs. Leslie said she meant being High, to which Rose replied that, good gracious, he wasn't a monk, and anyway he was quite shatteringly well off, which quite resolved Mary Leslie's doubts.

"But I don't quite *see* anyone for him," Mary said, looking earnestly in front of her at nothing.

"One doesn't," said Rose, whose long and varied experiments in being engaged to the wrong people and subsequent extremely happy marriage made her something of an authority. "But quite suddenly one does."

To dispose of the hand of a well-to-do bachelor is one of the nicest parlour games. Rose at once suggested Miss Pettinger, the almost universally disliked Head of the Barchester High School, but not in a very serious spirit, and both ladies had the giggles in arranging for the ceremony to be held in the School Chapel with the whole of the Sixth Form, in their gym tunics, as bridesmaids; and so loud was their laughter, especially Rose's who had no great sense of humour and laughed all the more uncontrollably when she did see a joke, that the other ladies could not hear themselves speak and wanted to know what it was all about.

"Oh, it was rather silly," said Mary Leslie, though still laughing. "We were thinking of people for Canon Fewling to marry and Rose said Miss Pettinger."

"Rose would say that," said Mrs. Birkett dispassionately. "She never had any sense about young men. It was pure luck that John fell in love with her just before the war and married her out of hand, or heaven knows who it would have been."

Rose, apparently taking this as high praise, said John was divine and who did they think Tubby could marry?"

Mrs. Morland, pushing her hair back in a very unbecoming way, said it all depended so much, and having made this sibylline utterance looked at Mrs. Birkett for help, which she hardly got when Mrs. Birkett said Assistant Masters' wives were one thing and Rectors' wives quite another.

"But," she added after a moment's reflection, "you know that nice Mrs. Villars at Northbridge, Laura."

"Canon Fewling couldn't very well marry *her*," said Mrs. Morland, "considering her husband is alive and she has two sons, Amy."

"Really, Laura, you take no pains to understand *anything*," said Mrs. Birkett. "Of course Mrs. Villars wouldn't dream of Tubby. But there are several nice middle-aged women in Northbridge and Mrs. Villars might know if he likes any of them. We took the Rectory, one summer before the war, and saw quite a lot of them. There was that very nice Mrs. Turner whose husband drank himself to death and quite a number of quiet unmarried women with very trying old parents of one sort or another who are probably dead by now."

"Well, Amy," said Mrs. Morland, "I don't think they would do at all. You seem to forget that the really important thing is for Cannon Fewling's wife to be persona grata—if that is what I mean—to the people *here*. I mean someone who will fit. Otherwise I'd say Eileen would be exactly the person," and the three other ladies agreed that Eileen, who still presided with robust and cheerful efficiency over the bar at the Red Lion in Southbridge, would make an ideal wife for the Rector as they had so much in common in their figures, their good temper and their sound bottom of common sense, at which point the gentlemen came in which, as Rose afterwards said to her husband, was too shattering and spoiled everything.

"Do come and sit by me, Canon Fewling," said Mrs. Morland. "It is so nice to talk to people at other people's parties. At one's own parties one is always wondering if something will be overdone or underdone."

The Rector said that his Mrs. Hicks was really an excellent housekeeper and very kind to him.

"So is my housekeeper," said Mrs. Morland. "And she adores all my grandchildren when they come to stay. But I sometimes think how restful it would be if she weren't there. And then I reflect that it would really be quite unrestful, because of having to get odd help in or doing it all myself not very well, which would annoy her so much when she came back."

As all Mrs. Morland's old friends knew, she was apt to talk aloud to herself about herself when entertaining guests, or in this case a fellow-guest, but Canon Fewling, who had had plenty of experience of talkative ladies when he was priest in charge at St. Sycorax and adored by his almost entirely female flock, took it in good part and pointed out very kindly to Mrs. Morland that after all this was Mrs. Fairweather's party, so none of her guests needed to bother about the food or the service, both of which had been excellent.

"Now," said Mrs. Morland, "that is *exactly* what I wanted to ask you about, because of course it is always better to go right to the *source*."

Any ordinary man might have gone mad at this point, but Canon Fewling's apprenticeship to rather adoring middle-aged females at Northbridge had in some ways enlarged his experience of human nature.

"I quite agree about going to sources," he said kindly. "But if you would be so kind as to tell me what sources in particular I could perhaps better answer whatever questions you might like to ask," and then wondered if he had perhaps been a little severe with a Writer, knowing from experience of Miss Pemberton at Northbridge how non-understandable, not to say peculiar, female writers could be, being often (or to his conclusion he had come), so immersed in a world of their own creating that they came up to breathe with straws in their hair, as it were.

"Well," said Mrs. Morland, pushing her hair earnestly and unbecomingly away from her face, "it is the question of Marriage," and then fell silent, leaving her kind hearer entirely in the dark. "Not for myself, of course," said Mrs. Morland, "which would be absurd and of course I have left all the money I have earned equally between my four sons and would not *dream* of bringing in a Mr. Murdstone, but in general."

This all-embracing statement did not make things any clearer to the Rector, who very bravely said so.

"I know, I know," said Mrs. Morland, "and that is the worst of being a writer. I don't mean An Author, which sounds pretentious, but someone who does earn enough money to live on by writing, and I did manage to educate all the boys who, I am thankful to say, are all married, not but what it comes rather expensive with presents to all the grandchildren on birthdays and Christmases, but one does think extraordinary things inside one's head. At least they seem quite ordinary while they are inside, but when they get out they seem to get out of control; and though I must say I never missed my husband at all who, I must say in his favour, was really nothing but an expense, I mean not at all unkind or anything, there are sometimes moments when one feels a man about the place would be almost useful."

Here she paused, further to untidy her hair, which gave the Rector a chance to say that he would be only too glad to help her in any way if only she could manage to explain what it was she was saying.

"And pray do not take this as unkindly meant," he added. "I do assure you that I am *most* ready to help if I knew what it was."

"I am *sure* of it," said Mrs. Morland, "and as someone says somewhere in Shakespeare the readiness is all; but, of course, Shakespeare simply could not always have known what he was saying because he was not for an age but for all time," upon which she sat back with the air of one who has at last solved a problem.

Canon Fewling was a very kind man and a man of good common sense and natural courtesy, but he could willingly have shaken his distinguished co-guest. He looked round for help, but the rest of the party were talking and laughing and so, by his canons of politeness, not to be disturbed.

"It is only about clergymen getting married," said Mrs. Morland, with a voice of relief that he had learned to dread when the good ladies of Northbridge would discuss their uninteresting little sins of omission and commission with him. "Is it always all right?"

"I should think so," said Canon Fewling, wondering what peculiar doubt had assailed the gifted novelist and why. And we may add, at this point, that he did not for a moment suspect her of having any designs upon himself, though the good ladies of Northbridge had given him what, in confidential talk with Mr. Wickham, he had called a Fair Sickener of Sisterly Affection that he didn't want. "But if you would explain *exactly* what you were thinking of——?"

"Only a book I am writing," said Mrs. Morland, at which point Canon Fewling felt that a burden as heavy as Christian's had miraculously fallen from his shoulders. "One of the people in it is an *extremely* nice clergyman. Rather like you, if you see what I mean," which rider Canon Fewling accepted at its exact value without fear or irritation. "I mean rather High—in the *best* sense, of course," she added, but by now Canon Fewling was prepared for anything and more amused than alarmed. "And he has fallen in love with a really delightful woman of a suitable age with some money of her own, and if he can't marry her it will be too *dreadful* and I shall have to rewrite half my book."

"But why shouldn't he marry her?" said Canon Fewling, adding with great courage, "Is it anything to do with divorce? If it is, might I know what you want to say? Of course a great many people have violent and personal opinions one way or the other, but the church stands on the indissolubility of marriage."

"Good gracious, no!" said Mrs. Morland. "I might *talk* about divorce in a dashing way in private, but it would never do for my books at all. The people who read them wouldn't like it. I was only wondering, as the clergyman is a bit High, would it mean it would be awkward for him to get married?"

At this moment there came to Canon Fewling, one of the kindest and most charitable of men, a strong wish to take his distinguished fellow-guest by the shoulders and shake her till her teeth chattered. But the conventions discourage such behaviour, especially from a clergyman who is dining with quiet local friends in an atmosphere of extreme and very happy respectability, so he contented himself by asking what exactly she felt the awkwardness would be.

"Well, I mean his being very High," said Mrs. Morland, with the admirable pertinacity of her sex. "I mean, would it be All Right? Or could someone Bring an Injunction against him, or Unfrock him, or anything?"

At this moment there came into Canon Fewling's mind a memory, preserved by tradition, of how the wife of a Bishop of Barchester, some hundred years ago by now, had been rebuked by a penniless clergyman for intromitting in clerical affairs.

"Are you interested in the history of Barchester, Mrs. Morland?" he asked.

"But of *course*," said Mrs. Morland indignantly. "Ever since before I can remember. Why?"

"I was only thinking," said Canon Fewling, almost talking aloud to himself, "of how difficult Mrs. Proudie was about Mr. Crawley and the day when he came to the Palace. Do you remember the story about it?"

Mrs. Morland looked at him, was evidently puzzled and then suddenly began to laugh so much that two of her large tortoiseshell hairpens fell onto the floor. The Rector stooped, picked them up and returned them to her.

"Oh, thank you *so* much," said Mrs. Morland. "They *will* fall out, apparently of themselves. But of course I remember. And you ought to say to me, "Peace, woman! The distaff were more fitting for you." And so it is. At least I am sure it would be if I knew exactly what a distaff is or what one does with it. Have I been *very* silly?"

"Not a bit," said the Rector, relieved and also a little ashamed of himself. "The pen, or the pencil, whichever you use, is highly fitting for you and I hope you will go on writing for ever. But pray do get it out of your head that to be what is commonly called High means that one is a monk. It is one of the great glories of the Church of England that so long as you behave decently you can be as High or as Low as you like. And if I may tell you something in confidence——" and he paused.

"*Do*," said Mrs. Morland.

"Well, when I was at Northbridge I used occasionally to wish that I *were* a real monk, nicely shut up. You have no idea, Mrs. Morland, how the middle-aged spinsters—I use the word with great respect—*would* adore me. And why me, I shall never know," he added, looking with a slight tinge of sadness at his stout though not flabby form. "We are told that things are sent to try us, and those kind ladies certainly were. But I could get married at any moment if I and some lady—one whom, I may say, I have never met and hardly expect to now—were agreed that our happiness would not interfere with anyone else's."

"Well, thank you *very* much," said Mrs. Morland seriously. "Now I can go ahead with a clear conscience. And I do hope you will meet some lady one day who will be the one. Not that St. Paul knew *anything* about it at all," she added rather crossly. "He is one of the people I certainly would *not* ask to dinner," which entirely novel view of a great missionary struck Canon Fewling very much. Mrs. Morland appealed to the rest of the females of the party to support her, and after a rapid survey of history from Adam and Eve to the present day it was agreed with hardly a dissentient voice that broadly speaking No One in History would really be a help at a dinner party, except Charles II. The men were then asked to choose suitable females from history, but all professed themselves entirely satisfied with the present day and the present company, and so the talk rambled off into other matters.

At this point Rose Fairweather, who could be as tenacious as a bulldog when once an idea had got into her lovely head, tackled every single member of the company about the necessity of visiting Admiral and Mrs. Phelps as much as possible while the Croftses were having their holiday, which was almost at once. She then produced paper and a pencil—which rather surprised some of the party, who had a general idea, and a not unreasonable one, that she could neither read (except film captions) nor write (except to her husband or her parents, who had got used to her writing)—and with that tenacity and singlemindedness of which very lovely stupid women are capable made a kind of roster, by which some friendly emissary from Greshamsbury was to visit the Phelpses on at least four days of each week. For the three other days Rose pledged herself to collect supporters from Southbridge where, as the ex-Headmaster's daughter, she had many friends.

"Well, Rose, that's that," said her father, who was rather bored by it all, though secretly proud of his elder daughter's thoughtfulness and her capacity for organising people whether they wanted it or not. "And now we must be going. I am behindhand with my work as usual."

Canon Fewling asked what Mr. Birkett was working on.

"The Analects of Procrastinator," said Mr. Birkett, doing his very best not to give the impression that he was laying pearls in front of not exactly swine but some more pleasant and equally unappreciative animal.

"I wish I had ever got as far as them," said Canon Fewling wistfully. "I wasn't bad at Latin at school, only there was the war and the navy and I got so rusty that I felt ashamed. But I do read Virgil with a crib and Lucretius, though he's a bit stiff because one is never quite sure if he really knows what he is saying or is putting down everything that came into his mind and meant to sort it out later. But when does your fellow come out, Birkett? I should like to get a copy as soon as possible."

Mr. Birkett, suddenly feeling rather humble before a man who had given up the classics for his country, said that an advance copy would reach Canon Fewling from the Oxbridge Press, if he would accept it. Everyone felt slightly emotional for no particular reason, goodbyes were said with a quite Christmas-ish warmth and the party dispersed. At least the Birketts and Mrs. Morland did, for they had some way to drive, but the Leslies and Canon Fewling lingered in Rose's warm comfortable room. The men were talking desultory naval shop, Rose Fairweather was putting in some excellent though quite unnecessary work upon her lovely face, and Mary Leslie began to play softly on the piano, singing to herself in a small true voice.

"I wish I could do that," said Rose, bringing herself and her powder and lipstick over to the piano. "I did have an ocarina when I was engaged, but John was quite beastly about it and wouldn't let me take it on our honeymoon."

"I really got engaged to my John because of a song I was singing when I didn't know he was in the room," said Mary Leslie. "It all feels like a hundred years ago now. Mr. Leslie and Lady Emily were alive, and John was being a disconsolate widower, and I was just a niece by marriage of Lady Graham—Lady Emily's daughter—and spending the summer at Rushwater. It is all such old, old history now."

"What was the song?" said Rose.

"Only a very, very small song by Bach," said Mary. "'Bist du bei mir' is its name," and she began to sing it very softly.

"You ought to ask Tubby to play," said Rose, who had waited politely till the little aria had come to an end. "He has an absolutely wizard touch on the piano. Have you ever heard him?" but Mary hadn't.

Canon Fewling had heard the soft strains and neglecting

the other guests came over to the piano to enquire what was happening.

"Tubby plays too divinely," said Rose Fairweather. "Come on, Tubby. Play something. I absolutely adore your playing, and considering what a lot of trouble I've taken about the Phelpses the least you can do is to play for us. I'm going to see them twice a week at least while the Croftses are away. They'll need it. I say, Tubby, what do you know about Admirals' pensions?"

Canon Fewling, rather taken aback, said he had never thought about them, adding with a pleasant touch of shamefacedness that he had never hoped to be an Admiral.

"Well, I'll tell you," said Rose firmly. "It's not a bad pension, but if the Admiral dies first his widow gets next to nothing. So it would really be better for Mrs. Phelps to die than the Admiral. They've stepped it up a bit, but it's only a bit. And whichever dies it's going to be hard going for Margot Phelps. That's partly why I want to keep in touch with them. I can't stop anyone dying, but I can see that Margot isn't stranded. Thank goodness John has some money—and so shall I when Daddy and Mummy die," she added, not at all callously but simply as an interesting fact.

There was a silence while the company digested this information.

"I don't want to seem at all unfriendly," said Captain Fairweather, "but you are taking on rather a lot, Rose. I like Phelps immensely, and his daughter is a first-rate fellow, but you really can't take them on as a permanence. And Mrs. Phelps too. And probably no one will die for years," to which Rose only replied "Oh, John!" in a voice of tender reproach, while her lovely eyes began to brim with tears.

"Well, do what you like," said her husband, "only don't say I didn't warn you," and then rather spoilt his effect by adding, "Darling."

"Of course I won't say anything of the sort," said Rose, hurling herself into her husband's arms to the considerable embarrassment of everyone present. *"Angel!* I say, Tubby, do play something to cheer us up."

Canon Fewling, deeply moved by the sight of Rose's emotion, though the detached part of his mind noticed that her eyes were barely wet, obligingly sat down at the piano and began to extemporise.

"Lucky man," said Mary Leslie. "We all practise before breakfast for years and then you come and do it all by nature. I suppose you sing too."

Canon Fewling, going rather pink in the face, said only for fun, when he was alone.

"Then do have some fun," said Mary Leslie. "Pretend we aren't here. I heard you singing not long ago when I was coming back from a Women's Institute Meeting, after dark. You were singing 'Who is Sylvia.' Oh, *do* sing it."

The last thing Canon Fewling wished to do was to sing in public, even to so small a circle of intimate friends, but his code of courtesy forbade him to refuse, so he did as he was told. Unless one has known a man long and intimately it is difficult to believe that he has the enchanting gift of making drawing-room music, and no one had suspected that the Rector's stout form and unromantic appearance might have immortal longings in them. Before the end of his song everyone was almost uncomfortably emotional, but, exercising the fine English self-control which is so baffling to outsiders, no one showed more than decent gratitude for a charming song. Except perhaps Mary Leslie, who had music in her and felt, with faint discomfort, that the song was addressed to a real person. And as Mrs. Birkett and Mrs. Morland had been some time gone and it was obviously not directed towards herself, it could only be to Rose. Yes, beauty certainly did live with kindness in Rose, however trying and however sluttish at her dressing-table (as the dowager Lady Lufton and others could bear witness). And if her championship of the Phelpses was not kind, well, what was it? There was no obvious answer, so she took her husband away and asked Canon

Fewling if he would walk back with them, which he did, and when they got to the Old Rectory the Leslies very naturally asked him to come in for a good-night drink.

"I'd love to,"said Canon Fewling, "only I think I'd better put my car away first."

"Why not wait till you get home?" said John Leslie. "Nobody's likely to steal it. The whole county police know that car of yours, Fewling. In fact the way they turn a deaf eye, I mean a blind ear, to the way you speed about is quite disgraceful. It will be all right in your drive."

"Well, you see, it isn't there," said Canon Fewling apologetically. "It is all my fault. I do try to cure myself of my faults, but it is such hard work."

"As a temporary naval man of World War One to a naval man of World War One, what the hell are you talking about?" said John Leslie, who but rarely showed emotion. "Have you left your car at the garage, or at the Palace, or where? Or lent it to the Phelpses?"

By this time he had opened his front door and the light was full on Canon Fewling's face, which exhibited a variety of emotions to which the Leslies had no clue.

"Really, Leslie, you misjudge me," he said. "I admit I have been foolish—but one can't help one's feelings."

"But what on earth *are* your feelings, Tubby?" said Mary. "Come in and have a drink and explain."

As a naval man the Rector could not refuse a direct invitation from a lady and he followed Mary rather shamefacedly into the drawing-room, where the comfortable remains of a fire were not beyond encouragement to a blaze. John Leslie gave everyone whisky and soda, apologising for the apparent ostentation by saying he had won it in the West Barsetshire Conservative Club's Christmas raffle and been keeping it for a suitable occasion.

"And now, out with it, Fewling," he said. "If you have killed a policeman and left him and the car on the top of the downs, you might say so. I know I'm a J.P., but I'm off duty this evening."

"I cannot tell you how much I apologise," said Canon Fewling to Mary Leslie. "It was an impulse."

"Then you'd better confess it. You'll feel better," said John Leslie, who did not suspect his Rector of any breach of the law, but felt puzzled.

"All right. I'll tell you exactly. But I won't *confess*," said Canon Fewling. "You know at Northbridge the older ladies of the town—the ones that came to St. Sycorax—*would* confess things to me. I cannot tell you how dreadful it was. I tried so hard to avoid it, but they were very earnest, and against my better judgment I consented. It was *dreadful*."

"Well, I can't imagine any of those old cats at Northbridge having anything really exciting to confess," said John Leslie. They couldn't have cheated, even over a bus fare."

"But that is exactly what I mean," said Canon Fewling. "They *would* ask me to hear their sins, and if all the things they told me had been heaped together and squared or cubed it wouldn't have made more than child's-play. "Of course in my church I could deal with them. It was my duty and I did. But they would attack me at tea-parties. I used, I fear, to wish at times that one of them would really do something *dashing*—something like shoplifting or even kidnapping. But it was all little things like having spoken rather unkindly to the daily woman when she broke four tea-cups, or not having remembered to put the cat's saucer of milk out when they went to the Barchester Odeon. I began to long for a good murder, or forging a will."

"Well, no one wants to confess at a tea-party in Greshamsbury, I hope," said John Leslie. "If they do, I ought to know about it, as your churchwarden."

"I know. And I do number that among my mercies," said Canon Fewling. "Not," he added hastily, "that I would willingly discourage anyone, but, as nobody has yet suggested it, I have thought it best to leave well alone."

"Good fellow," said John Leslie. "And now we have got rid of this red herring, Fewling, where *is* your car?"

Canon Fewling, after fortifying himself with a drink of the raffled whisky, said it was in the Fairweathers' drive, the dark bit round by the rhododendrons.

"But why?" said Mary Leslie, her kind heart divided between exacerbation and a feeling that the Rector must be allowed to defend himself.

"Well, I'll explain," said Canon Fewling resolutely. "I suppose you know John Gilpin."

"If you mean with the Caldecott pictures, of course I do," said Mary. "We had them all at home and all our boys were brought up on them. Heavenly, heavenly pictures, and so English that I almost cry when I look at them. I am keeping them for which-ever of the boys marries and has a family first."

Her husband said that was a very correct attitude, but she must let the Rector get on with what he was saying—though his tone as he said these words was highly unhopeful.

"You know when the Gilpins had been married twenty years——" Canon Fewling began.

"Just like us. 'These twice ten tedious years'," said Mary, looking with deep affection at her husband.

"Yes, darling, but we have had quite a lot of holidays," said her husband. "And now do let Fewling get on with what he is trying to say about the Gilpins."

"Sorry, Tubby," said Mary, at which warm words the expression of stern anguish on Canon Fewling's face melted.

"Well, as you know the Caldecott pictures," he said, evidently much reassured by his audience's attitude to that enchanting artist, "you will remember when they hired a chaise and pair to go to Edmonton they would not let it drive up to their door——"

"—lest folk should say that they were proud," said the Leslies with one voice.

"Well, I feel rather like that about my car," said Canon Fewling. "I know I can, owing to a lucky inheritance, quite well afford it. But sometimes when I am driving about the country and often—far too often, I fear—overtaking other cars, I feel I am being puffed up. I could quite well have walked down to the Fairweathers, but I do love the feeling of that car under my hands. It's the next best thing to handling a small boat in a gale. And then I felt it was ostentation and I ran it into the side drive behind the rhododendrons so that no one could see it. I did hope I could drive someone home, but the Birketts and Mrs. Morland both have cars. And when you asked me to come back with you it seemed almost showing-off to get her out of the shrubbery. So I thought I'd leave her there while I visited you and then slip back and fetch her."

"And wake the Fairweathers by doing it," said Mary Leslie, rather unkindly.

"No, no, I do assure you, Mrs. Leslie," said the Rector, "that she doesn't make a sound when she starts. It's as quiet as casting off and letting the boat drift for a moment while you get your oar or oar sculls going."

"And, anyway, you could have started a jet plane without our Rose hearing it. I had the room next to hers at a house-party somewhere once, and the racket that beautiful moron made going to bed you wouldn't believe," said John Leslie most unchivalrously. "What with turning the bath on for hours so that no one else could get any hot water and gabbling nonsense through the door to Fairweather and turning everything upside down because she couldn't find some filthy toy animal that she liked to take to bed, and even sending her husband in to ask if I had taken the wretched thing by mistake, it was like Waterloo Station in the war. And, once asleep, nothing could wake her—at least I suppose Fairweather could, but he doesn't. And as for driving a car, she has a cool head and she knows how to speed all right, but give her a chance and she'll strip your gears clean as a whistle and then look at you like an angel and get away with it. I sometimes wonder why Fairweather hasn't murdered her. Mary and I will walk back to the Fairweathers' with you and you can drive us home first and then yourself. Come along."

Encouraged by his churchwarden's words and by Mary's kind

laughter, he did as he was told. The Fairweathers' house was dark except for one upper window from which dance music from Hamburg was pouring at the top of its voice. The Leslies got into the car which, under Canon Fewling's loving and skilled hands, slipped with hardly more than a purr up the little drive and into the village street. He landed the Leslies at the Old Rectory, drove quietly back to his home and put his beloved toy away.

As he went to bed he reflected upon the occurrences of the evening and how kind Rose Fairweather was in organizing help for the Phelps family while their Vicar and his wife were away. But we are compelled to confess that, deeply though he admired her beauty and her kindness (and trying though she could be, we also freely admit both), what at the moment he most admired was her grasp of facts. Facts that were going to make a good difference to other people's lives. What she had said about an Admiral's pension, for instance. And he decided to find out as soon as possible exactly what pension a Rear-Admiral had and how much of that pension would remain to his wife should the Admiral die first. For Canon Fewling had been badly off in his time and had also seen the widows of his senior colleagues in the Royal Navy making both ends meet. One had taken such things for granted when one was young and had no responsibilities. Now, and he thanked his Creator humbly for it, he was well off as things go now and, what was more, a bachelor, with no nephews or nieces. Perhaps just as well for a priest, he thought, and then laughed a little at himself, for he had never undervalued human affection. But it was obviously his duty to find out how the Phelpses stood. Probably Colonel Crofts, the Vicar of Southbridge, knew, but now, confound it, he was away. Well, there were other ways of finding out, and one had old friends in the Senior Service who would give one all the necessary information. And having made these decisions he went to sleep almost at once.

CHAPTER 5

C anon Fewling did not forget about the pension of a retired
Rear-Admiral. Being in Barchester a day or so later, he
went to the Public Library, where Mr. Parry the City Librarian
was quite a good friend of his, and asked whether such information was in a book anywhere. Mr. Parry, who knew what was
in every book in the library whether he had read it or not, was
able almost at once to produce two or three books which would
give facts and figures of naval pensions and left Canon Fewling
to deal with them. An ex-naval man who is a bachelor with a
comfortable private income is not likely to know much about
pensions, and what Canon Fewling read was to him surprising
and rather dispiriting news. It appeared that if Admiral Phelps
were to die his widow might with luck get £150 a year, subject to
income tax and a means test. About grown-up daughters at
home he could find nothing. Although it was no business of
his and not in his parish, he could not help feeling disturbed
about the Phelps family and hoping, though with no particular
grounds for the hope, that perhaps Mrs. Phelps had some
money of her own, or that Miss Phelps, who had been so prompt
and helpful with the fowls, would get married. Both these hopes
were rather wishful thinking and as he could not give any
immediate help, he put the subject out of his mind as far as
possible. But it was never very far; and when he considered the
fact that since 1944 a distinction had been enforced between

officers' widows as capable or not capable of going out to work, amounting to an official pronouncement that they must if possible go out to work and so relieve the State of part of their pension, he felt inclined to go and kill someone. But one cannot kill people now. Alternatively, it would be a good thing if Admiral Phelps could be retrospectively killed in action, as it would almost double his widow's pension—which was impossible. And so bewildered and so indignant did he feel on behalf of families who were not only grieving for a husband and father lost but at the same time reduced to a scale of living which any trades unionist would scorn, that he began to wonder where England was going.

For the present there was nothing to be done. The Admiral was alive and would probably resent in a lively way any intromission of a junior ex-officer into his affairs. But he thought about it a good deal and began corresponding with friends who had influence, finding, to his great pleasure, that opinion in this matter of pensions for naval men's dependants was becoming very strong, not to say fierce, and that there was a probability of improvement before long. Such things move slowly and meanwhile he had his own work to do and many friends. But he determined to keep his eye on Jutland Cottage, and more specially during the spring and early summer when invalids so often wane with the waxing year, having exhausted their strength in fighting cold and poor feeding through the winter months.

A day or so later he met Rose Fairweather after lunch in the post office which also sold picture postcards, haberdashery, cigarettes, sweets and toys, besides having a small and totally inefficient circulating library at twopence per book for an unlimited period. As Rose was buying stamps he looked through the library, finding that such books as still had a binding, or half a binding, seemed to have been used chiefly as paper for shopping lists, and that in several cases the first or last pages were missing, not to speak of both.

"Hullo, Tubby," said Rose who, totally immune to the rigours of an English early summer, looked more than usually ravishing in a blue and white frock belted round her elegant waist with a wide piece of scarlet webbing ornamented with brass stars. "Are you coming this afternoon? We'd better use your car—it's much nicer than ours; besides, John has taken it to Barchester. Really too too self-making."

A combination of interest in this new word of Rose's with the awful feeling of guilt that one has when someone suddenly asks if one is going to go somewhere or do something which one has obviously promised to do and quite forgotten, made him lose all power of speech for a moment.

"I didn't think *you* would forget, Tubby," said Rose, turning reproachful blue eyes upon him.

Confounding himself in excuses for an omission of which he was at least temporarily unconscious, Canon Fewling took his engagement book from his pocket and anxiously looked at the current week.

"Mr. Aggs, Mr. Baggs, Mr. Caggs AND Admiral Phelps," said Rose, with a kind of careless self-consciousness, at the same time looking under her long lashes to see how the Rector would take her words.

Canon Fewling could hardly believe his ears. The lovely Rose Fairweather, in whom illiteracy almost amounted to genius, was quoting from Dickens. It was almost as surprising as if a tropical bird had perched on one's shoulder and spoken in human words. But even greater than his surprise was his horror when, looking in his engagement book, he saw, in his own neat handwriting, that he was due to have tea at Jutland Cottage with the Phelps family.

"I know what's happened to you," said Rose, who at intervals surprised her nearest and dearest by suddenly showing a quick social intelligence. "You put it down to remind yourself, because you really didn't quite want to go. I don't mean you didn't want to go *horridly*, but just because you didn't. I never put *anything* down because then I'd forget it, and anyway I don't put things down that I don't want to do. Then it doesn't matter if I don't do them. Like old Lady Norton's horrible parties on cold days to look at her nasturtiums and things in her ghastly garden. But really, Tubby, I am quite shattered about you forgetting."

Canon Fewling said he was shattered too, but he hadn't really forgotten; he had only forgotten that he had put it in his book, and he was quite free and would of course take Rose over in his car with the greatest pleasure, adding that he didn't know she knew her Dickens and was delighted by her use of his words.

Rose opened her eyes as wide as possible and said what on earth did Tubby mean and Dickens was quite shatteringly old fashioned, like that film called *Pickwick* and the one about Shylock.

Canon Fewling, who found trying to keep pace with Rose's swallow flights a stimulating mental tonic, said he thought she must be thinking of Shakespeare.

"No, no; not Shakespeare—that's *Hamlet*," said Rose, who had seen that tragedy several times with a very popular actor in the title role and, so far as her friends could tell, thought it comprised the whole of the Bard's output. "I mean the one with the burglar that murders a girl and has a faithful dog. There's a wonderful child-actor in it. There's a branch of the Dickens Society in Barchester——"

"Fellowship, not Society," said Canon Fewling, whose soul revolted against careless talk.

"—and someone gave a Reading out of Dickens," Rose continued, being apparently under the impression that the two great writers whom she mentioned had written the one a book called Shakespeare, the other a book called Dickens, "and there was a bit when he was saying a lot of names like Aggs and Baggs and it made me laugh," in proof of which she did laugh and then smiled so enchantingly that an old tag from his schooldays came back to Canon Fewling's mind about a girl who so spoke and smiled.

"Lalage," he said, partly to himself, partly addressing Rose, who being quite used to not quite understanding what people were talking about, laughed and smiled again.

"Well, anyway, you will take me to Southbridge, won't you, Tubby," she said, with the placid obstinacy of her nature, "and let me drive over the downs. I'd love to get sixty-five out of her."

"Certainly not," said Canon Fewling. "There is only one woman in Barchester that I would allow to drive my car and it is not you."

"Who is it then?" said Rose as they walked down the street together. "Not that sister of Jessica Dean's who married a Spaniard or something and drives racing cars?"

"Do you mean Helen Fanshawe?" said Canon Fewling. "She used to drive racing cars, but her husband is as English as I am."

"Then why is he called a Don?" said Rose. "I've heard Daddy call him one. Anyway, who is she? The woman, I mean."

"Lady Cora Waring, of course," said Canon Fewling.

"Oh well," said Rose carelessly, perhaps feeling that to be outclassed in driving by a duke's daughter was not a thing to be ashamed of. "I say, Tubby, Mr. Wickham came in last night and brought two bottles of curaçoa for us. Do you think Admiral Phelps would like one?" on hearing which words Canon Fewling's kind heart was full of contrition for having misjudged Rose, though as they walked up the street together it did occur to him that Captain Fairweather might have been consulted. Still, that was not his business.

At the gate of the Fairweathers' house Canon Fewling said goodbye and promised to fetch Rose about half-past three, at which she pouted, if we may use so gross an expression about her, and said Why so shatteringly late? Not really shattering, said Canon Fewling, but he believed the Admiral sometimes slept in the afternoon and it would be a pity to disturb him.

"Well, they can't *all* go to sleep," said Rose. "Look here, Tubby, let's go quite early and then we could take Mrs. Phelps for a drive. Or Margot Phelps. They don't get about much, you know. Then we could be back in time for tea when the Admiral has woken up."

Again and again had Rose's least loving friends been reconverted to admiration by her quite unaffected way of thinking what other people would like. Finely self-centered in many ways, she had what one can only call a natural instinct for knowing what kind of treat people would like and really going out of her way to see that they got it, even if it were, as in the present instance, at someone else's expense—which indeed it usually was. Canon Fewling blamed himself severely for not having thought that a drive would be a treat for Mrs. Phelps or her daughter and felt like a murderer. But this feeling he did not let Rose see, nor would she, we think, have understood it if he had, for to her happy extrovert mind everything was ordinary and could be taken in one's stride, from a film of *Oliver Twist* to taking a retired Admiral's wife for a drive.

"I might ring up and ask," said Canon Fewling.

"Good gracious, I'd quite forgotten," said Rose.

As this appeared to be the beginning and end of her sentence Canon Fewling ventured to ask what it was she had forgotten.

"I was only suddenly thinking," said Rose, "that the Phelpses haven't got a telephone."

"I didn't know that," said Canon Fewling. "Does it get on the Admiral's nerves when he is ill?"

"I don't suppose so," said Rose, who was capable of letting the telephone ring itself to death if she was doing what she called reading a book, by which, in common with the great majority of women in this enlightened age, she meant a fashion paper or a magazine of potted and predigested articles supposed to help people to know all that was happening everywhere about everything. "But it costs too much."

"But then, if he is ill what happens?" said Canon Fewling, seriously perturbed by Rose's report.

"I don't know," said Rose. "There's the post office almost next door and the Vicarage just up the road and anyone in the village would let them use their telephone. But we must look into it, Tubby. Seriously, I mean. It's simply too shattering to think about, so I must do something," and with a wave of her well-manicured hand she went into her house.

About two o'clock, in obedience to Rose's suggestion, Canon Fewling took her aboard and set his course for Southbridge. They drove in silence, which for Rose was unusual. Suddenly she said, "Tubby, do you ever tell lies?"

Canon Fewling, not quite sure whether he was being appealed to as a pastor, an ex-sailor, or just a friend, was quite unable to find a ready answer. As far as he knew he was pretty truthful, partly by nature, partly because he rarely found himself in a position where a lie would be helpful. Also he knew that not only would he be found out at once but would have such remorse for what he had done that he wouldn't be able to sleep and, worst of all, though he had considerable confidence in his Creator's power of understanding and forgiveness he would never be able to forgive himself; which indeed is our worst punishment.

"I don't mean *real* lies," said Rose. "But if I could talk to Mrs. Phelps, and say we were all so worried about her and the Admiral not having a telephone and there was a Society of Friends of Retired Admirals or something that would like to contribute, would you back me up?" which ingenuous proposition took Canon Fewling so completely aback that he pulled up at the side of the road just where it ran level over the top of the downs.

"Quite honestly," he said, "I don't think I'd mind telling the lie, because I should get my punishment at once—I mean I would have a bad conscience. But I'm not sure if it is a useful lie. Would Mrs. Phelps believe it?"

"I had thought of that one," said Rose with great candour, "but I hoped you wouldn't. But look here, Tubby, there's another thing. The Croftses are away for a fortnight or three weeks and the man who is doing locum is pretty ghastly and so is his aunt. I saw them in Southbridge when they were there before.

I'm sure they'd be beastly about people using their telephone. We'd better wait and see what happens, perhaps."

Much relieved by Rose's attitude (though he had greatly admired her kindness in thinking about the telephone), Canon Fewling drove on and soon they were in Southbridge. The car was parked in the yard of the Red Lion, not lest anyone should think that Canon Fewling was proud, but because the little High Street was narrow and if he had left the new car outside Jutland Cottage it might easily have been scratched or banged by a reckless lorry driver.

Miss Phelps, in her usual outfit of trousers and shabby sports coat, received them with great cordiality and took them into the sitting-room where Admiral Phelps was reading one of Lisa Bedale's thrillers about Gerry Marston, the famous detective.

"Hullo, Admiral Phelps," said Rose. "I've brought Tubby over, at least he brought me, but I reminded him we were coming," at which remark the unfortunate Canon Fewling went very red in the face, but thought it better not to interfere. "How is Mrs. Phelps?"

"Oh, mother's quite all right," said Mrs. Phelps, a trifle too quickly and brightly perhaps. "She's just lying down for a bit, but she'll be down to tea."

"Well then, I'll talk to the Admiral, Tubby," said Rose, at once organising the party, "and you go and help Margot with whatever she's doing. And John sent you a bottle of curaçoa with his love, Admiral Phelps, and he said not to share it with *anyone* and keep it in the family."

The Admiral expressed genuine pleasure and Rose sat down just provocatively enough to make him feel that he was still a dashing sub-lieutenant, though he hadn't the faintest intention of behaving like one, while Canon Fewling obediently followed Miss Phelps into the kitchen.

"Do sit down," said Miss Phelps, flicking the seat of a kitchen chair with a duster. "I've only got to fry the onions and put them in the stew for supper and then if you don't mind coming into the garden I'll get on with a bit of digging."

"I like the smell of fried onion more than anything," said Canon Fewling, "but if you don't mind we won't go into the garden. I have to go over to Northbridge to ask Mr. Villars about something. I wish you would come with me. I promise to bring you back in plenty of time for tea. And if I may make a suggestion, you could put the onions in a very slow oven and leave them to fry themselves. About on One, or even A Half, and then they can't burn."

Miss Phelps looked perplexed.

"Oh, *gas* you mean," she said. "But we have a proper range," and she pointed with some pride to what Canon Fewling, used to more modern ways and well able to afford them, had not noticed; a small old-fashioned kitchen range with a large coal hod beside it. "Still, it's an idea. I could push the damper right in and leave them in some fat. Even if they aren't quite done I can finish them when we come back. But are you sure you really *want* to take me over to Northbridge—like this," she added, looking at her clothes and her hands.

Anyone who contracts the habit of receiving an invitation of whatever kind, from whomsoever, by asking if the giver really *means* it, is showing very bad manners, or at any rate very silly ones, embarrassing and annoying to the giver of the invitation. But with Miss Phelps it was so evidently a real and, so her guest thought, quite unnecessary humility. True her hands were work-stained and her clothes very unbecoming, but if Canon Fewling could take them in his stride surely Mrs. Villars could. He assured her that Mrs. Villars's hands were usually dirty with gardening and in fact that hardly any self-respecting woman had immaculate hands now, unless her trade or profession demanded it.

"Mrs. Fairweather has such lovely hands," said Miss Phelps wistfully, but at the same time rapidly cutting up her onions and putting them in a fireproof dish with a bit of dripping saved from last Sunday's bit of meat.

"Let me put the dish in the oven," said Canon Fewling. "Do you need any more coal putting on?" and with an expert's hand he took a kind of poker with a bent end from its corner by the range, lifted the round lid from the hole where one stokes the oven, tipped the hod over the hole, put the lid back, replaced the poker and said, "She'll do."

"How *do* you know all those things?" asked Miss Phelps, rapidly and carelessly washing her hands at the sink and part-drying them on a rather objectionable cloth. "Sorry the towel looks so filthy," she said. "I meant to wash out three today and somehow I didn't. Are you sure you *really* want me to come?"

A knock-down blow would have been a suitable answer but Canon Fewling, with admirable self-restraint, said he hated driving alone, which specious words Miss Phelps accepted if not as Bitter Truth at least at their face value and taking a rather toothless comb from her jacket pocket, gave her hair a stroke or two and followed her guest out of the kitchen.

"I left the car at the Red Lion in case it got scratched outside the house," said Canon Fewling. "You see, it is my new toy— almost my ewe lamb at the moment. What it really needs," he added, as they walked into the Red Lion's yard, "is one or two good scratches, or a dent in one wing. Then one wouldn't mind *what* happened next."

"Oh, but you *mustn't* let her get scratched," said Miss Phelps, looking with admiration at the sleeping monster. "She's as good as a first-rate destroyer. Gosh! What a good job! Can I look at the engine?"

Not displeased by the compliment, Canon Fewling lifted one side of the bonnet. Miss Phelps looked long and earnestly.

"She's a *marvel*," she said reverently. "How many cyclonic super-het revs?" or if those were not the exact words any others would be equally unmeaning to us.

Fascinated by his guest's professional knowledge, Canon

Fewling plunged into highly technical explanations, to all of which Miss Phelps listened attentively, putting in an intelligent question or comment from time to time, and so overcome by her competence was Canon Fewling that he asked her, with some hesitation, whether she would like to drive.

"Oh, Canon Fewling! I *couldn't*!" said Miss Phelps. "I mean it's most awfully kind of you, but I don't think I ought to. She's such a beauty. We had to give up our car. I mean she got so old that she cost too much in repairs and we didn't like to do hire-purchase, because you never know what might happen."

"But I don't suppose you have lost your skill," said Canon Fewling, which was very noble of him and not quite true.

"Well, not exactly," said Miss Phelps. "Miss Hampton and Miss Bent let me drive their car for them sometimes and she's a fairly new model. Miss Bent usually drives, but if she is too busy Miss Hampton gets me to drive her. She pays me too, which is quite useful."

"Can't she drive herself then?" said Canon Fewling who, in common with most people who did not know those ladies intimately, thought that Miss Hampton was, in all honour, the man of the party.

"Oh dear no," said Miss Phelps. "She doesn't know a thing about cars, or really about anything. It's Miss Bent who does all the things like putting in fuses or a new washer on the tap. You see, Miss Hampton has her work to think of."

"Well, well, well," said Canon Fewling, sitting down on an empty beer crate much as Miss Betsy Trotwood sat down in her garden path. "I thought I knew something of the world. But I don't. And that's that. And now, Miss Phelps, if you'll take the wheel I will sit beside you and try not to give advice."

Miss Phelps, apparently quite unable to speak and almost purple in the face with emotion, got into the driving seat. Canon Fewling took his place beside her and tried to think quickly of a suitable prayer. Not for himself, but for his beloved car. No words came to his mind, but what he was confusedly thinking was that surely a merciful Creator would not take advantage of an offer made with a real wish to give pleasure to someone who did not have much of it to the extent of allowing anything detrimental to happen to a new and rather expensive car. Having put up this unformulated prayer, he shut his eyes tightly and with the feeling that a mother may have when she is forced by circumstances to allow the adoption of a child by outsiders sat quite still and tried to resign himself to the will of Providence.

As Miss Phelps started the car, turned it out of the yard, took it kindly but firmly into the High Street, round by the Police Station and so onto the river road to Northbridge, the owner of the car gradually unstiffened and, once over the bridge, went so far as to open his eyes. To his shamed horror his guest, without taking her attention off the road, looked at him and smiled. Good fellow as he had thought her, he had grossly underestimated her gifts, and it became horridly obvious that not only was she a first-class driver but had also fully realised how anxious, not to say frightened, he was. A small herd of cows wandering under the charge of a highly incompetent hireling from a gate on the river side of the road to a gate on the other, or land side, appeared to offer no difficulty to Miss Phelps. As the last cow turned into the field she accelerated, took the next little hill like a bird, drove swiftly and smoothly beside the river, swung round to the left over Northbridge's elegant bridge (rebuilt about 1816 by a pupil of Rennie), up the High Street, past the little town hall on its stone legs and so down the lane to the Rectory, where she pulled up, quietly and competently, exactly opposite the gate.

As she got out she gave the steering-wheel the kind of pat that one gives to a good horse. Then she walked round to the other side of the car, facing Canon Fewling, who had already opened the gate.

"Thanks, Tubby," she said. "Thanks a *lot*," and went past him, up the flagged path.

What might have been an emotional moment was saved by

Mrs. Villars, who rose from the ground rather like Erda in The Ring and taking off a very dirty, damp gardening glove, shook hands with Canon Fewling in a very friendly way and then with Miss Phelps.

"You remember Miss Phelps, the day we went up the church tower," said Canon Fewling. "She drove me over. Her father is Admiral Phelps at Southbridge," which did not really explain anything, but Mrs. Villars was well used to people coming to the Rectory who were unable to give any coherent account of themselves and often mistook her for Someone Working in the Garden, as indeed she was, only unpaid, while she had to find out indirectly whether they were the Sunday School Outing, or Cruelty to Children, or the Wolf Cubs' Annual Entertainment, or which of the many charitable efforts which gave up time and energy to making both ends meet, all full of zeal in general and each distinctly jealous of the others.

"I'm Margot Phelps," said Miss Phelps, grasping Mrs. Villars's rather earthy hand in her own. "You know the Croftses at Southbridge. They are awfully good to father."

Mrs. Villars, who combined being a delightful and charming not-so-young woman with being one of the best clergy-wives in West Barsetshire—or so her husband said—almost at once took in Miss Phelps's words, remembered how Mrs. Crofts had once told her that the Phelpses were as poor as church mice, only naval mice, which was more of a come-down because the Admiral had had good pay when on the active list, and everyone knew that they practically lived on selling the best of their fowls and garden produce and eating the nasty bits themselves. This was of course just Mrs. Crofts's way of putting it, but Mrs. Villars, the latter part of whose life had been spent in a little town populated largely by old and elderly people living on pensions or such savings as the war had left them, had seen that life at close quarters and, we may add, was always using her garden, her hens, or her bees to help people who were too poor to have treats and too proud to speak about it.

"Gregory is in the study, Tubby," she said. "Do go in. Would you like to look at the garden, Miss Phelps? It's not at its best, I'm afraid."

"They never are," said Miss Phelps. "At least that's what I find. But what I'd like to see is your bees. Tub—I mean Canon Fewling told me about them."

"We all call him Tubby," said Mrs. Villars, pulling off her other glove. "We miss him dreadfully here, but we are so glad he has got good preferment and we hear all the gossip about him from his housekeeper who is a Northbridge woman. You'll stay to tea, won't you?"

Miss Phelps had at once taken a liking to Mrs. Villars and would have loved the treat of having tea at the Rectory. But she had left her mother lying down and felt she ought to get back and see about the tea before her mother began worrying about it.

"I'd love to," she said, "only I don't know—I can't quite explain, Mrs. Villars. I told Tubby I must get back. You see, father's rather an invalid and mother does really need a proper rest in the afternoon. Rose Fairweather is taking care of father, so *he's* all right."

"A quite *dreadful* girl she was," said Mrs. Villars placidly. "Her people could never control her. But her husband got the upper hand at once and he's never let go. She used to have quite frightful rages when she was a girl and practically drummed with her heels in the attic," and though this allusion passed over Miss Phelps, whose mother had not brought her up quite properly owing to their books being nearly always in store somewhere while she followed the flag, she thought it might have fitted a younger Rose quite well and liked Rose the better for it, having a pretty strong temper of her own which circumstances and her excellent heart had helped her to subdue.

"Well, if you can't stay, I will tell Gregory to hurry up with whatever he is talking to Tubby about," said Mrs. Villars, which showed true kindness. "I'll just show you the bees and we'll go in."

So the bees were inspected and admired and Miss Phelps asked some intelligent questions about what kind of bees and what price and then her hostess took her indoors.

"I expect you'd like to wash," she said. "Looking at other people's gardens always seems to get on one's hands and under one's nails."

"I'm afraid everything's always on my hands and under my nails, though I do keep them as short as I can," said Miss Phelps.

"One can't help it in a garden," said Mrs. Villars, showing her own hands. But there was a difference and Mrs. Villars, a great deal of whose life was spent in doing things quietly for other people, felt that this was the moment to tell Miss Phelps some of the more useful facts of life.

"I'll show you what I do," she said, taking Miss Phelps into a small room with six grey marble basins in a row. "One of the former Rectors had a small school for backward little boys here—not lunatics, just a bit slow—and he did very well by them. That's why there are so many basins. I use it as a flower room. I suppose you wash with soap?"

Miss Phelps said she washed with anything. Sometimes with the yellow soap, sometimes with some of the soap powders if she was washing out clothes, only one's hands seemed to get horrider and horrider.

"Now, I am going to tell you something interesting that I am sure you would like to try," said Mrs. Villars, assuming unconsciously rather the voice in which she gave Talks to Women's Institutes or the Conservative Association's Local Branch. "The first thing is to *start* the day with absolutely clean hands."

"I do," said Miss Phelps obediently. "I always have a bath before I go to bed, only the boiler eats fuel so fast that I don't have a very hot one."

"Tepid chalk and water," said Mrs. Villars. "*I* know the Southbridge water. Luckily we've got a well here. So you can have a good wash in soft water," and as if Miss Phelps were a little girl she half filled the basin for her and took some pleasure in watching her guest's face as the soft soapy water melted the dirt from her rather rough hands.

"How *lovely*," she said, as she dried them. "I do wish we could have a water softener, but they cost so much. No wonder your hands look so nice."

"I haven't as much to do as you have, my dear," said Mrs. Villars. "Northbridge is still rather feudal and I can get some servants. It was difficult when tea was rationed, and I had to buy China for myself, which the lower orders don't like, or I would never have had a cup to give to my guests. Now, my dear, I'm going to give you some good advice and a present, only you must promise to do exactly as I tell you."

"I promise," said Miss Phelps, more like a good little girl than a not very young house and garden female worker.

"I am going to give you this jar of cream stuff," said Mrs. Villars. "Have you a rain barrel, by the way?"

"Well, we have, but last summer it got empty and I forgot about it and of course it had got spilt."

"We'll talk about that later," said Mrs. Villars, now running the First Aid Instruction Class, as she had done during the war. "Anyway, wash first thing, the moment you get up, and rub quite a little of this cream well into your fingers and round your nails. It will dry almost at once. Then carry on with the cooking and the housework, and when you want to wash again the dirt will come rolling off with the cream. I shall ring up to ask if you are remembering and find out when you need a new pot, because it is very difficult to get," which was quite untrue, but Mrs. Villars felt, correctly, that Miss Phelps would believe anything she said.

"Oh, *thank* you," said Miss Phelps, her face bright red with embarrassed pleasure. "Only would you mind if I wrote to you? I don't mean that anyone would listen or anything, but we haven't a telephone."

"Well, send me a postcard," said Mrs. Villars placidly. "Now come and meet my husband before you go," and she took Miss

Phelps to the study where her husband, having polished off what he wanted to discuss with Canon Fewling, was going over with him the happy days of the war.

"My present priest-in-charge at St. Sycorax isn't a patch on you, Fewling," said Mr. Villars. "One doesn't see queues on winter mornings for the early service now. I don't know what the old women are coming to."

Canon Fewling was about to argue this with the Rector when he saw Miss Phelps looking at him in a kind of dumb agony.

"I am so sorry," he said, getting up with the swift movement that always surprised people. "I am quite ready."

"Miss Phelps has to get back to Southbridge because her mother isn't well, Gregory," said Mrs. Villars.

"I am indeed sorry," said the Rector. "I was somehow under the impression that it was your father. Nothing serious, I hope."

"Well, it is father, really," said Miss Phelps, "because he gets such bad bronchitis and it is bad for his heart. But mother gets so awfully tired that I try to make her lie down, and then this afternoon Mrs. Fairweather came over with Canon Fewling and she said she would sit with father while we just came over here. But if mother gets up and finds I've left father she might worry. Thank you very much all the same and thanks most *awfully*, Mrs. Villars, for the stuff. I'll try hard to use it and I'll see if I can get someone in the village to mend the rainwater barrel," and she might have gone on thanking people for ever had not Canon Fewling taken her, very kindly and politely, by the elbow and almost run her down the path, out of the gate and into the car.

"I'll drive," he said. "You just try to rest. We'll be back by a quarter-past four exactly."

For the next few months, or rather as long as his friends could bear to hear him telling the story, did P.C. Haig Brown (nephew of Mr. Brown at the Red Lion, Southbridge) bore his circle of acquaintance by his epic story of how the car belonging to the Reverend Fewling (a form of address which appears, horribly, to have become part of Modern English Usage), coming along the river road from Northbridge, had almost collided with Lady Waring's car (for there are still a number of people who hold, with what dim atavistic stirrings we cannot say, that it is rude to say Lady Mary Brown or Dame Mary Brown and so darken counsel and confuse the issue by saying Lady Brown and Dame Brown) turning off to the road over the downs, and how he, Haig Brown, seemed to come over queer being as he'd never had to deal with a car accident and couldn't remember which side of a cut you ought to tie a handkerchief round a person's arm on if the blood was Gushing out of it, and how, owing to the great skill of both drivers, nothing had happened at all. Lady Cora pulled up and signalled to Canon Fewling, who slowed down.

"Sorry," said her ladyship. "My fault."

"Not a bit," said Canon Fewling; "I was doing a good sixty. Fewling's my name."

"Mine's Cora Waring," said her ladyship. "I've heard about you from Mr. Wickham, the Mertons' agent over at Northbridge. I hope I didn't frighten your passenger."

"So do I," said Canon Fewling, though quite kindly. "I expect your husband knows her father, Lady Cora. Rear-Admiral Phelps, retired, Jutland Cottage, Southbridge."

"If he doesn't, he shall," said her ladyship, and with a friendly wave of her hand she sped up the downs road.

"Lady Cora's husband was in the Royal Navy, but he had an old bit of shrapnel or something in him and has been retired," said Canon Fewling, starting the car again.

"Like father," said Miss Phelps, not without pride.

"Very much the same," said Canon Fewling placidly. "They both do a lot of good in their different ways. You know Wickham. You must get him to tell you about the Warings. He knows Lady Cora quite well. Here we are and only twenty minutes past four," and he stopped at the door of Jutland Cottage.

"Thanks most awfully," said Miss Phelps. "I do hope father and Mrs. Fairweather won't think we are late. Come in."

There was an unexpected sound of voices from the sitting-room. Miss Phelps cautiously opened the door a very little way to look. An elderly man and woman, unknown by sight to Canon Fewling, were seated in a determined way in the drawing-room; the man, if collars are any criterion, a clergyman.

"Goodness," said Miss Phelps, backing Canon Fewling and herself into the passage. "It's that Mr. Horton who is doing locum for Colonel Crofts and his aunt. Oh dear! It will tire mother so dreadfully."

Canon Fewling, suddenly speaking with authority, said he was sure Rose Fairweather was more than a match for any callers, and if Miss Phelps would begin getting tea ready he would go and help to defend the Admiral and, what was more, would get the visitors away by fair means or foul if they seemed to be tiring her father. Casting a flurried but grateful look at him, Miss Phelps went to the kitchen, where she could be heard rattling the poker between the bars of the fire, the better to encourage it to burn, while Canon Fewling went into the drawing-room. A quick glance showed him that Rose had, with skill and prudence, put herself between the Admiral and his visitors obviously as a protective measure.

"Hullo, Tubby, I *am* glad you're back," said Rose. "It's Mr. Horton and his aunt, stopgapping for Colonel Crofts. They were here for a bit—just after the war, wasn't it?" she added, turning to the guests with the air of a schoolmistress who hopes her young scholars will not disgrace her in public.

Mr. Horton, a tall, elderly bony man with a kind of ecclesiastical grizzled side whiskers, rose and shook hands with Canon Fewling. He then sat down again, folded his long bony hands, finger-tip to finger-tip, and gently beat the air with his right leg, which was crossed over his left leg. His aunt, a tall gaunt woman with a long face and bony ankles, also shook hands, and then, turning to her nephew, remarked that she had been telling him for the last five or six years that he ought to go to a better tailor, which remark, obviously induced by the sight of Canon Fewling's clerical outfit, made no apparent effect at all upon him.

"I would give you my tailor's name with pleasure," said Canon Fewling, rather uncertain which of the visitors he should address, and as the only result of his kind offer was to make aunt and nephew look at each other with considerable want of affection, he felt he might as well have held his tongue.

"We gather that the services have become, shall I say slightly more ultramontane, since I had the charge of Southbridge," said Mr. Horton.

"No harm in that, Dunstan," said his aunt.

"No, Aunt Monica?" said Mr. Horton.

Had Mrs. Francis Brandon, she who used to be Mrs. Arbuthnot, been present, she could have told the company that these bickerings between aunt and nephew meant nothing at all, but to unaccustomed onlookers it was disconcerting.

"I always think," said Rose Fairweather, who had obviously never thought at all in her life, but was a creature endowed with a happy instinct for keeping things smooth, however foolish she appeared, "that it's six of one and half a dozen of the other. I mean, when Tubby—that's Canon Fewling—was at Northbridge he was *frightfully* High because all the old ladies liked it, but when he came to Greshamsbury he *most* kindly got lower, because they like it. And after all St. Paul said he was made all things to all men," and she looked round for approval. The Admiral was obviously too tired to hear or understand. Canon Fewling, having suddenly found that beauty lived not only with kindness but with a sound knowledge of the Epistle to the Romans, was so busy grappling with this double manifestation of the goddess—not that he would have consciously applied the word to Rose—that he felt unequal to any comment.

"Well, it was most shatteringly nice of you to come," said Rose, getting up, "and I think it would really be too too kind if you didn't come again while you are here, because the Admiral gets so tired. And if he gets tired absolutely *anything* might happen," she added, leaving her hearers to decide whether the anything might be a stroke or a violent personal attack on themselves. "So goodbye," she went on, "and it was awfully nice to meet you, and Canon Fewling was awfully pleased too—weren't you, Tubby?"

Canon Fewling, who had been entirely absorbed in admiration of Rose's shock tactics, came to with a start and said it had been a great pleasure.

Aunt and nephew then said goodbye. Canon Fewling took them to the front door and had the pleasure of observing that a violent quarrel between them must be brewing, for they walked down the little path in single file and Mr. Horton almost slammed the little gate behind him in his aunt's face.

"You go and talk to the Admiral," said Rose, "and I'll go and help Margot with the tea," so Canon Fewling went back to the drawing-room and asked the Admiral exactly what part he had taken in the Battle of Jutland. Once started, the Admiral's look of patient endurance melted away and he spoke almost with fire of that glorious fight, addressing Canon Fewling as if he had been a junior officer in the flagship, much to that cleric's delight, so that by the time Mrs. Phelps, followed by Rose and Miss Phelps and tea came in, everything was calm, and after tea Canon Fewling said he must be getting back.

"So must I," said Rose. "I say, Tubby, can I drive going back?"

"That," said Canon Fewling firmly, "is the one thing I cannot nor will not do, even for you," which words, for some reason not very clear to her, gave Miss Phelps great pleasure.

"Well," said Rose, as the car soared up the road by the downs, "I think we've done a good day's work."

"You have," said Canon Fewling. "Not I. I couldn't have given them their congé as you did. I daresay the Hortons think Admiral Phelps is a criminal lunatic by now, but it was worth it."

"*Can* I drive for a bit?" said Rose, we will not say snuggling up against Canon Fewling, but conveying an aura of snuggling.

"Again, certainly not," said the Canon. "I admire your skill and your courage with those visitors more than I can say, but that is quite different. Please don't ask me again. I do hate saying no, but no it will be."

"You let Margot Phelps drive," said Rose, almost pouting, if we may use that old-fashioned word, but in a most attractive way.

"I did," said Canon Fewling, "and for two reasons. One is that she has hardly any treats in her life, the other is that she has quite excellent hands and road sense."

"Haven't I nice hands?" said Rose, in her pouting voice and laying her right hand, which if not beautiful was exquisitely cared for, on Canon Fewling's left hand.

"Now, don't do that," said Canon Fewling. "That's the way nine out of ten accidents happen. You have very nice hands, but Miss Phelps has capable hands—a workman's hands, if you like. And she hasn't the time and I'm pretty sure she hasn't the money to try to keep them nice."

Rose did not answer, evidently thinking, or doing what passed in her mind for thinking, about Miss Phelps's state. Canon Fewling drove in silence, miserably wondering if he had hurt Rose, yet feeling that he was right to speak as he did—a situation that we all find ourselves in far too often.

"You win, Tubby," said a chastened voice beside him. "You know I can't think. That's what's wrong with me. But John knew that before he married me and that's partly why I adore him so. I can't tell you how wonderful it is to have a husband who adores one even if one is silly."

"Or because one is silly," said Canon Fewling, but he said these words in an abstracted way, as if thinking aloud to himself.

There was silence for a time and now, as they began to go down again towards Greshamsbury, Canon Fewling wondered if he had been too harsh.

"I say, Tubby, you are quite shatteringly marvellous," said Rose suddenly. "I always wondered why John adored me and now I know. And what is so nice," she continued in a voice of deep satisfaction, "is that I shall never disappoint him, because I can't help being silly."

"Now that's enough," said Canon Fewling, whom the events of the afternoon seemed to have brought into closer relation with Rose and perhaps into a clearer understanding of her. "You women are all alike," at which Rose pouted and took out her powder and lipstick. "You like to pretend you are everything you are not. Don't forget, my girl, that I was a clergyman in Northbridge for a good many years, and just because I had a cassock practically every woman over forty-five, or even forty, I regret to say it of your sex, had a kind of—I really don't know how to put it——"

"I know *exactly* what you mean," said Rose, her lovely refurbished face alive with interest; "like having a crush on the Science Mistress. We all had a crush on someone at the Barchester High School, but we all got uncrushed again. And when I met some of the mistresses at an Old Girls' Meeting after I was married, which I never did again for it was quite shatteringly boring, I couldn't think how I could have been so quite frustratingly silly," to which Canon Fewling replied calmly that it was a perfectly normal part of life and speaking for himself, he had feelings for the Head Prefect at his prep. school only just this side idolatry.

"So then I got married," said Rose, "and of course I adored John and always shall."

"And I didn't," said Canon Fewling.

"Was there Someone?" said Rose.

For a moment Canon Fewling did not understand what she meant. When he did he rather shocked her by laughing quite loudly.

"I have often thought," he said, "that it would be very nice to *be* married, but as I have never met any girl—or woman—that I could bear the thought of being married to, I have remained a bachelor. And a very happy one, I must say, especially since I came to Greshamsbury, where no one pursues me."

"Like the wicked flea," said Rose meditatively. Her companion asked what on earth she meant, rapidly substituting the words What on earth for What the hell, which had more easily occurred to his mind.

"Oh, it's only a kind of joke," said Rose, which naturally made Canon Fewling ask what kind.

"Well, it's rather irreligious," said Rose, turning her lovely eyes full on him to see how he would stand it.

"That's what I'm here for," said Canon Fewling. "I don't want to boast, but I don't think anyone could hurt or annoy me about what I revere and trust. Fire away."

Encouraged, though more by the last words, which she understood, than by the first to which she had not paid much attention, Rose said, in the voice which was encouraged by Miss Hippersley in the Upper Fifth Literature class at the Barchester High School, "'The wicked flea, when no man pursueth but the righteous, is bold as a lion,'" at which we regret (not really) to say that Canon Fewling, who had somehow missed that crusted bit of schoolboy wit, laughed loudly and appreciatively and finally pulled the car in to the side of the road, the better to enjoy it.

"Really, Tubby, you don't seem to know *anything*," said Rose, out of her experience of life.

"Sorry," said Canon Fewling. "Being in the Navy does get one a bit out of the way of knowing ordinary things and living in Northbridge was rather the same. I think Greshamsbury will be much more helpful. And now I'll drop you at your house. And thank you more than I can say for what you have done. If the Phelpses are kept safe till the Vicar and Mrs. Crofts come back, we shall be all right. And doubtless the warmer weather will be a help to the Admiral."

"I suppose as I'm a woman I can't help thinking about women," said Rose, who was by now standing on the path and had to bend a little to speak to the Rector, owing to the lowness of modern cars, "and it's Mrs. Phelps that worries me. She's the wrong colour. And I know she has a heart. I think I'd better have a word with Dr. Ford. Goodbye, Tubby," and she went into the house.

On the same evening Rose had a long talk on the telephone with Kate Carter, whose husband was the Headmaster of South-bridge School. Though Kate was older than Rose and far more sensible, she was fond of her and realised that Rose had excellences which were quite out of her own line. Kate gladly agreed to become one of the Friends of the Phelpses and said she would see that one or two of the nicest Senior Masters and their wives, if they were married, should look in from time to time, and that she knew Matron would love to pop in, which, she explained, was Matron's way of putting it, not her own, though she might have saved her breath, as Rose was completely uncritical of anything except deliberate bad manners or unkindness. And the better to further the plans of the Friends of the Phelpses, she promised to have a sherry party within the next week and make a kind of list, so that someone would look in on the Admiral every day.

"What we need," said Rose, "is to get Margot out a bit too. If someone could just sit in the house in the afternoon, while Mrs. Phelps rests, Margot could get right away for a couple of hours. I'm going to get Mr. Wickham onto it, because he is frightfully kind and was in the Navy in the war. We must rally till the Croftses come back and then they'll help to cope," which words, though highly inelegant, Kate thought quite sensible. And then Rose, upon whom heaven in addition to her beauty and her silliness and her underlying kindness of heart had bestowed the great gift of never worrying, took her mind off the Phelpses altogether and went to stay with her parents for a few days and then to London with her husband, for her boys were safely at school and her little girls had a perfectly good Nanny.

Kate Carter, whose husband often compared her in his mind with Dr. Johnson's General Oglethorpe, driven by strong benevolence of soul, was as good as her word and had a small informal sherry party in the Headmaster's house, inviting Mr. Shergold, the Senior Housemaster, who had done war service in the Navy, and all the inhabitants of Wiple Terrace, from Miss Hampton and Miss Bent at one end, through Mr. Traill and Mr. Feeder, to Mr. Feeder's mother. All her invitations were accepted and the Red Lion benefited therefrom, as it was the habit of Wiple Terrace to celebrate any small local festivity by carrying on the party till a late hour at one or other of their houses.

About half-past five on the day of the party Dr. Ford, who had been rather unsympathetically inspecting two very light cases of measles in the sanatorium, dropped in at the Headmaster's house, nominally for a cup of tea but really to unburden himself to Kate Carter, for whom he had a great liking, of some of the county gossip. Everard Carter had said rather unsympathetically that Ford was the Man with a Load of Mischief, but on being reminded by his wife how good Dr. Ford had been when the children had chicken-pox he repented. It was one of the usual chill summer days, and when Dr. Ford saw a fire in the drawing-room he expressed approval and told Kate she was a very sensible woman.

"So is Mrs. Morland," he added. "Her house is always warm, even in summer. Why we all go on living in England I don't know."

"Mostly because we can't get out of it," said Everard Carter. "One can't take enough money to have a proper holiday. Also one gets rather ashamed of having to count every franc, especially as I still think of francs as about twenty-five to the pound instead of seven or eight million. And one could buy something with twenty-five francs then. How are the measlers?"

Dr. Ford said as near malingering as made no odds and had they heard that Lady Silverbridge had another boy, which somehow cheered everybody, for if we are to keep our aristocracy they must have some heirs.

"Too many peers, all the same," said Dr. Ford. "I remember

when old What's-his-name threatened to create a couple of hundred new peers to swamp the House of Lords politically what a row there was. Now every Tom, Dick and Harry gets a peerage. Just look at Aberfordbury or whatever his name is, Sir Ogilvy Hibberd that was. Man who wanted to get Pooker's Piece built on, but old Lord Pomfret spiked his guns."

Kate Carter asked how.

"Bought it," said Dr. Ford. "And he managed to get it cheap. The only man who ever got the better of old Hibberd."

"How *does* one get the better of people?" said Kate Carter. "I never can."

"Don't ask me," said Dr. Ford. "Pomfret did it by being gloriously rude and paying no attention to what the other fellow said. I sometimes think that Adams, the man who married Lucy Marling and owns the big Hogglestock works, is the nearest approach to old Lord Pomfret that we've got. He just makes up his mind what he wants to do, and when he is perfectly sure he does it. Mind you, he's not a pirate and he'll listen to reason. If you can prove to him that he is wrong he isn't above acknowledging it."

"What about Gillie Pomfret?" said Everard Carter, speaking of the present Earl.

"First-rate mind and heart," said Dr. Ford, speaking in a professional voice. "And plenty of character, but not enough stamina behind it. His elder son is going to be like him. Now Lady Emily and the Honourable Giles are pure Pomfret, tough as they make them. And of the three, Emily—she's about twelve now—has far the most character. Too many of our women have more character than the men now. Can't say why. May be the war, or it mayn't. But I get about the county a good deal and I see it again and again."

Kate, at once turning from the general to the particular, as our sex is apt to do, said certainly Angela ruled the nursery, but she thought Bobbie and Phil had plenty of character and anyway Bobbie was at school now. Which really did not prove anything.

Then the sherry party began to drop in. Dr. Ford said he must go, but Kate said Certainly not, as he was an Interested Party, because they were going to talk about what could be done for the Phelpses and they were his patients. All the more reason, said Dr. Ford, not to interfere. Doctors, he said, had to be careful.

"Not all doctors," said Mrs. Feeder from Edith Cottage, the widowed and extremely active mother of one of the Assistant Masters. "Certainly not you, Dr. Ford. Did you or did you not let my son know that I had broken my wrist, just when he was going to Switzerland last winter? If I hadn't rung him up myself with a trunk call to London and told him not to be silly he would have been hanging about Wiple Terrace being a nuisance instead of getting some good bracing air."

"And breaking his ankle skiing," said Dr. Ford.

"It did him no harm," said Mrs. Feeder. "The Swiss doctors know their job and he got splendidly brown. And I was perfectly safe. You looked in—not that there was anything to look at with plaster all over my arm—and everyone from the Terrace came and had drinks with me. You must let old people kill themselves in their own way, you know."

Dr. Ford said that was a true word, and when Mrs. Feeder was an old person he would think about it, at which Mrs. Feeder, who was certainly as old as he was and probably older, cackled in scorn, though we believe she liked the flattery all the same.

Mrs. Feeder was followed by Miss Hampton and Miss Bent. Sherry was circulated and as soon as they were released from their other duties Mr. Shergold the Senior Housemaster came in, followed by Mr. Traill and Mr. Feeder. Kate said she would not apologise for the sherry, but she had made a vow, a very unwilling vow, against gin because it cost so much, which she said, made her feel rather horrid.

"No need at all, my dear," said Mrs. Feeder. "None of us in Wiple Terrace have children to think of."

Mr. Feeder, overhearing this remark, asked what about himself?

"If you read your Bible," said his mother, fixing him with her Ancient-Mariner-like eye, "you would know that when you were a child, which you certainly aren't now, you spoke as a child and very backward you were; and understood as a child, which didn't amount to much; and thought as a child which, goodness knows, you often still do; and when you became a man I really didn't find much difference except that you became very expensive till you got a job," by which gloss on First Corinthians, chapter xiii, verse 11, the School Chaplain, known to everyone as Holy Joe, who came in at that moment, was impressed and slightly alarmed, for he had a feeling—in which we may say he was perfectly correct—that Mrs. Feeder might say absolutely anything.

"And it is no use your telling me if I want to learn anything to ask my husbands at home, like St. Paul," said Mrs. Feeder, instantly forestalling any possible attack, "because my husband— and, anyway, I only had one—has been dead for several years. And even if I had asked him he probably wouldn't have known the answer," which so terrified the Chaplain, who had no idea of telling Mrs. Feeder any such thing, that he took refuge with the ladies from Adelina, who in spite of their manly bearing were extremely kind.

"Now," said Kate, feeling that this discussion had better be closed, "that we are all here and Doctor Ford too, I am glad to say, we can really talk about Jutland Cottage," which was a tactical error, for each person present began to say what she, or he, thought.

Everard Carter, who had been talking to Mr. Shergold, stood up and the talking died down.

"It is simply a question of what we can do to help Admiral and Mrs. Phelps," he said.

"And Margot," said Miss Hampton. "Good girl with no nonsense about her. Can get the better of a billy-goat. Seen her do it."

"And of course Miss Phelps," said Everard. "It really boils

down to this. The Admiral isn't well, as we all know. Mrs. Phelps must have a rest between lunch and tea or she will break down. Margot is one of the best and kindest daughters I have ever met, but she has the vegetables and the animals and all the cooking and most of the housework. No one gets a holiday. Colonel Crofts and his wife do a good deal for them, but they are away. Now this isn't my idea, it is Rose Birkett's—I mean Rose Fairweather. If we can run a kind of Friends of the Phelpses society, quite quietly, we might be able to help. For instance, Rose Birkett—well, she *was* Rose Birkett and I'll stick to the names as we all know it—suggested that if someone could drop in between lunch and tea it would be company for the Admiral, who never sleeps in the daytime, it would give Mrs. Phelps a chance to have two hours' complete freedom to rest without worrying, and it would set Margot free to do her animals and vegetables."

"It's Margot that carries it all, you know," said a voice from near the door. Everyone turned to look and there was Mr. Wickham, who was almost universally welcome in the county. "It's not setting free to work that she needs. It's a change. Something to take the girl out of herself. Rose rang me up and told me about the Friends of the Phelpses, and I had to come over to see Brown at the Red Lion, so I thought I'd come along. Any objections?"

None was raised, nor was there any place, we think (except perhaps at the Palace, where Mr. Wickham would not have dreamed of setting foot) where he was not welcome for one reason or another. And we may add that though his frequent gifts of spirituous liquor were gratefully received and fairly shared, he would have been just as welcome had he come dry-handed.

"I suppose, Dr. Ford," said Miss Bent, "it would not be in order to ask your professional opinion."

"Well," said Dr. Ford, "as I haven't the faintest idea what you want to ask me, I couldn't say. All I will say is that Mrs. Phelps and Margot are killing themselves. The Admiral luckily doesn't see it, or he'd never sleep again, and with his bronchitis he doesn't get much sleep, anyway. If I thought they could do him any good in London I'd drive him up myself. It's bound to come."

"The really important thing," said Miss Hampton, screwing her monocle into her eye, "is to keep Margot alive till her parents are dead, or one of them. If she cracks—and crack she will at this rate—it will mean hospital for her and then what happens to the Admiral and Mrs. Phelps? Canon Fewling is extremely kind to them, but he has his own parish to run."

"Excuse me, madam," said Edward, the highly respectable ex-odd-job-man who had been butler in the Headmaster's House since his predecessor went to the Jorams in the Close, "but it is the Reverend Fewling at Greshamsbury wishing to speak to Mr. Wickham if he is here."

"Well, you can tell him I jolly well am here and well do you know it, considering you let me in," said Mr. Wickham, getting up. "Will you allow me to leave you for a few minutes, Mrs. Carter?" and he followed Edward to the telephone, while the meeting went off onto the subject of the very dashing new perm with a henna dye lately acquired by Eileen at the Red Lion, so that his return a few minutes later was almost a disappointment.

"Sorry, all," said Mr. Wickham. "Just a job Tubby wants me to do at Jutland Cottage. Rain-barrel's leaking and Tubby doesn't know who can mend barrels. Look here, Carter, what about your school carpenter? Snow's the name, isn't it? He'll know. Do you mind?" to which Everard of course replied that the sooner it was done the better and he thought Mr. Wickham would find Snow at the Red Lion, which was in any case on the direct route to his cottage.

"Then I'll be off," said Mr. Wickham. "Thank you for letting me come, Mrs. Carter. And I'll see the old Admiral gets his grog all right. As a matter of fact I've got a bottle of Navy rum in my car. Fellow called Jones—you wouldn't know him, we had a drink or two at Sheerness once—was passing my way the day before yesterday and brought me a couple. If I'd known about the Friends of the Phelpses I wouldn't have drunk the other bottle, but when an old pal gives you a drink you *must* go halves."

"Quite right," said Miss Hampton. "Fairdooze, I always say, Fairdooze," after which Mr. Wickham said goodbye to the Carters and drove down to the village. With unerring instinct he went into the tap-room of the Red Lion and enquired for Mr. Snow, who came forward slowly, as befits a master carpenter.

"Wickham," said that gentleman. "Agent for Mr. Melton over at Northbridge. I remember you when you were doing up Editha Cottage for Mrs. Arbuthnot and her sister-in-law. Bookshelves, four six and a half, wasn't it, and a nice job too. What's yours?"

Pint of the usual if it was all the same, said Snow, which is clear enough if you get it clear. Yes, he added, four six and a half it was. Those ladies, he said, wanted four foot three, but seeing as he had some nice bits of wood, good wood too, four six and a half, what he said was why not *have* them four six and a half.

After disposing of this question and another pint, Mr. Wickham carelessly asked if Snow knew a cooper. There was a rain-barrel, he said, in Admiral Phelp's back-yard and they'd forgotten to fill it up and after that dry spell one of the staves was a bit loose and it stood to reason the longer it stood like that the worse it would get.

With this Snow agreed and over another pint made the suggestion that he should come up with his mate next day and see what he could do. Coopering, he said, was coopering, but nowadays there was hardly a tradesman as properly knew his trade. His mate, he said, was what you might call a bit soft, but give him a saw and a bit of wood, or a hammer and some nails and you wouldn't think him soft. And, he added, his mate had been at old Pilward's Brewery and knew a bit about casks and he didn't mind having one more if the gentleman was agreeable. Mr. Wickham was highly agreeable and Snow promised to go up to Jutland Cottage next day and see what he could do. No man, he said, could do more than he *could* do, but if that bit of work could be done, done it should be. So they had another pint and Mr. Wickham got into his car. He rather thought of stopping at Jutland Cottage and breaking the news, but it might seem as if he wanted to be thanked, so he went quietly round to the back door, which was open, and put the Navy rum on the kitchen table. As he was going out he met Miss Phelps, who had been feeding the hens, and said he hoped she wouldn't mind if the School carpenter came up and repaired the rain-barrel next day, to which her only answer was "Oh," but not a disapproving Oh.

"And please could you tell me how much it would cost?" she said.

Damn all women! said Mr. Wickham to himself, but aloud he said that was nothing to do with her because it was a present from a friend and a surprise for her father.

"Oh, Wicks," said Miss Phelps. "A most extraordinary thing. There's a bottle of Navy rum on the kitchen table. Can it have got there by mistake?"

"It's from a pal of mine," said Mr. Wickham. "He thought your father might like it. I didn't want to disturb you so I just shoved it into the kitchen. That's all right. Have some yourself too—boiling water and sugar. Make you sleep. Goodbye," and with a kind of naval salute he went away.

CHAPTER 6

Mr. Wickham, as all his friends would agree, was a chap who would always do anything for a chap who was down on his luck. Not that he didn't enjoy the company of those who were on the top of the wave, but almost anyone who, in his own language, told him the tale was pretty sure of sympathy and a generous uncorking of bottles. His duties as general bailiff and overseer for the Noel Mertons were never neglected; and out of office hours, which hours were capricious in the extreme, so long as the place was looked after, his employer turned, as Mr. Wickham said, a deaf eye to things. The county had of course married him to more than one lady, and it was commonly believed that he had proposed to Miss Arbuthnot, she who was now the wife of Colonel the Reverend Edward Crofts, but he kept his own counsel and remained one of the most popular men in West Barsetshire, with friends everywhere from Gatherum Castle, where the Duke and Duchess of Omnium still managed to live in a corner of their hideous and fairly ancestral mansion, to the cottages at Grumpers End, which had been condemned some dozen years earlier and luckily overlooked, for if their inhabitants had been turned out there would certainly not have been anywhere to put them, partly owing to shortage of houses and partly because they were all so happily dirty and slovenly that any house they were put in would, in Modern English Usage, have deteriated within a week beyond recognition.

Mr. Wickham had always liked the Phelps family. For the Admiral he felt a proper respect, being an ex-naval man (temporary) himself. In Mrs. Phelps he found a pleasant, motherly, easy affection which he much enjoyed, having (as he rather loosely put it) never had a mother himself, and for Miss Phelps he had what we may best describe as the unemotional affection felt by Mr. Wemmick for Miss Skiffins, though if he had gradually slipped his arm round her waist it is quite possible that she would not have noticed it, having spent so much of her life among junior naval officers that she looked upon them all, on the whole, as younger brothers who merely required something to eat and a listener. And if we do not say drink, it is because the many lieutenants and sub-lieutenants who had at one time or another frequented Jutland Cottage had kind and thoughtful hearts for a retired Admiral and more often than not brought a bottle of something with them.

Meanwhile the Society of Friends of the Phelpses had not been wanting in zeal. For every day while the temporary Vicar and his aunt were in residence would one or other of the Southbridge members look in, both morning and afternoon, often bringing a bit of garden produce, or a couple of tins out of one of the generous parcels from U.S.A., or a book. From Greshamsbury Rose Fairweather or her husband came with some naval gossip, or to show the Admiral Rose's newest style in cosmetics, and through them the Greshams visited Jutland Cottage; and as Captain Gresham had been a prisoner of war in the Far East during the 1939 war and the Admiral had been on duty there during the 1914 war they were able to discover, with considerable interest, that they had practically no people nor places in common. But they liked each other and the Admiral, much to his own satisfaction, had been able to introduce Captain Gresham to Admiral Mahan's *Influence of Sea-Power on History*, going so far as to lend him his own copy which Captain Gresham accepted gratefully, took home and kept for three weeks and then returned to the Admiral with profuse thanks.

He afterwards, when telling his wife about it, said he had felt a double-faced brute, as the real truth was that he had read it a long time ago and admired it and didn't want to read it again, but as the Admiral did all the talking he had not been found out. Much to Miss Phelps's pleasure several of the elder boys took to dropping in with offers of help in kitchen or garden. Leslie Minimus managed to break a tine of the old garden fork while turning the earth, as he had been specially warned not to do, too near the roots of a particularly gnarled, obdurate old pear tree. Frank Gresham helped Miss Phelps to make toffee by spilling it all over the top of the stove, making such a smell and mess as brought the Admiral in from his armchair, full of quarter-deck wrath. But no one could be angry with Frank Gresham for long (and well he knew it, with the devilish insight of boys) and the end of the matter was that Frank and the Admiral cleaned the stove together while Miss Phelps consulted Snow, the School carpenter, who with his mate was reconstructing the rain-barrel, about the broken fork.

"Varmints, that's what boys are," said Snow, but without rancour, "and that young Gresham, he's another. You give me the old fork, Miss Phelps, I'll see to it," which Miss Phelps gladly and trustingly did, and what with a couple of pints at the Red Lion and one thing and another the blacksmith who, we are glad to say, still found some work to do in an agricultural and hunting county, routed out from the miscellaneous heap at the back of his shop a perfectly good fork with a broken handle, and out of the two wrecks he and Snow produced a good, solid tool.

"She," said Snow to the Admiral, who was smoking a pipe in the little orchard before lunch, "ought to do a tidy job of work now. And the old rain-butt, she's finished now, sir. Me and my mate we've made a good job of it. Last you a lifetime, she will, if she isn't allowed to stand empty. Now a rain-butt, she's like a man's innards. Needs filling, she does. It stands to reason if a man's innards aren't filled that man's no use, and no more is a rain-butt."

"Thanks very much, my man," said the Admiral, after inspecting with admiration the shipshape appearance of the butt. "All we want now is the rain to fill her, but that's a matter for Providence."

"Don't think I'm taking a liberty, sir," said Snow, "but it isn't no good waiting for she. I'll run the water into the butt with your hosepipe, sir, and then when we get some nice rain you turn the tap and let some of the water out and that there old spout from the roof she'll do the rest."

The Admiral, though slightly confused by the number of females who seemed to be implicated in Snow's speech, quite saw what he meant.

"And what do I owe you?" said the Admiral.

"Well, sir, Mr. Wickham and some of the other naval gents, sir, they said they'd settle that," said Snow.

"Nonsense," said the Admiral.

"Well, sir, that's as you say," said Snow, "but Mr. Wickham he's a gentleman I wouldn't like to disoblige. Nor I wouldn't like to disoblige any of the other naval gents, sir."

"What about me?" said the Admiral, half annoyed, half amused.

"Well, sir, that I couldn't say," said Snow, who had by now packed his tools into his carpenter's bag. "Me and my mate—he was with Pilwards the brewers, sir, in Barchester and knows his job proper—we carried out Mr. Wickham's instructions and a man can't do more, not if he tried till he bust."

"All right," said the Admiral, who knew when he was beaten and also knew that he would have killed to do the same by an elderly brother officer under similar conditions. "Will you and your mate have a pint before you go?"

"No objection to that, sir," said Snow, relieved that the affair was settled, "and my mate, he hasn't got none neither. Have you, George?" he added rather threateningly.

George, who like many good tradesmen kept what wits he had for his work and left everything else to his wife, said he couldn't rightly say that he hadn't. So the Admiral put his head in at the kitchen window and asked his daughter to bring out some beer and glasses, which she willingly did. Glasses were filled, a general sense of embarrassment overwhelmed everyone, the beer was drunk and the Admiral and his daughter went into the house.

"Fine old gentleman," said Snow. "*He* won't see another winter out," which was said not with unkindness, only in the countryman's way of seeing all things moved round in earth's diurnal, or annual, course to their common end.

"Might be him, might be the lady," said George.

"Well, George, you're less of a fool than you look," said Snow. "Never struck me it might be the Admiral's lady. Come to think of it she's got a look of my Aunt Emma. Just faded away she did and Dr. Ford said if people had a call to go, go they must," with which oracular words the discussion closed.

Just as Miss Phelps, having seen her mother safely on her bed with a warm rug over her and a hot bottle to her feet (for true as the saying is that you should not cast a clout till May is out it can be equally true that, given an average English post-war summer, you would do better not to cast it at all), and her father established in the sitting-room with the *Daily Telegraph* (for *The Times*, at double the price, does mount up), had begun to wash up the lunch things, Mr. Wickham looked in at the kitchen window.

"I've a message for you from Mrs. Carter," he said. "She is coming at two o'clock, that's in twelve minutes, to take on for the afternoon. You wash your hands and face and come out with me. Mrs. Carter will make the tea for your people and I know Mr. Shergold is coming over after school to talk to your father about Grouses in the Gunroom," a naval witticism new to Miss Phelps.

"I'd love to, Wicks," she said wistfully. "Only I must be back in time to get supper and I haven't even started it."

"What are you giving them?" said Mr. Wickham.

"Well, I don't exactly know yet," said Miss Phelps. "Eggs, I expect. The hens aren't laying well, but we might as well eat the eggs while they're there. And baked apples. The ones I put in the attic last year haven't lasted badly."

"No wonder you're looking peaky," said Mr. Wickham, when to his horror Miss Phelps raised a soapy hand to her eyes, which of course made her cry even more.

"Look here, my girl, that's enough," said Mr. Wickham. "Here, wipe your eyes and blow your nose," and he handed her a large bandanna.

"Pre-war, I needn't say," said Mr. Wickham. "Colours don't run, so you needn't worry. Now, look here," and from the suspiciously capacious pockets of his old tweed jacket he produced a tinned ham (or canned, as we should learn to say in gratitude to our American friends), a large tin of baked beans and lastly, extricating it with some difficulty, a fine piece of real cheese.

"Finished with my handkerchief? That's right," said Mr. Wickham. "Give it back, there's a good girl. There's your supper. Now go upstairs and clean yourself. Hi!" he added, as Miss Phelps, hypnotised by his martinet attitude, was going out of the kitchen, "are you still using that stuff for your hands that Mrs. Villars gave you?"

"I truly did," said Miss Phelps, "but it got used up."

"Just like a woman," said Mr. Wickham. "Mrs. Villars told me with her own mouth that you had promised to let her know when it was done. I was over there this morning. I said I'd wager sixpence you wouldn't. I've won."

Miss Phelps remained silent, a prey to shame and remorse.

"Well then, don't do it again," said Mr. Wickham. "Here's a fresh jar, double size, and mind you use it."

"Is it from you?" said Miss Phelps.

"Never you mind, my girl," said Mr. Wickham. "As a matter of fact it is from Mrs. Villars. And if you aren't careful I shall buy you the next jar myself. Only for the Lord's sake *use* it. You can't go putting your friends to all this trouble and expense for nothing. And now go up and get ready and don't dawdle."

Miss Phelps looked at him with a kind of horrified yet fascinated gratitude and went upstairs. In a minute or two the bell rang, so Mr. Wickham went to the front door and admitted Kate Carter.

"All shipshape," said Mr. Wickham. "The Admiral is doing the *Daily Telegraph* cross-word. Don't help him *too* much; he doesn't like it. Can you manage tea?"

Kate said nothing would be easier.

"You're one of those women who can find the tin-opener by instinct," said Mr. Wickham admiringly, to which Kate Carter replied that she was sure he could always find the corkscrew.

"Now, I'm taking that girl over to tea at my house," said Mr. Wickham, returning to business. "Lady Cora is coming and perhaps one or two others. I've put the fear of the Lord into Margot about not using the hand cream Mrs. Villars ordered her to use. As for her hair, we'll have to leave that to Rose Fairweather. I think myself she cuts it with the nail-scissors, or bites it. We've got to get her going somehow," and at his serious way of speaking Kate Carter smiled and said they would have to get some vanity into her before they could begin.

Then Miss Phelps came down, looking slightly sheepish.

"What on earth have you done to yourself?" said Mr. Wickham.

"Well, I thought perhaps you wouldn't like me in trousers for your house," said Miss Phelps.

"Like you anyway, at any time," said Mr. Wickham gallantly. "And it must have been a good suit."

"Oh yes, it was," said Miss Phelps, ignoring, or not realising this backhanded compliment. "It was one Rose Fairweather brought me. She had it when she was expecting——" and her voice tailed away into embarrassed silence.

In different company both Kate Carter and Mr. Wickham would have laughed, but to both there seemed something rather simple and touching about Miss Phelps's acceptance of a coat and skirt made for so different a person, in such different circumstances. Kate, who was always practical, said they had better go if they were going, so they got into Mr. Wickham's ramshackle but highly capable little car and drove towards Mr. Wickham's house which was over on the other side of Northbridge.

It was not a particularly interesting brick house, about a

hundred years old, solidly built and well arranged for a bachelor. As the rest of the tea-party had not yet arrived Mr. Wickham offered to show Miss Phelps over the property, which consisted of two rooms and kitchen premises on the ground floor and three bedrooms and a bathroom above.

"It's good enough for a fellow like me," said Mr. Wickham. "But what I'd like you to see is the garden," and he took her round the house to the back. The garden had no special features of interest, being a large lawn with a flowerbed on one side and a gravel path on the other; but his vegetables, which lay beyond the lawn, were famous. Miss Phelps, used to her own spare-time gardening, was enthusiastic about the beautifully kept borders and the exquisite regularity of the rows.

"We do practically all the watering from those," said Mr. Wickham, pointing to two gigantic rain-water butts which stood against the back of the house. "My old gardener believes in loosening the soil and watering by hand."

"So do I, if only I had a little more time," said Miss Phelps. "*You* don't have to have hens, do you?" she added rather wistfully.

"Wouldn't if I did," said Mr. Wickham cryptically. "But my gardener's wife keeps them. She lives in that cottage on the side of the lane and she does for me," a description which all sensible readers will understand. "I told her she could keep all she liked and I'd pay for the feed, but I wouldn't buy the eggs and she mustn't let her cocks make a nuisance of themselves. It's a bit awkward, you know, if you have a couple of pals to spend the evening and one way and another you don't get to bed till pretty late and then a cock gets up and behaves like an alarm clock."

"They *are* awful," said Miss Phelps. "But father and mother sleep on the far side of the house, so it doesn't matter. I'm simply *sick* of fowls," she added, almost as if she were talking to herself.

"Bloody nuisances—sorry, Margot," said Mr. Wickham.

Miss Phelps wanted to say how much she agreed and how unnecessary it was for him to apologise for a word that by sheer usage has now practically no meaning at all, but she was confused by his use of her name. It is true that she had known him on and off for some time, that he had been more than kind and thoughtful about her people, but as far as she could remember he had always called her "you" or occasionally "my girl." It then occurred to her that she did not know his Christian name and it would seem rather silly to ask someone whom she had seen so often and at such domestically close quarters what his name was. So she made no comment.

The sound of a car in the lane, obviously a good car by its purring sound, interrupted these reflexions. Mr. Wickham, saying, "That's Cora," went round the back of the cottage into the front garden. But far from being Lady Cora, it was Canon Fewling.

"Hullo, Wicks," he said. "And what a pleasure to see you, Miss Phelps. Lady Cora should be here in a minute."

"And how do you know *that*, Tubby?" said Mr. Wickham, at which Canon Fewling looked rather uncomfortable, but Mr. Wickham did not notice it, for at that moment another deep purring noise came round the corner of the road and was Lady Cora with her car.

"Are you all right, Lady Cora? Sixpence, please," said Canon Fewling.

"Devil!" said her ladyship, though without heat. "Look here, Wicks, I passed Canon Fewling on Fish Hill and then he passed me and then I passed him and we had sixpence on it and then he did the roundabout at about eighty, on one wheel. I can only hope a policeman saw him. They are all on my side. Here you are, Canon Fewling," and her ladyship gravely counted a three-penny piece, two pennies and two halfpennies into her hand and held it out to him, adding, "Simony. That's what it is."

"The great advantage — at least one of the *many* advantages of being a priest," said Canon Fewling, "is that you are in some respects slightly less ignorant than a few other people. Not simony, Lady Cora, though one might be had up under an obsolete Lord's Day Observance Act for illegal betting."

"If it were the Lord's Day," said Mr. Wickham. "But it isn't. I mean not in the strict sense, though I suppose any day is the Lord's Day, come to think of it. Look here, Cora. This is Margot Phelps. Her father is Admiral Phelps at Southbridge and she handles a car as prettily as you'd like. In fact," he added, "there's very little to choose between the two of you except that you have a car, so you get more practice. But if Margot had a week with your car, Cora, she would drive it up Scawfell like a lamb."

Lady Cora smiled very kindly at Miss Phelps.

"We will make a plan," she said. "Look here, Tubby. Suppose you let Miss Phelps drive your car with Wicks as passenger and I'll drive mine with you as passenger. Straight up Fish Hill and then down by the sunken lane and then into the straight up to Gatherum. We'll let my father give the prize. He adores giving prizes."

Miss Phelps, dazzled by excess of light, hardly knew what to make of this suggestion and with the courage of despair said it was awfully kind of Lady Cora, but she didn't think she could leave her father and mother for so long. She then felt she had been ungracious to a very kind person and was in general a Peri outside the gates of Paradise and wished she were at home.

"You don't know what you are taking on, Lady Cora," said Canon Fewling seriously. "Miss Phelps is a remarkably good driver. She was with me the day you nearly ran me down on the Northbridge Road," at which her ladyship laughed and said it was the nearest squeak she had had since she rashly did a measured mile in the avenue at Gatherum with that Helen Fanshawe who was Jessica Dean's sister. That *was* a day. At least it was nearly dark, she added.

"Noctes coenaque motorum," said Mr. Wickham unexpectedly, at which Canon Fewling said he didn't know anyone remembered that poem, and entirely forgetting or ignoring the ladies they quoted in strophe and antistrophe the brilliant production of a former Public Orator at Oxford about the Motor Bus.

"So like men," said Lady Cora to Miss Phelps. "Not a bit interested in Us. Let's go into the garden and not be bored. Have you seen the summerhouse?" Miss Phelps hadn't, so Lady Cora took her to the far angle of the little estate, round the corner from the vegetables, where a brick garden-house of two stories was built against the mellow red-brick wall. The lower storey was a toolshed. The upper was approached by a flight of brick steps built against the wall, with a brick balustrade, and at the top was a small room with a door in one wall and a window in each of the other three. Two of the windows overlooked the garden. The third looked over the world outside, across fields, away to the downs.

As they stood there in silence the clock sounded from the tower of Northbridge Church, across the fields.

"Is it only three o'clock?" said Miss Phelps. "But it *can't* be. I wish it were, though."

Lady Cora asked why.

"Well," said Miss Phelps, loosening a bit of dark hairy moss on the wall as she spoke, "it is such fun to have a holiday, and I thought if it could really be three I would have an hour more. I mean I am very happy and I love being at home, but this is different."

"I wish I could say it *was* three o'clock," said Lady Cora, "but I'm afraid it is four. The clock at Northbridge doesn't like being altered for Summer Time and I must say I rather sympathise with it. Are you in a hurry?"

Miss Phelps, moved by such consideration, said it wasn't exactly that, but she had to be back to get her father's and mother's supper.

"I don't mean that it's a bother, or anything," she added, fearful lest this new friend should think her unfilial, "but it *is* such fun to have a holiday."

Lady Cora, although her father and mother were quite badly off as dukes and duchesses go, because of the increasing taxation imposed on people who have lived on their own land for many years and have in most cases done well by their land and their people, had (we are glad to say) never known the narrowness of the quiet poverty forced upon so many who have served their country by land and sea. For a moment she found it difficult to say anything.

"Do you ever come over our way?" she said. "We live at Beliers Priory, near Lambton. Lunch? Or tea?"

Miss Phelps went red in the face with pleasure and was struck dumb.

"Or is it difficult?" said Lady Cora, feeling pretty sure Miss Phelps's parents had not got a car. "Look here I'll tell Wicks to run you over. He can always get about if he wants to. I'll ring you up."

Miss Phelps looked at her, but was apparently unable to speak.

"Have I put my foot in it?" said Lady Cora.

"Oh no," said Miss Phelps. "It's only that mother isn't very well and father isn't either, and if they get any worse I wouldn't be able to get about much. And we haven't got a telephone."

"Then I'll write," said Lady Cora, "and soon. I find it often saves a lot of trouble. If I really want letters to get anywhere I don't stamp them and the post office comes rushing round with the letter to collect the excess postage." So they went back to the house for tea.

In deference to the ladies present Mr. Wickham's tea was tea, and we may add that though his housekeeper was his slave, she was one of those slaves (who must have been the ever-present plague of antiquity) that had her employer well under her. There were of course bounds to her tyranny. Once Mr. Wickham's evening meal had been served and cleared away he could do as he liked; whether putting a wet towel round his head and dealing with the Mertons' estate accounts, or making a night of it with one or two of his extensive and peculiar circle of friends, though we must in fairness add that owing to his excellent health inherited from a long line of Barsetshire yeoman-farmers and his integrity in all business matters, he was never a day late with his accounts or a penny out and was up by seven every morning. His housekeeper, who would have liked of course to be a tyrant but found it impossible, made a virtue of necessity by boasting to all her neighbours that Mr. Wickham was as good as an alarm clock and when she heard him a-hollering and a-bellering in his bath she knew it was a quarter-past seven without having that old wireless on, and so could go over and prepare his breakfast. When we add to this that Mr. Wickham, whatever god-like feasts and nights he had spent, always put the glasses and things (his housekeeper's expression, not ours) neatly by the kitchen sink before he went to bed, leaving the sitting-room windows open the while to air the room, we my conclude that he was a most satisfactory employer. The only fault his housekeeper could find with him was that he didn't seem to fancy the ladies: perhaps an unusual complaint from a bachelor's housekeeper, actuated, we think, by a feeling that it would be very pleasant to have some gossip to retail. But though Mr. Wickham was much liked by the ladies of Barsetshire, no one of them had ever been seen leaving his house unaccompanied in the small hours of the morning, and we may add that none of them had wished to, and he—if we may be pardoned a muddle whose grammatical name we do not know—least of all.

After a very pleasant meal and a short professional talk between Lady Cora and her host on the subject of rabbits and their omnivorous habits and how Jasper Margett, the half-gypsy keeper at Beliers Priory, had invented a new snare of surprising ingenuity which enabled him to sell even more rabbits unofficially to his large and rather shady circle of friends, Lady Cora, whose consideration for the needs of others was partly atavistic, coming as she did from county families who had been good landlords and mostly lived on their estates, and partly a genuine natural kindness for anyone who seemed to need protection, said she must be going and she knew Miss Phelps wanted to get back to Southbridge.

"Look here, Wicks," she said. "I'll drive Miss Phelps home. It's hardly a mile out of my way and you have plenty to do. And then I shan't be tempted to race with Canon Fewling. That's pure kindness on my part. The police wouldn't bother me—we are all friends—but they might think it funny to cop a parson for speeding."

If Canon Fewling was disappointed he concealed it very well, and indeed the thought had occurred to him that if he tried his car against Lady Cora's and against her superb driving he might find himself in trouble, and it would be a great pity to give any handle for unpleasant talk from the Palace. So goodbyes were said and Lady Cora took Miss Phelps aboard. When they had come to the end of the lane which led to the high road she stopped.

"Look here, Miss Phelps," she said. "Would you like to drive?"

Miss Phelps went so red in the face that Lady Cora, talking later to her husband, said she must have been bright red all over, and uttered some incoherent words of thanks.

"She's as soft in the mouth as you'd wish," said Lady Cora, when the ladies had changed seats. "We shan't meet anyone along this bit of road unless it's one of those ghastly motor coaches on an excursion, so take your time," and she sat back, relaxed (to use a word which is far too often used on every unsuitable occasion) and ready to help. But help was not needed. Gently Miss Phelps did whatever it is one does to start a car, gradually the handsome animal quickened its pace under her firm, capable hands and took its even course along the road, keeping below the speed limit by the smallest possible legal amount. Two motor coaches of the Southbridge United Viator Company, packed with a Women's Institute outing, were by-passed by Miss Phelps without a tremor. A dog, undecided whether to cross the road or not, was warned by a blast of the horn that made him rush to safety; and a cat, who had been thinking of crossing the road herself, pretended she was only washing her face on the grass outside her cottage, thus ostenta-tiously showing her scorn for everybody and everything. The only moment of anxiety was when a young stoat who wished to see life thought it would cross the road in front of the car, but its mother, furious at being interrupted while listening to the wireless, rushed after it, boxed its ears and pushed it back into the ditch. All too soon for Miss Phelps the treat came to an end and she drew up at Jutland Cottage.

"May I come in and meet your father and mother?" said Lady Cora.

Miss Phelps, pleased if embarrassed, could not refuse this request, so both ladies got out.

"Oh, Lady Cora, is it all right to leave your car here?" said Miss Phelps, pausing at the little gate.

"No one steals my car," said Lady Cora. "The police know it too well."

"But I mean, it might get scratched. The High Street is rather narrow," said Miss Phelps.

"Now that is very kind and sensible of you," said Lady Cora. "I'll have a look."

So she went back to gauge the width of the little High Street when the policeman, Haig Brown—nephew of Mr. Brown of the Red Lion and christened after a general of the 1914 war in which his father had served, for which he rather blamed his parents as the village wits found a perennial source of pleasure in calling him Scotch and Splash, or Neat Scotch—happened to come by.

"Oh, Brown," said Miss Phelps. "This is Lady Cora Waring. I was wondering if she ought to leave her car here. Those lorries go so fast and it might get scratched."

"Good afternoon, your ladyship," said P.C. Brown who, largely owing to his uncle of the Red Lion, had been well educated; for a man who owns a public-house in a little town— for such Southbridge was becoming—where most people know who other people are, needs to know who's who, not to speak of what's what. "Anything I can do for you?"

"Good afternoon, Brown," said Lady Cora, who heard most

things and forgot very little. "If you think she's all right I'll leave her here. If you think I'd better move her, say the word."

"Well, your ladyship, it's not for me to say," said Brown, "but if you won't be long I daresay I'll be about. If any of them lorries comes along I'll give them the word."

So Lady Cora gave Brown a smile, which he rightly interpreted as a promise of largesse to come, and followed Miss Phelps up the path and into Jutland Cottage.

In the sitting-room the Admiral was alone, reading.

"Oh, father," said Miss Phelps, "this is Lady Cora Waring. She let me drive her car back from Mr. Wickham's. It's even better than Canon Fewling's. Where's mother?" and without waiting for an answer she went off to find her mother and stop her, very kindly, doing whatever she was doing, for though it was the Admiral who had a heart, his wife was, like so many women of her age in England, paying the penalty of the old years of war-work and the perpetual claims of housework, not to speak of trying to make both ends meet.

Mrs. Phelps was in the kitchen, standing on a wooden chair in front of an open cupboard above the dresser.

"I say, mother, what *are* you doing?" said Miss Phelps, who had for her mother the exacerbated affection which Dickens has so perfectly described in the relations between Mr. Guppy and his mother that we will not attempt to describe it and hope that such readers as do not know it will look it up at once and when found make a note of.

"Only the cupboard," said Mrs. Phelps rather guiltily. "Mr. Shergold came and had a talk with father after tea, so I thought I'd tidy a bit. You know those extra saucepans we put away?"

"You mean the big ones?" said Miss Phelps, for a great many housewives, finding their pre-war batterie de cuisine too large for the much smaller amount of food they were getting, had put some of their cooking utensils on half-pay as it were.

"I was thinking of that saucepan we used to boil the Christmas pudding in," said Mrs. Phelps. "We might as well use it for the hens. Their one has *really* got a hole in the bottom now and it does so mess up the stove when I do their food. Is father all right?"

"Oh, Lady Cora Waring is with him," said Miss Phelps. "She brought me back from Mr. Wickham's, mother, and she let me drive. It's a marvellous car, almost better than Tubby's."

"How nice of her," said Mrs. Phelps, alluding, we think, rather to Lady Cora's visit to her husband than her kindness to her daughter.

"I wish there were something useful one could do with saucepans when they go," said Miss Phelps, a remark which we shall not insult our readers' intelligence by explaining, "but there isn't. Unless," she added hopefully, "we had another war and used them as helmets for air-raid wardens. Do get down, mother, I'll find it for you."

Obediently Mrs. Phelps did as she was told and sat down on an old basketwork chair which had gradually come to the kitchen for its declining years. Miss Phelps took a duster and got onto the chair.

"There are about a million things we don't really need, mother," she said. "I'd better send some to the Scouts for their jumble sale. There's a whole lot of kitchen gadgets. And here's the big saucepan," and she handed a variety of objects to her mother, who put them on the kitchen table.

"I wonder who on earth really uses all those things?" said Mrs. Phelps, examining what her daughter called the kitchen gadgets. "It seems to me that the more things you have to make cooking easy, the difficulter it is. I *never* could use that patent potato-peeler."

"And we don't really need a special thing for getting the pips out of grape-fruit," said her daughter, "nor a thing for coring cherries—I mean taking the stones out of them. Let's give the whole lot to the Scouts."

There are few things so agreeable as the sacking of a city or, on a smaller scale, the ruthless turning-out of a cupboard. Miss

Phelps got everything down and put it (or them) on the kitchen table to be tried and sifted, at which moment Lady Cora came in.

"Forgive me, Mrs. Phelps," she said, putting out her hand. "I'm Cora Waring. Your husband was telling me about the Battle of Jutland. My husband would have *loved* to be there, but unfortunately he wasn't old enough. I do hope I haven't let him tire himself," which last words were spoken with such obvious sincerity that Mrs. Phelps took a liking to her at once and said nothing did her husband so much good as talking about the first war. Lady Cora then further won her heart by asking what all those things were on the kitchen table and telling her the amount of useless kitchen things she and her husband had found at the Priory when his uncle and aunt were dead. Miss Phelps, with a grateful look at Lady Cora, took the hens' supper which was in the large saucepan and went away.

"I hope my husband didn't bore you," said Mrs. Phelps, sitting down again—rather too quickly, Lady Cora thought, as if her strength had suddenly failed.

"No sailor could possibly bore me," said Lady Cora. "My husband was all through the last war, but he had a piece of iron or something inside him and when it was taken out the Admiralty didn't much want him. We are starting a kind of home for naval orphans at the Priory. It is the most hideous house in Barsetshire," she added proudly and gratified Mrs. Phelps by a description of some of the more peculiar horrors of her home.

"You have been so good to Margot," said Mrs. Phelps. "She hardly gets any treats. And she never grumbles."

This tribute to a daughter from a mother touched Lady Cora and she asked if the Phelps family would come to tea and see the Priory one day, adding that she would see that they were fetched and returned with punctuality and dispatch.

"How kind of you," said Mrs. Phelps, "but my husband finds getting about so tiring, even in a car. And I am really too tired to go anywhere now. Dr. Ford makes me lie down all afternoon."

"I *am* so sorry," said Lady Cora, with real if temporary concern.

"But Margot would love it, I am sure," said Mrs. Phelps. "We have so many kind friends here who will come and spend the afternoon with my husband and I do feel so grateful to anyone who takes Margot out—like Mr. Wickham. It's no life for her to look after rather useless parents. She could easily have got jobs, again and again, but she has such a sense of duty. And she doesn't think it *is* duty," said Mrs. Phelps, showing an insight regarding her daughter which surprised Lady Cora, who had been thinking—not unkindly—that the Phelpses did rather put upon Margot, who at that moment came back from feeding the hens, empty-handed.

"I gave the old saucepan to Ernie Brown and his brother," said Miss Phelps. "I can't that what they'll do with it, but thank goodness it's gone. And now we'll use the other one. And I saw Mrs. Brown over the hedge and she said she would come and collect all that kitchen junk for a jumble sale."

"And will you come to lunch or tea at the Priory? It is so hideous that it is really worth seeing. I'll fetch you and bring you back and you can drive," said Lady Cora.

Self-abnegation, which is often a positive vice, was sticking out of Miss Phelps at every pore, but her mother, somehow encouraged by Lady Cora's presence to assert herself, said she was sure Mrs. Carter or Mrs. Fairweather or one of their friends would do locum for the afternoon if they had a little warning, and over Miss Phelps's head a day was arranged between her mother and Lady Cora, just as if she were a little girl, which indeed Lady Cora felt in some ways she was.

"And the Croftses will be back on Saturday, mother," said Miss Phelps, "and thank heaven Mr. Horton and his aunt will go."

"A clergyman and his aunt who were here while our own clergyman was having a holiday," Mrs. Phelps explained to Lady Cora. "I know one oughtn't to hate people, but I could not stand them, clergy or no clergy. They nearly killed my husband when they came to see him one afternoon, while I was resting. Oh, how I *hate* having to rest," she added, half to herself.

"I really think father would have *died*," said Miss Phelps, "because his heart and his breathing are so bad. But Rose Fairweather was here and she saved his life."

"What a lovely creature she is," said lady Cora. "I have met her off and on since they came to Greshamsbury. We must ask them to dinner."

"She is the kindest, most beautiful woman I have ever seen," said Mrs. Phelps. "Her father, Mr. Birkett, used to be Headmaster at the school here. Her husband is a sailor, at the Admiralty just now," and then she wondered if she said too much. But Lady Cora, like most good-looking women, admired beauty in other women and said she must meet her and now she must really go.

In the lane she found P.C. Brown, who saluted smartly and said there hadn't been any trouble with lorries, but he had to keep them kids away from the car. There'd have been enough fingerprints on it to keep Scotland Yard going for a month, he said, and his own kids were as bad as the rest. Mad about cars they were and collecting the numbers off number-plates. Still, that was better than the Pools, he added philosophically.

"Is one of your boys Ernie?" said Lady Cora.

"That's right, your ladyship. Called after my uncle Ernie Brown, like," said P.C. Brown. "I've two lads."

"Well, Miss Phelps has given them the old saucepan she used to do the hens' food in," said Lady Cora, "and they are going to use it for a helmet, I believe. You'll probably have to take one of them round to the blacksmith to have it got off. I know boys. Thank you for keeping an eye on the car, Brown," and, putting into his hand a generous tip, she drove away. P.C. Brown, whose time on duty was about up, went home for his tea and reported faithfully to his wife the events of the day.

"She's a real lady, Lady Cora is, and I ought to know, my

auntie having a temporary at the Castle when she was in service," was his wife's answer. "Those kids are yours, Haig! Miss Phelps gave them an old saucepan and young Ernie put it on his head and couldn't get it off. Screaming the place down, he was, and his brother not much better."

"What did you do, mother?" said P.C. Brown, placidly eating his tea. "Take him to the blacksmith?"

"Much sense you've got, Haig," said his wife. "If I'd have done that, every kid in the place would have been sticking his head into that saucepan. I got a bit of lard—at last that's what the rations calls it, though it's no more lard than I am—and I melted it and I made young Ernie bend right over and I poured the lard down his neck into the saucepan and it came off quite easy. About all that ration lard's fit for. And I told him Dad would give him a good hiding if he did it again."

"You *are* a one," said P.C. Brown admiringly. "But you tell young Ernie to tell the other kids that anyone as gets his head stuck in that saucepan again, there won't be no lard. It'll be the blacksmith, and if he's busy the saucepan will have to wait. Give us another cuppa, old girl."

On her way back—or, to be correct, well out of her way back which did not lie in the least in that direction—Lady Cora had a whim or fancy to go via Greshamsbury and see if she could get more information about the Phelpses. It was a queer thing, her ladyship thought to herself as she went over the downs, that there were some people whom everyone wanted to help, and others, truly in need of help, who didn't get it. And the rum thing was, she thought, and wishing while she thought that her husband was with her because he always understood everything, that one could never be sure. Take the Phelpses. They were obviously people of determined independence who had always lived on what they had (and precious little of that with prices what they were, her ladyship thought) and had never asked for anything: yet help had come to them and what was more, they were taking it and being grateful, with complete dignity. She then thought of her parents' odious connection by marriage, the Honourable Juliana Starter, for many years a lady-in-waiting to Princess Louisa Christina of Cobalt-Herz-Reinigen, whose income was a first charge on the diminished estate of the present Lord Mickleham and how she took paying guests whom she starved and from whom she demanded an outrageous rent, and yet was always complaining of her poverty.

"Fine fun for *me* to talk like that," said Lady Cora to herself, "with enough to live on. Well, well," and she slowed down as she got to the outskirts of Greshamsbury. It was quite in order that she should ask the Fairweathers' address from (*a*) a tripper who had never been there before, (*b*) a child who was too frightened to speak, and (*c*) a postman who said it was his first day on that round and he was waiting for his predecessor to go round with him, though he did not put it quite like that. She was just wondering whether she should park the car and go into the post office, unless it was early closing day, which it practically always is, everywhere, if one happens to be there, when an elderly woman coming along the road stopped, looked at her and came up to the car.

"Excuse me, my lady," said the elderly woman, "but if I'm not mistaken, Lady Cora Palliser."

"Yes, indeed, only it's Waring now," said Lady Cora. "Now don't tell me. Gatherum. The housemaids' cupboard on the nursery floor and Nurse scolded me for going into it and she scolded you for letting me. Bessie. Bessie Bunce, from North-bridge. Your uncle was a regular bad lot you told me."

"That's quite right, my lady," said the elderly woman. "I remember the cupboard quite well and what a telling-off Nurse gave me and I cried so much that Bertha—she was the head housemaid then—asked what the matter was and she went to Nurse about it."

"How *fascinating*," said Lady Cora. "And what happened next?"

"Well, we shall never rightly know, my lady," said the elderly woman, "but Her Grace heard about it and she passed the remark that she was always in the housemaids' cupboard herself when Her Grace was a little girl and then I married Hicks."

"Was he at Gatherum?" said Lady Cora.

"Not so as you'd notice it, my lady," said the elderly woman, now recognised by Lady Cora, and ourselves, as Mrs. Hicks, "being as he was only tempery in the boot-room. A beautiful hand at polishing boots and shoes he was, and he'd always take the laces out before he put the blacking on and put them back when he'd finished polishing. But his father had a little business in Northbridge, so we took it on, and when he died I had a lovely funeral for him and then I took lodgers."

She appeared to have come to the end of her life-story, but Lady Cora wanted to know why she was in Greshamsbury now.

"Well, my lady," said Mrs. Hicks, "when the Reverend Fewling was at Northbridge he lodged with me. One of the nicest gentlemen I ever see, and if he did have his ways about fasting as he called it, well, we're all peculiar one way or another. I couldn't fancy a cake with caraway seeds in it not if you was to hand it to me on a golden plate. And if he didn't have breakfast some days I always made it up to him for lunch."

"Then you are just the person I wanted to meet," said Lady Cora, which left Mrs. Hicks quite unmoved, for like all the respectable women (and when we say respectable, we may be understood to mean respect-worthy) one knows, her opinion of herself was a rooted conviction, partaking of direct inspiration rather than any mental process, that she was, if not perfect, at any rate more perfect than other people. "You will be able to tell me where Mrs. Fairweather lives."

As their conversation had taken place a few yards from the house this was not difficult. Lady Cora got out of the car and shook hands with Mrs. Hicks, saying that she was sure her mother would like to hear all about her and what she was doing, all of which Mrs. Hicks received as her due. Lady Cora, hearing young voices from the side of the house, went in at the gate and found an enchanting tableau of Rose and her two youngest children, both with a quite unfair amount of good looks.

"May I come in?" said Lady Cora.

The elder child looked at Lady Cora and said, "You can't come in, because this is out."

"That's why I came in; because it *was* out," said Lady Cora gravely. "If it had been in I'd have rung the bell. May I stay for a few moments, Mrs. Fairweather? I have just come from the Phelpses and I thought you would like the latest news."

"Of course," said Rose. "Say how do you do to Lady Cora, darlings, and then go along to Nanny. It's nearly bath-time."

If Lady Cora had admired Rose before for herself, she now admired her even more for her complete mastery of her young. The children came up to Lady Cora, shook hands, said "Good-bye" and went to the house.

"*What* nice children," said Lady Cora with conviction.

"Of course they can be quite too shatteringly dreadful," said Rose, "but we like them. John is somewhere about. I'll tell him to bring the drinks," and she took Lady Cora to the far side of the lawn where, under a brick wall, were really comfortable garden chairs, and a view of Captain Fairweather, R.N., who was trimming the edge of the lawn, guided by a length of string stretched between two pegs, all very taut and shipshape.

Rose had said all she wanted to say and quietly did a little work on her face. Lady Cora almost envied her, not for her beauty, which she admired, but for her ease. There were few situations in life that Lady Cora would not have faced with quiet assurance, but to sit with a guest and not make any effort to talk was a thing she could not have done. The thought did cross her mind that Rose said nothing because she had nothing to say, but she dismissed it as unworthy. When Captain Fairweather came back Lady Cora told him and his wife about Mr. Wickham's party and how she had let Miss Phelps drive her car and what beautiful hands she had.

"Fewling told us the same thing," said Captain Fairweather, "and he's as finicky as an old maid about anyone driving his new car."

Rose said it must be too shattering not to have a car.

"Much more shattering, my girl, to have had one and had to give it up," said her husband. "They did have one and they ran it till it wouldn't run any longer, and that was that. Cars cost money, not to speak of running expenses."

"Couldn't we have a subscription or something," said Rose, "like the time we had the raffle in Malta?" which suggestion fell very flat.

"You can't do any more for independent people than you are doing," said Lady Cora. "They wouldn't let you. It's like seeing a ship on the rocks, being battered to pieces, and you can't help," which naval comparison touched Captain Fairweather professionally and increased his admiration for Lady Cora.

"I must go," said Lady Cora. "I've got to meet Cecil at Barchester Central. Oh, before I forget, I asked Margot Phelps if she would come to the Priory one day. If I made it at a weekend would you both come? We will talk to Margot about the importance of a good foundation belt, though why not stays I never know; our old nurse always said stays. Of course, hers *were* stays," said her ladyship, summoning to her mind's eye a nursery vision of Nurse dressing with clicks all down the front. "And you and Cecil can talk shop, Captain Fairweather. What about tea next Sunday?"

Tea next Sunday suited everyone, and Rose said she and her husband would collect and bring Miss Phelps and also return her.

"It will be a good day," said Rose, whose mind, when not concerned with powder and lipstick, was extremely practical, "because the Croftses come back on Saturday and the Admiral will be able to go to morning church properly, which he loves, and he's a churchwarden."

Lady Cora said she didn't know he hadn't been able to go to church.

"Not *properly*," said Rose, "because he couldn't help disliking that Mr. Horton all the time and then he got remorse. Would you like to see the children in bed before you go, Lady Cora?" which invitation Lady Cora accepted with pleasure. So they went up to the nursery and found two very clean bright-eyed little girls in their cribs, who at once asked for a story.

Lady Cora's mind went back to a summer before her marriage when she had been to visit the Priory School, which lived in a wing of Beliers Priory, and how she had been taken to see the little boys in their dormitory and told them how when she was a little girl her parents had let her and her brothers sleep in a hut in the woods and had a channel cut right across the floor of the hut so that a little stream could run through it, and how the little boys had jiggled and jumped in their beds with excitement. But something told her, and we think correctly, that Rose Fairweather's children would not have romantic feelings, so she invented a story about a little girl who had straight brown hair and wanted golden hair, and how a fairy had waved a magic wand and made her hair turn into golden hair, but she must promise to be good or it would go brown again; and, furthermore, how the little girl was disobedient next day and her golden hair did go brown. So then she was *very* good next day and her hair turned gold for ever and ever—which piece of idiocy went down so well that she was ashamed of herself.

"My hair's gold, so I am *very* good," said the younger little girl virtuously.

"Mine's brown and I don't *like* being good," said her elder sister, "so I can be as naughty as I like," then Lady Cora kissed them both, said goodbye to the Fairweathers, picked her husband up at Barchester Central and so home.

CHAPTER 7

On Saturday morning Mr. Horton and his aunt left the Vicarage and went back to St. Aella's Home for Stiff-necked Clergy. On Saturday afternoon Colonel the Reverend Edward Crofts and his wife came back amidst universal rejoicing. Bateman, his ex-soldier servant and now combining the offices of house-man and sexton, had the best cleaners in the village mobilised on the Saturday ready to rush into the Vicarage the moment the Hortons left it and clean it from head to foot. This was, if we are to be fair, which we hate being, a work of purest supererogation, as Mr. Horton's aunt had kept everything in excellent order, but we think the village (who were still finely primitive under a veneer of wireless and television) looked upon it as a form of exorcism and enjoyed themselves immensely. Miss Hampton and Miss Bent at Adelina Cottage issued invitations for a welcome party from eight o'clock onwards, and it was generally understood that the whole of Wiple Terrace would be keeping open house till midnight.

"But not one minute later," said Miss Hampton to Mr. Shergold, the Senior Housemaster, whom she met going into the Red Lion just as she was coming out. "Keep the Sabbath," to which Mr. Shergold replied, "What price Cinderella," and Miss Hampton went back into the Red Lion with him, the better to discuss it.

As for Admiral and Mrs. Phelps, words cannot express their

quiet pleasure at the thought of their own Vicar back in his place. They had both been to church on the two Sundays of Mr. Horton's ministrations, but in spite of all their efforts to think of the loved and majestic words each confessed afterwards to having been conscious of little but the way Mr. Horton read or said them and the way his aunt had sat in the Vicarage pew as if it belonged to her. In which last they were quite unjust and unreasonable: but what else are we here for?

The Friends of Admiral Phelps Society had talked a great deal on a great many telephones, and it had been decided to ask Kate Carter, the Headmaster's wife, if she could spare time to sit with him between tea and the evening service with which Colonel Crofts was, as it were, to re-inaugurate himself, for she was so sweet and yet so firm that it was almost impossible to be excited in her presence. This she did and so cleverly managed to keep him talking about his naval experiences in the 1914 war that Mrs. Phelps had to remind them of the time. Kate, kind and thoughtful creature, had brought her little car and drove them to the church, where she sat with them. She and Mrs. Phelps had consulted together about letting the Admiral go and very sensibly come to the conclusion that he had better do what he felt like. When the service was over the Admiral went into the vesty and greeted his old friend, but did not stay long, for there were many others waiting. Kate drove them home, handed them over to Miss Phelps and said she was almost sorry the Croftses were back, as she had enjoyed visiting Jutland Cottage so much and hoped they would let her come in when she was passing.

"You've been wonderful, Mrs. Carter," said Miss Phelps, taking her as far as the little front gate. "People have been so good to mother and father."

"And to you too, I hope," said Kate, who had wondered more than once if Miss Phelps had been much considered.

"Indeed, yes," said Miss Phelps. "I went to tea with Mr. Wickham, and Lady Cora let me drive her car and so did Canon

Fewling. And Lady Cora asked me to tea at the Priory. And she said she would have me fetched and brought back," all of which Kate retailed to Everard at supper, and they both felt that the Friends of the Phelpses Society had done some good.

"And now, my love, I suppose we must look in at Adelina," said Everard. "Next time I'm offered a Headmastership I'll have Westminster or St. Paul's. There is too much life in the country. We will go to Adelina because we had to say we would, but go to Louisa or Editha or Maria I will not. What I really would like to know is how much the Inland Revenue benefits from Wiple Terrace during the year."

So to Adelina they went and found it already very hot and full of cigarette smoke, after which they escaped unnoticed, quietly walked round to the back of Wiple Terrace and so along the lane towards the church. Being June, the evening was chilly and grey.

"I think I can see a fire in the Vicarage drawing-room," said Kate. "Shall we just go in for a moment? I should love to see them. If they don't want us Bateman will know. He knows everything."

So they went up the little hill to the Vicarage and rang the bell. Bateman, sexton, butler and so confusingly the Vicar's former batman, opened the door.

"When I saw you coming up the hill from my pantry window, sir," he said to Everard, "I said to myself, Now the Colonel and Mrs. Crofts *will* be pleased to see Mr. and Mrs. Carter," and he took them to the drawing-room, where there was indeed a delightful glowing fire, tempering the chill June evening. Colonel Crofts and his wife looked very well after their holiday and, being very intelligent people, they did not try to tell the Carters about it, for other people's holidays are of no interest at all. Rather did they ply the Carters with questions about the school and the village, and particularly about Admiral Phelps.

"I really did have him on my mind," said Colonel Crofts, to which his wife replied that to her certain knowledge he had never once mentioned him, not even when he talked in his sleep, and they looked at each other with great affection.

Kate Carter gave as good a report as she could, describing the activities of the Friends of the Phelpses Society in a way that made the Croftses laugh a good deal.

"But quite seriously," said Kate, "people have been quite extraordinarily kind. And people who don't belong here. Canon Fewling and Rose Fairweather and even Lady Cora Waring. And everybody came more than once. And Mr. Wickham fetched Margot and took her over to tea at his house. That was where she met Lady Cora. And she and Mrs. Phelps cleared out that big cupboard high up on the kitchen wall."

"Lady Cora did?" said Mrs. Crofts, willing to believe but requiring to be better informed.

"Oh no, Margot and her mother," said Kate, "and they gave us a splendid lot of rubbish for the next jumble sale. The only bad patch was when the Hortons *would* visit them."

Mrs. Crofts looked at Kate with surprise.

"You don't mean to say that dreadful woman went district visiting on the Phelpses," she said. "I *am* so sorry. I particularly told Mrs. Horton when I was writing that he was an invalid and mustn't be excited."

"I don't think she excited him," said Kate. "She just sat there and Sapped his Vitality."

"I'll take two guineas off her nephew's wages for that," said Colonel Crofts. "I will *not* have my churchwarden exhausted by a locum, a mere temporary."

"Luckily," said Kate, "Rose Fairweather was there and she was quite gloriously rude; only she said it so nicely that no one could mind, and in any case nobody could snub Rose. They never could, even when she was at the Barchester High School. She told me about it herself, and she has always been extremely truthful," to which her husband ungenerously added that she hadn't the wits to tell a lie. But here we think he was wrong.

"All the same," said Kate, who never forgot what she really

wanted to say, however far removed from the subject immediately in hand, "I don't think Mrs. Phelps ought to have cleared that cupboard."

Her husband, who had not particularly noticed what she had said earlier in the evening, asked what cupboard.

"You know, darling," said Kate without the faintest sign of patience (and we beg the printer's reader, otherwise our shelter from the stormy blast, *not* to query this last word, for all married people will understand exactly what we mean). "That big cupboard high up in the wall of the kitchen at Jutland Cottage above the dresser. It means standing on a chair and reaching up, which is very bad for Mrs. Phelps. You know she has a heart. That's why Dr. Ford says she must lie down between lunch and tea."

"Well, I didn't know," said Everard.

"I did," said Mrs. Crofts, "because Dr. Ford told me. I *never* met such a gossip. But I sometimes wonder if the gossip isn't part of being a good country doctor. I half think he told me about Mrs. Phelps on purpose, so that I could occasionally see what she was doing and tell her not to. I hope she didn't overdo it."

"It was Margot who told me," said Kate. "She came back from tea with Mr. Wickham and found her mother standing on a chair reaching up for things and made her get down. I felt sorry for Margot. She hardly ever has a treat, and just the one afternoon she went out her mother had to stand on chairs in the kitchen."

There was a minute's silence and then Mrs. Crofts, feeling that the subject had been exhausted and, anyway, there was nothing that could be done about it now, asked after Kate's three children, all of whom were well and at their various places of education, and posted herself in the local news, while the Vicar and Everard talked of things like the Barsetshire County Council Election and the plans Southbridge were making for Coronation Festivities next year.

"How is the Coronation Committee getting on?" said the

Vicar, for Southbridge, an eminently loyal place, had already formed a Committee to make people's lives even more difficult for them during the Coronation than they would in any case have been.

"I am thankful to say," said Everard, "that I don't know. Kate is on it—she rather had to be, of course—but she is extremely sensible and is letting them all talk their heads off for the present. You haven't escaped anything, Crofts. Just wait. I think we—I mean your wife and you and Kate and I—can stand pretty firm, and I gather that Miss Hampton is going to support us in anything we say. She will attend the meetings, because she has a conscience about doing what she has promised to do, but as a yes-man for you and Kate. Or should I say a yes-woman?" to which the Vicar, in a manner quite unworthy of his cloth, said he thought yes-man would be the more correct. "It is difficult to say," said Everard.

Mrs. Crofts, who had heard their last words, said Miss Hampton was the yes-woman and Miss Bent the yes-man; at least Miss Bent could drive a car remarkably well and Miss Hampton had never driven at all, and, remembering a conversation that she and Canon Fewling had with those ladies earlier in the year, she began to laugh.

"We are a rum lot in Southbridge," said Everard thoughtfully. "Of course, wherever you get a large school you get oddities. Just as well. They will be evened out by life."

"Not all of them, I hope," said the Vicar. "One or two of your assistant masters, excellent fellows, seem to have kept a good deal of individuality. Shergold, for instance, and Feeder, and even Traill. And look at yourself."

"But I'm not a character," said Everard indignantly. "My Governors wouldn't like it."

"Oh, wouldn't they?" said the Vicar. "Just look at them. Characters nearly every one. You've got Sir Edmund in Pridham, and that man who was Solicitor-General, and the Air-Vice-Marshal who would fly a new machine to Scotland just to show he could and came down in a fog near Orléans. And you can't say Pomfret isn't a character, though a quiet one; he can bring the temperature of a meeting down better than anyone I know. And what about that man who was an old boy and got away with two years for falsifying company accounts and made a million as soon as he came out, and that man Hacker at Redbrick University, a former pupil of yours if I am not mistaken, who exchanges venomous letters about Aulus Gellius with every Latin scholar in Europe and keeps a chameleon? Sorry, Carter, but you are a character whether you like it or not."

"In fact, my boy, you've had it," said a voice from the door, identifying itself at once with Mr. Wickham, who had stood for several minutes unnoticed while the argument raged. "Good evening, Effie; may I come in?"

Of course Mr. Wickham was welcome, as always, and Mrs. Crofts asked him if he had been to Wiple Terrace.

"As a matter of fact, I haven't," said Mr. Wickham. "They did ask me. And when I say They I meant it, for I can't at the moment remember how many invitations I had. Four certainly, but I rather think Miss Hampton and Miss Bent each sent me a separate invitation, so that would make it five."

"It's not like you, Wicks," said Mrs. Crofts. "Is anything wrong?"

"If it's anything at all serious we could take you to the School Sanatorium at once," said Kate, scanning his face with the eye of an experienced mother and Housemaster's wife for the nasty look that heralds the spotty diseases.

"No, no, not serious," said Mr. Wickham. "I must say it would almost be worth pretending to be a schoolboy and having chickenpox if Nurse Heath is there. I met her once and adored her, only I could never remember whether she was herself or that nice woman who was a pal of hers—Nurse Ward, that was it."

Kate Carter said in her gentle voice that they were only temporary the year chickenpox was so bad and extra help was needed.

"There's nothing wrong, I hope, Wickham," said the Vicar, who liked Mr. Wickham as much as his wife did and thought all the better of him for having had the good sense and good taste to propose honourable marriage to Effie Arbuthnot, as she was then, before he, Colonel Crofts, had really known her. "Anything I can do?"

"Nothing, thanks, old fellow," said Mr. Wickham.

"But there *is* something wrong," said Kate Carter. "Whenever I have met you here, or anywhere, Mr. Wickham, you have always brought a present with you. I mean a bottle," she added, feeling that this was no moment to be mealy-mouthed.

"Good God! No more I have," said Mr. Wickham. "I did mean to, Effie. It was a bottle of rye I got off a pal back from the U.S.A. Filthy stuff, but, oh, believe the donor's heart sincere. Sorry."

"Excuse me, sir," said Bateman, coming in with a tray and glasses and a strong air of having listened outside the door before entering, "but they told me at the Red Lion that there's a mad dog loose over Northbridge way. Been worrying sheep, he was, and the men were out after him."

"That will do, Bateman," said the Vicar. "And you needn't wait in the hall."

"Thank *you*, sir," said Bateman, quite unmoved. "Good night, sir," and he went out, shutting the door a little too ostentatiously.

"Sorry," said Mr. Wickham. "No, nothing to drink, Crofts, or just a glass of beer," which Colonel Crofts gave him, and then offered something to the ladies, who preferred orangeade. "It's all right about that dog. He wasn't mad, but pretty vicious. No one knows where he came from, but he had got at one henhouse and I wasn't going to have him get at mine. It was my housekeeper who found him trying to get into the roost and all the hens yelling blue murder and she banged one of those zinc things she does her wash in on top of him and stood on it and screamed till I came."

"What *would* she have done if you hadn't been there?" said Kate Carter.

"Stood on it till I got home," said Mr. Wickham more calmly. "But I *was* home, so I sprinted across and I wrapped my hand in a towel—thoughtful woman, my housekeeper, she ran in and got one at once while I stood on the tub—and I got him out and trussed him and took him away."

"Do you mean to your house, Wicks?" said Mrs. Crofts.

"Not on your life, my girl," said Mr. Wickham. "I took him to the vet and we had a look at him. He's either mad, or a professional hen-killer, or both. So the vet took him home."

"But I thought you said you were *at* the vet's house," said Everard.

"So I did," said Mr. Wickham. "But the vet took the dog back to his master. And who do you think *he* is. It was on the collar."

There was silence. Mrs. Crofts boldly said, "The Bishop," but her husband said the Bishop hadn't got a dog. Dog licenses, he added in an abstract way, cost money.

"Don't bother to guess," said Mr. Wickham. "Lord Abbotsfordbury."

There was a reverent and grateful silence, broken by Everard Carter saying, "The one that was Sir Ogilvy Hibberd."

"The one," said Kate Carter, losing all sense of decency in her joyful excitement, "that has the dreadful son who is a director of the National Rotochrome Polychrome Universal Picture Post Card Company that does those *awful* coloured cards of beauty spots; and didn't get into Parliament when he stood against Mr. Gresham."

A great calm descended upon the company and everyone had some more beer or orange drink, except Mr. Wickham.

"There's something wrong with you, Wicks," said Mrs. Crofts. "Are you sure the dog didn't bite you?"

"It's not that," said Mr. Wickham, "and, anyway, I expect I'm too pickled to catch anything at my time of life. I've had a shock."

"Then tell us all about it," said Mrs. Crofts calmly, even if she felt anxious inside. "If it's anything we can help with, you know we will."

"Good girl. I know you would, and Crofts too," said Mr. Wickham. "It's not so bad really, but I wasn't expecting it. You know my old uncle over Chaldicotes way?"

Mrs. Crofts said she remembered Mr. Wickham speaking about him once and she had thought he didn't sound very pleasant.

"Right as usual, Effie," said Mr. Wickham. "He was stingy and unpleasant in his life, but in his death——" and he paused.

"Well, do go on, Wickham," said Colonel Crofts, using, which he rarely did, his old tone of military authority.

"He was my mother's only brother and a close-fisted mean old skunk to her even if he is dead," said Mr. Wickham. "And he's left me everything. Must have gone mad before he died."

The news was so exciting and there was so much that everyone wanted to ask that for a moment there was complete silence.

"And how much is it?" said Kate Carter, coming to the point at once with her kind and practical mind.

"If the lawyers are speaking the truth," said Mr. Wickham, looking straight in front of him as if he were reading the words off a blackboard, "there will be enough when the death duties are paid to bring me in about six hundred a year. Don't tell me farming doesn't pay."

There was complete silence after this dramatic announcement, till Kate, whose social conscience was always alert, as it ought to be in a good wife of a Headmaster, said it was the best news she had heard since Bobbie got his scholarship, and the floodgates were opened and everyone drank his health in whatever drink they had, and both ladies nearly cried, which is a heavenly feeling when done in joy. Colonel Crofts got up, went to the drawing-room door and opened it quickly.

"All right, Bateman," he said. "You've heard the news. Now bring some more beer and you can drink Mr. Wickham's health," at which words Bateman, for once rather abashed, saluted and went away to get the beer. Mr. Wickham's health was drunk, standing, and Bateman said goodnight respectfully and went away.

"And what will you do?" said Mrs. Crofts.

"Do?" said Mr. Wickham. "What I've always done, of course. Carry on with the Mertons' property till they sack me, or superannuate me, and then do a spot of farming and gardening on my own."

"You really ought to get married, Mr. Wickham," said Kate Carter. "It makes *such* a difference," at which her husband told her to leave the man alone, and it wasn't everyone who could be sure of getting the right wife, with which Colonel Crofts concurred.

"All very well for you chaps with your wives," said Mr. Wickham. "If I'd known this was coming I'd have asked you again, Effie. It was in 1946 I told you I loved you. In fact I went further—I asked you to marry me and you wouldn't. I hope you're sorry."

"I hated hurting you, Wicks," said Mrs. Crofts, "but how could I be sorry?" and she held out her hand to her husband, who pressed it.

"You win," said Mr. Wickham generously. "And I may say, as we're all old friends, that the moment I'd asked you to marry me I wished I hadn't. It's always taken me that way. Well, some chaps have all the luck," and he raised his glass to Colonel Crofts and got up.

"'Back to the Army again, Sergeant,'" he said. "It's a bit late to think of getting married. My children would be as young as my grandchildren. No, I'll go on at the estate work. I like the Mertons and they are fair and they are generous. Good night all. And if," he added, pausing in the doorway, "I hear any more about old What's-his-name's mad dog I'll let you know, Crofts," and he went away.

"Stay a few moments," said Mrs. Crofts to the Carters. "I wanted to speak to you about this Coronation Festivities Committee, Kate. Could you ask Miss Hampton and Margot Phelps and me to tea one day and we could settle what *we* want? I'll have a talk to Eileen. She has more sense than ten of the other village women put together. And she really is leaving the Red Lion next year because Bateman says he won't go on walking out with her unless she does. And, considering they've been walking out for six years, I daresay he is right. Not but what she is mostly up here in her off time and cooks quite beautifully."

"They used to walk out for *ten* years when my mother started housekeeping," said Colonel Crofts, "or fifteen. But we must move with the times," and with affectionate good nights the Carters left the Vicarage and went down the hill. In Wiple Terrace every window was brightly lit to cheer the chill dusk of summer-time. From Maria came the full blast of Mr. Traill's gramophone, and from Louisa the ear-rending bellow of Mr. Feeder's wireless, while from Adelina and Editha came a noise, like the French Revolution, of well-bred people talking to one another.

"Thank goodness we didn't go further than Adelina," said Kate. "Mr. Traill and Mr. Feeder won't mind, if they noticed it at all, nor would old Mrs. Feeder. But I think Miss Hampton would have felt it very much. And now Mr. Wickham *must* get married, Everard, don't you think?" to which her husband replied that Wickham always had done exactly what he liked and always would. A wife, he added, was not a bad investment for one's old age.

"But I might die first," said Kate, who was very practical.

"Then I would marry again," said Everard, quite unmoved.

Kate, in a rather challenging way, said, "Who?"

"Whom," said Everard rather priggishly. "Oh, anyone. Why not Margot Phelps? Her parents will probably be dead by then, and she could look after the children nicely," and both of them laughed at the thought of Margot Phelps as a Headmaster's wife.

"One thing, Everard. If you marry her she *must* wear a skirt," said Kate, "because I know Matron would not allow a Head-master's wife in trousers," and then they got tired of this silly conversation and hurried home, as some nasty cold summer rain was falling.

Lady Cora had inherited a strong will and a managing dispo-sition, largely, we think, through the heiress Lady Glencora MacCluskie and the American Duchess Isabel Boncassen, who had both married into the Omnium family in the last century—from which last she inherited her exquisite legs and elegant slim feet, for her father, the Duke, had them, while the Duchess's legs, though worthy of all respect, had never been her strong point. She had also an excellent memory for faces and for promises made—two things much in her favour. Having con-sidered the matter of Margot Phelps, she put her views before her husband.

"Do exactly what you like, darling," he said. "Have the Fair-weathers by all means, and we'll make it a naval party and get Fewling to come. We might knock off the Greshams too," but Lady Cora said she thought not; and as Sir Cecil never ques-tioned his wife's views in domestic matters he was content to leave it at that. "We could go over to the other wing and see the Winters after tea," he said. "Now they are going, Cora, I rather wish they weren't," to which his wife very sensibly replied that he could not have his cake and eat it, and as Philip Winter needed larger quarters for his prep. school and her husband had his plan of a home for little boys of naval men, he must really be content.

"If suppose I must," said Sir Cecil. "And I shall be when they've gone, but I don't like to think of it. And I shall miss Nannie Allen. I gather that she is moving with the school, to be with Selina," for Mrs. Allen, who had been Nannie in the Waring family nearly fifty years ago, had now for many years been a kind of pensioner and had her little cottage in the village, though she spent most of her days at the Priory School, where her daughter Mrs. Hopkins was cook. Here, by the mere fact of her nannyhood, she frightened the raw village girls who came to work there so much that several of them became quite efficient and even used their cheap make-up with discretion.

A good deal of telephoning went on during the next few days between Lady Cora and Rose Fairweather and several things were said that made Lady Cora want to have the giggles. But as Rose's sense of humour, or even fun, was not up to her standard, she refrained.

In due course Sunday came, as indeed it always does. Rose Fairweather, who in spite of her apparent silliness was extremely practical, went over to Southbridge after lunch, according to promise, and collected Miss Phelps, who for such an occasion had again crammed herself into her coat and skirt with a rather depressed shirt or blouse of mud-coloured imitation silk and was carrying a pair of hogskin gloves. Miss Hampton, who was sitting-in for the afternoon, waved her approval, and Rose took Miss Phelps away.

"Now," said Rose, when they were out of the village, "will you drive?"

Miss Phelps looked rather than spoke her pleasure, and Rose pulled up at the side of the road.

"What nice driving-gloves," said Rose, seating herself beside Miss Phelps with a fine display of her lovely legs.

"They are nice, aren't they?" said Miss Phelps. "Mrs. Carter gave them to me for Christmas five years ago, but my hands seem to get bigger and bigger and I can't get into them. But I brought them with me because it seemed a pity to leave them at home," and she started the car in a workmanlike way.

Rose, who in all her life had never worried about anything though she was ready to deal in her own way with everything, sat back, made no comment and wondered idly if men's gloves wouldn't be better for Miss Phelps.

"I looked the road up on Miss Hampton's map," said Miss Phelps, "all but the last bit. When we get to Worsted will you let me know," and then she gave her mind to a gaggle of bicyclists who were riding all over the road, some of them (of opposite sexes, we regret to say) holding hands as they rode. Though, on reflection, if they had been of the same sex it would have been even sillier and just as dangerous to traffic.

"We're stuck now till we get to Skeynes," said Rose, with the resignation that even our boldest spirits are at last feeling under the general tolerance of lawlessness.

"No worse than cows," said Miss Phelps placidly as, to Rose's surprise and admiration, she edged her way past the bicyclists, just not ditching the car on the wrong side and then shot ahead, letting out a long hoot of derision from the horn as she did so.

"I couldn't have done it," said Rose admiringly, to which Miss Phelps replied that she hadn't run the Girl Guides for nothing and her father had always said attack was the best defence.

"Suppose you'd run over one of them," said Rose, but as Miss Phelps hadn't there was no more to be said. Passing Pooker's Piece, that Debateable Ground saved from Sir Ogilvy Hibberd (as he was then) by old Lord Pomfret's patriotic action, Miss Phelps turned north, past the gates of Staple Park, and was soon in Worsted.

"We turn up in about a mile," said Rose, once they were clear of the village, "just in front of the Sheep's Head," so Miss Phelps obediently turned up and in a few minutes had reached the end of the winding drive, with Beliers Priory full in view.

"I say!" said Miss Phelps, slowing down the better to look at the most hideous mansion in Barsetshire.

"It *is* pretty shattering," said Rose, gratified by Miss Phelps's surprise. "Of course, it isn't as big as Gatherum Castle, but I think it's much ghastlier."

Then they drove up to the front door and were taken to the other side of the house where Lady Cora was in her sitting-room overlooking Golden Valley.

"Hullo, I'm awfully sorry John isn't here," said Rose, "but he's coming in the little car. Here's Margot Phelps. She drove all the way. There were some quite shattering bicyclists all over the road and she simply frightened them out of their wits."

Sir Cecil came in and immediately won Miss Phelps's heart (having been carefully coached thereto by his wife) by saying that the Admiral's name was still remembered as one of the glories of the Iron class of destroyers, and, whether it was true or not, it gave such pleasure to Miss Phelps that it was well worth it.

Captain Fairweather then appeared.

"I hope I'm not late," he said to Lady Cora. "I had to go over to see Canon Fewling about something, and while I was there Mrs. Crofts rang up with the news about Wickham."

"Is he going to be married?" said Lady Cora. "It's high time he did something about it," and then Captain Fairweather told them about Mr. Wickham's legacy which gave universal pleasure. And if Miss Phelps felt particular pleasure it was simply because his thoughtfulness and kindness had touched her, for if you hardly ever have a treat you are grateful to someone who gives you one, even if it is only going out to tea.

Miss Phelps had secretly wondered whether Lady Cora would be wearing something very beautiful and rather hoped she would, so she was a little disappointed that her ladyship was, like most countrywomen in an average English summer, in tweeds. But even Miss Phelps could see that Lady Cora's tweeds were quite different from her own and, quite without envy, wished hers weren't quite so thick and shapeless. But she comforted herself by reflecting, very sensibly, that in England warmth is, on the whole, even more important than food. When they had finished tea Lady Cora showed Miss Phelps some of the chief hideousities of the Priory, including her own bedroom which had windows and woodwork of quite first-class revoltingness (even though painted cream instead of the artificially grained dark brown of her predecessors' days), but also the view across the valley.

"*How* I wish I could paint," said Miss Phelps after a silence.

"So do I," said Lady Cora. "I can't even draw a pig with my eyes shut. Oh, Miss Phelps—may I say Margot, it's such a nice name?—I wanted to ask you something. Rose Fairweather tells me that your father and mother are having their Golden Wedding soon."

"I expect father told her," said Miss Phelps. "He loved talking to her when she sat with him and got rid of Mr. Horton and his aunt. She *is* so kind. I feel rather awful letting everyone come and sit with father while I go off and enjoy myself."

"Have you any brothers or sisters?" said Lady Cora.

"I did have a brother," said Miss Phelps, "but I never saw him because he died before I was born and then father was on foreign service. I was born before the war—I mean the war father was in. I was forty last birthday."

"You don't look it," said Lady Cora and in all seriousness, for Miss Phelps's life of a ceaseless round of toil, combined with her total lack of interest in herself, made her look more like a hearty fifty. "But about the Golden Wedding. I don't know your people very well and they might think I am pushing in where I wasn't wanted, so Rose and I want to give *you* a present which I hope will please your people. It was the best way we could think of celebrating their anniversary without seeming to intrude," and if she swallows *that*, said Lady Cora to herself, she'd swallow a camel.

"Oh," said Miss Phelps, going purple in the face in a highly unbecoming way. "It's most awfully kind of you. But I couldn't."

"Why not?" said Lady Cora.

"Well, I don't know," said Miss Phelps weakly. "It is *most* awfully kind of you and I didn't mean to be ungrateful."

"It's not much," said Lady Cora. "It's only a length of tweed that I don't know what to do with. And if you will have it, Rose will see about it being made up. She knows a very good little tailor in Barchester and he will do it for practically nothing, and, of course, that is part of the present. So that is settled. I am so glad. I simply can't bear being disappointed. And now we will go over to the Priory School and see the little boys," which was a well-calculated stroke on Lady Cora's part, for all little boys were to Miss Phelps midshipmen in embryo and so came into her large affection for the Royal Navy.

So they went downstairs and the whole party walked across the garden to the Priory School, where the Headmaster, Philip Winter, and his wife, Sir Cecil Waring's sister, were in their drawing-room with one or two of the Junior Masters and a young woman whom Miss Phelps had never seen—dark, elegant, of middle height.

A great noise of greetings burst out, and Lady Cora, taking Miss Phelps firmly under her wing, introduced her to the Winters.

"How nice to meet you," said Philip Winter to his guest. "I was a master at Southbridge before the war and I remember Admiral and Mrs. Phelps very well. Weren't you at the Christmas party they had at the School for the evacuated children, Miss Phelps? Everard told me about your mother doing the Christmas tree. I was in the Army by then. How are your people?"

Miss Phelps remembered Mr. Winter quite well now, with his flaming red hair, and felt safe, so she confided to Mr. Winter that her father was rather an invalid now and so was her mother, but everyone was very kind, and while Colonel and Mrs. Crofts were away one of their friends came in every afternoon and how, owing to this kindness, she had been to Northbridge and to tea with Mr. Wickham: to all of which Mr. Winter listened with a kind of compassionate interest, though we may say that the compassion, in Miss Phelps's opinion had she known of it, would have been entirely misplaced.

"I don't suppose you would remember me, Miss Phelps," said one of Philip Winter's staff coming up to her. "I was at Southbridge before the war. Eric Swan. I was in the same form with Tony Morland and old Hacker," and, of course, Miss Phelps did remember and enquired after Mr. Swan's friends. Tony Morland, he said, was happily and heavily married, and Hacker held the chair of Latin at Redbrick University; and so, talking South-bridge shop, they got on very well indeed, so well that Miss Phelps forgot everything except how much she was enjoying herself, and a very good thing too, thought Lady Cora, looking benevolently at them. Rose Fairweather then joined them, whom Swan had also known in old Southbridge days as his Headmaster's daughter, and of whom he and his friends had the poorest opinion for her absolute silliness and her habit of find-ing a new catch-word and running it to death. But marriage to a devoted husband who stood no nonsense had vastly improved the former Rose Birkett, and Swan had to acknowledge her more mature beauty and a sort of universal benevolence which had not been apparent in her younger days. Not everyone, he thought, having picked up the news from his Headmaster's wife, Leslie Winter, Sir Cecil Waring's sister, would have taken such trouble about the not so young nor attractive daughter of an elderly Admiral, and, seeing that Mrs. Winter had designs on Miss Phelps, he continued his talk with Rose.

"You know Justinia Lufton?" said Mrs. Winter, bringing the dark, elegant young woman up to Miss Phelps. "She works at the St. John and Red Cross Hospital Library in Barchester and does a bit of secretarying for the Dean." Miss Phelps didn't, but with good-will on her side and Justinia's pleasant manners they got on quite well, finding a common ground in hens.

"You know mother and I live in the village since my brother married," said Justinia. "It's an awfully nice house, and we've got an old man who does the garden and cleans out the hen runs and their quite revolting houses, but he has bronchitis in the winter and gets drunk regularly on Saturdays. He doesn't come when he's drunk, which is perhaps just as well, but I have to make their revolting mashes or whatever one calls it. And I never know them apart unless one of them has a wooden leg," which surprised Miss Phelps till she realised that Miss Lufton was making a joke.

"We've had hens for ages," said Miss Phelps, "so I don't really mind doing the food. I only sometimes wish they weren't so ungrateful. However hard you work for them, they are never pleased." She smiled, to show that she wasn't really grumbling, and Justinia thought what very nice teeth she had.

Tea was at a large table and Miss Phelps wondered where she ought to sit, among so many people who knew each other so well. Leslie Winter was keeping an eye on the nice, rather gauche woman Lady Cora had brought, and looked at Swan, for the assistant masters were used to being a kind of honorary A.D.C. when they came to meals.

"May I sit next to you, Miss Phelps," said Swan, pulling out a chair for her. "You have Sir Cecil on your other side, so you will be quite safe. Do tell me what Southbridge is like now. I am always meaning to go over, but being an assistant master keeps one pretty busy, and in the holidays I go up to Scotland to my mother. And do your people still live at Jutland Cottage?"

This may have been just a polite question, but we rather suspect that Swan was throwing a lifebelt to Miss Phelps (if we may use a naval comparison for an Admiral's daughter), because his intelligence, and we may add his kind nature, told him that she was for the moment on foreign soil—or, shall we rather say, in uncharted seas.

As Swan said afterwards to Philip Winter, it was a great mistake to have tact and savoir vivre and savoir faire, because they always got you into trouble. Miss Phelps at once rose to the bait and told Swan all about the house and garden and how she sold most of the eggs and how that nice Canon Fewling had bought some hens and how kind Mr. Wickham had been in driving her over to tea at his house and how kind it was of Mrs. Fairweather to fetch her in the car and how she had found her mother turning out that cupboard in the kitchen over the dresser and mother oughtn't to have done it because she had a heart and how kind Lady Cora was and had given her a length of tweed, till Swan devoutly wished he had never begun being kind himself. Then, to his great relief, Sir Cecil Waring, on the other side of Miss Phelps, claimed her attention and told her about his plan for a kind of home for the orphans of naval ratings with a view to educating them to follow their fathers' calling, all of which she heard with real interest, though when Sir Cecil said he supposed the end of it would be that they would all go into the films or the black market she thought perhaps he was being funny. Leslie Winter, keeping an eye on everything, as a good Headmaster's wife should, wondered if she ought to rescue her brother, but Miss Phelps looked so happy and eager that she left things alone.

"No, we will *not* sit in the veranda, my love," said Philip Winter to his wife, when tea had come to an end. "Not on an English Sunday afternoon." So they returned to the drawing-room, where there was a fire, and Miss Phelps did feel rather hot but didn't like to take her jacket off, and noticed that most of the other ladies were indeed wearing tweed skirts, but each had what she had always longed for: what is called a twin set, namely a jumper (or jersey, as we used to call them) and a cardigan. And as she looked at them, her thick tweed jacket and the mud-coloured imitation silk blouse suddenly became rather hateful to her. But one does not cry in public, especially if one is an Admiral's daughter, so she choked back her feelings and told herself how extraordinarily lucky she was to be having such a treat and to know that Miss Hampton wouldn't mind if she was a little bit late.

It was at this moment that Rose Fairweather, mindful of her responsibilities, said she expected Miss Phelps would be wanting to get back.

"Oh, but you must see the boys first, Miss Phelps," said Leslie Winter. "I told them a real Admiral's daughter was coming and they are so excited," and, of course, Miss Phelps could not say no to this, so Leslie took her to a large room where a lot of small boys were painting, or being very important with model railways, or practising boxing with friends, and any other activity which suggested itself to their cheerful minds on a cold summer's afternoon with a drizzle of rain outside.

"Here is Miss Phelps," said Leslie. "Her father is an Admiral. He was in the Battle of Jutland."

"Has he got one arm?" said one little boy hopefully. "Mummy's uncle's only got one arm; he's a Captain."

Various other little boys then boasted of physical defects, not all attributable to war, in their various older relatives.

"Don't all talk at once," said Miss Phelps, feeling herself at last in her own element, "and I'll tell you all about it," and sitting down on a playbox she regaled the company with an account, directly taken from her father's experience, of heavy shelling from the German ships, fires breaking out, guns out of action, men blown to pieces (at which the little boys shrieked with delight), and how Admiral Phelps (only he wasn't an Admiral then) and his Captain (who had a great cut on his forehead and one arm broken) did finally collect their victorious and shot-shattered ships and so came home.

"Please, Miss Phelps," said one of the boys, "would you tell it all over again," to which Miss Phelps replied that she had to go back and take care of her father and mother, but if Mrs. Winter would let her come another day she would tell it all over again and bring a splinter from her father's ship. She further, in response to various shrill requests, said she would ask her father to write his autograph for anyone who wanted it. Every arm shot into the air. Miss Phelps laughed, because she felt more like crying, said goodbye to the boys, with some difficulty refraining from kissing some of the smaller ones, and followed Leslie to the house.

"I can't thank you enough, Miss Phelps," said Leslie Winter. "You *must* come again. Will you? My husband would come over to fetch you and take you back," for her sister-in-law, Lady Cora, had explained to her that the Phelpses had not got a car. To this Miss Phelps agreed with deep pleasure, and then Rose

Fairweather said they really must go and hurried her through the goodbyes and into her car.

"Oh!" said Miss Phelps, when they were halfway down the drive. "My tweed that Lady Cora gave me."

"I knew you'd forget it," said Rose. "It's in the back of the car. We must see about having it made up. What's your best time?"

Miss Phelps did not answer for a moment. When Lady Cora had showed her the tweed her gratitude and joy had completely drowned her usual practical way of thinking. Now she suddenly realised that the present was likely to be not a joy but a very worrying responsibility. A sailor's daughter must face facts and always tell the truth, so, not without a rather horrid feeling that she might cry, or even as bad sniff, she said, "Oh, Rose, I'm awfully afraid I'd better not have the tweed. Quite honestly I can't afford to go to a good tailor and I *couldn't* let a bad one touch such lovely stuff. And," she continued, her courage rising with the sound of her own voice, "I don't think I could afford a bad one either."

She then sat silent, quite ready to be turned out of the car and told to walk home.

"Oh, but the tweed and having it made up are all part of the present," said Rose. "Of *course* Lady Cora wants you to go to her tailor—not her London one, of course, but a good local man. She would be shatteringly hurt if that lovely tweed wasn't properly cut and made up. You tell me a day you're free and I'll run you into Barchester."

Miss Phelps, completely surprised and routed by Rose's air of effortless superiority, meekly said that Wednesday was the best day for Barchester because she could always get someone on Wednesdays to sit with her father while her mother rested.

"Splendid," said Rose, rather alarming even the intrepid spirit of Miss Phelps by taking both hands off the wheel to powder her face, though so swiftly was it done that Miss Phelps's fright went almost as quickly as it came. "Look here. I've got to go to Barchester next Wednesday to have my hair set—*too* shattering, but I'll look like nothing on earth if I don't. If I picked you up about a quarter to twelve, could you manage?"

With the courage of despair Miss Phelps said she thought it would be all right.

"Oh, I say, I'm sorry, would you like to drive?" said Rose, slowing down at the crossroads, but Miss Phelps, rent by so many unusual events and emotions, said please would Mrs. Fairweather go on driving because she drove so well, to which Rose replied that, please would she call her Rose because all her friends did, and then overtook a large lorry which hadn't a mirror by the driver's seat and nipped past it in the face of one of the Southbridge United Viator Passenger Company's motor coaches, to Miss Phelps's deep and outspoken admiration.

"Now don't forget," said Rose Fairweather, as she stopped outside Jutland Cottage. "Next Wednesday. I'll be here at a quarter to twelve if you can manage it, and I'll bring the tweed with me. Or," she added, with one of the moments of understanding which occasionally surprised her nearest and dearest, "would you rather have it yourself?"

Miss Phelps, who had felt for a moment like an unmarried mother who has to leave her child in an orphanage, said she really would like to have it and show it to mother.

"Here you are, then," said Rose, reaching for the tweed and shoving it into its owner's arms. "I won't tell anyone about it, not even Tubby. It'll look quite crashingly shattering when it's made up. Goodbye till Wednesday," and she kissed Miss Phelps carelessly, watching her get out and open the gate of Jutland Cottage, waved her hand and sped homewards. As she went through Greshamsbury she saw Canon Fewling cutting off dead roses in his front garden and pulled up her car.

"Hullo Tubby," she said. "Come over for a drink."

Canon Fewling looked up and came to the garden gate.

"I can't," he said. "I'd love to, but Miss Hopgood's aunt is coming over from Northbridge by the bus to have supper with me."

"Well, I must say it sounds quite foully shattering," said Rose, "but just as you like. I suppose you are going to talk about stars. I must say I think stars are quite perfectly pretentious, if you see what I mean."

Canon Fewling did not quite see what she meant, but any feeling of mortification he may have had was swallowed up by his scientific interest in Rose's new word. Every year in Rose's happy life, as far back as her parents and friends could remember, had been marked by a fresh word, applied indiscriminately to animals, vegetables and minerals, and her friends sometimes wondered how anyone as illiterate as Rose could think of so many. Swan, who had known her since his schooldays at Southbridge when her father was Headmaster, had a theory that she had kind of private aerial that picked up from the ambient ether any word that was travelling through space and one ought to be thankful that "wizard" had not yet reached her. Canon Fewling, though without the advantage of having known Rose since she was in her 'teens, had already been struck by this phenomenon and, perhaps rather unfairly, asked Rose exactly what she meant.

"Oh, you know," said Rose. "Having all those Latin and Greek names and really not a bit like what they are called. I mean, no one's ever seen a person that shape."

Canon Fewling, interested scientifically and personally in Rose's science of stars, asked which person.

"You know. Orion," said Rose. "I suppose he was an ancient Roman or something, but he couldn't have looked like that. I mean, if I just had a star at the end of my arms and legs and a kind of tail hanging down, you wouldn't call it a person—I mean, if it was only stars and I wasn't there. Too shatteringly like those ghastly things in exhibitions all made of wire and holes."

"Perhaps not," said Canon Fewling, even his kindly nature feeling a desire to smack Rose—though all for her good.

"But I'll tell you something *really* nice, Tubby," Rose went on. "Are you in a hurry?"

"Not a bit," said Canon Fewling, who all through his life as a priest had done his best never to be in a hurry if anyone wished to talk to him, in case he might cause discouragement. "Fire away."

"You know Margot Phelps," said Rose. "Well, Lady Cora and I have had a consultation about her, to see that she gets some treats. She did get a treat when Mr. Wickham took her to tea at his house, but that was only one thing. So Lady Cora has given her some very good tweed and I'm taking her to Barchester to get it made into a suit. Of course, it's absolutely top secret. Lady Cora is going to pay to have it made up and I'm going to give her a few other things. Now, Tubby, don't say you disapprove, because that would be too quite shatteringly pretentious," and she laid her hand on his arm.

"I couldn't disapprove anything you do, or Lady Cora either," said Canon Fewling. "All I wonder is—but doubtless you have thought of that—whether Miss Phelps will accept it. The Phelpses are desperately independent—as I know to my cost," he added.

"Now I'll tell *you* one," said Rose, her lovely face flushed as much with the plan for giving pleasure as with the delicate pink foundation and the discreet dusting with pink powder on her cheeks. "She may be independent, but she is grateful. Oh, I know *I* haven't really done anything for her to be grateful about," she added, "unless it was getting that dreadful Mr. Horton and his aunt out of the house, but she thinks I have, which is exactly the same. So now she has got to do something to pay me back and that's it," with which rather muddled explanation she sat back in the car.

"You are a very remarkable woman," said Canon Fewling.

"Me?" said Rose, in complete and ungrammatical surprise. "Really, Tubby, you are quite shatteringly un-understanding. *Nobody* could not be kind to Margot; but she does quite shatteringly need a proper belt," which to Canon Fewling's in some ways innocent mind meant a strap with a buckle at one end and some holes at the other. "Well, you can't look at stars till it's dark. Bring Miss Hopgood's aunt over after supper. Mr. Wickham gave John a bottle of Scotch whisky and we're going to celebrate."

If the sentence sounded a little vague, Canon Fewling was used to that, but Rose did not mean to let him off so lightly.

"You might ask *what* we're celebrating," she said, with what in other women would have been a pout, but only made her look more ravishing. "It's Lord Aberfordbury's dog that tried to get into Wick's hen-roost and Wicks's housekeeper put the washing-tub on the dog and then Wicks took the dog to the vet and the vet took it to old Aberfordbury next day and it's coming up before the Bench. You *do* miss things, Tubby."

"Yes, I do," said Canon Fewling. "But there are other things I don't miss, you know."

"Like your church," said Rose gently. "Well, whoever says what, I think you are quite *crashingly* good. Bring old who-ever-it's aunt it is in for a drink after supper, anyway," so Canon Fewling said he would and Rose drove home to see her younger children in bed and have a long delightful talk to her husband.

"Don't go overdoing it," said Captain Fairweather. "It's all very well to start a good thing, but you've got to go through with it, my girl. I'm all for giving Margot Phelps a hand, she's a good girl, if a bit long in the tooth, and she deserves it. Only if she takes to being grateful and pestering the life out of you like that woman in Lisbon when you took her to the maternity hospital by the skin of her teeth don't blame *me*."

"Oh, Margot wouldn't be grateful," said Rose, at which her husband laughed, but had to admit to himself that his Rose was, as she usually was about human relationships, absolutely right. Margot was no beauty, but she was a thoroughly good girl—if girl one could call her—and had all her admiral father's integrity and more. If more people could accept kindness without making the giver's life a plague by going on expressing gratitude, it would be easier for all parties, which led him deeper into philosophical paths than he could go, so he very sensibly thought about something else.

As the evening went on the sky became clouded and there was no star-gazing to be done. Canon Fewling gave Miss Hopgood's aunt a very good supper and heard all the latest Northbridge gossip and then took her over to the Fairweathers', where Miss Hopgood's aunt put down her whisky like a gentleman and after some uninteresting talk said she must catch her bus.

"I'll run you over," said Captain Fairweather. "I haven't put the car away," which offer Miss Hopgood's aunt accepted.

"And," said Rose rather severely to Canon Fewling when they were left alone, "don't have remorse and think *you* ought to have taken her. You've put your car away and John hadn't. And don't go thinking you've missed doing a good deed, Tubby, because that is quite too shatteringly self-conscious. Just be unselfish and think about what fun it will be for me to take Margot to Barchester. Which reminds me," and she went away to the telephone. Before long she was back.

"*That's* all right," she said. "I rang up Mrs. Crofts and she is going to ask the Admiral and Mrs. Phelps to lunch and then she'll go back with them and sit with the Admiral and see about tea."

"How thoughtful you are," said Canon Fewling.

"One has to be," said Rose. "You're quite shatteringly thoughtful yourself, Tubby. I shall take Margot in the morning and dump her in the shop while my hair's done and then give her lunch and see about the tweed and have her back at Jutland Cottage by tea-time."

"I have to be in Barchester on Wednesday," said Canon Fewling. "Will you both honour me by lunching with me at the County Club?"

"I knew you would think of something nice," said Rose and then, rather to Canon Fewling's annoyance, she put the wireless on. It was not so much that he minded hearing the ten o'clock news which he had already heard at nine o'clock, as that he would have liked to sit quietly with Rose. But one must not be greedy. Captain Fairweather soon came back and Canon Fewling went home, thinking how practical Rose was, how kind and thoughtful for that nice Margot Phelps whom everyone had always taken for granted. And what a *good* girl Margot Phelps was. A phrase of Mr. Adams, the rich ironmaster, came to his mind. "The best stainless steel and then some." That was Margot Phelps. And as for Rose, the words for her had come into his mind quite a long time ago now. Not so long by days and weeks perhaps, but during those days and weeks he had thought so often of Rose's beauty that lived with kindness. And very often he had thought of Margot Phelps, her pleasant unaffected devotion to her parents, her complete absence of any thought of herself and, even more, her splendid want of self-pity. To know two such women was, he felt, something he hardly deserved and he gave most humble and hearty thanks for all the blessings that had been vouchsafed him since he came to Greshamsbury.

CHAPTER 8

So strange and interesting had Miss Phelps found her half-holiday with Lady Cora and Rose that she would almost have thought it a dream had it not been for the tweed, which she put away in her own room as soon as she got home and said nothing about it till next day, when the Admiral had gone out for his usual morning walk, which often included the Vicarage or one of the cottages in Wiple Terrace. Then did Miss Phelps ask her mother to come and see what Lady Cora had given her and deep as was her gratitude to Lady Cora for the gift, her gratitude was doubled when she saw her mother's pleasure and how lovingly she handled the material.

"It's as good as pre-war," said Mrs. Phelps, "I mean pre-1914. I had such a lovely tweed suit in my trousseau, tailor-made. It cost seven guineas, I think, and everyone thought Granny was being frightfully extravagant. But it lasted and lasted and lasted. I think this will last. It feels like real wool to me. I wonder where Lady Cora got it," and inside herself she wondered how much it cost.

Miss Phelps had wondered the same, and after an excited and on Mrs. Phelps side almost tearful discussion about what sort of buttons would look nice with it and how she would knit a jumper to go with it, it was decided not to tell the Admiral.

To this Miss Phelps had no objection. Partly because she felt the tweed was almost too sacred to mention to a man, deeply though she loved her father, and partly because there was just a chance that the Admiral might feel it was charity, which would spoil it all. So it was wrapped up and put away again and the two ladies began to make plans for a sitter, or even a series of sitters, for the great Wednesday.

Most luckily Mrs. Phelps, while out shopping on the following morning, met Mrs. Crofts, who asked if she and the Admiral could lunch at the Rectory on Wednesday, when Mrs. Francis Brandon was coming. The Phelpses had known and liked Mrs. Francis during her brief stay in Southbridge when she was Mrs. Arbuthnot. Mrs. Phelps accepted the invitation and then made a clean breast of everything to Mrs. Crofts and how Margot was being as it were abducted to Barchester by Rose Fairweather who was having a lovely length of tweed, the gift of Lady Cora Waring, made up for her.

"Only we don't want my husband to know," she said, "in case he feels it is charity, or dishonourable or something silly. Men *can* be so dense."

"But won't he notice it when Margot is wearing it?" said Mrs. Crofts.

"Not for several days," said Mrs. Phelps, and a look passed between the two women expressive of how trying and often stupid men were, "and then I shall say it is a length I had by me only I'd forgotten it," which Mrs. Crofts found a very sensible idea and so became yet one more conspirator in this innocent plot.

To Miss Phelps it appeared that Monday and Tuesday would never pass, but pass they did (as they always do) and a little before twelve Rose came to the gate. To Miss Phelps's slight annoyance her father, who was doing some mild gardening in front, greeted Rose's appearance as a kind thought for himself and showed her how well his standard roses were doing. But a sailor's daughter must be brave, so she came into the garden and looked at Rose, whose candid countenance became more innocent than ever.

"I've come to ask Margot to lunch with me," she said.

The Admiral replied that as he and his wife were going to the

Vicarage it would be very nice for Margot not to be alone, which words made Miss Phelps feel that she was frightfully guilty and ought to confess, but she just had the sense not to.

"Then I'll take her along with me," said Rose, for which the Admiral thanked her, saying in a perfectly audible aside that Margot didn't often get out and how kind it was of Rose, upon which Rose winked at Miss Phelps, who felt like a murderess, though this was quite unnecessary. So Miss Phelps, kissing her father and telling him to give her love to the Croftses and Mrs. Arbuthnot—she meant Mrs. Brandon—got into Rose's car with the tweed in a parcel, and the Admiral went on cutting dead roses off his standard trees.

Once out of Southbridge, Rose stopped the car, made Miss Phelps change places with her, and sat quite composedly thinking of nothing in particular till they reached the outskirts of Barchester.

"Which way?" said Miss Phelps.

"Bostock and Plummer," said Rose, this being an old-established Ladies' Emporium dating from the eighteen-seventies or so. "You'll have to park in Barley Street—it will come in handy," though for what she did not say.

Luckily it was not market day. The car was easily parked and Rose walked with Miss Phelps to Bostock and Plummer, where the respectable county still did its shopping. Rose led the way upstairs—for Bostock and Plummer never having had a lift did not propose to have one—to the underwear department, where she approached an elderly shop assistant and said, "Good morning, Miss Spragge. I'm Mrs. Fairweather. Do you remember when my mother, Mrs. Birkett, used to bring me here for my belts?"

Miss Spragge, who was dressed in the severe black of a past generation, said what a pleasure it was to see Miss Rose again and how was Mrs. Birkett keeping? Rose said her mother was very well and would be so glad to have news of Miss Spragge and would Miss Spragge let her see some nice belts for Miss Phelps, to wear with a new tweed suit. Miss Spragge, who was used to every eccentricity among her older clients, serving as she did old

Lady Norton and the Bishop's wife, gave a knowing look at Miss Phelps and said she knew just what Mrs. Fairweather meant. She then took them into a small fitting-room with a looking-glass in a dark corner, went away and reappeared with an armful of belts, or slightly boned corsets, or whatever one pleases to call them. Into a selection of these belts Miss Phelps was then pulled and pushed and coaxed by Miss Spragge's masterful hands.

"Now, Miss Birkett—really I keep on quite forgetting it is Mrs. Fairweather now," said Miss Spragge—"I think we have the idea."

Rose thought so too and Miss Phelps was too fascinated and indeed overawed to say a word.

"That's the one," said Rose. "You'd better keep it on, Margot. You'll need it at the tailor's. And how is your mother, Miss Spragge?"

As Miss Spragge's old mother had been ailing, at her daughter's expense, for the last twenty-five years or so, this was a purely honorary question, but Rose knew that Miss Spragge liked to be asked and would enjoy telling her mother, who was very deaf and rather wanting in the intellect, that Mrs. Birkett's daughter had been in the shop that morning, so with her usual lavish and impersonal kindness she did what would give pleasure.

"And not a nice brassière, Miss Spragge," she said. "*Not* uplift."

"It's nice to hear a lady say that, madam," said Miss Spragge. "A customer of mine—but I do not name names—who lives not a hundred yards from here, asked me for an uplift and I said in my pointed way, for I can say quite pointed things, I assure you, Miss Birkett—Mrs. Fairweather, I should say—as I was saying, I said quite pointedly, "Uplifts are in the Juveniles, madam," and I can assure you that she went quite a beetroot red."

"How like her," said Rose who appeared to have a clue to the customer, though Miss Phelps hadn't. "Uplift at the Palace, how too pretentious," upon which Miss Spragge smiled a kind of shocked approval, went away and returned with an armful of what in the earlier years of our life were called bust-bodices.

Miss Phelps, by now quite sure she was in a dream, submitted to being tried on by Miss Spragge until that lady and Rose were satisfied.

"Miss Phelps will wear those," said Rose, "and I'll take another of each, and please put them down to mother's account— Mrs. Birkett. I'll pay her back. Just put the other ones in a parcel. Mother will be too terribly pleased to hear about you," and then Miss Phelps got into her depressed suit again feeling, Lawka-mercy on me, this is none of I.

"Now I must simply fly to my hairdresser," said Rose. "Come along," and they walked to the Maison Tozier, Barchester's best beauty parlour, with what they called a Sports Department upstairs which included stockings and a good selection of what we can only describe as Woollies, owned by a cousin of Messrs. Scatcherd and Tozer, the well-known Barchester caterers, where she was warmly greeted as one of the firm's best advertisements.

"Just the usual set, Miss Dahlia," she said to the young lady who stepped gracefully forward to conduct her to her cubicle. "And this is my friend, Miss Phelps; her father's an Admiral, and she's too busy farming to bother about clothes. Do let one of the girls take her upstairs and find her a really suitable twin set. She wants to wear it straight away. Here's a scrap of her tweed suit for a pattern. On my account, please," and leaving a rather distracted Miss Phelps to her fate she gave herself over to the ministrations of Miss Dahlia and thought very comfortably about nothing.

Meanwhile Miss Phelps, extremely frightened, but somehow heartened by the comfortable support of the belt and brassière, was delivered to a young woman who was of a charitable disposition and felt she must do her best by a customer who obviously didn't know her own mind. Taking one look at Miss Phelps, she went behind a curtain and came out with an armful of what are called twin sets, though if one had twins one of whom had long arms and the other arms that stopped well above the elbow it would be disconcerting. Taking no notice of Miss

Phelp's wistful looks at beige, dirty green, or muddy turquoise blue, she produced a jumper and cardigan of a soft golden-brown shade which Miss Phelps, greatly daring, tried on and at once fell in love with.

"Quite madam's style," said the young woman, who was much less frightening than Miss Phelps thought she would be. "Will you wear them, madam?" said Miss Phelps, by now becoming quite reckless, said she would, feeling that if the worst came to the worst she could change into her Cinderella jumper in the garden shed before going into the house, and then went down to the hairdressing department.

"Mrs. Fairweather will be ready in a few moments, madam," said one of the attendant nymphs. "Would you like a book?" and she laid before Miss Phelps several illustrated fashion journals which she looked through with an unseeing eye, being by now quite dazed by the morning's experiences. Presently Rose came out looking, to Miss Phelps's eye, exactly as she had looked when she went in, or in other words perfectly neat and lovely.

"Let's see what they gave you," said Rose. "You *do* look nice in that browny-gold. It goes so well with your hair. I wish we had time, but we haven't. Dahlia," she called to the girl who had been setting her hair, "what would you do with Miss Phelps's hair? She lives in Southbridge and is frightfully busy and can't possibly come in more than every six weeks."

"Well, madam," said Dahlia, "the lady's hair has a nice bit of natural wave and if I could cut it properly it would need very little doing to it. In fact if there were many ladies with hair like that we wouldn't keep going, it's a fact. Thank you, Mrs. Fairweather," she added as Rose gave a generous tip.

"Got your parcels?" said Rose, always practical. "It's a pity we can't get your hair properly cut, but we mustn't keep Tubby waiting. Come on. It isn't worth taking the car," and after a few minutes' walking they reached the County Club, where Canon Fewling was waiting in the hall.

The County Club was a handsome if heavy early nineteenth-

century house, bought and very nicely restored by the old
County Club which had grown out of its premises between the
wars. Canon Fewling took his ladies through the spacious hall
with its high curved staircase to where, covering a good deal of
what had been the garden before the house fell on evil days, was
a large bar; a post-war innovation much disapproved by the
elder members, who with a fine large-mindedness used it so
much that the younger members complained they could never
get near the bar.

"Dry sherry, please," said Rose.

"And what for you, Miss Phelps?" said Canon Fewling.

Miss Phelps, flown with the morning's work, said a small
whisky, adding that she wished her father were there, as he
couldn't afford whisky now except on doctor's orders.

"If I had a large one, would you too?" said Canon Fewling.

Almost shocked, but upheld by the belt and brassière, Miss
Phelps said, Yes, please, and then wondered if he would think
her a Scarlet Woman.

"Splendid," said Canon Fewling. "I never like drinking alone.
Wine, yes. But cocktails or spirits, no. Two double whiskies and
a dry sherry, please," and the waiter went to get their orders.
Canon Fewling and Rose Fairweather fell into a kind of county
chat and though they did not mean to exclude Miss Phelps, her
daily circle was so small that she did not know most of the
people they were talking about. However she was quite happy to
sit, rather bolt upright owing to the new belt, and listen and look.

A good-looking dark-haired young woman stopped opposite
them in whom Miss Phelps recognised the Miss Lufton she had
met at the Priory School. To her surprised pleasure Miss Lufton
recognised her (which was not difficult) and stopped.

"I'm waiting for Eric Swan," she said. "I told mother about
my meeting you, Miss Phelps, and she said she remembered
dancing with your father just after the first war," at which
pleasant remembrances of her father Miss Phelps went brick red

and somehow managed to introduce Canon Fewling, who pulled a chair across to his table and offered it to Justinia.

"Father gave up dancing quite a long time ago," said Miss Phelps. "He and mother can't do much now. But he will love to hear about your mother. It's Lady Lufton, isn't it?" and Justinia said yes, it was, only she was the dowager now, because Ludovic had married Grace Grantly and she was the real Lady Lufton.

"I wish more people would be Dowagers," said Canon Fewling. "I find it much more distinguished than Poppy, Lady; or even Corinna, Duchess," which led to a rather uninformed discussion as to the proper nomination of dowagers if there happened to be more than two living at the same time, till Eric Swan appeared.

"I don't apologise for being late," he said to Justinia Lufton, "because the Cathedral clock is just striking one and yonder is the moon," an allusion which meant nothing to Justinia Lufton or to Canon Fewling, nor did Swan expect it to. As for Rose, we doubt whether she even heard the words on account of her lipstick which had stuck and needed coaxing.

"That's out of the *Golden Treasury*," said Miss Phelps, plunging into the conversation with a courage born of the new belt and brassière and fortified by the whisky.

"May I sit beside you for a moment?" said Swan. "It is so pleasant to find anyone who understands what one says. I don't suppose any of the young people read Wordsworth now."

"Well, I don't really, either," said Miss Phelps, "only I'm not very young, and as a matter of fact I remembered that bit because I had to learn it by heart when I went to stay with my grandmother—mother's mother—when I was a little girl. I had to learn something by heart every day and say it to her before breakfast, and that was one of them. I hated it."

Swan looked benevolently at her and asked Justinia if she was ready for lunch.

"Don't forget you are coming to see us," said Justinia to Miss Phelps as she got up. "What about a day next week?" upon which Miss Phelps fell into a bog of muddled thoughts. She wanted to accept Justinia's invitation very much indeed, but she would have to plan a day with her mother and see if she could do the journey to Framley by a series of motor buses. Swan, remembering her hard-working life from his schooldays at Southbridge, realised with a quickness of sympathy peculiarly his own that her parents and the question of transport were the difficulties.

"I have a kind of extra day off on Thursday fortnight," said Swan. "I am coming over to Southbridge to lunch with the Carters. Could I pick you up in my little car and take you over to Framley for tea, Miss Phelps? I would also return you to Jutland Cottage with punctuality and despatch."

"A very good plan," said Justinia Lufton kindly. "We'll expect you both for tea, then," and she went away with Swan.

"It's absolutely marvellous the way Eric Swan plans things," said Rose, who was looking at her lovely face in the mirror of her powder compact (silly word, but there it is, so we must use it) and applying a freshener of powder which most people would have thought quite unnecessary. "He was always like that at school. He and a boy called Tony Morland were camping on Parsley Island the year I was still engaged to Philip Winter and Daddy and Mummy took the Rectory at Northbridge for the summer, and we had a picnic with them. Let's have lunch, Tubby," all of which Miss Phelps found rather confusing, but it was part of the curious and not unpleasant dream she was in, so she accepted it as she had been accepting everything and they went into the dining-room where Canon Fewling treated them to the best, including some red wine. Rose, whose abstemiousness was always a surprise to those who did not know her well, said she would like water, so Canon Fewling and Miss Phelps had a bottle between them, Miss Phelps taking her fair share with naval aplomb.

"I wish I could drink like that," said Rose with undisguised envy, "but I go red in the face and go to sleep, and anyway I don't like the taste much."

"I'm a hardened drinker myself," said Canon Fewling. "But never alone."

"Wicks is the best," said Miss Phelps. "It doesn't matter if he's alone or not. At least he says so. And he is very generous. He nearly always brings father a bottle of something. In fact we've got three bottles of whisky put away in a cupboard because we don't want to hurt his feelings if he sees them."

"What would you do if he asked you?" said Rose.

"I don't know," said Miss Phelps, "but I think we would say we had enjoyed them very much, which would be quite true, because if we had drunk them we would have enjoyed them," which neat piece of casuistry was rather beyond Rose Fair-weather's powers of apprehension.

Canon Fewling signed his bill and said they would have coffee in the library, where it was quieter, and took them up to a fine room overlooking the scrap of garden, with the Cathedral spire white in the sunshine beyond the market place. One or two of his friends or acquaintance were sitting there, each of whom had something pleasant to say to Miss Phelps as soon as they knew who she was, for her hard-working life in Southbridge had cut her off from the outside world more and more. Captain Belton, R.N., he who had married Susan Dean, the sister of the well-known actress Jessica Dean, had served under the Admiral for a short time in the Far East. Sir Edmund Pridham, the doyen of the county, remembered the Admiral dancing a horn-pipe on the table some fifty years earlier, though whose table he had forgotten. Lady Pomfret, taking a brief rest between com-mittees, smiled at Canon Fewling who got up to greet her and introduced his guests. Lady Pomfret said how valuable Captain Fairweather was on the Barsetshire Solders' and Sailors' Families Association and how much they would like to see the Admiral on it.

"I know father would love it," said Miss Phelps, standing up because she was being spoken to, "but he isn't very well and we haven't a car now. He is awfully keen about the S.S.F.A.," to which Lady Pomfret replied that perhaps Miss Phelps would allow herself to be put up for the Council, which naturally deprived that lady of her powers of speech. Lady Pomfret, taking her red-faced silence for consent, said she must mention it to the committee and asked a quiet middle-aged woman who was with her not to let her forget, and they must ask Miss Phelps to lunch at the Towers and so passed on her way. It was all very exciting, even intoxicating, but Miss Phelps, whom nature aided by circumstances had made very unselfish, felt a little anxious about Rose Fairweather who, though not in the least excluded form these passing conversations, was not exactly in them. But she need not have worried, for wherever she went Rose collected her own circle, largely of male admirers who fluttered round her light, but also of a number of people of both sexes who in her opinion needed some kind of help; and we may confidently say that in spite of her beauty she had never made an enemy, or to use a better word, an unfriend.

"Who was that nice kind-faced friend of Lady Pomfret's?" said Miss Phelps.

"Oh, Miss Merriman," said Rose "She was a governess or something and stayed on and is most frightfully practical with committees and things," which is a lesson to us all as to how we are misrepresented with the kindest intentions by people who have not exact knowledge, for Miss Merriman had never been a governess in her life. Secretary, companion and true friend to the old Countess of Pomfret she had been, and at her death had transferred her care to Lady Pomfret's sister-in-law, Lady Emily Leslie; and then, after Lady Emily's death, had come back to help the younger Lady Pomfret. That she had once, years ago, felt very deeply about the present Lord Pomfret, then only the young cousin who would inherit the title, was her private affair kept within her secret heart and now but a shadow of a shade.

"Good gracious," said Rose. "A quarter-past two. Thank you a million times for the lovely lunch, Tubby. Come on, Margot, or we shall be late getting back," and without much ceremony she hustled Miss Phelps away and back to Barley Street. Here she got the tweed out of the car and took Miss Phelps up a narrow staircase, past the first landing where a door bore the inscription Madame Tomkins on a brass plate and up to the second floor. Here on the door facing them were the words Hamp, Tailor and Cutter, in white paint. Rose went in and there was Mr. Hamp, the tailor and cutter himself, sitting cross-legged upon a kind of counter, like the Tailor of Gloucester.

"Hullo, Mr. Hamp," said Rose. "This is Miss Phelps. Her father is Admiral Phelps at Southbridge and she's got some lovely tweed for you," with which words she laid the parcel on the counter.

"Dear me," said Mr. Hamp, laying down his work and opening the parcel, "a lovely length, madam. It's not often you handle material like this now. Dear me. I remember altering a skirt for Lady Waring, in nineteen forty-two it was, when old Sir Harry Waring was still alive, and that *was* tweed. No, I'm mistaken, it was her ladyship's black skirt; a lovely bit of material. Not but what this isn't good. I wonder where it came from. The last I did in this material was for Miss Jessica Dean, and how she got it past the Customs, brining it from Yewessay as she did, I couldn't say."

"Well, you'd better measure Miss Phelps," said Rose, "because we've got to get back to Southbridge."

"In a hurry, that's what all you ladies are," said Mr. Hamp, climbing down from his table. "It's not hurry that measures a suit, nor cuts it out, nor bastes it, nor sews it, though when I say sew it's machines nowadays. Now, if you'll stand still, miss," which Miss Phelps did, while Mr. Hamp with his yard measure in his hand circled about her, first standing and then on his knees, keeping up a running accompaniment under his breath of "twenty-five, forty-two, sixteen and a half, twelve and a half," or if not exactly those numbers, something that sounded remarkably like them. He then got up, took a very dirty little book out of one pocket and a stump of pencil out of another and giving the pencil a good lick, wrote down his figures.

"Do you never get them wrong?" said Miss Phelps, much interested.

"I couldn't, miss," said Mr. Hamp with the appalling confidence of the artist. "Though I may say," he added with an Ancient Mariner gleam in his eye for his audience, "that there's one place where my memory isn't what it was and that's if I'm doing a pair of gent's evening trousers and we come, if you ladies will excuse the expression to————"

"Then that's splendid," said Rose, whose social security sense never failed her. "Now when can you give Miss Phelps a fitting?"

After some consulting a day and time were fixed. Miss Phelps said she would talk to her mother about not letting father know, and Rose said she would fetch her as before and getting away from Mr. Hamp's eloquence as best they could, they went downstairs and so back to the car. Again Rose remembered to let Miss Phelps drive and they were in Southbridge as the church clock struck four.

"Will you come in?" said Miss Phelps. "Father would so like to see you," but Rose, who wanted to get home, left her love for the parent Phelpses and sped away.

Miss Phelps stood for a moment on the doorstep, feeling that her golden crown, her sparkling dress and her glass slippers were fast vanishing. Then she remembered that she was wearing the belt, the brassière and the twin set which were certainly as good as one glass slipper—and there was still the suit to come. So she took a deep breath, gave a sigh for past glory and went into the house, with the unnecessary sense of guilt that only the guiltless know. Softly she opened the sitting-room door, softly she went into the kitchen and then upstairs, but all was empty. Instead of coming at once to the conclusion that both her parents had been murdered and their bodies buried under the fowl run, her good sense told her that they had probably stayed to tea at the Vicarage, so she took off her coat and skirt and hung them up, lovingly took off the twin set and put them or it in a drawer and then undid the parcel in which with her other new belt and brassière her old underwear had been packed. Tucked under the string was a large envelope, bearing the name of Bostock and Plummer, and on it, in Rose's generous scrawl, the words, "To wear when you wear the suit with love from Rose." She opened the envelope and found two pairs of the very best brown thread stockings. If she had been in the church she would have knelt down with a prayer of thanks, not only for the stockings but because Rose had so cleverly known that thread was what she would wear. Nylons were a beautiful thought, but not in her line, when one little bit of unfiled nail, one roughened finger, might turn the whole delicate fabric into a tangled mess. Her eyes to her surprise were blurred and to her confusion and fury she found herself crying. But not for long. There were the fowls and the supper to be attended to and various little things that she had left undone in the morning, so that when her father and mother came home they found Cinderella going about her work very cheerfully.

During supper she told her parents about the expedition, though she did not mention the visit to Bostock and Plummer nor the adventure in the Sports Department of the Maison Tozier. Not that she really wished to deceive them, but a Something told her that so much good news might not be good for them and that there was always a possibility that father might suddenly be proud, or independent. But when supper was cleared away and the Admiral had gone out to syringe his roses because of the green fly, Miss Phelps showed her mother the presents. Mrs. Phelps was loud in her admiration of everything and ready to conspire wholeheartedly for her daughter to get to Barchester for the tweeds to be fitted. While Miss Phelps was reverently putting the twin set, in its tissue paper, into a drawer, her mother was looking out of the window. Miss Phelps heard a slight noise and turned round to face the appalling sight of her mother trying not to cry. Not in the black winter of 1947, when it was colder than the oldest inhabitant could remember and the coal deliveries were held up by snow-blocked roads and Miss Phelps carried home two gallon cans of oil which the School had smuggled to her and everyone was wearing most of their clothes night and day, and the Admiral nearly had pneumonia; never during that or any period of stress had Miss Phelps seen her mother cry. It is an experience that, luckily, many people never have, for parents try to control themselves (little as their offspring may feel it at the time) and by the time the children are grown up they have mostly passed the age of tears. So Miss Phelps was frightened out of her wits and begged her mother to tell her what it was, and got her a drink of water.

"Nothing, really," said Mr. Phelps. "You wouldn't understand, Margot," to which Miss Phelps replied that even if she couldn't understand, perhaps she could help; and had her mother found the day too tiring, because if she had then she, Miss Phelps, certainly wouldn't go to Barchester again.

"It's not that, darling," said Mrs. Phelps. "It's that I can't ever give you nice things. I did want you to have fun like the other girls, but the war came at the wrong time and you were so good with those horrible goats and hens," then she had to stop and wipe her eyes.

"Well, that's all right, mother," said Miss Phelps. "I like goats and hens and gardening and cooking. All the girls have jobs now, only mine happens to be at home. I'd hate not to be at home. And we've lots of friends, the Croftses and Wicks and Tubby and all the School and Lady Cora and Rose. *Please*, mother."

Mrs. Phelps, furious with herself for want of self-control, drank some more of the water and tried to smile.

"Listen, mother," said Miss Phelps. "It isn't because of Rose giving me those things, is it? I don't really want to go to the Warings or the Luftons or *anywhere*, if it makes you unhappy."

"Unhappy?" said Mrs. Phelps, who now had herself well in hand. "I'd like you to go everywhere and see everybody and have new clothes and go to beauty-parlours and dances and theatres."

"Well, mother, I've been to Barchester and I've seen the Warings and those nice boys at the Priory School and I've got a lovely twin set and I'm going to have a tweed suit. And if you mean it is charity," she said, thinking she might have found the clue to her mother's depression, "well it isn't. It's people doing kind things because they *want* to do them. Like Mrs. Villars giving me the stuff to keep my hands clean, only I keep on forgetting to use it and she has sent me another jar. And if Lady Cora gives me things it's because she *likes* it, and if Rose gives me things it's because *she* likes it. So you see, mother, I'll have to wear them or they'll be unhappy," and though her pronouns were muddling Mrs. Phelps did understand.

"You are quite right, Margot darling," she said, and she only rarely used words of endearment. "In fact very sensible and level-headed. And I'm glad you have friends to give you pretty things. And you must get out more and see some people."

"And then I can tell you and father all about them when I come back," said Miss Phelps, much cheered. "I'm to go to Barchester with Rose Fairweather next week to be fitted for the suit and I hope it will be ready when I go to the Luftons," which was news to Mrs. Phelps. So then Miss Phelps told the story of her day in Barchester from the beginning and how the girl at the beauty parlour had said if her hair could be properly cut it would hardly need anything done to it and how glad she was that she had that very good pair of brogue shoes that Kate Carter had given her because they didn't fit.

"Well one thing I will say," said Mrs. Phelps, now all eagerness, "you get your legs and feet from my side."

"Oh, mother!" said Miss Phelps, unused to such praise.

"You could go anywhere with them," said Mrs. Phelps rather vaguely, "and I must say I think they are every inch as good as Rose's. And with that belt and brassière you look like your Aunt Poppy, my eldest sister whom you won't remember, because she died in India when you were three. Only then one couldn't see women's legs unless it was in the Lancers," and her mind went back to some dashing balls of her youth when the girls were swung off their feet by their partners and dreadfully scolded by their mothers afterwards.

Miss Phelps, intensely interested by her mother's words, sat down on the edge of her bed, pulled her old skirt well up and looked at her legs, now in their Cinderella cotton stockings and battered gardening shoes, and thought perhaps her mother was right.

"It's round the hips you're too big," said Mrs. Phelps, "like me. But I like you just as you are. Oh, *such* good news about Mr. Wickham."

"Who is it this time?" said Miss Phelps, for Mr. Wickham had more than once, to the intense interest of the whole of West Barsetshire, made offers of honourable marriage to ladies of a suitable age, the present Mrs. Crofts, as we know, being one, but in every case he had been declined with thanks and with many expressions of affection, mostly because the ladies were already smitten by, or plighted to someone else. And we may add that after each rejection he had gone home and given himself a good stiff drink with congratulations on his own luck. So Mrs. Phelps told her daughter that Mrs. Crofts said Wicks had come into some money from his old uncle over Chaldicotes way, and Miss Phelps pretended she had not already heard the news and said how glad she was that Wicks was going to have the money.

"Well, I'd better put on my old belt now and do the hens," said Miss Phelps, now quite cheerful again, and so she did, and then she got the supper, and the evening passed as usual. And the days passed as usual till the following Wednesday, when the Admiral had been invited to lunch at the Carters, not without some scheming by Kate Carter and Mrs. Phelps, and never knew that his daughter had gone to Barchester and back with Rose Fairweather for her fitting. To Miss Phelps's surprise and gratification the coat and skirt, mostly inside out, with intricate tackings of white thread everywhere which Mr. Hamp ruthlessly tore away in most places, was an almost perfect fit. Emboldened by all her experiences, Miss Phelps asked when it would be ready.

"Say a fortnight today?" said Mr. Hamp. "It's the jacket. Jackets must be humoured, not drove," at which words Miss Phelps looked helplessly towards Rose.

"It simply must be ready by next Wednesday, Mr. Hamp," said Rose. "You can't let Miss Phelps go to Lady Lufton's on Thursday in that suit she's wearing. I shall come and fetch it myself. If Lady Lufton sees her in the new suit she's bound to want one like it. I don't mean old Lady Lufton, I mean young Lady Lufton. You know, she was Miss Grantly."

Mr. Hamp, who had worked for most of the county, except those who were rich or misguided enough to go to a London tailor, said that, of course, altered things a bit.

"That's better," said Rose. "It would be quite too shattering if Miss Phelps went to Framley Court in her old suit and young Lady Lufton thought you had made it," at which horrible thought Mr. Hamp went quite pale, all but the top of his bald head which had been kicked by a mountain battery mule at Mutta Kundra in 'fifteen and was apt in moments of cold or emotion to assume a violet hue, very terrifying to those who weren't used to it. And then, rather to Miss Phelps's alarm, Rose took her again to the Maison Tozier where Miss Dahlia, with skilful hands or rather scissors, trimmed her hair just enough to make all the difference, and so skilfully was it done that the Admiral never noticed it, though we must say that Miss Phelps tied her head up in an old scarf when she got home and as her father was used to seeing her tied up, everything appeared normal.

There was then the question of whether the Admiral would notice the new suit and Ask Questions. Rose, being over at Southbridge on the Sunday, lunching with the Carters, dropped in on Mrs. Phelps to make enquiries.

"I rather wish I had told Irons from the beginning," said Mrs. Phelps, for Rose was such an old friend that this familiar name did not need an explanation. "I'm beginning to wonder if we haven't been too deceiving about it."

"You simply can't deceive men too much," said Rose. "They can be so shatteringly stupid. Ever since I had my hair done with an auburn rinse in Rio and John didn't notice it till I told him and then he went *quite* off the deep end like the Bible, I have been careful not to tell him anything he wouldn't like to know and it works perfectly. If I hadn't told him I don't suppose he'd have noticed. Men don't, really too pretentious. Anyway, about the suit, I've got to go to Barchester myself next week, so I'll bring it over and wrap it up to look like something else," by which kind thought Mrs. Phelps was really touched even as she vaguely wondered what on earth Rose could find as a disguise.

"I do hope Irons won't notice it," said Mrs. Phelps. "Usually he notices nothing, but with men you never know."

Rose thought, so profoundly that she quite surprised herself.

"I know," she said. "I'll tell Tubby to come and sit with the Admiral while you have your rest. He was saying only yesterday that he wanted to see him about pensions or something. He seemed quite pleased about it. It's as good as one of Mrs. Morland's thrillers. I say, Mrs. Phelps, what about the hens?"

Mrs. Phelps looked unquestioningly at her.

"I mean their tea, or whatever they have," said Rose. "That ghastly stuff in a pail that smell like nothing on earth. Tubby won't let Mrs. Hicks do it in the kitchen."

"Goodness knows one doesn't *want* to do it in the kitchen," said Mrs. Phelps, "but there isn't anywhere else."

"Well, Tubby has a wash-house at the back that isn't used, so he told Mrs. Hicks to do it there," and Mrs. Phelps wondered, as many of Rose's friends had wondered, how anyone could be so lovely and so silly and so practical, all in one breath; nor was her wonder lessened when Rose, with her always unexpected practical side, went doggedly back to her question of the hens' tea.

"Oh, I can get Mrs. Brown to do that," said Mrs. Phelps, "our policeman's wife," and Rose, used to the intricacies of village life, seemed to think this quite in order.

"Margot gave her children some old kitchen things to play with and one of the boys got his head stuck in a saucepan that he was wearing for a helmet," said Mrs. Phelps, as if that explained everything; and as Rose did not ask any questions we presume that it did.

It was of course inevitable that Miss Phelps should imagine every possible blow of fate that might stop her going to Framley, for even a mind as sane and matter-of-fact as hers could not help the superstitious feeling that something nice that is going to happen won't happen. But in the long rather chilly summer days she was too much occupied with her work in house and garden and the Girl Guides and the house-to-house collection of jumble for the Sea Scouts' Sale to worry overmuch; not to speak of the evening when Mr. Feeder at Louisa Cottage had the whole of the Meistersinger from Covent Garden on his wireless with the window open, and Mr. Traill at Maria Cottage had, as a form of counter-attack which is one method of defence, played through the whole of the Meistersinger upon his very powerful gramophone, also with the window open; and old Mrs. Feeder from Editha had come out and banged on both their doors and told them not to be fools; and Miss Hampton from Adelina, coming back with Miss Bent from the Red Lion, had said Boys would be Boys, and Mrs. Feeder, with one of her terrifying grins, had said it was better than Girls being Girls and taken Miss Hampton and Miss Bent into her house and given them drinks until the operas were over and the gentlemen could join them. Not that Miss Phelps was personally implicated in these last activities; but although Southbridge was spreading quite alarmingly in its outskirts, it was still at heart a village and everyone knew everything, usually incorrectly, within an incredibly short time.

*   *   *

Thursday dawned damp and chill, but that is English Summer Usage, so no one noticed it, except perhaps Miss Phelps, who was secretly rather glad, for she had been afraid of a really hot day, the sort of day when the right sort of people had dresses of printed linen, or even silk, and wore sandals. But now her tweeds would be all right. Kind Rose Fairweather had been to Barchester the day before, stood over Mr. Hamp while he sewed on the last button, paid him (which rather shocked him, for he had been brought up in the old school of tailoring when good clients were expected to keep their tailor waiting till their other debts were paid, or, even better, borrow money from their tailor to pay debts of honour) and brought the suit over to Jutland Cottage looking, we must confess, exactly like a suit wrapped up, but the Admiral was out on his morning constitutional and did not see her.

"And don't try to wear a hat," said Rose, who was nearly always bareheaded herself. "Just pat a very little brilliantine on your hair."

Miss Phelps said she hadn't got any.

"Then use your father's," said Rose, "or whatever he does use for his hair, the old darling. And have a lovely time," and with a careless kiss she had gone away.

So after lunch, when her mother was safely lying down and her father happily engaged with Canon Fewling, Miss Phelps, who had managed to remember to use Mrs. Villar's hand cream for a whole week, went upstairs with a beating heart, took off her Cinderella clothes and put on her ball dress and her golden slippers, or in other words her new belt, brassière, stockings, jumper (though not the cardigan) and suit. Her best shoes were old but of good leather and kept polished by herself with almost masculine devotion. She took a good look at as much as she could see of herself in her looking-glass and went gently into her mother's room.

"It *does* look nice," said Mrs. Phelps, bursting with pride and pleasure. "I *wish* you had some pearls, darling," to which Miss Phelps, choking down a sudden pang, said then she would be just like anyone else.

"Well, I'd better go down and wait for Swan," she said. "I do hope father won't notice anything," and her mother said not if he was talking shop with Canon Fewling, so she went downstairs.

"Hullo, Tubby," she said. "I'm awfully glad you're here."

Canon Fewling got up with the swiftness that still surprised his friends and shook hands. Miss Phelps sat down with her back to the light and the men went on with their talk. She did not pay much attention to it, for she had now invented a fresh fear for herself, namely that Swan would not come. And so strong was this foolish self-torturing (and those of us who are given to it will sympathise), that when Swan drove up to Jutland Cottage and walked up the path into the house she came back, almost with a jump, into real life.

"May I come in, sir?" he said. "My name is Eric Swan. I don't suppose you will remember me, but I was at Southbridge before the war, when Tony Morland and Hacker were there and Philip Winter was Junior Classical Master."

The Admiral, thus briefed, did almost remember, and when Swan took out his spectacles and put them on he quite remembered.

"Now," he said in his precise voice, "you boys were at the School at the beginning of the war, when Mrs. Carter and my wife had that party for the evacuee children in the School gymnasium. And what are you doing now? Fewling, do you know Eric Swan? Sit down, my boy, and have a talk," at which words Miss Phelps's heart nearly broke.

"I'm very sorry I can't, sir," said Swan. "Miss Lufton asked me to go over to Framley for tea and to bring Margot. But if I might have a talk with you when I bring her back that would be delightful. Come on, Margot."

"So you are going to Framley, Margot?" said the Admiral. "I

daresay you did tell me, but I forget so many things now. Have a nice time. And if you see Lady Lufton, will you tell her that I had the pleasure of waltzing with her, somewhere about 1919."

"That would be the other Lady Lufton," said Swan, finding himself rather embarrassed—an unusual state of mind for him— to describe her. No one said Dowager now, and to say Old Lady Lufton would be a gross overstatement.

"Of course, my boy," said the Admiral. "I saw that her boy has married a Grantly. All very suitable. And now, Fewling," he said, having obviously no further interest in the younger people, "tell me again what you were saying about the proposal to increase the pensions of naval widows. It interests me very much—and very personally, Fewling, though I wouldn't say it to most people, but as you were in the Navy you will understand."

Miss Phelps, vastly relieved by her father's complete want of interest in her, went out with Swan to his car.

"I did think," said that gentleman, when he had shut her door and got in on the other side himself, "of pinching Tubby's car and leaving mine instead."

"Why didn't you?" said Miss Phelps, whose spirits were soaring.

"Partly that I don't like getting into trouble with the police," said Swan, "and partly because he is such a remarkably good fellow. Oh, I forgot," and he rummaged in a pocket. "I ran into Rose Fairweather in Barchester yesterday and she said I was to give you this," and he handed her a small parcel of tissue paper. In it was a row of pearls, with a diamond clasp—or as good as, to Miss Phelps's eyes.

"Rose said you were to wear them and they aren't real so it doesn't matter," he said, elliptically, but Miss Phelps understood him and was quite truly grateful for a present that could not have cost very much (though we may say that she was mistaken in this, for they were Superior Artificial Pearls and Diamonds and had cost as much as two guineas).

"Do you think I ought to wear them, Swan?" she said. "Oh, I'm sorry."

"What about?" said Swan. "Do you mean calling me Swan? It's not a bad name, and, after all, you knew me when I was a horrible schoolboy. I'm an old Schoolmaster now."

"Not old," said Miss Phelps, who had a very accurate memory. "Thirty-something. For a man that's nothing. Look at me."

"And very nice too," said Swan approvingly.

"I'm very well over forty," said Miss Phelps.

"Don't try to come it over me, my girl," said Swan, but very kindly. "Do what Rose tells you and you needn't worry about over forty. And do put that necklace on or it will slip down into the gearbox and get scrunched," which horrible thought so alarmed Miss Phelps that she put the pearls round her neck and felt the snap go home.

"Now have a look at yourself," said Swan, obligingly tilting the mirror in her direction. "Jerseys and pearls and SENSIBLE shoes," he sang aloud in a pleasant voice, adding as a coda, "I don't mean anything. It's out of a silly revue that made me laugh. In fact I went three times and laughed every time till all my stomach muscles were contracted and I could hardly breathe. Now, you go on calling me Swan—Eric's a poor name, anyhow— and I'll call you Margot. Bargain?"

"*Rather*," said Miss Phelps with schoolgirl violence.

Swan drove well and easily and it was a good make of car, but somehow Miss Phelps had no desire to be at the wheel. Perhaps it was because Swan's driving was quite as good as her own; perhaps because she had her one good pair of wash-leather gloves on, as yet unwashed, which however carefully you do it makes all the difference. They did some remembering about pre-war days at the School and wondered how Mr. Bissell, head of the evacuated boys' school from the Isle of Dogs, was getting on and then Swan turned down a lane just opposite of Framley Court and drove up to the Dowager Lady Lufton's residence, known as the Old Parsonage. This was a pleasant unpretentious house with good outbuildings and a very manageable garden which in the days when the clergyman still lived in the Parsonage had been a lawn with a gravel path all round it and a flowerbed along the far side, but after various periods of neglect, and then the house being let during the war to a firm that only wanted space for furniture-storage, it had rather run to seed. To reclaim it had been Lady Lufton's constant care during the past year and an excellent job she had made of it. Not without help, for Mr. Macfadyen, the wealthy manager and part-owner of Amalgamated Vedge, who was paying a very handsome rent for a wing of Framley Court, had taken a professional and friendly interest in Lady Lufton's gardening and a good deal of its success had been due to his kindness. And to his generosity, for he had from the outset made it clear to Lady Lufton that he would not take a penny from a fellow gardener, which offer she, with we think equal generosity, had accepted. So barrow-loads of Vimphos, or Sang-Bono, or whatever was best on the market, were trundled across from the Court to the Old Parsonage, a man with a scythe was lent to take the tall rank grass and weeds off the lawn, other men in Mr. Macfadyen's employ practically ploughed and sowed and reaped and mowed and carried their last load and weren't overthrowed, the lawn was well forked and levelled and rolled and resown, suitable climbing roses were put in the border that ran under the south windows of the house and, probably encouraged by these signs of returning prosperity, a large magnolia which had done nothing within memory of man but grow more and larger shiny leaves, suddenly produced as fine a crop of huge, creamy-petalled, almost nauseatingly sweet-scented flowers as one would wish to see.

We need hardly say that all that part of West Barsetshire (and also our reader, who so very kindly includes these neither very short nor very simple annals of the county under the heading of "A Nice Book" and puts the name of the next one down on her list at Gaiters' as soon as it is announced), and even as far afield as the Close and Gatherum Castle and Pomfret Towers and even, we believe, Hartletop Priory though this is not confirmed, had decided that the Dowager Lady Lufton and Mr. Macfadyen would make a match of it, and indeed, if loads of best manure and seedlings and man's time and labour are the Food of Love, there was proof enough. But we may say that, though each liked and respected the other, no such thought had entered their heads. Lord Lufton, talking it over in confidence with Eric Swan, had said he had no particular feelings about widows remarrying, but he was hanged if he thought his respected mamma was contemplating matrimony, with which Swan entirely agreed. Not that either of these gentlemen had any specific grounds for such belief, not having given the matter much consideration, but we may say at once that they were probably right, and Lady Lufton and her tenant would go on being very good friends in their different spheres as long as Mr. Macfadyen was a tenant at Framley Court.

Lady Lufton was not in her garden but in her sitting-room, a large room on the first floor, facing south over the walled garden and westwards towards the lane with a view of Framley Court, considerably obscured by trees at this time of year. It was furnished mostly with things from the Court and here against the wall, well away from draughts, Lady Lufton had her very good grand piano, and by one of the windows a large desk covered with papers where she did all her County Work. There was hardly a deserving society in West Barsetshire but had her on its list of patrons, sometimes as its president, always on its Committee. As chairman she was much in request. She had also within the last year become a J.P. and sat on the bench regularly, so that, as she once said to Mr. Macfadyen, no one could say she was not public-spirited, but she would far rather be private-spirited, as she was when her husband was alive; to which Mr. Macfadyen could find no answer.

Lady Lufton greeted Miss Phelps very kindly and gave her hand to Swan who, much to Miss Phelps's interest, bowed over it and kissed it.

"A slight affectation, Margot, which I am sure you will

excuse," said Swan gravely. "I was rash enough to do it once—just pure showing off—and I couldn't stop," at which Lady Lufton laughed and said, "Silly boy," but not as if she meant it.

"Now, I will tell you what I have planned," said Lady Lufton. "I should like to show you the house, Miss Phelps, unless it would bore you. My daughter Justinia will be back presently and afterwards we will go over and see my daughter-in-law. Ludovic—my son—had to go to a meeting in Barchester, and I'm afraid he won't be back in time. And we might look in on Mr. Macfadyen. Do you know him?"

"I don't think I do," said Miss Phelps, "unless he is the Amalgamated Vedge man? Father used to meet a Mr. Macfadyen at the club, but he gave it up," and she said no more, leaving her hearers, however, with a curious sense that she had checked herself for some reason.

"That's the one," said Swan, "and he is hand in glove with Mrs. Sam Adams. They market-garden together like one o'clock. Do you know her, Margot?" but though Miss Phelps had often heard of the Miss Marling who married the rich ironmaster she had never so much as set eyes on her and felt deeply conscious of not belonging—a phrase which, we hope, does not need explanation.

Then Lady Lufton enquired after Admiral Phelps.

"Oh, father is pretty well, thank you," said Miss Phelps, "but he can't do much. He asked me to say that he did remember waltzing with you in 1919 and he had never forgotten it," which, we may remind our reader, was not a faithful reproduction of Admiral Phelps's words, but did her great credit.

"How nice of him," said Lady Lufton, with obvious sincerity. "It was at Barchester Town Hall, in aid of something, and I was on the Committee. I had to dance with the Mayor who trod on my toes, and then with a Major somebody who smelt of whisky, and then your father was introduced to me and it was quite perfect. I felt like those little figures one used to have as a child that you put on a little round box and wound it up and they went round and round till the machinery ran down. If you can imagine dancing with a very reliable soap-bubble that couldn't possibly burst, that is what it felt like. A rather solid, stout kind of soap-bubble."

"Oh, I *do* know that kind," said Miss Phelps, her shyness falling off her in lumps. "I always seemed to get them at naval dances, and I used to long for someone tall and dark and romantic," which made Lady Lufton laugh, though very kindly, and Miss Phelps had to laugh too.

"And now," said Lady Lufton, suddenly becoming the good hostess, "I expect you would like to see the rest of the house."

"No, dear Lady Lufton," said Swan. "She would not. She is a girl of the wide open spaces and what she would really like to see is—or do I mean are?—the hens and things," at which Lady Lufton smiled and said, Certainly. But Miss Phelps, with great courage and feeling the moral support of her new suit and her lovely pretence pearls, said she simply adored houses.

"Dear Lady Lufton, much as I honour and adore you," said Swan, who had been standing by the window that commanded the drive as he spoke, "I do *not* want to see the house again. May I stay here and play with your piano?"

"Of course," said Lady Lufton. "Shall we go upstairs first, Miss Phelps? What is your name, my dear? Your father did speak of an only daughter with great pride. There wasn't a son who was killed, was there?"

Miss Phelps said she was an only child because her brother had died before she was born and her name was Margot.

"A charming name," said Lady Lufton, leading the way upstairs. "My elder daughter who married Oliver Marling is Maria, and my younger daughter, whom you know, is Justinia. I wanted you to see these rooms, because I am doing them up for my grandchildren when they come here. A day nursery and a night nursery and a bathroom, only of course I shall have everything properly painted and papered and bars put on the windows. And along the passage two more quite nice rooms if one ever had proper servants again. I have heard of a man and wife who might do. And here is a little back-stair down to the kitchen, so convenient."

"Then you'll need *two* gates?" said Miss Phelps.

"How do you mean, my dear?" said Lady Lufton, but quite kindly and interestedly.

"Well, I mean you'll need a nursery gate at the top of the nursery stairs, won't you?" said Miss Phelps, hoping she had not put herself forward too much. "And another at the top of these stairs in case the children run along the passage and fall down-stairs."

"*What* a good idea!" said Lady Lufton, stopping short at the stairhead and looking at Miss Phelps with admiration. I can't think why that never occurred to me. I shall see about it at once. Naval people are always so intelligent. And I believe there is a kind of safety catch so that the children can't open it themselves. I think Cora Waring showed me one at Beliers, though of course her little boy hardly needs it yet. Still, just as well to get it done in time. One doesn't want broken arms and legs."

"How many grandchildren are there?" said Miss Phelps as they went down again. Lady Lufton, a step below her, turned and looked up with a face of amused self-deprecation.

"You will think I am putting up gates on false pretences," she said. "Maria's little girl is one year old."

"Is that all?" said Miss Phelps, who had not unnaturally imagined a horde of rebellious babies.

"Well, practically all," said Lady Lufton, adding in a long parenthesis as she opened various doors, "and here is Justinia's room and her bathroom, my younger daughter. This is my bedroom, and I have a kind of dressing-room here and my own bathroom. Of course, the sitting-room where we were was really the best bedroom when the vicar lived here, but it was so large that Mr. Macfadyen suggested I might turn it into a music-room, and I do my county work up there too. It is like having a flat in a country house, you see."

"Then it is only one grand child?" said Miss Phelps.

"Only one at present," said Lady Lufton. "But, of course, my daughter-in-law, Ludovic's wife, will be having some, though even if they are very precocious, gates won't really be needed for some time. But one might as well have them put in while the rooms are being done up, otherwise there is always a grumble about the carpenter having spoilt the paint when he put a gate up and not made it good," which sounded to Miss Phelps so like things her father said that she suddenly felt quite at home.

Sounds of music came from the sitting-room.

"Dear Eric, he adores my piano," said Lady Lufton. "The nicest boy. Is he an old friend of yours?" and when Miss Phelps said she had known him as a boy at Southbridge School Lady Lufton was delighted.

"You know," she said when they got to the ground floor, "last year—this is the drawing-room with the long windows out to the garden, lovely in summer but it takes a great deal of heating in winter—when Ludovic and Grace were not yet engaged— and this is the dining-room, it was Mr. Macfadyen's idea to have a service hatch put in from the kitchen to the dining-room— Eric was over here quite a lot. I thought he came to talk to me—this is our little kitchen, and Mr. Macfadyen had the excellent idea of taking a couple of bricks out of the larder wall for ventilation—but of course it wasn't that a bit—and you see the yard outside is in beautiful order, and the outbuildings are let to Mr. Macfadyen to store his seeds and things, and he had to put some heating in so he said it would cost hardly anything to run it through to the house which makes an *enormous* difference not only in winter but practically all the year round being England—it was Grace."

By this time, Miss Phelps, considerably addled by her hostess's way of carrying on two different conversations simultaneously, rather timidly asked who Grace was.

"Oh, *Grace*," said Lady Lufton. "My daughter-in-law, Ludovic's wife. Her father is the Rector of Edgewood, one of the

Grantlys. She is a darling and makes Ludovic *so* happy. And even if they have a daughter first there is plenty of time. I had two daughters before Ludovic was born. That's why he is the youngest. Now I daresay you would like to wash your hands after walking all over the house and then we will go over to the Court for tea. Use my bathroom," and as in their peregrination they had come back to the first floor again, she left her guest in the bedroom and went into the drawing-room, where Swan was playing the piano, to himself.

"I can't think how you remember it all," said Lady Lufton, "and why you have such a heavenly touch, I don't know. It is extremely unfair. I can play *far* better than you, but as for touch——" and Lady Lufton made a gesture of throwing something away.

Swan got up from the piano and sat by her.

"Dear boy," said Lady Lufton affectionately. "That nice Phelps girl has made some very practical suggestions. You know, Eric, it really worries me to see all the girls like her—well, women really—going on doing the useful jobs and getting themselves nowhere."

"It's not for you to talk of jobs getting people nowhere," said Swan. "You run half the county, and remarkably well too. If your job had been looking after a rather invalid father and mother you'd have done it just as well."

"But what future is there for all those good, not-so-young girls," said Lady Lufton, "that stay at home and look after their parents? And there can't be much money."

"There isn't," said Swan. "I happen to know, through Rose Fairweather, whose name would convey nothing to you, that they are getting along on his pension and if he dies first—which is probable—there will be just enough to starve on."

"Could I find any paid job for her?" said Lady Lufton, whose many county organisations were always in search of the Absolute; otherwise the perfect secretary with shorthand, tact, typewriting, good manners, a knowledge of office work, ability to get on with a duke or a dustman, a good appearance and private means; and if a little car (the petrol to be paid for by the office of course), all the better.

"Not possibly," said Swan. "She has been the slave—the happy and wiling slave, I grant you—of her parents all her life and will be till they are both dead. After which she will probably go mad because her occupation is gone—like Othello—or live with another indigent woman and keep hens. I wonder," he added, "if her parents ever think of that."

"I expect they do—rather more than you realise, dear boy," said Lady Lufton, and Swan threw up his hand in a kind of salute and said, "You've won."

"Someone ought to marry her," said Lady Lufton firmly.

"Somewho, if that's a word?" said Swan.

"Well, surely *someone* could," said Lady Lufton rather in her chairman's voice. "She isn't exactly pretty, but it's an extremely nice face and good skin, and she had nice hair and dresses very suitably. And nice feet—I couldn't help noticing that. The pearls are imitation of course, but that's nothing now and it saves the insurance."

"I am glad you are wearing *your* pearls," said Swan. "I had a horrid feeling that you might give them to Grace."

"I would have," said Lady Lufton, "gladly. But her father gave her a beautiful row that had belonged to a Grantly grandmother, I think. I shall give mine to Justinia when she marries, but she is like them all, she never thinks of marrying."

"Lots of people don't, you know," said Swan.

"You?" said Lady Lufton looking at him, her sad, deep-set eyes full of compassionate affection.

"If you mean am I in love with Ludovic's wife, I am *not*," said Swan. "I was. And it was plain hell when I saw that she loved Ludovic. But you were so good to me. And now, on my word of honour, that feeling is as dead as a doornail. I didn't even bury it. It gently drooped and withered and died. Honour of a Swan," and he took her elegant if rather garden-roughened hand and kissed it. "And what the dickens is Margot doing?" he said. "Trying all your make-up, Lady Lufton, I expect."

"I was *not*," said Miss Phelps, appearing indignantly in the doorway. "I was looking at those old photographs in your room, Lady Lufton. I loved those two children in pinafores sitting on a sofa. The ones that have Mary and Susan written underneath."

"Susan was my younger sister. She died a long time ago," said Lady Lufton. "Mary is myself. A funny fat child I was. I hope one of my grandchildren will be a Mary. But of course I shan't suggest it. And now we had better go over to the big house."

So they walked down the little drive, across the road and so to Framley Court. Miss Phelps admired the grass verges, so neatly clipped, and the herbaceous borders.

"Macfadyen for twopence," said Swan. "Is there *anything* he doesn't do here, Lady Lufton?"

"Not much," said Lady Lufton. "I do try to stop him, but one does not wish to appear ungrateful and he has a great gift for listening very politely and going his own way. It is like being up against a wall sometimes."

"A granite wall," said Swan. "If it was brick one could loosen the mortar. I am a countryman of his, Margot, in spite of my name, and I may tell you that sometimes it frightens me."

Miss Phelps not unnaturally asked why. Swan said he couldn't explain, except that being Scotch was not the same as being English, and luckily they were now at the house so that conversation came to an end. The front door was open in the pleasant country way that still goes on. Lady Lufton opened the inner door and called, "Grace," and out came young Lady Lufton with a hug and a welcome to her mother-in-law and took them into her little sitting-room, where Justinia Lufton was talking to Mr. Macfadyen.

The whole family, including Swan, seemed to become one person and Miss Phelps felt a little out of it. But only for a moment. Justinia said how glad she was to see her again. Grace said she had heard of Admiral Phelps from that nice Canon

Fewling whom she met at the Deanery and wondered if he had known her old uncle Commodore Grantly who was at Portsmouth in nineteen-fifteen, which Mr. Macfadyen said he had more than once had a talk with the Admiral at the club about the shipyards on the Clyde.

"And when I say I had a crack with him, I should more correctly say a one-handed crack," said Mr. Macfadyen, "for I knew even less about shipbuilding than your father did about the chemistry of agriculture, and that was a practically negligible quantity. So I held my tongue like a douce man and let him go full steam ahead. How is the Admiral, Miss Phelps?"

For a brief moment Miss Phelps thought of saying, Quite well thank you, and so avoiding questions or sympathy. But Mr. Macfadyen seemed so pleasant that she thought it would be unkind.

"Well, father is pretty well," she said, "but he can't do much. It's very lucky that they have been at home, because I can look after them."

"And how do you look after them, Miss Phelps?" said Mr. Macfadyen, who had taken a fancy to this very pleasant-faced, suitably dressed woman, whose hands—for she had taken off her gloves—were working hands.

"Oh, just helping," said Miss Phelps. "You see, mother has a heart and she simply must lie down every afternoon, Dr. Ford says, and father isn't too good either. But he goes for a walk in the village every morning and people are awfully good about coming to see him. Mr. Wickham comes quite often and so does Canon Fewling—oh, lots of people. So I do the cooking and the housework and the hens and the vegetables. We did have goats in the war, but no one wants their milk now, so we sold them. I was really rather glad, because you wouldn't believe how strong they are if they want to go in the other direction."

"And you manage to look as you do in spite of all you do," said Mr. Macfadyen. "Like my mother. She had a hard life and little enough to give me. I was all she had—there were other weans, but they left the world almost as soon as they entered it, but that's neither here nor there. Aweel, she's dead long syne."

At these words Miss Phelps was torn by varying emotions, the chief of which was, quite unreasonably, that Mr. Macfadyen must think her very heartless for coming out in a good tweed suit, good thread stockings and what looked like a pearl necklace. For one moment she felt, like Cinderella, that she must rush home as fast as she could or her borrowed plumes would fall off and expose her as an impostress, dressed above her station by charity. She looked round. All the others were talking about family matters and absorbed in them.

"Oh, Mr. Macfadyen," she said, "if you ever come over to Southbridge, *do* come and see father. He would so love to talk about shipyards on the Clyde. You see, he has given up the club. It is rather expensive, and he did once have a sort of heart attack in the club and mother was so frightened that he said he would stay at home.

Mr. Macfadyen, with suitable caution, said he was but seldom over Southbridge way, but he would make a point of getting over before long and perhaps Miss Phelps would let him see her garden.

"Oh, I really *couldn't*," said Miss Phelps. "You'd simply *despise* it. It's only a few vegetables. But the hens aren't bad."

"I have yet," said Mr. Macfadyen, "to see the garden I would despise, unless it were the garden of the sluggard. If your father and your leddy mother will receive me, the Admiral and I will smoke a pipe together," and then Grace Lufton summoned the company to tea.

"I say, Swan, we needn't stay too long, need we?" Miss Phelps managed to say as they went to the tea-table.

"Not a moment longer than you wish," said Swan. "What is zero hour?"

"If I could be back by six, or really earlier, please," said Miss Phelps. "If I'm not I *know* mother will do the hen food."

"And your golden ball dress will turn into rags and your glass slipper fly out of the car and hit Everard Carter on the nose," said Swan, but kindly. "I'll see to it. Word of a Swan."

Miss Phelps found tea very pleasant. Young Lady Lufton whose father was the parson at Edgewood knew all about Colonel and Mrs. Crofts and expressed most orthodox views about the Bishop. Justinia and Swan were talking their own talk, rather out of Miss Phelps's line, but they both smiled to her, and Lady Lufton asked her if she would come onto the Committee of the Friends of Distressed Gentlewomen, to which she could only reply that she would like to very much, but didn't think she could leave her parents for long and the buses to Barchester were so bad.

"Well, we must find some way of doing it," said Lady Lufton, with the splendid confidence of the true Committee Woman. "Goodbye, my dear, if you must go, and you must come here again—to the Old Parsonage," she added, reminding herself as she often had to do that Framley Court was not now her home. And we must say here that never had her daughter-in-law shown any annoyance at this form of speech for the very simple reason that she sympathised with her mother-in-law and thought of and for her perhaps more than Justinia did.

"Can I come with you?" said Justinia, speaking as it were to Miss Phelps and Swan jointly. "And then you come back to dinner at the Old Parsonage, Eric, unless your school wants you."

Swan, politely opening the door of the car, said by all means, and he would love to come back to dinner as, like Hervé Riel, he had a good whole holiday with leave to go ashore, a reference which was entirely lost on both ladies, who had got into the back of the car the better to talk about things.

So Swan drove back to Southbridge and deposited Miss Phelps safe and sound at her own front gate, saying as he let her out that he would stand by in case the fowls had attacked and eaten her parents. After a few moments she waved to him from the sitting-room window as a sign that all was well.

"Oh, you are in the front seat now, are you?" said Swan. "What is the good of being an eligible bachelor? I offer to drive two ladies and instead of fighting to sit next to me they go and sit behind."

"I wanted to talk to Miss Phelps," said Justinia. "I like her and she needs liking. By women, I mean—and *not* what you mean, Eric. As far as I can make out she has no female friends of her own age. Don't interrupt me. Of course, I'm not as old as she is, because she told me she was over forty, not that she looks it, but as far as I can make out she doesn't see any women that are her equals. They all think of her as Poor Margot Phelps. If she isn't careful she will marry Dr. Ford," which made them both laugh.

"You always go too fast, Justinia," said Swan. "There is already a Society of Friends of the Phelpses, with Rose Fairweather at the head of it."

"Oh, I have met her, but I don't know her people," said Justinia, with no snobbishness at all, but thinking of the many divisions of society.

"Naval wife, daughter of ex-Headmaster of Southbridge School," said Swan. "Divinely beautiful, pure nitwit and excellent mind for getting things done. The trouble with you Framley people is you don't mix enough. Your mother is marvellous about committees and Maria seems to combine dogs and a baby and a husband very competently, but that's as far as they get. And you——"

"Well, what am I?" said Justinia.

"A very useful member of society," said Swan rather pompously. "But otherwise bornée in the extreme. Hospital Libraries are your end and your beginning. At least Miss Phelps sees life."

"What an extraordinary thing to say," said Justinia.

"Well, you *are* extraordinary," said Swan. "And here we are at your front door. Do you still want me to stay to supper?"

"But of *course*," said Justinia. "That's why I told mother to ask you," so Swan followed her into the Old Parsonage and the door shut upon them as it had shut upon Miss Phelps.

CHAPTER 9

July was drawing to a close. The Priory School had broken up a little earlier than usual, for during the summer holidays everybody and everything except the little boys were to move over to Harefield House, into more spacious quarters. The Headmaster, Philip Winter, would only be able to take a short holiday, but the job had to be done and both he and his wife had health, strength, energy and common sense.

Philip was working in his study when Swan came in.

"Can you spare a moment, sir?" he said.

Philip said it all depended on whether a moment meant a moment or half an hour and laid down his pen.

"It's only this, sir," said Swan, going back to the days when he had been a schoolboy at Southbridge with a devilish gift for annoying his masters. "You may remember that I had an idea of a fellowship at Oxford."

"At Paul's," said Philip, who remembered everything, "where your promising career was cut short by being called up. And you went back and took a second," he added. "It's a good safe class."

"If I had worked harder it might have been a first," said Swan. "But the summer term at Paul's, with the river almost in the back garden. How *can* one work, sir? Unless of course," he added, to forestall any objection, "you are simply dotty about the classics, like Hacker."

"And look where it got him," said Philip. "The chair of Latin at Redbrick University. And don't look at me through your spectacles, boy!" an echo of Southbridge days before the war that made both men laugh.

"Well, it's this, sir," said Swan. "I would like to do both, which, as Euclid used to say, is impossible. If I did try for the fellowship, sir, would it upset your plans?"

"And you have to choose this moment to ask me that, boy?" said the Headmaster, his temper rather out of hand what with the end of term and the prospect of working at least sixteen hours a day during most of the holidays so that his little boys would find everything ready for them. "Toss up. Or ask someone else."

"There is only one other person I could ask," said Swan. "And that person may not choose to give me advice."

"If it is Margot Phelps," said Philip, with a perspicacity that took his subordinate's breath away, "marry the girl out of hand. She will be an admirable Housemaster's wife. Only you must see that her parents are kept in order. I don't mind their living in Harefield in the village, but in the School quarters, no. Well, can't you answer?"

"Certainly, sir," said Swan, putting on his spectacles and looking at his Headmaster. "Margot is as good a girl as they make them, but her heart it is another's and it never can be mine, leastways I meantersay," he added, being well grounded in his Dickens, "that though I have the highest respect for her, I wouldn't marry her for the lost books of Livy," to which his Headmaster, amused but at the same time extremely busy, said who the hell was it then.

"Si vous croyez que je vais dire, Qui j'ose aimer," Swan began sententiously.

"Well, I don't," said his justly exasperated Headmaster. "Ask whoever it is and let me know. And before the middle of August, because I am taking Leslie abroad for a fortnight not leaving any address and you will have to keep an eye on things."

"Then I take it, sir," said Swan, "that the idea of a possible fellowship does not smile on you?"

"Go AWAY, boy!" said Philip Winter; so Swan went away to consider his future and, very conscientiously, the future of the School. Lady Lufton had invited him to spend a few days with her as soon as the School broke up. They were to play duets on the piano together and Swan had promised to encourage her to destroy a great many entirely valueless letters from her late husband's great-aunts who lived in Leamington and their might be some rough shooting, for the rabbits were being a nuisance.

Accordingly he drove himself over to the Old Parsonage at Framley, now the home of the Dowager, who was still known as Lady Lufton by all the neighbourhood pending their gradual recognition of her Dowagership, while the present Lady Lufton was called Young Lady Lufton, a state of affairs which both ladies accepted, knowing that time would set matters straight. Here he was told by one of the Podgens family who was acting as general utility under her despotic mother's orders that her ladyship was up at the Court and please the gentleman was to go there. Swan took his suitcase out of the car, put it in the hall (where, we may say, it remained till his return as Phoebe Podgens, remembering her mother's instructions not to go meddling with things, was afraid to take it up to his room lest worse might befall her) and drove up to the Court. Here he found his hostess together with her daughter-in-law and, to Swan's pleasure, her son, with whom it was his habit to speak in what we can only call Regency Buckish.

"The pox take me but 'tis a deucedly long time since we saw your ugly phiz here, sir," was Lord Lufton's greeting, to which Swan replied agreeably that stap his vitals, he would have driven over in his curricle far sooner had it not been that the beggarly usher (by which disrespectful epithet he meant his Headmaster, Philip Winter) had kept his nose to the grindstone. To Lord Lufton's great admiration, he bent over the Dowager's hand and then, saying "The pox take me, my lord, but I must presume," kissed young Lady Lufton. But as everyone kisses everyone now, Grace Lufton took his kiss sedately.

"It is very interesting," said the Dowager, "to watch the change in manners. I should not be in the least surprised if the Dean were to kiss me," to which Lord Lufton replied, with unfilial disrespect, that he'd like to see the Dean do it.

"But really," said the Dowager, "one cannot call it kissing. It is people pushing their cheeks together without thinking."

"I know," said Swan. "One just does a little cheek-pushing as a matter of course. When I really love people—female people, I mean—I kiss their hand. When done with an air it looks well. And how is that nice Margot Phelps? I have meant to go over and see her, but my beggarly usher—I mean my Headmaster— has kept me working twenty-five hours a day."

"Grace drove me over to call on her people," said Lady Lufton, "and I liked them very much. Miss Phelps was doing the hens, or the garden, in trousers. I cannot say that I like trousers, but she was extremely pleasant. I think Mr. Macfadyen is over there this afternoon advising her about manure. And now, Eric, tell us all about the great move."

Swan said there was really nothing to tell as yet. Charles and Clarissa Belton had already moved into married quarters in one of the wings of Harefield House and the kitchen staff would move in as soon as they had had their holidays and the School staff as soon as the kitchen was settled, so that by the middle of September all should be ready for the boys.

The Dowager said she could not help feeling sorry, in a way, for Mr. Belton, the owner of Harefield.

"Pray do not waste your pity, Lady Lufton," said Swan. "Mr. Belton is a delightful old codger if I may use the expression— you know I spent the Christmas holidays there last year—and he is getting such a kick as I cannot adequately describe out of meddling up at the School. He comes nearly every day and talks to the workmen and when the kitchen staff come he will be up there twice a day at least."

"Who will be where twice a day?" said Justinia Lufton, the Dowager's unmarried daughter, just back from her Hospital Library work. The whole company explained the position to her.

"I don't think so," said Justinia. "If any of you know old Nannie Allen, the cook's mother, she won't allow Mr. Belton to gossip in the kitchen. She holds with the gentry *being* the gentry. One state visit and that will be all."

"Poor Mr. Belton," said Lady Lufton, who knew what it was to be an exile from what had been one's home, but there was not any arrière pensée, for although she and Justinia had moved to the Old Parsonage when Lord Lufton married, his wife had kept the doors of Framley Court wide open for them.

Then Lady Lufton as we find it easier to call her, keeping the name young Lady Lufton for the former Grace Grantly, took Justinia and Swan back to the Old Parsonage and after tea set them to work at the Sisyphus task of weeding the flagged walk along the side of the house while she clipped the dead roses. Any work that entails destruction, or rather in this case eradication, is agreeable, but kneeling, even on a padded rush mat, makes the joints ache and is bad for the trouser knees or, if one is wearing them, the nylons.

"It *would*," said Justinia, as a stitch ran swifter than lightning from knee to ankle. "I put them on because Lady Pomfret came to the Red Cross Library this morning, and I meant to change them."

"You will get yourself into trouble, Justinia," said Swan. "St. John and Red Cross Hospital Libraries, my girl. Do be correct."

Justinia said well everyone said Red Cross; and before Swan, with his Scotch delight in argument (especially when he was right on a technical point) could draw her any further she said, with the air of she could an if she would, wasn't Grace looking well.

"They mostly do and good luck to them," said Swan. "I entirely agree with his late Majesty King Charles the Second. Don't let me shock you, my girl."

"You couldn't, said Justinia. "Or if you did you wouldn't know it."

"I suppose you have been doing nothing but count on your fingers," said Swan, at which Justinia couldn't help laughing and Lady Lufton wanted to know what they were laughing about and had they seen her secateurs, after which it got too cold, as it nearly always does, so they put away the gardening things and went indoors.

"I can't tell you how nice it is to be in a warm house in an English summer," said Swan to Lady Lufton while they were having some pre-dinner sherry. "I wonder if the Romans kept their central heating going all the year round when they lived here."

Lady Lufton said she had once been taken to see some excavations of a Roman villa near somewhere and they seemed to have quite a good system. A holocaust, she said, but not with much assurance, and looked at Swan as the scholar of the party. Swan said that would do quite nicely.

"Do tell me, dear boy," said Lady Lufton, "what happens to your classics, because always going back to the beginning every year must be a little———" and she hesitated.

"Yes, it is in a way foully dispiriting, as our Rose Fairweather used to say when she was Rose Birkett," said Swan. "But as old Lorimer used to say—he was Senior Classical Master at Southbridge when I was a boy—whatever the trials of a schoolmaster, we do follow the gleam. And occasionally we have a pupil who makes it worth while. Young Dean, one of Jessica Dean's nephew's, who left us last year, is shaping very nicely at his public school, I hear. You never know with the classics. His aunt is our most brilliant actress, his grandfather a very well-off intelligent man of business, his parents nice but rather dull. Then suddenly, out of these three Deans there comes not a fourth Dean but a born classical scholar," and as neither of his companions recognised his misquotation he left them to make of it what they would. Lady Lufton said no one need change for dinner because they could go on with the weeding afterwards, at which Swan and Justinia exchanged glances of despair. But most luckily, while they were having coffee after dinner in Lady Lufton's sitting-room, Mr. Macfadyen came in.

"Have you had dinner, Mr. Macfadyen?" said Lady Lufton. Her tenant thanked her and said he had had a very pleasant meal over at Southbridge with Admiral Phelps and his wife and daughter, but would gladly take coffee with them if her ladyship would invite him.

"You know I *always* invite you, Mr. Macfadyen," said Lady Lufton, who had very comfortable friendly relations with her rich tenant. "And how were Admiral and Mrs. Phelps? When their daughter came here the other day with Eric Swan I was very much taken by her. She was so sensibly dressed and so pleasant."

"She is a remarkable woman," said Mr. Macfadyen. "I cannot just exactly say that trousers become her as her tweed suit did. There are very few women who can wear trousers without looking the worse for it. But in a job like hers she needs them. I have never seen fowls better kept—unless it were my mother's, but that is an auld and sang now. As for the vegetables, she has a genius for making the best of the worst bit of ground in Southbridge. And her fowls; the hen-houses may be patched up with odd bits of wood and wire, but she has the root of the matter in her. Then the Admiral and I had a crack about the shipyards on the Clyde and I just let the old gentlemen talk, for it gives him pleasure and I would say 'Aye' to what he said and just sometimes I would say 'No', or question him, that he would not be thinking I was a gawping idiot. But here am I letting my tongue run on. How is all with you, Lady Lufton?"

Lady Lufton was glad that her tenant or rather, as she carefully reminded herself, her son's tenant, had spent so pleasant an afternoon and said she must ask Miss Phelps over again.

"Then Mr. Macfadyen must fetch her and take her back," said

Justinia. "Eric told me the Phelpses haven't got a car and the
buses between Southbridge and Framley are quite impossible."

"Or I could offer myself as fetcher and carrier," said Swan.

"But you are going to Scotland, aren't you?" said Justinia, to
which Swan replied that his mother was most accommodating,
after which a good deal of argle-bargle-ing took place and
nothing particular was decided for the moment. Mr. Macfadyen
asked Lady Lufton if she would play for them and she said
certainly, if he would sing. So the two elders went to the piano
and turned over the leaves of song-books, and Lady Lufton
would play the beginning of a song and Mr. Macfadyen would
sing, very pleasantly and unaffectedly, rather for himself and his
hostess than for the younger people. To Swan it was an écho du
temps passé, or rather of a time that was now dead for him; those
few weeks or even few days when he thought his heart had
been broken, when Mr. Macfadyen had sung in Lady Lufton's
sitting-room at Framley Court and he had seen Lord Lufton
look at Grace Grantly and known his fate. But time had passed
since then and far from drowning or shooting himself he had
gone on, conscientiously, with his schoolmastering and found
when he had time to think, which in term-time was very
seldom, that though his admiration for Grace Grantly remained, there was not one smallest fraction of his heart that beat
of her. Quite a pleasant feeling too. Being an evening of late
summer a fire had been lighted, which made the chill late
twilight much more bearable.

"Shall we go over to the fire?" said Justinia. "Mother and Mr.
Macfadyen don't notice anything when they begin their music,"
so they sat and looked at the tongues of flame leaping round the
logs and the glowing coal below.

"How long will it take you to get the School settled at
Harefield?" said Justinia.

"As far as one can tell," said Swan cautiously, "we shall be
settled within two days after the beginning of term. Everything
has been thought out, down to the last brass farthing—if there

is such a thing. But that isn't all," and he stopped, looking into the fire.

"You mean the Ship that Found Herself," said Justinia.

"Clever, clever girl," said Swan admiringly. "That's it. From our dear Selina Hopkins in the kitchens, through Matron and the beggarly ushers—I allude to Charles Belton and myself and the rest—we have got to get into tune with Harefield, or get it to meet us halfway. It isn't quite clear in my mind, but we—I mean Philip Winter and the rest of us—have got to put our guts—our last ounce, if you prefer—into the School and possibly push it uphill for a year, for two years, till it is launched on an even keel. And what the dickens that means," he added, "I have not the faintest idea."

Justinia said it sounded difficult but rather fun.

"The alternative, as far as I am concerned," said Swan, "is a possible fellowship at Paul's—my old college—where I can grow old and drink port and at least discourage young men from reading P.P.E.—if reading it can be called," he added, talking aloud to himself rather than to Justinia.

"P.P.E. is what?" said Justinia.

"Philosophy, Politics, Economics. Not a school at all," said Swan. "Hora novissima, tempora pessima sunt, vigilemus, which means that if we don't keep civilisation alive in these years to come it will be lost. As it was lost in the Dark Ages."

"So it would be better to be with the little boys? I mean, to make a good foundation for them—at least I can't quite explain what I mean," said Justinia.

"I expect you are right," said Swan, after a pause which made Justinia wonder whether she had somehow offended him. "Yes, I think you are right."

Then they sat in silence, Swan looking for his future in the glowing caverns of the fire, Justinia watching him, till Lady Lufton left the piano and came to join them.

"We shall have to put the central heating on if this summer lasts much longer," she said, to which Mr. Macfadyen replied that she only had to say the word and he would see that the fuel reached her.

If Rose Fairweather had been conceited, which she certainly wasn't, she could have congratulated herself warmly on the success of her plan for helping the Phelpses. From that plan had sprung so many others that the Phelps family had hardly seen so much society since Portsmouth and Devonport days. Rose, to whom envy or jealousy of any kind were unknown quantities, was frankly delighted that Margot Phelps had found so many friends and patrons. That Margot should suddenly be in the Lufton set gave her real pleasure, though she thought it all sounded quite ghastily dim, and with all her children for the holidays and her husband having a week's leave she was perfectly happy.

On the following Sunday she asked Canon Fewling to come to lunch, an invitation he gladly accepted. Not that he ever felt lonely, but he very much enjoyed the Fairweather family life. Rose also, in common with the rest of that part of the county, had become increasingly fond in a most respectable way of her pastor, treating him rather like a very nice large dog who could be patted and would not presume. As for Canon Fewling, falling in love, even like the mildest curate going, was not at all in his line, but he occasionally wondered when examining himself (whom he treated far more severely than he would ever have treated any of his flock, however erring) whether, if he had been younger and less stout and Rose had been unmarried, he might have done something about it. And then he dismissed this thought as a work of supererogation, forbidden to clergy and laity alike by the Fourteenth Article.

"You know, Tubby, it's ackcherly hot today," said Rose after lunch. "Let's sit in the garden. You can have the hammock."

"Certainly not," said Canon Fewling. "If you have no respect for my cloth, I have. I don't mean that a clergyman can't sit or recline or whatever you like in a hammock, but they make your coat and trousers look like noughts and crosses."

Rose said it was much worse with velvet, because though you weren't likely to lie in a hammock in black velvet you couldn't ever sit on a chair with a cane seat or a rush seat, which was quite foully depressing. So Rose, in a very simple and quite expensive summer dress of a golden colour that matched her fair hair, reclined on a great many cushions in the hammock while Canon Fewling sat on a comfortable low chair and talked with her—or, to be more truthful, listened to her artless prattle about her husband, her children, her parents and the new book from the libery she had been reading. Her word, not ours.

"It was really what people call griping," she said. "It made you think."

"First, my girl," said Canon Fewling, who owing to Rose's incurable ungrownupness about most things found himself treating her as if she were sixteen—as indeed in some ways she still was—"you don't mean griping, you mean gripping, though even that isn't a word I'd use."

"Of *course* not," said Rose, her lovely blue eyes infused for a moment with a gleam of sense; "the gripes is what's on the label of that medicine that the children——"

"And there we will let it stay," said Canon Fewling. "What was the story that griped—I mean gripped you."

"Well it was one of Lisa Bedale's—you know, the one that she's Lady Silverbridge now—about her detective called Gerry Marston and he finds a quite shatteringly lovely girl being blackmailed *entirely* because she had been engaged to a man who was a crook and he kept all her letters. So I thought what a good thing it was I hardly ever wrote any letters, not even when we were engaged, because it's so much easier to telephone."

Canon Fewling said he sometimes wondered what her telephone bill was, as he had hardly ever found her line disengaged.

"Oh, sometimes quite shatteringly enormous," said Rose, "but John pays it, so that's all right."

"Certainly, if he can afford it," said Canon Fewling.

"Now, Tubby, *don't* behave as if you were a clergyman," said Rose.

"Well, I am one," said Canon Fewling, almost pettishly, and Rose looked at him with her deep-blue wide-set eyes and he felt ashamed of himself, though he knew he was in the right. But this happens to all of us.

A very discordant hoot was heard from the front of the house.

"That's Wicks's horn," said Rose. "Isn't it quite foully shattering. I adore it. I hope he's coming in," and in a kind of Folies Bergères whirlwind of lovely legs and a tempestuous yellow dress Rose hurled herself out of the hammock, almost turning a cartwheel in her excitement, to greet Mr. Wickham who came round the corner with Miss Phelps, both of whom Rose embraced warmly.

"Hug me if you like, my girl," said Mr. Wickham unchivalrously, "but none of your lipstick on my face. That's the way single men are trepanned into matrimony."

"But I *couldn't* marry you, Wicks," said Rose, "because of John."

"And thank God for that, hullo, Tubby—sorry," said Mr. Wickham. "I was over at Southbridge with a bottle of port for the Admiral. Real port, mind you. I drove like a lamb the whole way and it will settle again quite nicely. And I found Effie Crofts there, bless that woman I do like her, and there was Margot cleaning the kitchen range, so I said Captain's Orders, go and clean yourself and come for a drive, my girl."

"Wicks does bully me," said Miss Phelps, "but he said we might go to Greshamsbury, so I thought we could come and see you—if you don't mind," she added.

"Hammock for me," said Mr. Wickham, swinging himself into it with practised ease. "Makes me think of the good old days: Battle of the Nile, Battle of Copenhagen and all that."

"But you weren't at Trafalgar, Wicks," said Miss Phelps. "If you had been there wouldn't have been any rum left to bring

Nelson's body home in," at which neat attack Mr. Wickham laughed so much that Canon Fewling had to laugh too and Rose said it was too, too shattering about Nelson, and if he had been alive now he couldn't have driven a car with one arm.

"Oh, couldn't he?" said Mr. Wickham. "Then you don't know old What's-his-name over Hartletop way. He's got a special wheel with all the gadgets on it so that he can use his two feet and his one arm. Nelson wouldn't have let a little thing like that get him down, my girl. I say, Tubby, have you heard what old Admiral Palliser at Hallbury said to the policeman at the cross-roads?"

"Come in with me," said Rose to Miss Phelps. "It is too shattering when those two begin talking. We'll get some beer to keep them quiet. And I want you for a moment," sometimes ominous words, but Miss Phelps had a perfectly clear conscience—or as clear as our unpleasing anxious conscience will ever allow itself to feel—and went into the house with Rose and followed her upstairs to her bedroom.

"Now, look here, Margot," said Rose, "I have just *got* to talk to you. Look at yourself."

Most people did what Rose told them. Miss Phelps looked rather anxiously at herself in the long mirror and saw a woman who had a handsome head of short brown hair with some natural wave, wearing a shapeless artificial silk dress of mustard yellow with brown flowers on it, with very nice legs and beautifully polished shoes.

"I do look rather awful," said Miss Phelps meekly.

"That's what I wanted to talk about," said Rose. "I look quite ghastly myself in the morning before I've done my face—and your face hardly needs doing at all. And I have to go to Dahlia for a set nearly every week and your hair stays put of itself."

"But you have such a lovely figure and such lovely clothes," said Miss Phelps, without any touch of envy, rather with genuine admiration. "If only it hadn't been such a hot day I'd have put on that lovely suit, but I'd been doing the range and I simply *couldn't* get into tweeds. I *am* so sorry," and, though she didn't cry, her eyes were dim. "I did put the belt on, though," she added, hoping to give satisfaction, "and the brassière."

"That was the one sensible thing you did," said Rose kindly. "Now look here. I've got two summer dresses put away that are much too big for me, and don't ask me why," she added darkly, which frightened Miss Phelps. "If you had been wearing your old belt I wouldn't have mentioned them, but now you could wear them beautifully. Come on."

Miss Phelps looked round for help, but none was forthcoming so she did as she was told. One was a very neatly tailored dress of grey linen buttoning all down the front, the other a slightly dashing black and white check silk. Both by some miracle (or so it appeared to Miss Phelps, though not to Rose, who had bought them in the sales with a view to her protégée's welfare) could be worn without any alteration.

"There," said Rose. "You keep the grey one on and I'll put the other in a box with your old frock to take home with you. Gosh! I wish I had your skin," and she sat down before her mirror and did a little work on her face.

"And I'm glad to see," she said, kindly but severely, to the reflection of Miss Phelps, who was standing behind her, "that you put the thread stockings on. And mind you keep them for best. Whatever you do, *don't* think you can do the pigs or whatever it is in them if you're in a hurry, because you can't. I say, you *do* polish shoes well. John can do them quite shatteringly, but I can't," when, to her eternal surprise, the meek Miss Phelps, the household and garden drudge (though all done cheerfully and with love), said, "Did you every try?"

Rose almost gaped, if such a term can be applied to so lovely a face, but, as her parents and husband knew, with all her peculiar faults she was what in her own words she would have described as quite shatteringly truthful.

"Once," she said, rather inarticulately because of twisting her mouth to get the lipstick on right. "But I made such a quite shattering mess that John said, Never again on your life, my girl. So I never did."

"Well, I sometimes wish I didn't," said Miss Phelps, who had by now perched on the edge of Rose's bed and was secretly admiring herself in the long mirror. "You know, the great thing in life is *not* to be able to do things, because then they are *always* done for you. But father and mother had to do things for themselves when he retired, so of course I did things too and then there was the war and then it was a habit. And now it is simply one's life, because I *must* look after them," all of which she said with no apparent self-pity. "Oh, and thank you again for those *lovely* pearls. I look at them every day."

"Why didn't you put them on today?" said Rose. "No. Don't answer. You were quite right. They wouldn't go with that ghast—that frock of yours."

"It *is* ghastly," said Miss Phelps calmly. "It was charity from a cousin of mother's and the stuff is so good that I expect I shall be dead before it wears out." But, said Rose, just the thing for the garden and the hens; and then they went downstairs again, got beer out of the enormous super-fridge (a term which our female reader will understand if she has got as far as this) and glasses from the pantry and so rejoined the gentlemen, both of whom rose to their feet and relieved the ladies of their trays.

"Holy Jumping Jellicoe!" said Mr. Wickham. "Have you been to the Caledonian Market, Margot?"

"Don't be so shatteringly stupid, Wicks," said Rose, who was not drinking beer for the very good reason that she didn't care for it. "The Caledonian Market is for odds and ends. I once got an ivory pig there with a gold ring in its nose and I lost it next day because the pig fell off the ring and I cried for *weeks*," to which Mr. Wickham unchivalrously replied that he could believe the first but not the second. Canon Fewling did not say very much, for he was puzzled and a little afraid. Here was Margot Phelps, for whom as herself and as a daughter he had a deep admiration, who could drive a car almost as well as Lady Cora Waring, whom he liked and trusted; but a new Margot Phelps. He had seen her in her tweed suit and, like a man, had merely thought that she was in a tweed suit. But seeing her today, suddenly, as his imagination had never conceived her, able to hold her own with any woman of her age, the steadfast sailor's heart which had never been touched—except in a very happy and friendly way by people like Mrs. Villars and Rose Fairweather and a good many others all respectably married—was suddenly overcome. He went on talking and they all laughed and the men drank their beer, but underneath there was turmoil. Once, in his youth, he did remember having fallen in love with a Commodore's wife, more than twice his age with a large family, whose name he said aloud to himself at night, "Oh, Mrs. Collerton," just as David Copperfield had said "Oh, Miss Shepherd," but since that experience (of which no one but himself ever knew, as the Commodore was posted to the Australia station within a few weeks) he had never looked upon women except as extremely nice, friendly people so long as they didn't want to tell one about their souls—which as often as not meant that they had had words with Mrs. Smith over leading that heart, and having lost their temper hoped to shift the burden onto someone else. But nothing of this showed in his round, pleasant face and when Miss Phelps said to Mr. Wickham that she ought to get back to Southbridge now, Canon Fewling shook hands and said he would like to come and spend an afternoon with the Admiral soon, if she would let him know when it suited her father.

"Don't go just yet," said Rose. "I'm almost saying goodbye myself. Oh, I don't mean for ever, goodbye, goodbye like that shatteringly tear-making record, but John and I are going down to join the children near Bognor next week. They are having a splendid time. There are tennis tournaments for under-twelves and lovely sands and even donkeys."

Mr. Wickham said Rose would look top-hole in a swimsuit.

Canon Fewling doubtless felt the same, but it would hardly have been becoming in him to say so.

"Oh, by the way," said Canon Fewling, "I have had an extraordinary piece of good luck. The Dean——"

"What about a spot more beer, Rose?" said Mr. Wickham. "Must celebrate old Tubby's luck and he's drunk it all. I'll go and have a look-see. Trust me," and he went off to the house where he at once spotted the refrigerator, and by the same instinct—rather like that of a truffle-hunting dog—found where the rest of the beer was, shoved a few in the fridge for luck (his words, not ours) and brought out the cold bottles.

"Out with it, Tubby," he said. "Are you going to marry Miss Hopgood's aunt? Considering all the nights you've sat up star-gazing with her, you ought to, you know."

"Not yet," said Canon Fewling, to which Mr. Wickham replied, "Kamerad," and threw up his hands. "No," Canon Fewling went on, addressing himself more to Rose and Miss Phelps after Mr. Wickham's heartless interruption. "I have heard that the day is fixed on which, as an Honorary Canon, I am going to preach in the Cathedral."

"Well, well, what the devil!" said Mr. Wickham.

"Really, Wicks," said Rose, "that is too shatteringly foul of you. Don't notice him, Tubby. How lovely. Can I come and listen to you?"

"Everyone can, as it is in the Cathedral," said Canon Fewling. "If you do come it will add to my pleasure. But what does delight me is that it is almost an anniversary," and he paused.

"Well, I'll buy it," said Mr. Wickham. "When is it?"

"Sunday the twenty-eighth of September," said Canon Fewling.

"Can't think of anything that happened then," said Mr. Wickham. "The twenty-ninth is Quarter Day, worse luck, and then there's nothing till pheasant shooting on the first of October."

"Well, it isn't absolutely an anniversary," said Canon Fewling, "but what with summer time one day more or less doesn't seem to matter very much. The 29th, the very next day, is Nelson's birthday. And exactly one hundred and ninety years afterwards," which news so paralysed, or shall we rather say hushed his hearers, that he was almost grateful when Rose said she had no idea he was as old as that.

"Good old Tubby," said Mr. Wickham, rapidly refilling Canon Fewling's and his own and Miss Phelps's glass and pouring a little beer into a glass for Rose. "Well, here's to Horatio Nelson coupled with the name of—what the hell *is* your name, Tubby? I've known you for donkey's ears, but we always said Tubby."

"I can't help it, but it's George," said Canon Fewling.

"Well, you weren't there when you were christened," said Mr. Wickham tolerantly; "at least you know what I mean, you weren't responsible, non compos and all that. Well, here's to Horatio Nelson and George Fewling and now we'll forget it," and he drank the whole of his beer in one draught. Rose drank a little of her beer and looked at Canon Fewling, her thoughts busy with the problem of what would be beset to wear in the Cathedral at the end of September with probably no heating anywhere, her eyes expressing, as they often did, nothing at all except the beauty of their colour and setting: while Miss Phelps, putting her beer down like a man, thought how interested her father would be.

"Well, that'll be one in the eye for the Bishop," said Mr. Wickham, on no grounds at all. "And I must be off, Rose. I've got a couple of men coming to spend the evening. Haven't seen them since I was in Valparaiso. By the way, did you chaps know I had come into a spot of money? An old uncle over Chaldicotes way that I hardly knew."

The news had not unnaturally spread through most of West Barsetshire since the night Mr. Wickham had told his news to Colonel and Mrs. Crofts with the Colonel's ex-soldier servant listening outside the door, but everyone behaved as if they had not heard it. Canon Fewling in particular was loud and sincere in his congratulations and asked what he was going to do with it. Miss Phelps was also delighted by the good news, but felt too shy to say anything, for it seemed to remove Mr. Wickham into a higher sphere.

"First I'll tell Merton to put my wages up," said Mr. Wickham. "It's always worth a try and if you have a spot of money people respect you more. Of course he won't, and there's no reason he should. Then I shall give the house a good over-haul and do some painting and papering and perhaps another bathroom. It's quite a good thing to have another bathroom if you have chaps to stay," and thanking Rose warmly for her party, he collected Miss Phelps and went away.

Canon Fewling also went home to prepare himself for the evening service. It was very fairly attended now and he liked to have a time in which to attune himself to the words he was going to say. But it was a little difficult to get away from the atmosphere of the afternoon. The interest that Rose had taken in his preaching in the Cathedral (though one fears that Rose had, in her artless way, made her feelings appear deeper than they were) had touched him a good deal. Wickham had been extremely nice and sympathetic, even if "What the devil" was hardly an appropriate comment. But they had both been naval men and he thought Wicks a thoroughly good fellow.

Then, with a quicker heart-beat, he wondered if Margot Phelps would be interested. He had always liked her and respected her and today she had seemed more than usually likeworthy and respectworthy. And why he hadn't noticed before how good-looking she was he couldn't imagine. Then he went to his church and set his thoughts on the noble words he was to read and the eternal spirit that informed them. But through them there ran, quite uninvited, the question, Why had he never before properly noticed Miss Phelps.

CHAPTER 10

Although the summer holidays do not have the disintegrat-ing effect that they have in London, they do make changes. The Fairweathers took their family to the sea, the Carters went to Spain. Miss Hampton and Miss Bent had gone on a cruise among the Greek Islands, spurred thereto by the discovery in a *Times* cross-word puzzle that Sappho (anag.) was Paphos, and hoping to learn something thereby. Mr. Traill went to Switzer-land and Mr. Feeder and his mother to Monte Carlo, where Mrs. Feeder had a good many friends who could be relied upon for meals and alcoholic beverages, and by her not inconsiderable wits kept herself nicely in pocket money. The Croftses, having taken their holiday earlier in the year, were in residence at Southbridge and Canon Fewling had no intention of deserting Greshamsbury and the flock which had gradually accrued to him, so the Phelpses saw a good deal of both of them. There was at first a slight difficulty about Canon Fewling's car being left outside Jutland Cottage where every passing boy and girl sounded The Gentleman's Hooter, but P.C. Brown, after hav-ing been invited by Canon Fewling to handle the car as far as Bolder's Knob when off duty one Wednesday, said if the Rev-erend liked to leave his car in his, P.C. Brown's, yard at the side of the cottage the way those perishing kids couldn't get at it, he was welcome; an invitation of which Canon Fewling took every advantage.

"You are getting quite a Regular, Tubby," said Mr. Wickham when for the fourth or fifth time he had found Canon Fewling sitting with the Admiral. "Battle of Jutland as usual?"

Canon Fewling said it was. And though, he said, he gloried in the thought of that battle and wished he had been old enough—he meant young enough—oh well, anyway he meant the right age to have been in it—he occasionally wished it had never happened.

"I get you, my boy," said Mr. Wickham. "Well, it's my turn to take the wheel now," and he went into Jutland Cottage while Canon Fewling went home.

It was not difficult to see that Mrs. Phelps's health was not improving, though her daughter worked harder and harder to keep her mother from overdoing it. But if you leave your mother in a chair on the lawn and go and see about taking some week-old chickens over to the Red Lion one of whose hens has gone broody, and then come back to find her among the raspberry canes in the sun and annoyed at being found, what are you to do? And when Mrs. Phelps looked tired the Admiral worried and then Mrs. Phelps worried and felt more tired, so that sometimes Miss Phelps would go away to the end of the paddock where the hens lived and shed a few tears by herself. Here, one afternoon, she was surprised by the appearance of Dr. Ford.

"I knew I'd find you somewhere," said Dr. Ford, settling himself not very comfortably on the shaft of a wheelbarrow. "This barrow's too heavy for you, Margot," at which Miss Phelps laughed and said she could wheel the barrow with Dr. Ford in it twice round the School cricket ground, adding, "How are they?"

"Fair to moderate," said Dr. Ford cheerfully.

"No, *honestly*, Dr. Ford," said Miss Phelps.

"Well then, moderate," said Dr. Ford.

"Look here, Dr. Ford," said Miss Phelps, busying herself with some revolting chicken food in a pail, her back to Dr. Ford, "you know they aren't too good. Will you tell me something if I ask you?"

Dr. Ford, who had a pretty good guess at what it was, said with professional caution that it depended.

"Well, they aren't well," said Miss Phelps, poking her horrible mixture with a stick. "Are they going to die?"

Dr. Ford did not make any answer.

"I suppose that's one of the questions you aren't allowed to answer by your old Trades Union," said Miss Phelps, with a rudeness most unusual in her. "Oh, sorry then."

"I can't possibly tell you what I don't know," said Dr. Ford. "Do try not to worry. It will only worry them and *that* won't help."

"If only I knew *which*," said Miss Phelps, who had at last given up all pretence of mixing the hens' food and faced Dr. Ford as she knelt. "If mother dies first I can't think *what* father will do. And if father dies first she will only have her pension," and she named the sum which seemed to Dr. Ford incredibly small. "Tubby says all the pensions for naval men's widows will be raised this year," she continued, "but even with raising I don't see how I can make her really comfortable. I could take a job, of course. I'm a pretty good driver and I know hens inside out— odious things——" and she kicked the bucket vengefully, thus causing two elderly hens to have hysterics and tell the others that the Cold War had begun. "But if I had a job I couldn't look after mother. Oh, well," and on these words of resignation, which are the only adequate comment on many of life's trials, she began mixing the hens' food again.

"Now, take it quietly, Margot," said Dr. Ford, getting up. "I give you my word of honour that if I see serious trouble ahead I'll tell you at once. Will you believe me?"

"Oh, I believe you," she said, not raising her head, "but that doesn't make it any better, you know," and went away up the garden.

"Good afternoon, Dr. Ford," said a voice from behind them,

which turned out to be Mr. Macfadyen. "I found your father and Mr. Wickham at the Battle of Jutland, Miss Phelps, so I came away down the garden," and he sat upon the back of the wheelbarrow.

It did occur to Dr. Ford to wonder why Mr. Macfadyen had come away down the garden, but he was a busy man and felt he had done all he could for the Phelps girl, who was certainly looking well in spite of her worries; and he wondered why he hadn't noticed before what a good skin she had and what well-shaped arms and good legs and how well her short hair with its little wave became her. But wondering does not get a busy country doctor through his round, so he said goodbye to Mr. Macfadyen.

"I'll set you a step on your way, Dr. Ford," said Mr. Macfadyen. "I'll be back, Miss Phelps. And what, if I may ask," he said as the two men walked towards the gate that opened from the paddock onto the road, "do you make of yon girl's father and mother?"

Rather surprised by the question, Dr. Ford turned his head and looked at Mr. Macfadyen.

"An unusual question," he said.

"Aye, I'm an unusual man," said Mr. Macfadyen calmly. "I saw my mother wearing away—I was but a lad then—and you can't mistake the signs. But it is of Miss Phelps that I am thinking."

"Well, damn it, so am I," said Dr. Ford, who hardly ever swore. "I brought that girl into the world and she's as good as they make them and far better looking now than she was when she was younger. Of course her parents are going to kill her unless they die first," said Dr. Ford, most unprofessionally, but he had considerable confidence in the manager of Amalgamated Vedge whom he had often met at the Club and elsewhere.

"Can I help them?" said Mr. Macfadyen. "I am a wealthy man as wealth goes now. Amalgamated Vedge is a growing concern and a safe one."

"Look here, you have no business to talk to me like this," said Dr. Ford, "and I've no business to listen to it, but the whole thing adds up wrong. If Mrs. Phelps were to die, Margot would have to give up a lot of her outdoor work to be with her father; and they depend a good deal on the garden and fowls. If the Admiral were to die, Margot and her mother would have to live on a widow's pension," and he named the sum. "The Admiral has often talked to me about it. Why the dickens that girl didn't marry I don't know," he added angrily.

"Has no one——" said Mr. Macfadyen and stopped.

"Not so far as I know, or anyone else knows," said Dr. Ford. "What chance does that girl have? She never sees any men except the Vicar and the masters at the School and Wickham, who comes over to talk shop with the Admiral, and Fewling, who has been over quite a lot and lets the Admiral tell him about the Battle of Jutland. If you can find anyone suitable, Macfadyen, send him along. She's a girl in a hundred and her parents can't live for ever. Mind you, I am not talking professionally."

Mr. Macfadyen, after a moment's consideration, said it was a fact that so far no one had lived for ever.

"Except the Struldbrugs," said Dr. Ford, hoping, we fear, to puzzle the wealthy market-gardener.

"And a puir fushionless lot they were," said Mr. Macfadyen calmly, "and though Dean Swift made a fine tale of it I have never believed it," and he looked gravely at Dr. Ford.

"Game to you and set," said Dr. Ford. "Look here, Macfadyen, I'll let you know if there is real trouble here. Goodbye," and he hurried through the gate and got into his car. Mr. Macfadyen went back to meet Miss Phelps, who had just put a dozen or so eggs into her pail and was taking them up to the house.

"Oh, thank you," said Miss Phelps as he took the pail from her. "Will you stop to tea? Mr. Wickham is with father, and mother will be down soon. We'll go in by the kitchen if you don't mind, because of the eggs."

So Mr. Macfadyen accompanied her into the kitchen, which room he praised highly for its tidiness and cheerfulness.

"Won't you go in to father?" said Miss Phelps, as he put her pail down, but Mr. Macfadyen said it reminded him of his mother's kitchen, only hers was smaller.

"And you have a look of my mother, Miss Phelps," he added. "She was a bonny, bonny woman, and when my father was killed in the South African war there was more than one man would have liked to marry her, but she would not. She died when I was barely twenty and I came south and stayed here, setting my wits against other men's in the gardening and then the market-gardening. And now I'm a man that is well known and respected," and if we do not write weel known and respectit it is because we trust our reader to know how Mr. Macfadyen spoke.

"She must have been *very* nice," said Miss Phelps, who was by now washing her hands in the sink. "Do you know that wonderful cream stuff, Mr. Macfadyen, that Mrs. Villars gave me? You rub it into your hands when they are clean and then when you wash it all comes off with a lovely splodge," and Mr. Macfadyen came to the sink the better to observe this interesting phenomenon and said he would not just say but it might be a good thing.

"Oh bother, I ought to have made the fire up first," said Miss Phelps, but Mr. Macfadyen, who had not forgotten his mother's kitchen which was also her living-room and how he used to make up the fire for her, took the poker, rattled the dead coal into the ashpan, lifted the round lid off the fire and poured in just the right amount of coal from the hod. By this time Miss Phelps had accepted him as a helper and they got out the tea-things and set the large tray.

"I say, Mr. Macfadyen, could you so very kindly make tea as soon as the kettle boils," said Miss Phelps, as she might have spoken to Kate Carter, or Mrs. Crofts, or any friend in the village, "while I just go upstairs and get a bit tidy," and she ran up to her room. It was far too hot for the tweed suit. She had shown

the summer dresses to her mother, who had nearly cried with
pleasure, but this was no moment for silk dresses with more
gardening to do after tea and her parents would wonder what on
earth Margot was doing. So she combed her hair and pushed its
natural wave into place and down she went, to find Mr. Macfadyen putting the lid on the tea-pot. He looked up and observed the goddess made manifest by her step.

"Can you carry the tray," she asked, "and I'll bring the kettle,"
and she led the way to the sitting-room, where Mr. Wickham
was not listening to what Admiral Phelps was saying, neither for
the first nor the twentieth time, about Their Lordships of the
Admiralty.

"Good girl," he said as Miss Phelps and her kettle came into
the room. "Hullo, hullo, who's here? Macfadyen of all people.
Like a French farce; people popping up when you don't expect
them. How are Vedge, old fellow?"

"Up three points on today's quotation," said Mr. Macfadyen.
He put the tray carefully on the table and went over to the
Admiral and shook hands.

"You are missed at the club, Admiral," he said.

"Out of sight, out of mind," said the Admiral, but Mr.
Macfadyen had no intention of letting him be sorry for himself
and asked if he knew anything about the new liner they were
laying down on the Clyde with an eight point six inverse ratio
scrutator: or if those were not the words they do well enough and
the Admiral delivered an impassioned attack on the folly of
people who didn't realize that taking the tonnage and overall
width into account it would play Old Harry with the bulging-
recession: and if our readers do not understand this, nor do we,
but readers must be content. Then Mrs. Phelps came down
from her afternoon rest and was treated by Mr. Macfadyen with
a courtesy that won her heart.

"Look here, Margot, anything wrong with you?" said Mr.
Wickham while the others talked. "You look queer."

"I don't feel queer," said Miss Phelps, quite truly. "I've been

down with the hens and Dr. Ford came in for a talk and then Mr.
Macfadyen, so I asked him to tea."

"Well, you are looking different," said Mr. Wickham. "Younger
and all that. May be a bit of a hangover with me, one never
knows. I had some fellows from the old *Andiron* and we saw the
sun rise and jolly beastly it looked. I say, Margot, what *is* wrong
with you?"

"Perhaps it's because I washed my hair last night," said Miss
Phelps, which was the truth and she had used a rinse given to her
by Miss Hampton and had pinned her hair as nearly as she could
in the way recommended by Dahlia at the Maison Tozier.

"You looked top-hole at Rose's in that grey dress, and I
thought it was just fine feathers make fine birds," said Mr.
Wickham with sad want of gallantry. "But I'm blowed if you
don't look top-hole in those awful bags," he went on with sincere
admiration; and, or course, as being admired always does one
good, Miss Phelps coloured a little and Mr. Macfadyen, looking
across the room, felt a sudden distaste for Mr. Wickham and as
soon as he had partaken of the family tea he took his leave.

"Next week," he said to Miss Phelps, who had come down to
the front gate with him, "I am taking Miss Lufton over to
Harefield. We are to meet Mr. Swan there and see the arrangements for the Priory School which is moving to Harefield
House. If you would come with us we would fetch you and take
you home."

Miss Phelps, perhaps not uninfluenced by the thought of
wearing one of Rose's frocks again, said she would love to, only
she must make sure that someone could sit with father that
afternoon. "It's as bad as having children," she said, not complaining at all, merely stating a fact, "but I'm pretty sure I can
manage it," and Mr. Macfadyen said he would be at the gate at
half-past three on the following Wednesday and so took his
leave. For some reason into which she did not trouble to enquire
Miss Phelps felt that the tea-things could wait and she would go
and pick some raspberries for supper, so she took a basket and

went down the garden. As always happens, a bird had managed to get through or under the net and was rushing about with mad squawks, telling all its uninterested friends and relations that the Secret Police had got it and of course when Miss Phelps came to its aid it recognised in her the Head Torturer and flapped about more wildly than ever.

"Take it easy," said the voice of Mr. Wickham, who came creeping under the net. "Lucky I've got a hat," and taking his disgraceful old felt hat in one hand, he advanced upon the bird, drove it into a corner, bonneted it, lifted the net and released it. The bird went angrily away to tell its friends about the cosh gang and how it had pecked one of them to death and escaped. Mr. Wickham went down between the canes to Miss Phelps.

"Thanks awfully, Wicks," said Miss Phelps. "Sometimes they stay in here all night, silly things. Are you going?"

"I am," said Mr. Wickham. "All clear up aloft and they are doing the cross-word puzzle."

"We really ought to take in a cheaper paper," said Miss Phelps, "but they do love their cross-word. What do you think, Wicks. Mr. Macfadyen is going to take me over to Harefield next Wednesday, to see where the Priory School is going. Isn't it kind of him? I shall try to get Mrs. Crofts to come to tea with the parents."

"Gallivanting about the county with single men," said Mr. Wickham. "What next?" to which Miss Phelps replied that she had gallivanted with him and why not with Mr. Macfadyen. Besides, she added, Miss Lufton was coming.

"People used to say he was after the Dowager," said Mr. Wickham, "but now it's her daughter. Well, well."

"Really, Wicks, *what* a thing to say," said Miss Phelps, for some reason annoyed at Mr. Wickham's suggestion, which of course might be true. "Giving people a lift doesn't mean you want to marry them, if that's what you mean. Think of all the lifts you've given me," to which Mr. Wickham replied, "Kamerad," and laughed and went away. Miss Phelps stood looking after him, but whether her thoughts were with him we cannot say. Then she picked up her basket and went back to the house.

All went well with the plans for Wednesday. Mrs. Crofts willingly came as sitter for the afternoon, the weather was settled and quite pleasantly warm. Miss Phelps felt justified in wearing the grey linen dress and the good thread stockings with her well-worn but well-kept shoes and took her good pair of wash-leather gloves. Kind Mrs. Crofts came punctually at three o'clock and Miss Phelps was able to give the next half-hour to being certain Mr. Macfadyen wouldn't come. But of course he did come, in his very good but not ostentatious car, Justinia Lufton sitting beside him. When Miss Phelps came down to the gate, Justinia was there with a welcoming smile.

"Would you like to go in front?" she said. "I'm going in the back," and Miss Phelps, rather shy of usurping Justinia's place, said she would come in the back too if nobody minded. Mr. Macfadyen, not very seriously, said something about the Monstrous Regiment of Women.

"Dreadful man, John Knox," said Justinia to Miss Phelps, who agreed on general principles though she did not quite understand what Miss Lufton meant. Then they sped over downland and through water-meadow valleys to Harefield, up the village street with its dignified red-brick houses, through the gates of Harefield Park and up the drive.

"Oh!" said Miss Phelps. And we agree with her, for Harefield House was certainly enough to make any who was seeing it for the first time want, like Man Friday, to say Oh. It was a large house of English-Palladian style with a handsome pillared portico. On each side of it was a pavilion, connected with the main building by a covered arcade whose curve was by many authorities considered to be the most beautiful in the county, if not in all England. A middle-aged man of military bearing who was standing on the steps came down and opened the door of the car.

"Mr. Swan told me to look out for you, sir," said the man.

"He'll be here in a minute, sir," and while he addressed Mr. Macfadyen he held the door of the car open for the ladies to get out.

"Sergeant Hopkins, isn't it?" said Justinia. "I've seen you and your wife at the Priory School. How is she?"

Hopkins said she was very well, which exhausted the conversation, but luckily Swan came up and Sergeant Hopkins moved a step back and stood at attention.

"How nice of you to come," said Swan, embracing all the guests in this greeting. "Shall we go over the house first, and then Clarissa Belton has asked us all to tea. They have the East Pavilion. I have the West, which I hope you will honour afterwards."

The guests were all content, so Swan showed them the ground floor where the big rooms had been slightly altered by partitions. Here were the dining-hall, the recreation-room for wet days and some classrooms. On the floor above were more classrooms and a couple of bedrooms for masters. The top floor was dormitories and more bedrooms for masters and prefects, for the overtaxed and generally ground-down middle classes have not abandoned the very English plan of paying more than you can afford for your children's education; nor do we think they will as long as the best private schools (known in England as public schools) and the best preparatory schools continue in being.

After admiring the view over the church and the water meadows away to the downs the party were taken to the basement, though this is not a quite accurate description as owing to the fine flight of steps and the slope of the ground the front rooms were on ground level and even at the back the ground had been artificially sloped back from the house, so that everything was light.

In the large old-fashioned well-cupboarded kitchen (but with up-to-date cooking arrangements) an elderly woman with steel-rimmed spectacles was sitting in an easy-chair, darning socks. A very pretty though not very young woman with silvery-brown hair curling like the tendrils of the vine was preparing food on a large old-fashioned kitchen table.

"I have brought Miss Lufton and Miss Phelps and Mr. Macfadyen to see you, Mrs. Allen," said Swan, presenting his party as if to seated royalty.

The elderly woman sketched a motion of rising (which she obviously did not intend to do in the least) and said she didn't get about much now.

"Your brother married Miss Grace Grantly, miss," said Nannie Allen to Justinia, who stood up to it pretty well and made a suitable reply though, as she afterwards told Swan, she had felt more inclined to say that the owl was the baker's daughter. "And you're the gentleman that does market-gardening, sir," said Nannie Allen in a voice of accusation calculated to make most market-gardeners tremble. But Mr. Macfadyen came from a country which has always produced domineering old ladies and quite unmoved said that his firm, Amalgamated Vedge, was one of the largest in the country.

"Well, sir, if it's vegetables you're interested in, you had better speak to my son-in-law," said Nannie Allen. "He understands them," thus exiling Mr. Macfadyen from the conversation.

"And this," said Swan, "is Miss Phelps. Her father is an Admiral and they live at Southbridge," and as one of Nannie Allen's ex-nurslings was now Commander Sir Cecil Waring, R.N., she was very gracious to Miss Phelps.

"Here, Hopkins," said Nannie Allen to a noise which had approached the kitchen door and was obviously about to retreat in good order, "come in. This gentleman is a market-gardener, so you'd better ask him about the asparagus beds. And he's having tea with Mrs. Belton, so don't forget."

As this was obviously a royal command, Mr. Macfadyen got up with amusement in his face, shook hands with Sergeant Hopkins and went away with him.

"And now, Mr. Swan, you'd better take the ladies to see the

gymnasium," said Nannie Allen, "and then Mrs. Charles Belton is expecting you all for tea. Thank you for coming, I'm sure."

"You wouldn't believe it, would you?" said Swan, as they walked towards the old stables, now converted to a gymnasium. "We are all terrified of her. Except Leslie Winter because she and her brother, Cecil Waring, were Nannie's babies once. If you think gymnasiums are as dull as I do, let's go over to the Beltons'," and he led them to the far end of the colonnade where lived Charles Belton and his wife, once Clarissa Graham, an old acquaintance of Justinia's. We have hardly seen Clarissa since her marriage, but looking at her now we think her beloved grandmother, Lady Emily Leslie, would have been happy about her lovely, difficult grandchild; or shall we say that Lady Emily is happy about it? We do not know.

In a few moments Charles Belton came in and though he greeted his visitors most pleasantly his eyes and mind so obviously went straight to his wife that Swan felt more moved than he would have wished. The desire not of a moth for a star (nor had he ever cared for Clarissa beyond a friendly tolerance and her ways) but of a normal man for a normal home; a light shining from the window and a pair of slippers warming before the fire, which romantic thought made him laugh aloud at himself.

"A penny for your thoughts," said Justinia.

"You couldn't pay it," said Swan. "Mr. Macfadyen could."

Clarissa asked why Mr. Macfadyen.

"He knows his Schubert," said Swan sententiously, and Mr. Macfadyen said he could not rightly say that he knew his Schubert, for though he could not state precisely how many songs Schubert had written, it would be in the neighbourhood of four hundred or more, adding severely that the *Oxford Companion to Music* might well have made a computation of his song.

"You sang something from the Winterreise in Lady Lufton's sitting-room, I mean Justinia's mother, last year," said Swan.

"Rückblick, it was. But, if you wish to know," he said to the company generally and with a courtesy which barely veiled his certainty that all of them were ignorant, "it was another song that was in my mind. You will know which I mean, Mr. Macfadyen. It is about the bunte List, Die hinter Eis und Nacht und Graus, Ihm weist ein helles warmes Haus."

Mr. Macfadyen said he minded it well but, he added patriotically, Burns was a far better poet than Müller, upon which he and Swan fell into one of those pedantic conversations so enchanting to the speakers, so uncommonly boring to the listeners. But they did not have to suffer long, for Clarissa, with a pretty air of hostess-ship upon her, led her guests to her little dining-room for a comfortable sit-down tea. The falcon was tamed at last, thought Swan and then chid himself for being so damnably poetical and sentimental and made Clarissa laugh by his account of Nannie Allen's reception of them.

"Does she live here now?" said Justinia.

Not exactly, Clarissa said, because nothing would induce her to leave her little house, Number One, Ladysmith Cottages, Lambton, because it was near Beliers Priory and Lady Cora might be glad of help with the baby, for Nannie Allen had no opinion of Nurse at all. And even, Clarissa added, if she came by the bus Sergeant Hopkins always had to drive her home, and as he hadn't got a car one of the masters usually had to lend his.

"If there were a French word for a female Tyrant I would say Conspuez her," said Swan.

"Probably femme tyran," said Mr. Macfadyen, but the conversation was getting rather donnish, and Swan noted with amusement how well Clarissa, with a light hand, led them all back to ordinary talk.

"I don't want to be a nuisance, Eric," said Justinia Lufton presently, "but I think we ought to take Margot back. Her parents, you know," and Swan blamed himself for being so thoughtless and apologised to Clarissa. Miss Phelps's parents were not very well, he said, and she did not like to be out too long, so they said goodbye.

"Will you just look at my bachelor residence," said Swan and took Mr. Macfadyen and the ladies across to the West Pavilion, which was exactly the same as the East Pavilion, three bedrooms, two sitting-rooms and what are called the usual offices, all on the small scale but perfect in proportion.

Mr. Macfadyen and Miss Phelps were still examining the little kitchen and Swan was alone with Justinia.

"What would you say? This, or a fellowship at Oxford?" said Swan.

Justinia thought before she spoke.

"I think *you* would be perfect for Oxford," she said, "but would your wife like it?"

Swan said that was a point he had not considered and asked her to expound.

"Well, to be a Don, or a Fellow, or a Master, or a Provost, or any of those things, is splendid," said Justinia. "But their wives have to know all the other wives, and some of them," she added darkly, "do folk-dancing in slacks. And some of the older ones wear mackintoshes and look as if they hadn't anything on underneath them, if you see what I mean," at which Swan nearly had the giggles, so well did this describe the wife of the Master of Barabbas, who also liked to sleep on a camp bed in the Master's garden during the summer term, thereby much inconveniencing undergraduates who were re-entering their college by the garden wall, the crockets of the chapel and so to the little door in the organist's loft, if you had been able to get the key from the last chap who had it.

"But I haven't a wife," said Swan.

"You did care for Grace, didn't you?" said Justinia, remembering a tea-party at Framley Court when Lord Lufton and Grace Grantly had dressed up in a peer's and a peeress's robes. "I saw you look at her."

"I didn't know I had made myself a motley to the view," said

Swan, with no bitterness, but sorry for the Swan of yesteryear who now seemed very far away and unreal.

"Oh no," said Justinia. "You didn't. I only happened to see because I was at the door, looking at Ludovic and Grace. I had helped them to put the robes on and was waiting to put them away again. Only I was so sorry for you. I hope you don't mind," and she looked up at him.

"You are just like the portrait of your great-grandmother at Framley," said Swan, thinking of the drawing by George Richmond, with the oval face and beautiful eyes.

"Really?" said Justinia, pleased with the comparison.

"There is only one thing wanting," said Swan gravely, so of course Justinia asked what it was, because to be noticed, even for a defect, is pleasant when the right person notices it.

"The high light on the tip of your nose," said Swan. "I suppose it was a mark of virtue then, for all the beauties have it in their portraits," and though Justinia was not interested in marks of virtue, it is always a compliment to know that one has been accurately observed and compared with a beauty.

Then Mr. Macfadyen and Miss Phelps came in and said they ought to be going, so Swan took them back by the colonnade and the flight of stone steps to where the car was patiently waiting.

"You go in front this time, Miss Phelps," said Justinia, who had put herself in the back, so Miss Phelps did as she was told and asked Mr. Macfadyen which was the best, Holman's Phospho-Manuro, or Corbett's Bono-Vitasang, or Washington's Vimphos. Mr. Macfadyen said there was not a penny to choose between them, but he and Holman had dealings together and he could easily get Miss Phelps as much Phospho-Manuro as she liked because he happened to have more than he needed at the moment and would send it over which, he said, would cost nothing.

Miss Phelps was beginning to make a protest against this generosity, but a generosity in her own nature suddenly told her that what was freely offered must be freely accepted, so she thanked Mr. Macfadyen very much and asked if he would like some of the raspberry jam that she was about to make; which appeared to please him. Then he set her down at Jutland Cottage and with thanks to him and a promise to ask Justinia to tea one day she went into the house.

Justinia got into the front seat, but neither she nor Mr. Macfadyen spoke much. Mr. Macfadyen was wondering how much Phospho-Manuro he could give to the Phelpses without seeming to force his gifts upon them, while Justinia sat in a pleasant dream of how nice it was to be told one was like one's great-grandmother.

The next visitor to Jutland Cottage was Lady Cora Waring who brought her husband, Sir Cecil Waring, R.N. Not without protest on his part, for he had planned a happy afternoon in Golden Valley with Jasper, the half-gypsy keeper, who had found a badger with a habit of sunning himself between three and four P.M. in an eligible position and would like to be photographed, which meant a great deal of caution and almost a certainty that the badger would (a) go to earth at once, (b) have moved to a different position, and (c) not have come out at all. But Lady Cora said it would be good for her husband, and the Royal Navy must stick together, so of course Sir Cecil gave in. The day was almost hot and the trees along their road, especially the elms, had that thundercloud air which they assume just as we are beginning to enjoy the three days of good weather.

"Though for thunderclouds, give me a sycamore," said Lady Cora. "Once you let them get a start they will fill up the whole sky and look like the Great San Philip and take all the air away. You will love the Admiral," and it is a tribute to Cecil's good sense that these words did not make him hate the Admiral at sight, for nothing is more annoying than to be told you will like anyone.

Mrs. Phelps was, as usual, having her afternoon rest when the

Warings arrived, so Miss Phelps was there to receive them, or rather came hurrying up from the garden when she heard their car. The meeting of the two naval gentlemen could not have been better if Aubrey Clover had staged it. The Admiral rose from his chair, assuming (so Lady Cora afterwards averred) a slight limp which he really hadn't got, while Sir Cecil came quickly forward and shook hands with a respectful air that showed he considered an Admiral on the retired list as on the whole for above a mere Commander who happened through no fault of his own to be a Bart and quite well off as things go and had married the daughter of a Duke.

As Mrs. Phelps was resting, her daughter did the honours and then asked Lady Cora if she would like to look at the garden. We cannot say that Lady Cora wanted to see it in the least, but she had been well brought up to think about other people's feelings and realised, after a quick look at the little house, that there was probably no other room but the kitchen.

"I don't expect you really want to see it, after the Priory," said Miss Phelps, "but we had to turn the other room, which was our dining-room, into a bedroom for father. You know he has a heart," to which Lady Cora said, How very sensible, and when her husband had been so ill, before they were married, his bedroom had been moved to the ground floor of the Priory. And then they went down past the raspberry canes to the little paddock to look at the fowls.

"You are looking extremely nice, Margot," said Lady Cora approvingly, at which Miss Phelps coloured in a not unbecoming way and said she washed her hair with a special rinse Miss Hampton had given her and pinned it into waves as the nice girl at the Maison Tozier had told to do.

"It takes a bit more time," she said, "but it only means getting up a bit earlier or going to bed a bit later. Oh, Lady Cora, I didn't tell you, but Rose Fairweather gave me two lovely summer frocks. Of course, I like the suit you gave me best," she added hastily, to which Lady Cora nearly replied, "Little liar," but her breeding and her real kindness told her that Miss Phelps might not recognise the quotation, so she said she was so glad and she hoped Margot remembered to wear a proper belt with it, for Rose had of course told her all about the visit to Bostock and Plummer and the Maison Tozier, adding that she had suggested that Miss Phelps should keep her new underwear for best because if you wore the same belt all the time it got broader than it was long and nothing to be done about it.

"Oh yes, I *always* wear it," said Miss Phelps.

"And what is more, you are wearing it now," said Lady Cora, but very kindly, as she looked at Miss Phelps's old slacks which had assumed an almost Savile Row appearance. Miss Phelps went bright red in the face and looked as if she might cry.

"Oh, I do hope you don't mind," she said. "I can't tell you how it helps me. I know it's extravagant, but when mother is very tired and father feels ill, it does cheer me up so dreadfully, and after all Rose did give me two belts," which rather tangled remarks Lady Cora quite understood.

"I think it is *extremely* sensible of you," she said, with the decision of a long line of ancestors who had bullied (and also thought for and often provided for) those in dependent positions and of more humble rank. "Anything that cheers you up is a good thing. Even drink, though goodness knows one has to make a bottle of gin last as long as one can."

Miss Phelps said firmly that she liked beer.

"It's cheaper in one way, but it depends how much of it you drink," said Lady Cora. "Mr. Wickham can drink six glasses without winking and it mounts up. Cecil and I have wine in a modest way, and you drink less in a wineglass than you do in a tumbler. I don't know."

"I hope you won't mind," said Miss Phelps, "but Miss Hampton and Miss Bent are coming to tea. They are back from a cruise in the Greek Islands and father will like to hear about it. Will you stay to tea? she asked rather timidly, for perhaps Lady Cora would prefer Dukes and Earls.

"The Miss Hampton who writes those divine books?" said Lady Cora. "My pet, you couldn't have arranged a nicer treat. Ever since I read *Temptation at St. Anthony's* I have simply adored everything she wrote. That was in 1939, I think."

Miss Phelps said she knew her books were very intellectual, but she couldn't quite understand them. They were funny, if Lady Cora knew what she meant.

Her ladyship did indeed know what Miss Phelps meant and sympathised in a most gratifying way while inwardly wondering how such people still existed, for though her ladyship's knowledge of life was extensive and peculiar, she had not often come up against the short and simple views of the Miss Phelpses of this world; and there are still, we are glad to say, a great many of them. But she had been brought up to face social emergencies and said, quite untruthfully, that she didn't always quite understand them herself, but so long as it was a good story that was the great thing; with which Miss Phelps quite agreed.

"And where do you get your books?" said Lady Cora.

Miss Phelps said from the Public Library in Barchester and Mr. Parry, the Head Librarian, was very kind in getting the sort of books her father liked. And what were they mostly, Lady Cora asked.

"Oh, mostly books about naval things for father," said Miss Phelps. "Anything about Nelson, of course, and his admirals and captains, and all about when the Navy was changing from sails to steam, and about the 1914 war, because father was in it. Oh, and books about people who explored, like Columbus and Franklin and Scott. You see it's really very lucky that he likes that kind of book, because there are such a lot of them and mostly they are pretty long. Father doesn't read very much at a time because he gets tired, but he *does* so enjoy it. Mother likes novels."

Lady Cora asked if one could get the new novels at the Public Library.

"Well, not absolutely new," said Miss Phelps, "but mother

likes things like Dickens and Thackeray and she has always taken her books wherever they were stationed."

"And you?" said Lady Cora.

"Well, I really hardly get any time for reading," said Miss Phelps, without a trace either of boasting or self-pity, "but I do like Mrs. Morland's books because they are all exactly the same. I mean, if you like one you like the rest. And I get some very good books about fowls and fruit and vegetables from Mr. Parry."

"I should think you could write one yourself by now," said Lady Cora, without any particular conviction to that effect, but obeying her instinct to say what would give pleasure.

Miss Phelps stopped dead, just by the back door.

"How *did* you know that?" she asked.

"If you can tell me what 'that' is, my pet, I'll tell you how I knew it," said Lady Cora. Then seeing a rather unbecoming shade of red suffuse Miss Phelps's face she added, "Don't tell me you're a dark horse."

"Well," said Miss Phelps, getting even redder if possible, "I don't quite know what you mean, but I did try to write a book about doing the hens and the garden and the cooking and the house. I did put in a bit about goats too, because we kept them in the war, but it's awkward to write about things you loathe." She stopped suddenly, feeling she had said too much. Lady Cora, enthralled by this new facet of Miss Phelps, enquired why you couldn't write about things you loathed.

"Well," said Miss Phelps, who had now put the kettle on and was collecting the tea-things, "if I said all I think about goats I think the Goat Association or something would be down on me. They stamp on your feet and you can't stamp on theirs because they don't stick out flat like ours," at which Lady Cora could not help laughing, but quite saw what Miss Phelps meant. "And personally I think their milk is foul," Miss Phelps went on, "but I do know quite a lot about them."

"Put it in too, my pet," said Lady Cora. "There are millions—

well, anyway, hundreds of people who think goats' milk is good for children, though I think it is stinking. We'll make a book of it and all the other things and Wicks shall get his uncle to publish it."

"Wicks's uncle? I thought he was dead and had left him some money and a bit of land over Chaldicotes way," said Miss Phelps.

Lady Cora, reminding herself severely how restricted Miss Phelps's life had been by narrow means and hard work, explained very kindly that Mr. Wickham's other uncle, Mr. Johns, was a partner in Johns and Fairfield, the well-known publishing firm that brought out the books with Mrs. Crofts's lovely bird-illustrations, she added, feeling sure that Miss Phelps had seen some of them at the Vicarage.

"Oh! But they are *real* publishers," said Miss Phelps, apparently under the impression that anything of that sort would be a piece of luck out of her star. "They wouldn't want things like mine."

"Look here, Margot," said Lady Cora, "publishers *want* books. If they haven't any books to publish they starve and so do their wives and children. Johns and Fairfield are doing what they call a Popular Series of little books on things like tomato-growing and artificial mushrooms and things of that sort. We'll ask Wicks. I'm sure Mr. Johns would jump at your book. Is it finished?"

Miss Phelps, even redder than before if possible, said in a small voice that it was and Miss Bent had typed it for her very kindly, in duplicate too, but *please* it was a secret.

"Well, that's all right," said Lady Cora. "We'll keep it a secret. You give me one copy, whichever is the cleanest, and I'll see that Wicks does something about it. Shall I take the hot-water jug?" and without allowing Miss Phelps any time to consider she gently pushed her towards the sitting-room, where Sir Cecil and the Admiral were deep in some new naval charts which Sir Cecil had brought with him. These Lady Cora very kindly and very firmly refolded and laid on the top of a bookcase, and Miss Phelps put the tea-tray on the table and said she would tell her mother tea was ready. Even as she went upstairs she heard voices at the front door, but as she knew that Miss Hampton and Miss Bent would not stand upon ceremony, she did not come down again.

"Well, Admiral," said Miss Hampton, advancing with a firm step into the sitting-room, "here we are. Come along, Bent," and in came Miss Bent, dragging by his lead the long, low, shaggy dog who had been their slave (and tyrant) for more than twelve years, though his Christian (if we may use the term) name had varied with the popular hero of the day. "Don't get up, Admiral. No need. Think of Benbow, 'When his legs were shot away, He fought upon his stumps'," to which the Admiral replied with some indignation that he could still show a leg, and rising slowly from his chair, he introduced the newcomers to Sir Cecil and Lady Cora Waring, upon which a great and rather confused shaking of hands took place and everyone sat down, though rather like musical chairs as there was one too few, but Lady Cora obligingly fetched one from the kitchen.

"And what is your dog called?" said Lady Cora to the ladies, giving it a friendly pat.

"At the moment No Name," said Miss Hampton.

Lady Cora asked if that was after Trollope.

"Yes *and* no," said Miss Bent. "The fact is, we have not at the moment any hero. Mr. Churchill of course goes without saying, but even to our Great Leader we must show impartiality; and No Name was Churchill twice, wasn't he, Hampton? We are at the moment waiting for Something to tell us. Mr. Feeder suggested Super-Sonic, but as no one knows what it means, we let that drop. It must be a name with Universal Appeal. But we can wait. Light will come."

Lady Cora, who had been looking with great interest at Miss Bent's full, flowered cotton skirt, her loose Russian blouse with long baggy sleeves and her wide belt made apparently of coconut matting secured by a large brass hook and eye, asked what they did when they wanted to call him.

"Never leaves us," said Miss Hampton, who had been admiring from an impersonal point of view Lady Cora's feminine county elegance of light tweeds, well-polished shoes and pearls which were obviously real.

"Oh dear," said Miss Phelps, returning to the party. "I am so sorry. I did mean to bring the extra chair in, but mother isn't feeling very well, so I said I'd take her tea up. Absolutely all right, father," she said in an aside to the Admiral. "It's only that mother did have a sleep and you know how horrid one feels when one has been asleep after lunch, so I said I'd take her up some tea," at which the Admiral let out a great breath of relief (though quietly) and said, "A good idea."

Miss Phelps collected some tea for her mother and went upstairs again. The Admiral looked helplessly at the tea-pot. "May I pour out for you?" said Lady Cora, whom long experience of societies and meetings followed by cups of tea had made proficient in hostess-ship. The Admiral, who hated dealing with tea-pots and was already Lady Cora's slave, gladly assented and by the time Miss Phelps came down everyone was served. Miss Bent was discussing a new type of racing car with Sir Cecil and the Admiral, while Miss Hampton was visibly melting before Lady Cora's impassioned queries about her next book.

"I must say I simply *adore* everything you have written," said Lady Cora. "Which is your own favourite?"

This, as all writers will know, is a very difficult question to answer. All one's children are dear to one, and sometimes it is the Beauty who takes first place, sometimes the child with a crutch who is obviously not fit for this rough world. Nor was Miss Hampton an exception.

"It is hard to name a favourite, Lady Cora," she said. "Sometimes I think *A Gentle Girl and Boy*, sometimes I think *Chariots of Desire*—about the sex life of lorry-drivers, of course. It was strong meat—not for babes or sucklings."

"Well, I'm not either," said Lady Cora placidly, "and I've a pretty strong stomach. I must say I simply *adored* your public-school one, *Temptation at St. Anthony's*. Do you find much material here?"

"Not *here*," said Miss Hampton, looking round the little room. "The Admiral knows nothing about the Lower Deck. As for Margot, she is of course a striking example of Sex-Frustration, but I could not *dream* of using her. Dog doesn't eat dog."

"But *you* aren't sex-frustrated, are you?" said Lady Cora, who, like many well-born women, took the greatest interest in life and manners and had not the faintest inhibition about discussing them.

"Certainly not," said Miss Hampton, putting the monocle (which she always wore on a broad black ribbon) into her left eye. "You see, I am perfectly balanced. Bent is, psychologically speaking, entirely unbalanced. So, between us, we make the Norm," after which elucidatory words Lady Cora, for perhaps the first time in her life, was quite at a loss for words. But blood tells and quickly recovering herself, she asked Miss Hampton what she was working on at the moment.

"Tell Lady Cora, Bent," said Miss Hampton, speaking across Sir Cecil Waring. "You will forgive me if I do not discuss my own work, Lady Cora."

"Hampton is going full steam ahead with all sails spread," said Miss Bent, at which words Sir Cecil and the Admiral looked at Miss Hampton with interest. "She is facing, courageously, a problem of modern life. The title will be *My Daughter is My Son*. It will be strong meat. Can England take it?"

As no one knew the answer to this question, the naval men went back to their talk and the ladies discussed the Mammoth Bring and Buy Sale that the West Barsetshire W.V.S. were organising for the beginning of September. Miss Phelps looked in to say she would bring some more hot water and then run up and see if mother would like another cup of tea. As she went out of the room Mr. Wickham came in from the front garden. He gave a kind of salute to the two naval officers and cordially shook hands with Miss Hampton and Miss Bent.

"Every time I shake hands with you girls I swear I'll never do it again," he said examining his fingers. "And Cora! Bless your eyes, my girl, what are *you* doing here?" which to any outsider might have seemed a peculiar form of address from an estate agent (even if he had come into some money from his old uncle Chaldicotes way) to a Duke's daughter who had married a naval baronet, but Mr. Wickham, on leave from being a temporary sailor in 1944, had worked with Lady Cora Palliser, as she was then, during what he called a Godalmighty blitz and struck up an enduring friendship with her.

"Look here, Wicks," said Lady Cora. "Do you know what Margot has done?"

Mr. Wickham said he would buy it. Lady Cora appeared to understand this and went on, "She has written a book about hens and vegetables and goats and things. It's up to you to get your uncle to look at it, Wicks," to which Mr. Wickham replied that he never knew Margot was a dark horse and this was just the moment when one needed a spot of something to drink, and he would jolly well see that his uncle took it.

"You had better hurry up," said Lady Cora. "It's all nicely typed and if your uncle doesn't want it I can send it to Hobbs and Bungay," whom she knew to be business rivals of Johns and Fairfield.

"Kamerad," said Mr. Wickham and then Miss Phelps came back looking rather troubled. When she saw Mr. Wickham she asked him if he would come and look at the kitchen tap which was leaking again. As soon as they were in the kitchen Mr. Wickham said, "And what's wrong, Margot?"

"Nothing really," Miss Phelps was beginning, but Mr. Wickham cut her short with the fond words, "Little liar," and said to spit it out and Uncle Wicks would see to it.

"It's only mother," said Miss Phelps. "She wasn't well. I don't mean ill, but that kind of faintness she gets sometimes. I've got the stuff Dr. Ford gave me and she's had a dose of it, but I don't like to leave her just yet. Could you hold the fort, Wicks? I mean don't let father think anything's wrong. Say I'm doing the hens. If she goes to sleep I'll really do them, so it won't be a lie, and I've got to do them sometime, anyway."

"Trust the Royal Navy, even if only for the duration," said Mr. Wickham and put one arm round Miss Phelps with a brotherly hug, so that she went upstairs reassured while he went back to the sitting-room and arranged with Miss Hampton and Miss Bent to meet at the Red Lion about six, after which those ladies took their leave, followed shortly by the Warings. Mr. Wickham's quick ear heard Miss Phelps go into the kitchen, so evidently Mrs. Phelps was asleep and the hens were now to be fed.

"She's a good girl, that Margot of yours," said Mr. Wickham to his host. "I don't know a girl I like better except the married ones. How is the cold war going, Admiral? I mean the pensions for our wives. Not that I've got any, and anyway I was only a temporary, so it wouldn't count, but if I had I'd like them to have something to live on when I hopped the twig."

The Admiral said it was almost certain that the pensions would be increased shortly and then they fell into naval matters and the Admiral set Mr. Wickham right on several points which Mr. Wickham had cunningly got wrong on purpose, and so agreeable was the argument that the Admiral did not notice his wife's continued absence, or if he did he probably thought she was in the kitchen.

Meanwhile Mr. Macfadyen, who had been in the south of the county on a professional job, was driving back by Southbridge where he turned off, the better to by-pass Barchester on his way home, though it was a curiously roundabout way of by-passing it. When he got to the gate of the paddock where the Phelps hens lived, he slowed down and saw Miss Phelps giving those insatiable birds their evening meal. As he had a bag of Holman's Phospho-Manuro in the boot he thought this would be a good opportunity to deliver it, though whether the combination of the bag and the route he was taking were designed or accidental, we cannot say. Miss Phelps had her back to him and did not hear him till he said Good-evening, when she turned and exhibited a face blotched and mottled with crying.

"I had brought you some of Holman's Phospho-Manuro," said Mr. Macfadyen trying to imply that he saw nothing peculiar about Miss Phelps's face.

Miss Phelps, putting up a valiant effort to speak distinctly, said *how* kind and would he put it in the shed over there. Mr. Macfadyen looked at her and carried the bag to the shed. He then dusted his hands one against the other and came back to her.

"Oh, *please* go away," said Miss Phelps, more blotched and crying than before. "I'm so sorry. It's only that mother wasn't well. She's all right now, but when I came to feed the chickens I couldn't help crying. *Please* don't look at me."

"If *you* are crying, Miss Phelps," said Mr. Macfadyen, "things must be pretty bad for you. I think you are like my mother. She never cried but the once in front of me."

This might not seem to most women a really flattering comparison, but it seemed to please Miss Phelps, who cried more than ever. And if our reader does not understand this we can but pity his ignorance and despise him. Mr. Macfadyen went up to Miss Phelps and gathered her quietly and firmly into his arms, where she cried if possible even more than before.

"My poor bairn," said Mr. Macfadyen as her sobs died down from sheer exhaustion. "I cannot let this happen again."

"But *how* can you make things all right?" said Miss Phelps, raising her blotched face with eyes bunged up with crying.

"Just because I am what the world calls a well-to-do man," said Mr. Macfadyen. "When you marry me you need want for nothing, for yourself or for your parents. I can wait. But whenever you want me, or whenever you need any help, send for me and I shall come at once. Unless," he added cautiously, "I were at a Board Meeting or in Holland. But even so, I would be with you as soon as possible."

Miss Phelps, though making no effort to extricate herself from his comforting arms, said she must go back or her father would be going upstairs to find her mother and stairs were so bad for him.

"Then let me know as soon as you want me and whenever you want me," said Mr. Macfadyen. "My mother would have liked you, Margot."

"There's only one thing," said Miss Phelps, who had accepted the large handkerchief offered to her by her wooer and mopped up her tears, "I don't know your name. I mean your Christian name."

"It is Donald," said Mr. Macfadyen. "And that goes well with Margot, I'm thinking. Well, I must be stepping."

"Are we really engaged then?" said Miss Phelps.

"I am, if you are not," said her wooer, adding rather illogically, "so you are too," and he went back to his car and drove away.

Miss Phelps stood motionless, looking at nothing in particular and so submerged by what had happened that she was hardly able to think of anything in particular. But the hens were fed and there was supper to be thought of, so she picked up the horrid hen pail and went back to the house. As she neared the back door Mr. Wickham came out to meet her. At once she knew that misfortune had overtaken her. While she was talking to Mr. Macfadyen her mother had become very ill—or worse.

"And a precious long time you've been about your chickens," said Mr. Wickham. "I've fought the Battle of Jutland with your father from stem to stern, and your mother has had a little sleep and come downstairs," on hearing which words of comfort Miss Phelps, already much disturbed by the events of that afternoon, sat down on an empty box in the back yard and began to cry again.

"What the dickens have I said *now?*" said Mr. Wickham. "There's no pleasing you girls. Your mother's as fit as a fiddle, Margot, and then you begin to cry."

"I can't help it," said Miss Phelps. "It was so awful, and then Mr. Macfadyen came and now mother's better."

"Look here, my girl," said Mr. Wickham. "It *was* awful if you like, and I daresay Macfadyen did come if you say so, and Mrs. Phelps has had a nice rest. What on earth *do* you want?"

"I don't know," said Miss Phelps, looking piteously at Mr. Wickham.

"Then stop it, my girl," he said but not unkindly. "Look here, Margot, you've had a bad spell, but you're one of the finest girls I know for your age. Now attend. We've known each other off and on for a long time. I'm a decent chap on the whole, and I'm not badly off now. Listen, my girl. Why shouldn't we get married? Then you could tell me all about it when you feel down in the mouth. Have your own bedroom if you like. I'm going to build an extra one, anyway."

Miss Phelps looked at him. She had stopped crying and had an expression on her face that he could not understand.

"Sorry if it's a bit of a shock," he said kindly. "I must say I never meant to say it, but having said it I'll stick to it. We'll find room for your people over at Northbridge."

"It's so kind of you, Wicks," said Miss Phelps, "but I couldn't. And father does so love the church here and being a churchwarden. He looks forward to Sunday more than anything and the Croftses are his best friends. He would die at once if he hadn't got Southbridge."

"Well, we'll cross that bridge when we come to it," said Mr. Wickham. "What about marrying me, Margot? It's a firm offer. Take it or leave it. But I'd rather you took it."

"But Wicks, I couldn't, even if I wanted to," said Miss Phelps. "You see I'm engaged to Mr. Macfadyen. At least I suppose I am."

"Great holy cripes," said Mr. Wickham. "How long has *this* been going on?"

"Only just now, down by the hen-run," said Miss Phelps, and there was silence till the sound of the church clock striking six floated across to them.

"Well, that's that," said Mr. Wickham philosophically. "But I promised Cora I'd send your book to Old Uncle Johns."

"My book?" said Miss Phelps.

"About goats and things. The one Miss Bent typed for you. Go and get it, there's a good girl, I'm due at the Red Lion. Can't keep Hampton and Bent waiting."

Miss Phelps, almost stunned by the experiences of the afternoon and her relief about her mother, went upstairs obediently and brought back a neat packet of typescript.

"That's the stuff to give the troops," said Mr. Wickham. "Well, Gobbless, my girl. I shan't break my heart, but you're a fine girl, Margot, and I'll come to the wedding. When is it?"

"I never thought of that," said Miss Phelps, so simply that Mr. Wickham stopped himself from laughing, gave her a kind of avuncular pat on the shoulder and went away. Miss Phelps put the pail in its place and went into the kitchen, washed up the tea-things, got the supper, washed up the supper, helped her father to finish the cross-word, saw her mother safely upstairs and then went to her own room, suddenly so tired that she could have lain down on the floor. But on reflection a bed seemed better and after a few incoherent words of gratitude for all the extraordinary things that had happened that day she quickly fell asleep.

After all the excitement Miss Phelps had gone through she slept late for once. When she came hurriedly downstairs she found her mother in the kitchen, scolded her very kindly and began to get the breakfast ready. Her father was not yet up, so she took his breakfast in to him on a tray as she often did, together with his letters. Then she had breakfast with her mother in the kitchen and told her what Mr. Macfadyen had said.

"But I'm not going to leave you and father," she said. "That's settled. So don't let's talk about it. And mother, it was really too extraordinary, but Wicks said he wanted to marry me too and have us all at Northbridge," at which bundle of news her mother, of course, had to cry and kiss her in a comfortable Victorian way. But Miss Phelps did not say anything about her typescript, because she was sure Mr. Wickham's uncle would despise it and told the hope at the bottom of her heart to hold its tongue and not bother her.

"Will it be all right if I go over to Greshamsbury this morning, mother?" she said. "I promised Rose Fairweather some chickens and I can easily take them on my bicycle. I'll leave lunch in the oven for you and father, and don't wait for me," to which her mother agreed. But by great good luck Dr. Ford came in, as he often did, just to look at the Admiral and said he would take Miss Phelps over as he had to see a patient there, and Miss Phelps said, with a new-found courage which surprised herself, that she could get Tubby to run her back—possibly with a hope of driving his car—and her mother said not to hurry, as she could manage lunch quite well.

After the emotions of the previous day everything felt safe and comfortable again. It promised, for once, to be really hot, so with a car in prospect Miss Phelps put on the grey dress that Rose had given her, but also very providently took a large apron in case the hens gave trouble. As was his custom with his old friends, Dr. Ford was extremely indiscreet about various patients and they had a delightful gossip about things in general till they got to Greshamsbury, where Dr. Ford left Miss Phelps at the Fairweathers' house.

"Stay to lunch," said Rose as soon as she saw Miss Phelps. "Eric Swan is coming and Justinia Lufton and Tubby, and John is down for a few days, so we want another woman," and Miss Phelps felt so strangely happy and carefree that she accepted at

once, but even in her exalted state she did not forget her parents
and asked Rose if she might ring up Mrs. Crofts, who said she
would tell the Phelpses and would be delighted to go to Jutland
Cottage directly after lunch and Margot mustn't hurry back.
Even the chickens were in tune with this holiday and allowed
themselves to be shepherded into their new home without any
trouble, after which Rose and Miss Phelps sat in warm comfort
on the lawn till Swan came with Justinia Lufton.

"You do know Margot Phelps, I think," said Rose. "She has
brought me some quite breathtaking chickens. Come and see
them."

So they walked over to the chicken-run and admired the new
arrivals who were behaving like real refugees, being extremely
selfish and disagreeable to their new hosts.

"Mr. Macfadyen told mother and me," said Justinia to Miss
Phelps while Rose was talking to Swan. "We *are* so pleased. He's
much too nice to be a bachelor all his life. When's it to be?" to
which Miss Phelps, flattered though a little confused, said it
depended on her father and mother, because she simply couldn't
leave them. Justinia said Mr. Macfadyen would see to all that,
because he always did everything for everybody and was an
angel, and they all went back to the house where Captain
Fairweather and Swan were having one of those talks about war
experiences which are so fascinating to the speakers if to no one
else. Captain Fairweather then took Miss Phelps to look at
some books that he thought her father would like and Rose went
to telephone to her mother, so Justinia Lufton and Swan sat on
the old-fashioned veranda with its curved roof painted green
and hideous tiled floor and looked across the shimmering mid-
day heat towards the church. There did not seem to be any
particular reason to speak.

"Silent Noon," said Justinia. "Eric, have you decided about
the School or a fellowship?" but she did not look at him as she
spoke.

"If it comes to quoting," said Swan sententiously, "I do like that little face of yours, outlined against a background of pure gold. But none of you girls know any poetry now."

"I do," said Justinia, still looking out across the lawn towards the church. "You heard me quote it. But I shan't say any more if you don't answer my question. School or fellowship?"

"You answered it for me, at Harefield," said Swan.

"Do you mean you will stay at the School?" said Justinia, never turning her head.

"You see," said Swan, "you expressed a dislike to the idea of living among intellectual Dons' wives, or possibly the intellectual wives of Dons, which is even worse. How could I go against your wishes?"

Still Justinia did not move her head and seldom, Swan thought, had he seen more delicately poised beauty than the line of face and neck.

"I do know poetry," said Justinia, in a voice strange to Swan. "This close-companioned inarticulate hour. . . ." and she held out her hand, still looking away across the garden to the church.

Swan took it, kissed it very gently and returned it to its owner.

"Then that is settled," he said.

"But what is far far more exciting," said Justinia, suddenly coming to life, "is that Mr. Macfadyen is going to marry that nice Miss Phelps, parents or no parents. Mother is delighted, because she wants good advice about her chickens and Miss Phelps knows them inside and out. And Mr. Macfadyen says he will wait a hundred years if necessary."

"Which," said Swan, "is more than I will. Listen, my love, I am rather well off and my mother will be enchanted. What about yours?"

But before Lady Lufton's attitude could be discussed Canon Fewling came up the drive and the rest of the party assembled on the veranda, where Swan and Justinia put their heads metaphorically into the sand with such violence that Rose at once knew what had happened and took credit to herself for having brought it off, in which she was quite incorrect, but one often is.

Lunch was very pleasant. The food was good, the drinks cool, the lovers tried so hard to behave normally that they almost succeeded and Miss Phelps, confident in the strange new happiness of her life, made everyone feel that she was pleasant to look at and remarkably well informed about animals. Canon Fewling had always liked her from the day when she brought over his chickens and to this liking and his real admiration for her driving and her selfless devotion to her parents there had during that summer been added a feeling that such a woman would be extremely pleasant company and that without her there might be times of loneliness. He had never seen her look so delightful or heard her talk so pleasantly as on this day and wished lunch could go on for ever. But lunch never does and this was no exception.

"Can I take you back, Margot?" said Swan. "I'd like just to see your people again. We had a terrific admiration for the Admiral when I was at Southbridge. The whole of the Lower School thought he had been at the Battle of Trafalgar and he used to show us how to do knots. I am taking Justinia home too," which offer Miss Phelps gratefully accepted.

"I wonder if you would come and look at my chickens, Miss Phelps," said Canon Fewling. "I mean the ones you so kindly brought me. They are doing splendidly. It is only a step to the Rectory and perhaps the others will pick you up there."

This was agreeable to all parties, so goodbyes were said and Miss Phelps walked up to the Rectory with Canon Fewling. The chickens, who were now young hens, were admired and Miss Phelps offered one or two bits of useful advice, after which they walked back to the gate.

"I can't thank you enough for your help with the fowls," said Canon Fewling, "nor for the privilege of visiting your parents. I hope the Admiral is well."

"Sometimes he is and sometimes he isn't," said Miss Phelps, "but I'm sure he'd love to see you again. Do come over some time. And I must tell you, because you have been so good to us, that a quite extraordinary thing has happened. Who *do* you think is kind enough to want to marry me?"

Canon Fewling said, in a voice he did not quite recognise, that he could not guess.

"Mr. Macfadyen," said Miss Phelps. "It is really rather secret, because our getting married will depend a little on how my people can be looked after. But I am so, so happy that I felt I must tell you."

A life that has been disciplined by its natural goodness, by the Royal Navy and by its religion, has learnt self-control and will mostly try to help others before it thinks of itself. The pause that followed Miss Phelps's words was so short that she did not notice it, though to Canon Fewling it was ten years of years.

"My true congratulations to you," he said. "May you be blessed and happy in every possible way. You have been a loving and unselfish daughter and will be, I am sure, a loving and unselfish wife. God bless you both."

"I knew you would be pleased," said Miss Phelps with the fine egoism of the beloved. "Thank you more than I can say. I shall tell mother how kind you were. Come over and see father soon."

"I will," said Canon Fewling; and then Swan came up in his car, with Justinia beside him.

"Get in, Margot," he said. "Do you mind going in the back, because Justinia and I have a good deal to talk about and I would have to drive with my head the wrong way round if she were behind me," and Miss Phelps laughed and got into the back seat, thinking that if she were in a front seat with Mr. Macfadyen driving she certainly wouldn't change. Canon Fewling watched them speed away and turned to his house. But just at the moment his home was not a home to him. He walked slowly towards the gate at the side and up the path to a House where there was comfort for all who sought it, and went in.

COLOPHON

This book is being reissued as part of Moyer Bell's Angela Thirkell Series. Readers may join the Thirkell Circle for free to receive notices of new titles in the series as well as a newsletter, bookmarks, posters, and more. Simply send in the enclosed card or write to the address below.

The text of this book was set in Caslon, a typeface designed by William Caslon I (1692-1766). This face designed in 1725 has gone through many incarnations. It was the mainstay of British printers for over one hundred years and remains very popular today. The version used here is Adobe Caslon. The display faces are Adobe Caslon Outline, Calligraphic 421, and Adobe Caslon.

Jutland Cottage was composed by Alabama Book Composition, Deatsville, Alabama, and was printed by Data Reproductions, Auburn Hills, Michigan on acid-free paper.

Moyer Bell
Kymbolde Way
Wakefield, RI 02879